Be Careful What You Swipe For

BY

JEMMA FORTE

Printed in the United Kingdom

First Edition

Acknowledgements

Thank you to the gang I like to think of as Forte Press - Dad and Sally, proof readers extraordinaire, and Imogen, my talented sister, who just happens to be a professional photographer. To not emotionally blackmail/bribe her into shooting my cover would have been silly, right? If you're on Instagram, do your eyes a favour and give her a follow @imogenforte

Thanks also to Lucy Townsend for all her professionalism and excellence. And to Carolyn Owlett from Super Super PR (there's a clue in the name).

Thank you to Jeremy Vine for letting me regularly rant on his show and to all the lovely people who work there. It's truly a pleasure and a privilege.

To beautiful Ali Keenan for your help and advice, all my wondrous famalam (especially Alfie, Georgie and Louie, they've helped loads – ha) and amazing friends, with special shouts to Laura Slader, Nigel Mitchell and Sarah Jane Robinson who have had to live vicariously through much of the inspiration behind the book, (my dating dramas), to Vonda Barnes for such helpful support and to Clare Edmondson for trying to read the book on your iPad even though it gave you a migraine (paperback on its way).

I'm writing this way ahead of publication, so thanks in advance, to anyone I know who reads, shares, posts or recommends. Writing is a solitary pursuit, helping people find your book isn't.

To Charlie, thanks for being the best ex-husband/father to her kids a woman could have (behind every working parent is someone who looks after the kids and doesn't mind being flexible) and lastly, to Lily and Freddie. You two are the loves of my life and apples of my eye. I'm glad you haven't started dating just yet, it's a jungle out there. But when you do, I've got your backs.

FOR EVERYONE WHO'S EVER BEEN ON A BAD DATE.

- JF

5

A therapist once told her (Natasha Devon) that 'everybody has the real them and the person that they present to the world. For some people, the gap between the two is narrow.' She spreads her arms. 'For some people the gap is that big. The space between those two people is where mental health issues arise, so the wider the gap, the bigger the chance that something's going to happen.' And I think about.... the gap between filtered, retouched images on Instagram and the faces that I see in real life; the gap between fantasy lifestyles reported on Facebook and the real lives online fantasies conceal - **Decca Aitkenhead**

Comparison is the death of joy – **Mark Twain**

I totally attribute my career to social media **– Kim Kardashian**

1

Current Status Update: January

What had I been searching for as I'd swiped away?

Left, left, left, left, left, right. For someone to go on holiday with? For sex? Validation? Love forever after, or all of the above? Whatever it was, my thumb hadn't put in so much effort to only get abject misery back. The big four-oh only a couple of years away and nothing as it *should* be, according to society.

Bleary eyed I take a swig from the vodka bottle which has taken up residence on my bedside table. Then I reach for my phone, open the camera and reverse the lens so I can see what my ruined face looks like.

The answer is.... rank. My hair's greasy and sporting a full inch of dark roots, my complexion's like suet, eyes are bloodshot. I take a photo, a permanent reminder of this new pathetic low.

I've missed loads of calls and texts.

> Mum Mobile: Charlotte why aren't u picking up? We need to talk. I've said sorry and if it helps I am also v angry on your behalf but u have to take some responsibility. Let me know if u want 2 get away 4 a bit. Perhaps I can help? (lady shrugging emoji)
> Dad Mobile: Call me please. Very worried. What's the latest from work? Have you been in?
> Keisha: I hope I haven't upset you. Please darling, if I have I didn't mean to. Just worried about you. Give me a call or text saying you're ok. love you lots. (sad face emoji, hug emoji)

Lindsay P: hey you. Know you're gutted. About everything. But call me. It'll all come out in the wash. Promise. Pls don't go quiet on me xx

I lean over and rummage in my bedside drawer until I find a pack of Marlboro Golds. Peeling off the cellophane, I clamber unsteadily out of bed and pad over to the sash window, grabbing a box of matches and lighting a cigarette on the way. I heave up the window, dragging deeply and instantly feel nauseous and faint. Then again, the last time I smoked with any real conviction was over twenty years ago, back when it didn't say ***SMOKING KILLS*** all over the packet.

In this moment, I decide dating apps should carry similarly brutal warnings. In CAPS. Superimposed over 'before' and 'after' pictures of me, capturing the sad Neanderthal I've become. They could warn: ***THE INTERNET RUINS LIVES*** or ***REMEMBER – MEN CAN BE LYING TWATS.***

My face shudders as I try not to cry but, while taking another defiant drag, a fat tear rolls down my face because actually it's not funny. At all.

The sadness arrives in a huge wave, hoovering up my energy, so I retreat back to bed, sobbing, narrowly managing to avoid standing on a plate of old toast crusts.

I pull the duvet over my head. I'm a mess.

After that dreadful day in December, when life went into meltdown, friends and family blithely advised me to 'stay positive.' And I've tried, maybe even with some success? But then things went from awful to unbearable so now 'being positive' is just something else I've failed at.

You've got stuff to live for. In time your friends and family will forgive you; you have a roof over your head; you'll get over James eventually; you've got all your own teeth and a job you could fight for. Things will change. You can get through this...

This pep talk comes courtesy of my determined, but increasingly desperate, inner voice.

It feels like rose- tinted bollocks. In truth, I can't face anyone. I've let everyone down. My career's ruined. James is gone. I'm devastated and too depressed to cope with any of it. My heart is broken and so is my head.

What the fuck am I going to do?

2

RYAN: THE RACIST

Where to start?

I'm not sure what point marks *'the beginning'* of the state I'm in now. I also tend to find reading about anybody's childhood faintly laborious, preferring to get stuck into the years where people make things happen as opposed to have things happen to them. So, with that in mind, I've decided to start with the worst internet date I've ever had. It's as good a place as any.......

Ryan was a particularly depressing date because he'd seemed so great on paper: *Steady job. Could write a decent WhatsApp. Looked good in pics. Messaged back nice and quickly. Age 36. No kids.*

We met via Elite Singles. After a lot of Tinder and Bumble, Mum had suggested that maybe you get what you pay for....

He lived in Leighton Buzzard, which I soon discovered was about fifty miles out of London. Despite a previous long-distance relationship disaster, I threw caution to the wind and agreed to a date on Ryan's home turf. The alternative was to spend the rest of my days wondering if he could have been *'the one.'* I hoped that by making the effort to go to him he would appreciate from the off that I wasn't time wasting, lazy, or high- maintenance.

I'd grown quite excited during the build-up, going as far as to splurge on a navy dress from Zara. I had my highlights done and spent time making sure my green eyes looked as attractive as possible, applying a beautiful, tawny eyeshadow from Mac, a sweeping slick of black eyeliner and a good coating of mascara. I'd caught my reflection as I'd left the house and remember feeling quite pleased, for once. My last relationship (Lucas Harcourt – 43) shattered my confidence but it appeared to be returning, slowly.

I took a quick selfie and uploaded it to Instagram with a post saying **'Dinner Date'** along with various hash tags **#lancome #zara #benefit #narsblusher #makeup #maclipstick #stila** and so on.

QUICK DISCLAIMER – If that sounds vain, don't worry. I'm not some sort of budget Kardashian, I'm a makeup artist. This kind of post was less about me and more about the cosmetics.

'Insta' is where I have.... sorry *had* my biggest following. Makeup obviously lends itself to visuals and, until recently, I used to post frequently about new brands and products and demonstrate how to achieve certain looks. These days, anyone working as a freelancer within a creative industry has to market themselves and, long term, I wanted to start my own brand, so the bigger 'following' I could grow, the more that pipe dream had a chance of becoming a reality. I'd post 'after' pictures of any celebrities I'd made up at my job on Daytime Live and, inevitably, a fair few selfies. A bit vacuous, sure, but genuinely important for work.

Plus, the dopamine hit my brain received when a picture got lots of 'likes' felt good (there's honesty for you). And yes, I can confirm it's true, when we receive responses to posts on social media, our brains are flooded with the same hormone that alcoholics, drug addicts, gamblers and sex addicts experience while enjoying their vices. So that's nice......

Ryan was an IT engineer, a job which admittedly sounded pretty dull. But dull could have its upsides. Dull meant security, and saving for a pension. His dull could be the yin to my 'creative, freelance' yang. So it was a huge disappointment when, after a two hour schlepp, Ryan, (who seemed far skinnier in life than he'd appeared in his pictures and who definitely had worse hair), put a dampener on things by speaking brusquely to the waitress when she came to take our order, demanding to know exactly what vegetables would come with his steak, without even a hint of a 'please' or 'thank you'.

The waitress, who was clearly used to people taking their vegetable chances, plodded off to find out, but I could tell what she was thinking, because I was thinking it too.

'Oh dear,' said Ryan, too loudly, 'Not the brightest spark.'

My stomach lurched unpleasantly. We hadn't eaten yet so I couldn't blame the food and I felt like running over to the waitress to explain that Ryan was nothing to do with me.

Still, I forced myself not to frown or to say anything too kneejerk. I was there, the date was happening, the night was young, I was in bloody Leighton Buzzard...

When the waitress returned with the vital veg info (creamed spinach), Ryan managed a 'thank you' and something approaching a smile. Meanwhile, I finally settled on the best adjective to describe his haircut. It was 'feathered' but, due to the fact he'd just redeemed himself with a 'thank-you,' reservations were shoved to one side.

Conversation resumed and, for the next ten minutes, things went OK. Then, over his garlic bread starter, Ryan announced that he'd never, in all his thirty- six years, been abroad.

My heart went out to him. When I was a kid, I was one of only three people in the class whose parents couldn't afford to send me on the school trip to France. I'll always remember how that felt. Money must be an issue if he still couldn't afford holidays. Dinner would definitely be on me.

'I'm sorry to hear that. I hope you get to go at some point in the future.'

'Err, I don't,' he said, belligerently.

I was confused. Reservations came flooding back.

'Oh, right?' I said, starting to wish I was at home watching telly. This was tiring. 'Why?'

If there was a reasonable explanation (lack of money, fear of flying, concern for the environment, having rabies, anything) I could understand.

Ryan sighed heavily, as if I'd asked something really stupid and replied, in a tone similar to the one he'd used on the waitress 'The question, Charlotte, shouldn't be why haven't I been abroad, it should be why would I *want* to go abroad? In fact, why does anyone ever want to leave the UK when everything's here?' he queried, sweeping his arms about the drab bistro. 'I've never queued for hours at an airport, been struck down with a dodgy tummy or had to battle to be understood. So, who's the clever one really?'

At that point I knew, beyond any reasonable doubt that, in terms of the two of us, I was.

'Did you not even have a rite of passage 'lads' holiday to Magaluf when you were young?' I asked, drowning in a wave of self-pity. Raising a child or spending Christmas with this man was so unlikely. I was losing the will.

'A lads' holiday? God no,' said Ryan, face aloft as he pondered this distasteful idea, feathery hair framing his visage in such a contrived way I had to suppress a quite violent urge to reach over and muss it up. 'I've always had very firm views on the subject of going abroad. I remember my parents urging me to go to Portugal with them one year, for Dad's sixtieth. I refused.'

'That's nice.'

'Yeah, I told my parents to put the money it would have cost into a savings account for me,' he said, grinning smugly at the memory 'I've saved loads of money over the years by not going away, which is why I drive such a high spec car now.'

Christ.

'Aren't you ever curious to see other places, or to try different food? Wouldn't you love a day trip to Paris, or a weekend in Amsterdam or to see the Taj Mahal?'

'Why? I'm eating great Italian food now; I don't need to go to India to know what the Taj Mahal looks like, and I've got no desire to go to a place where drugs are legal. And, let's be honest,' he continued, leaning in, tone conspiratorial, 'the *'PC'* brigade hate admitting it, but there's a reason so many foreigners speak English.'

'Because they're better at languages than us?'

'No, obviously not. It's because they all want to come here. They all know they're onto a good thing in this country which is why so many people are called Mohammed. Makes me sick.'

He made me sick. Hope died.

By the time our pasta arrived we were arguing like we'd bypassed dating, left out marriage and leapt straight to an acrimonious divorce. People were staring, but by then I'd downed the best part of a bottle of red and was past caring.

With hindsight, talking to him about anything was pointless, but we covered: travel, marriage, equal pay for women, how to raise kids, his prejudice, back to travel. Round and round we went.

Needless to say, it didn't end well. Strong dislike had turned into mutual, sour loathing ages ago.

I *could* have taken the high road and left with dignity intact. But I didn't. In fact, by the time we'd come full circle and arrived back at the subject of holidays and Ryan's own unique 'foreign policy', I'd plumped for the unseemly low road, positively marched down it in fact.

I let rip. Wine, frustration, PMT, I blame them all and admit, it wasn't my finest hour but I so badly wanted to shock the scathing look off his face. 'Oh, you can mock,' I hissed. 'But you know what? I've had some of my best times on holiday *and* I've had holiday romances, with 'foreigners'.'

Ryan looked utterly disgusted.

'I have,' I reiterated, warming to my theme 'and it was fun and I don't regret any of it. I might even have had sex on a beach before, with a very fit Portuguese man, so what do you think about that? I don't think there's much point us staying for pudding, do you?'

'Definitely not,' he hissed, looking repulsed.

The waitress approached with dessert menus, but retreated when she noticed our frantic scribbling gestures.

As soon as she returned with the card machine, I was on my feet, struggling to get my arms into my jacket. 'What are we going to do about the bill?' I said. 'Are you alright to pick it up? Only the thought of having to wait here for two different cards to be processed is unbearable. Plus, I had eighty pounds' worth of highlights for this and I had to pay for a peak time train ticket. Oh God,' I said, overwhelmed by the shitness of it all 'I've got such a long journey back.'

Ryan sneered as I manhandled my bag off the back of the chair. 'Good, and thank God you're going. You're all the same. You think you're so amazing, just because you've been away. Well I wouldn't touch such damaged goods if you paid me. You should go back to India and stay there.'

I pressed a tenner into the waitress' hand, knowing Ryan wouldn't. On the verge of tears and aware that other diners were staring agog I couldn't leave without some sort of parting shot.

'I tell you what Ryan, I'll leave another tip, only this one's for you. My tip is to update your profile. Be honest on it because at present there's no clue you live in the Dark Ages. Advertise your odd views on travel and admit you're an out of touch racist who's rude to waiting staff. Separate the wheat from the freaky chaff perhaps. Then you might meet someone as outdated as you and not waste normal women's time.'

And with that, I left.

Any sense of triumph quickly dissipated though when, upon arriving at the station, I discovered that all trains out of Leighton Buzzard were suffering major delays. In the end I forked out ninety-six pounds on a cab back to Clapham Junction where I then missed the last train to Twickenham, at which point I had no choice but to shell out another fifteen pounds in order to get home. It was that, or sleep on the pavement. In the cab, drained and unbearably sad I checked my phone only to find that my earlier selfie had clocked up four hundred and two 'likes.'

I looked at the picture; a happy, hopeful looking woman who'd made so much effort; green eyes fixed on the lens. The deflated, smudged, sad reality couldn't have been further from the image.

Hours and depressing hours after I'd left, I collapsed into bed, yearning for a hug and to be held tight by strong arms. Would I be ever again I wondered? As if on cue my phone lit up with a WhatsApp.

I'm in town. Fancy a visitor? For old time's sake? L x

It was annoying on so many levels. Firstly, Lucas, my ex, had assumed (correctly) I'd be on my own. Secondly, it showed a total lack of respect, and thirdly, I was half tempted to say yes which made me hate myself even more. Lucas was only interested in one thing so it was terribly unfair that he'd been so bloody good at it. Still, I decided to ignore him (which I knew he'd hate). Sure enough I could see him typing something else.

If you're not up for seeing me, at least send a sexy pic. Please?

I grimaced. He really was pitiful. I flicked through my camera roll as I often did when alone, looking at the pictures he'd taken of us that night in the hotel. They were completely X- rated. I'd thought many times about deleting them but probably never would. They were sexy and my secret to keep. One of them in particular was outrageous. I was doing unspeakable things to him all of which was captured in the mirror next to the bed. *aubergine emoji* Part of me was proud at how 'rock 'n' roll' I'd been that night, part of me was horrified, but the pictures never failed to turn me on.

No chance.

I replied before switching off my phone.

Right, I thought defiantly, trying to pull myself together as I nestled into my pillow, in future they could all come to me (apart from Lucas) or bugger off. Yes, from that moment forward, if they weren't prepared to travel to see me on date one, they could forget it I thought tearfully, more scarred (and scared) by the evening's events than I was ready to admit.

My last thought before falling asleep was that my thirty eighth birthday was approaching and that at one point earlier on in the day, I'd actually wondered if I might end up spending it with Ryan from Leighton Buzzard; actually hoped I'd have succeeded in changing my relationship status before the self- imposed milestone of my fortieth.

Yet perhaps it was better that I didn't know what was to come because the truth of what was in store was probably too cruel to contemplate. For I was going to discover that, as far as I was concerned, Alfred Tennyson's well coined phrase *'Tis better to have loved and lost than never to have loved at all'* really wasn't true.

3

SIGNIFICANT DATING HISTORY

NICK MADDOX *(Nicki)*

BIO - Amazing gift buyer, identical taste in house music, horrible breath in the mornings, great dancer, slight lisp, GSOH, gorgeous pecs and a real life six pack, cleanest student digs on campus, overly interested in my bottom and only really liked doing it doggy style.

MORE INFO - My first serious relationship. Met during my second year at Durham University. We were both 21. The two of us were pretty much inseparable until three months after we left Durham at which point Nick told me he had a crush on a barman called Pepé. Being left for someone else is always exquisitely painful, but when the person you've been left for has a beard, and massive biceps, it adds a different dimension to the pain.

ARJUN SIDANA *(Weird Incest Features)*

BIO – Met at a mutual friend's birthday party. His sister, Prisha, told him from the outset that he couldn't be with me long-term unless I converted. I was confused by this given that his parents (both strict Hindus) had been so much more welcoming. Handsome, a talented doctor, ambitious. Prone to bad temper tantrums. Very hairy chest and back. Amazing eyes with lashes I envied. Even more amazing brain and caustic wit. Couldn't say no to his sister though, and used to kiss her hello and goodbye on the lips, which was really odd and made me deeply uncomfortable.

MORE INFO - Knew I was going to break up with him when I started to wince every time I heard him talking about 'my (delete as appropriate) incredible/talented/beautiful/one-of-a-kind sister Prisha.' He was furious when I ended it and smashed a vase. Suspect I had a narrow escape.

ANDY GREENING *(Randy Andy)*

BIO- Bit of a lad. Good kisser. Not massively intelligent but easy going. Nice to his family. Steady job working for a travel agent so got discounted flights. Very irritating best mate called Darren. Broad shoulders, nice hair. Football bore. Disappointingly small penis and strangely tight ballbag. Had a tendency to bang on about women he fancied 'off the telly' as if that was OK because they 'weren't real.' Drank pints of fizzy drink every day, always with ice, and was addicted to Coronation Street. Volunteered once a week at a homeless shelter which was main reason I fell for him. Proved hidden depths. So hidden I never really found them. A charitable red herring.

MORE INFO- Met on Match. com. Andy lived in Northampton and was the previously- mentioned long- distance dating disaster. After seven relatively unsatisfying months all I had to show for the experience was raging gonorrhoea, knowledge that going to football matches wasn't my thing and a car with a massive amount of mileage on the clock. His Mum rang me when we split up and told me I was a stuck up little cow for thinking I could do better than her Andy. I didn't tell her my vagina was on fire thanks to her charming son, but wish I had.

JUSTIN HARTLEY FORBES *(Justin the poet)*

BIO – Perpetually unemployed. Lost out on huge trust fund (set up by his very wealthy, aristocratic parents) at age 23 when he was arrested for possession of marijuana at a music festival and they cut him off. Creative, soulful, useless at anything practical. Long hair and questionable dress sense (owned a truly embarrassing poncho). Huge fan of Che Guevara. Slept on a futon. Wrote poetry. Would go to bed at 2am and get up mid-afternoon the next day.

MORE INFO- We went out for just over a year having met on Guardian Soulmates. Justin was more than happy to borrow money from me and everyone else around him because he believed that if you were a 'creative' your artistry shouldn't be stifled by something as mundane as a job. 'Apparently' artists should be 'allowed' to nurture their craft and wait for their break. After months of being continuously overdrawn I told him (in a nurturing way) that he could stick his craft up his arse.

After Justin, anyone who had a job they weren't actually paid money for didn't pass go.

<u>LUCAS HARCOURT</u>

BIO-

More on him later.

4

My Bio

After Nicki broke my heart by going off with Pepé, there was a long period during which I chose to enjoy being single and to focus on establishing my career. I left Durham with thousands of pounds' worth of debt, a 2:1 in English literature and precisely no idea what to do with it.

Skint and desperate to get any form of job, I was delighted when my godmother managed to get me one, working as a runner on a television show. I was paid a pittance and spent most of my time making tea and photocopying, but this was the foot in the door which helped me realise what I wanted to do.

I used to watch in fascination as the makeup girls transformed tired, ordinary faces into flawless camera-ready ones with their brushes, bottles, palettes and glosses, their kits endless treasure troves. I loved listening to their opinions on which brands made the best products. It felt creative and artistic. Some may view my passion for makeup as shallow, invariably because they don't understand the power of a good lipstick, but makeup is armour. Not only that, it has been around for thousands of years. The Ancient Greeks, Egyptians, Persians, Geishas, Chinese Empresses and Native Americans were all savvy enough to figure out that nature can usually be improved upon with a dab of well-placed colour here and there. Cleopatra used kohl and green malachite paste on her eyelids. Elizabeth 1st used to smother herself in white lead and vinegar in a bid to look pale and interesting. The first Hollywood starlet, Mary Pickford, used makeup to allow her to play both a boy and a girl in movie The Silver King. I like to think if these formidable ladies were around today, they'd have Mac loyalty cards and be drawn to the bargains in Superdrug. I make no apologies for my passion. It's an art form.

I love the environment too. At any studio, the makeup room is always the most comforting, nurturing place to be. People open up, share secrets, laugh. 'The chair' has a similar effect to one in a therapist's lounge or hairdressers.

Finally discovering what I wanted to do was bittersweet; a relief in one way, frustrating in another. To learn my trade, I had no other choice but to take a specialist media makeup course which meant more years spent studying, more investment and having to take on jobs to pay for it. Still, I was determined enough so I did it. Once I was trained and qualified, I spent the next few years making contacts, building up my own impressive kit and establishing myself within the industry. I worked long, unsociable hours, only slowing down once I'd reached a certain level and built up an impressive amount of contacts. When I did stop and looked around, the majority of my peers had coupled up and the dating scene had changed.

The world of online dating sites had exploded and it seemed to make sense. You go to the web to find a car, clothes, music and books, so why not love? That was the theory anyway. Though if it was such a great one I wondered why it felt so sodding hard. At least with ASOS they deliver to your door and nine times out of ten the item you receive looks like it did in the picture.

Years of meeting strangers in strange bars or restaurants followed, which never felt less... strange but taught me what I definitely *didn't* want. Becoming more selective helped. Two dates flowered into what were ultimately short-lived relationships (Gonorrhoea Andy and Justin the poet...)

Then, in about 2014, apps such as Tinder became more mainstream, not just casual, hook up apps, at which point it grew harder for married creeps or sexual deviants to use them without being spotted by someone they knew, making them less seedy places to be. So, I installed. All of them. Admittedly some weirdos still insisted on sending unwanted pictures of their horrible penises, but they were very user friendly (highs and lows) and I didn't even have to bother writing a particularly witty profile. It was the photos that counted. Suddenly I could be rejected/courted/fancied/and/or disappointed for free.

Along with millions of others, I started swiping - mostly left (for no) but sometimes right (for yes). Along the way, I learned to avoid men who used *'lol' 'haha'* or *'winky face'* to denote humour. The odd emoticon was fine but five in one message was a sure-fire indicator that whoever was sending it wouldn't be ready to have children in the next five years.

I discovered a whole range of new pet hates, for example the over- use of exclamation marks. I had to cancel a date with one man because everything was *so amazing!!!*

> *You like spaghetti Bolognese!! Oh my god! So do I! You're a makeup artist! Wow! That's so cool! You live in Twickenham! That's quite far from me! But we should do coffee anyway!*

I've never found reading messages so physically draining. Not wishing to continue feeling so exhausted every time I looked at my phone, I unmatched (!!!)

I was keen to meet someone clever. An underrated quality these days but one I hankered after. I needed someone who 'got me' which was going to be hard, because in many ways I'm a walking contradiction. For instance, due to working in TV and being single, and probably due to a non- conformist maternal influence, I probably appear younger than I am. I've got about eight pairs of trainers and live in either skinny jeans or tunic dresses. In the winter I tend to don big parkas and love a good quality sweatshirt, from ASOS, Adidas, Whistles, or by designers like Bella Freud. No cardigans here! I also have a thing for gold earrings, the bigger the better. I love going out. To gigs, festivals, comedy nights, bars, restaurants, galleries.

Sometimes I go dancing, inevitably with younger, unmarried friends who are also A/ hoping to meet someone B/ don't have to worry about childcare, or being woken up at five am to watch Peppa Pig.

I live in a small, one-bedroom flat, whereas my uni mate, Chris (now a vicar) lives in the country in what can only be described as a pile. Many of my peers have houses now, some even with the kind of kitchens that come with islands or utility rooms. Baby gates are pretty standard as are patios with barbecues, ones they actually use in the summer. I often go to these barbecues and they can be lovely, until everyone starts discussing schools with varying degrees of angst. I'm sure I'd join in if I had a child but because I don't it's really, *really* difficult to keep looking interested.

I often find myself being interviewed by wild- eyed groups of knackered parents, like I'm an exotic bird because I don't feel tired, don't view sex as a chore, can afford great trainers and am intimate with the cocktail menus of most of the bars in Shoreditch.

Yet, I live in suburban Twickenham, not East London or Brixton and maybe, due to a far more conventional *paternal* influence, I'm a bit prim about laddish humour. I have more days off alcohol than on and am at my happiest when at a pub quiz or doing crosswords. When at these friends' barbecues I feel so envious of *them,* for having a husband. A man clutching tongs who they can share both life and the chores with. I'd like to know what it feels like to have the kind of kitchen you can 'entertain' in (actually sit in) and would love to get involved with the 'school' chat and *not* want to gouge my eye out with a skewer.

Jogging is starting to affect my knees, Topshop depresses me, and loud music in restaurants is annoying if I can't hear what people are saying. I've started to quite like going out for afternoon tea and sometimes, I record University Challenge then use the pause button and play it. Alarmingly I've started experiencing frissons of excitement in garden centres. My dream would be to meet someone who could get on board with all of that, all the conflicting aspects of me. It's not much fun playing University Challenge against myself. So, I'd love to meet someone who doesn't dress middle aged, but is middle aged, someone who likes going out, but ultimately knows that the best part of going out is coming home. Someone young/old, like me.

Am I overly fussy? Are my expectations too high? Is there anyone like that out there, or am I one of those socks that's never going to find its match and be forever on its own in the drawer until slung out?

I don't know...... and this is where a long-term singleton starts to lose perspective. You start to become paranoid that the reason you're alone is because you're too choosy, at which point it occurs to you that maybe if you stopped thinking you deserved all the above and just went for a total wanker, whom you weren't in the least bit attracted to, all would be well?!

When I reached my mid- thirties, my approach became more feverish and urgent. Then I had one brief relationship which didn't start on the internet but ended in disaster nonetheless. In fact, the whole thing was a sort of passion fuelled mini drama. I'd love to gloss over the whole thing but I want you to understand fully why meeting James was such a relief, so have no choice but to elaborate on Lucas Harcourt in Part Two of 'The Potted Version of My Dating History'.

Deep breath.

5

DATING HISTORY FOR CONTEXT: PT. 2

LUCAS HARCOURT *(Fucking Bastard Features)*

BIO – Sexy. Gorgeous. Passionate. Trouble. Amazing in bed. Funny. Famous. Bastard.

MORE INFO -

I'll never forget the first time I met Lucas. Meeting well known faces is a regular occurrence in my job and, whilst it never stops being interesting discovering if people are as their public persona suggests, you do become blasé about it.

So, I wasn't feeling remotely giddy about the fact that attractive, reasonably well-known soap actor, Lucas Harcourt was coming in. Yet the second he appeared in the room, even I could feel the sexual tension crackling. The man is stupidly gorgeous. He's got one of those very rare male faces which can be described as beautiful; aquamarine eyes which crinkle at the edges, dark hair streaked with a bit of grey, thick but artfully dishevelled. His skin's olive, his smile is a killer. If his face had been designed it would be by Prada, or something similarly high end. In fact, I like that analogy. Yes, despite his working class, Ipswich roots, his face is definitely designer. Whereas mine's more high- street (nice high- street though) unless it's first thing in the morning when it's strictly Poundland.

'Lucas Harcourt,' he'd said, extending a hand.

'Hello,' I'd replied, trying not to go red and ignoring Flo, my assistant who comes in to help when there are a lot of guests. She was making ridiculous faces at me, as if I couldn't see for myself how good- looking he was whilst simultaneously applying blusher to a novelist who had come in to promote her latest book. The novelist, having spotted Lucas, fought a hand out of her black makeup gown to wave at him.

'Hello, I know you. I'm a huge fan of your show. And of you,' she chirped, laughing heartily at her own gall.

He flashed her a winning smile 'Well, before you start blackmailing me for story lines and demanding to know who killed Sheila, I'm not telling.'

'How did you know I was going to do that?' she squawked delightedly 'I'm Helen by the way, Helen Thomas.'

'Oh I know who you are Helen,' said Lucas, gesturing at me to find out if he should sit down.

I nodded and he took a seat. 'My sister said The Silent Town's one of the best books she's read in ages. In her top five.'

'Is it?' Helen gasped.

'It is,' he replied 'have you read it?'

It took a second to work out he was talking to me, which was ridiculous. Course Helen had read it, she wrote it, but I'd been purposefully trying to distract myself from their conversation by searching through my bases to find the perfect one for his lightly tanned skin.

'Sorry, oh you mean me?'

'I do, so, have you?'

'Er, not yet, but I'm definitely going to. Happy to have a bit of base?'

He nodded 'You still haven't told me your name,' he said, winning smile flashed in my direction via the mirror. I wished I'd made more effort. My face was passable because I always apply makeup once I've set up, but my hair was scraped into a messy bun and I was wearing a baggy grey, Nike sweatshirt with fake leather leggings and trainers.

'It's Charlotte' I replied, avoiding eye contact 'nice to meet you. Now, I assume you're after a bit of this and some powder?'

'Yeah, whatever you think I need,' he said, giving me the onceover. I knew then he was a terrible flirt, no doubt with any female within a five-metre radius. I ignored him and got on with cleansing his face.

'Could you put a bit of something in my hair too please?' he asked.

The thought of running my hands through his lovely hair made me nervous for all the wrong reasons. And, when it came to it, I shouldn't have been so conscious of how nice it felt, or gone out of my way to give him a bonus scalp massage, which made his eyes roll with pleasure.

As soon as he left to go to set, a now done up Helen Thomas started giggling 'Oh my goodness, if I was twenty years younger. He is beautiful! And he definitely fancies you.'

'No he doesn't,' I answered, which made me look pretty stupid when he popped his head round the door five minutes later, looking cheeky and a bit embarrassed (a stupidly sexy combination) and handed me a card with his details on 'You're lovely,' he said 'Call me.'

Helen practically combusted on the spot.

'Bitch!' Flo hissed which I thought was slightly over the top.

Still, flattered as I was, I didn't phone him. It would have been unprofessional for starters but also, I knew I'd be asking for trouble. In my experience, when it came to women, men like Lucas were like shopaholics at a sample sale.

But Lucas ended up becoming a fairly frequent guest on 'Daytime Live' and every time he came in, either to promote something, or as a panellist, he pursued me relentlessly, seemingly stunned that I wouldn't fall into bed with him. This used to unnerve me. His obvious confusion over my rebuttal insinuated that ordinarily every woman said yes straight away, which in turn, filled me with unease.

Still, my caution seemed to increase his ardour to the point where eventually I agreed to a date, partly to put him out of his misery and partly because by now I was desperate to know what he'd be like to kiss. I'd also be lying if I said I didn't find being pursued intensely exciting, and yet I never felt totally comfortable about shagging someone I'd met through work. It just didn't feel right. I suspected he was the kind of man who ultimately just wanted to conquer and spread his seed around as much as was humanly possible. **#romantic #literallyseedy** I'm not stupid, he could have anyone he wanted and I was frightened of falling for him and ending up hurt.

One date turned into two though and, to my surprise, we started seeing one another on a regular basis. Lucas was surprised too. He'd say things like 'I think I'm just sick of dating stunners who don't have the conversation' or 'there's something so normal about you, it's incredibly sexy.' Backhanded compliments which I tried to accept as they were intended.

Still, there was more to Lucas than I'd originally given him credit for and although I still had my reservations, I hadn't foreseen how well we'd get on. He was a great conversationalist, incredibly funny and never dull. On the flipside, I became the subject of a lot of office gossip, which I hated. People were blatantly jealous and as our relationship progressed and we began to be spotted out in public, I began to receive some pretty hateful comments via social media. It was horrifying, not only to discover people thought I wasn't 'attractive' enough to be worthy of Lucas, but also that they would express this to me and the rest of the world. It seems unfair that when a man's 'punching above his weight' it's cause for a slap on the back, yet, when a woman is, it's an excuse for a 'slap on the internet'.

For a few deluded months I thought the hassle might be worth putting up with. I *thought* I was falling in love, though with hindsight was probably getting muddled up with lust. The sex was the best I'd ever had you see and that clouded my judgement about a lot of things. There was one session in a hotel I'll never ever forget. It was the sort of sex where you're almost a bit ashamed after. Less romantic, more... filthy. When I recall it, it's like I'm seeing a movie as opposed to remembering something I did, but I don't regret a second. It was pretty bloody extraordinary to tell you the truth.

Anyway, I'll 'nutshell' the rest of the tale because it makes me feel like an idiot and a cliché because needless to say he turned out to be a totally unreliable, selfish pig and at a certain point I found out he'd had sex with a hot up and coming model whilst going out with me. Turns out you should always trust your instinct. Turns out he wasn't *that* sick of stunners.

I was furious and devastated of course and finished it immediately. He didn't make it an easy process but I was absolutely firm and eventually he got the message, at which point I tried to write the whole thing off as a mistake. Easier said than done. I felt like a complete mug.

Dating, it's exhausting.

6

Current Status Update

My bare feet grow cold on the tiles as I stare into the fridge. My head swims as I try to work out what to eat, while on another level, my brain tries to decipher whether or not I should kill myself. Everything feels abstract. Both decisions are equally difficult to make. I do know how wrong that is.......

In the New Year the doctor said that because of everything that's happened I'm 'depressed'.

With respect, this didn't take a genius to work out. A/ I couldn't stop sobbing B/ What had happened would be enough to make anyone depressed C/I was wearing tracksuit bottoms, a sweatshirt with no bra underneath, a big coat and ankle boots. Not the best look but Dad had basically forced me out of bed to go to the appointment and I couldn't find my trainers.

I don't disagree with her diagnosis. I'm on a waiting list to see a therapist and she prescribed tablets (Citalopram) but they made me feel sick and achieved nothing. *Apparently* they take up to two weeks to work. Well, I waited two weeks and still felt abysmal so I went back in and she upped the dose and tried to fast track me for a therapist. I persevered with the higher dose for another week or so but then I chucked them away. Now I feel worse, I don't want to speak to anyone, so I didn't turn up to my appointment with the therapist when it eventually came through.

It's weird. People say they're 'depressed' all the time, but depression is terrifying. It's waking up at three in the morning drenched in such bad anxiety that you think you might die. It's not being able to see how things are ever going to improve whilst feeling like the biggest loser in the world. It's sobbing down the phone to your alarmed network service provider because he's told you they're going to put you on a better tariff (this did happen). It means feeling like you should avoid everyone you love because you're a hindrance but simultaneously needing everyone you love more than you ever have before. It's waking up frightened. It's not knowing who the hell you are. It's zero hope. It's being sucked into a dark vortex of emptiness. It's apathy. It's an ill heart, an ill head, an ill soul. It's absolutely fucking awful.

The concept of not feeling like this, not having to deal with anything anymore is appealing. It's not that I want to die. I just can't do *this*.

I'm crying so hard now I can't see properly. I wipe my face determinedly with the back of my hands and try to choose between a half- eaten packet of ham and pot of pea soup, or an uninspiring ready meal with a debatable use by date. It's nearly five o clock and I haven't eaten anything yet. My appetite's disappeared, along with my will to live.

This time last year my fridge was crammed full of food, lights would have been on, the telly would be blaring and the radiators blazing. James would have been here. Work was going from strength to strength, my family and friends were proud of me. Life was good. Not perfect but pretty damn OK.

So much has been lost.

I take the ready meal out of the fridge, stab the cellophane with a fork and shove it into the microwave. Once it's 'pinged' I transfer the insipid, creamy slop into a bowl, grab a spoon and head back to my dark bedroom where I plant myself back in front of the blue glow of my laptop. Not for the first time today, I scroll through my timeline on Facebook.

The first person to pop up is Ricky, one of the young researchers who works on Daytime Live. I feel like I've been stung. He's posted a picture of himself and his young mates getting ready for a night out. The status reads: **Three cans of Lynx between us, watch out ladies.**

I click onto his home page and unfriend him, amazed I haven't weeks ago.

The next post is by my Mum, Eleanor. She's in Venice on a mini- break with her boyfriend Gordon, whom she met on an online dating website for mature professionals. She's taken a picture from her hotel balcony and underneath has written: **Feeling 21 again. Most romantic city in the world.**

FFS.

Next up my old friend from university. Chris, the one who's a vicar and lives in a country pile and who's married with three small children. He's written: **Stew in the oven, bottle of red open, fire blazing and new box set ready to be watched once the nippers are in bed.**

I used to be so close to Chris but nowadays he comes across as...... smug. Plus, I'm not sure the word 'nippers' can be forgiven. It's too close to 'nipples' and very... Enid Blyton.

Everyone's happiness on social media amplifies the fact I'm a voyeur, not a participant. Facebook is the only account I have left now. Twitter and Instagram have both been deleted.

I scroll on, stopping to study the picture my oldest friend, Keisha, has uploaded of her toddler daughter Freya. Keisha is of Jamaican descent whilst her husband Dave has a lilywhite complexion. Their genetic combination means both their offspring have skin the colour of milky coffee and corkscrew black curly hair. Freya in particular has the face of an angel. She's such a beautiful child. My heart aches with maternal longing when I look at her.

I feel a pang of guilt as I think about all the hundreds of texts I've ignored.

Would Keisha miss me if I died? She'd be sad, I know that, but maybe she'd also be relieved not to have to feel sorry for me anymore? She could get on with being happy without her miserable friend lurking constantly in the background, reminding her that not everyone gets a happy ever after....

I continue to waste time clicking on links to articles to read, staring at pictures and then, at a certain point, while shovelling tasteless food into my mouth, which by now has grown cold, find myself typing the name 'James Ralphs' into the search bar. There's nothing new to look at on his timeline but I like looking at his photo.

After another hour or so spent peering at James and at other people's perfect lives, face wet with tears, I slip into a fitful sleep and dream of easier times.

7

#TinderFails

Once I'd recovered from the disappointment of Lucas Harcourt and his philandering ways, (I was pretty bruised for a long while) it was back to the internet.

After weeks of moping, I picked myself up and decided I'd wasted enough time entertaining an obviously risky choice. It was time to get serious, so I signed up to a total of five different dating sites, three of which I paid for on a monthly basis and two which were free. I hated the fact my attitude had changed from *'I'm just casually looking around to see who's out there'* to *'Shit, when oh when am I going to find someone to inseminate meeeee?'* but accepted it was inevitable.

Meanwhile, the pool of available, decent men was shrinking as they were snapped up by younger women than me, while I grew older and more cynical. Not a great combination.

Looking for a mate was time consuming. 'Finding someone' started to feel like 'what I did.' Another job which needed to be fitted in and around my *actual* job. 'Swiping' was an addiction, a mindless one, like staring at Instagram, but something I was compelled to spend hours doing nonetheless.

Of course, if I wanted to, thanks to Tinder, I could have unfulfilling sex every night of the week with someone I really didn't like and/or found physically repellent. Only that wasn't what I was after, (funnily enough).

So, the search continued but was now pursued with zeal. My checklist was:

- ☐ Must be roughly my age (eight years either side was fine.)
- ☐ Mustn't be obsessed with their ex
- ☐ Mustn't be thick
- ☐ Must have a job which pays (At least enough to cover their own rent.)
- ☐ Must be looking for someone for keeps. So, no creeps. Keeps not creeps

Oh, and if someone met all the above criteria but was wearing a cowboy hat in their profile pic, they were a no go too. So...

- ☐ No cowboy hats (Cowboy boot wearers also to be approached with serious caution.)

And I wasn't massively keen on the pictures of men wearing rented tuxedos which tended to be taken in conference rooms. And, on that note, though I hate to sound picky, I also had a deep distrust of anyone who wore sunglasses in *every* picture. I learned to trust this instinct when I met an otherwise nice-looking man called Martin who had eyes so tiny I couldn't contemplate staring into them romantically because it took so long to locate them. When I did, I realised one of them had a squint. I spent most of the date trying to work out if he was staring at my tits or the wall behind me. I think it was a bit of both. So....

- ☐ No sunglasses in every pic.

And, as for the man on Tinder, who was pictured sprawled on a bed, surrounded by guns, wearing nothing but a menacing frown, a tiny pair of Speedos and a chest wig so thick it looked like he'd rolled around firstly in glue and then onto a dead, wild animal, no, just no. Who did he think was ever going to swipe right? Or Jerome, Jerome who had a nice enough picture, rendered awful by what he wrote, which was as follows –

> **French croissant boy, handy with a pan. I fall for elegance and confidence but am happy whether you want to wear dungarees or a dress. Have a blooming 12-year-old daughter. My tadpole factory is closed but let's pool our munchkins and bake some cakes.**

When I read that I decided I really would need to be handy with a pan in order to date Jerome because he needed bashing with one, very hard, for ever thinking it was remotely acceptable to refer to his balls as a *tadpole factory*.

Still, there were a few potentials that I weeded out, vetted, met for dates then forgot about because I didn't like them, or they didn't like me, or the dislike was entirely mutual.

As the months rolled by, I grew more discerning and learned to make snap decisions based on various things. My personal rule of thumb (and it was the thumb that ruled) was that if someone had a lovely photo but hadn't bothered to write a bio, this demonstrated either a distinct lack of effort or a big ego - left!

If someone looked nice in a photo but was sitting on a revolting sofa it was also swipe left. Bad upholstery in general became a deal breaker after a terrible date with David (Bumble). Despite having quite enjoyed our texting, I'd had a nagging doubt about the truly vile, gold and red tasselled cushion on display in the background of his picture from the beginning. On our first and last date it became apparent that the cushion was the mere tip of his bad taste iceberg. I've said it before; you should always trust your instinct.

It was brutal when I think about it. But that brutality went both ways. I lost count of the times I got my hopes up only to have someone disappear. It was dating warfare, every man and woman for themselves, with every swiping decision requiring a keen mixture of healthy instinct, detective work, code breaking, psychology and a lot of hours.

What had started out as a bit of 'harmless dating fun' became a battle. I'd think about all the hours I'd put in and feel utterly bewildered. I'd always been in control when it came to making work choices, yet finding a man was something I couldn't crack. The one thing I couldn't decipher from a photo was chemistry. So, awkward drinks, after terrible coffees and averagely fun but not mind-blowing dinners, were consigned to the part of my brain marked with a wastepaper basket icon. And so it went on.

Then came my nightmare date with Ryan the racist, which, as you know, caused me to have an 'ease of location' epiphany and affected my dating future forevermore.

Hopefully, this sense of how shit things were going in the relationship department, helps explain why I was so ecstatic when James showed up and then, so devastated when he was gone.

SORRY.
I MISSED
YOU.
Lou
xx

8

BABY BLUES

'You put your best fruit out to the front of the stall,' Dad said. This was a couple of months after the Leighton Buzzard/Ryan debacle during one of my bi annual freak-outs during which I felt doomed to be single and childless forever. I was turning thirty-eight that week, on November 12th to be precise, and had read an article in Metro on the way to work which had graphically described the decline of a woman's ovaries and how any enjoyment of alcohol over thirty-five meant you had more chance of scoring a goal in the FA Cup than ever getting pregnant. Or something like that. I hated reading articles like this. In this day and age, it felt so unfair that these problems were only faced by one half of the population.

It feels like they're saying 'Yeah you women can vote, be a CEO of a huge company or become Prime Minister, but you can't make like Rod Stewart or George Clooney and grow up when you feel like it. So, don't go getting too carried away with that 'you can have it all' shtick.'

The tone of this particular article made it feel like it was my fault I hadn't got pregnant by now and that by living a little, I was condemning my unborn children to certain birth defects. But what was I supposed to do? Subsist on lentils and green tea in the hope of prolonging the shelf life of my ancient eggs? As a single, working Londoner this was never going to happen. Plus, every date consisted of meeting either for a coffee or a drink. Caffeine was supposedly another huge 'enemy of the ovaries' but imagine if I sat opposite men I'd only just met and ordered a celery juice.

'Not drinking?' they'd say, possibly deciding then and there that I was a bit dull. Not everyone would be so judgemental of course. Many might be teetotal themselves. But let's not kids ourselves, *generally* speaking, Brits love booze. It's a culture thing.

'No, I'm detoxing, so I can get pregnant.'

'Who with?'

'You, if you play your cards right and don't turn out to be a total bellend.'

Anyway, back to my impending birthday. I decided to organise a big meet up in a gastro pub on the Sunday. Only, as the week went by, I recognised I wasn't feeling particularly celebratory. Whilst it would have been nice to see my mates, to receive a few nice cards and scented candles and so on, and to eat a big slab of roast chicken with loads of gravy, there was a strong possibility that, when everyone peeled off and went home to their respective partners and children I'd feel lonely and maudlin. So I cancelled.

At that point I examined how I really wanted to spend my birthday weekend, if I couldn't spend it in bed with the man of dreams, which I couldn't, because he didn't exist.

My eventual conclusion was that I wanted to be looked after a little bit and that ideally it would be quite nice to indulge in some self- pitying chat, rather than having to appear positive and hopeful, which got boring after a while.

I felt like I needed my mum only she was off to a writing retreat in Dorset with latest beau, Jeff (the one before her current one). To be fair she offered to pay for me to come with them and said that while they wrote (what I suspected would be their terrible novels) I could go for some long walks and that we could all have dinner together in the evening. I appreciated the offer but the thought of Jeff feeling sorry for me was too much to bear. Jeff wore bum-bags, was a terrible cook and had a grey ponytail. By rights I should feel sorry for *him*. But Jeff was really happy and had managed to keep Eleanor's interest for a whole eleven months, which by my flighty mother's standards was a long time. Of course, the irony never escaped me that in stark contrast to myself, my mother managed to find boyfriends with almost startling regularity, like it was an utter bloody breeze, which made me feel even more hopeless and undesirable.

So I'd phoned Dad. And actually, he did a great job of allowing me to indulge in my misery. I was very grateful. Graham lives in Addlestone, in Surrey, on his own in a three-bed semi with a dog called Wallace. Wallace is an English Mastiff so is fairly large and has slightly smelly breath but (breath aside) I've grown extremely fond of him over the years. And by the way, I know referring to my parents by their first names is slightly unusual but it was their idea when I was a kid. I don't think my Mum (Eleanor) liked being labelled a mother. She's always been a bit bohemian. Or tried her hardest to be. Think neurotic hippie.

I drove down to Addlestone after finishing work on the Friday. I'd been working for the past three days on a big commercial shoot at Acton studios. We'd shot three adverts for a well- known supermarket so the money had been great and the work relatively easy because the brief was to make the actors look natural and ordinary. The shoot inevitably ran over so I didn't arrive in Addlestone till eleven at night but, on Saturday morning, we got up and decamped to Graham's favourite café for a badly cooked, flaccid, bacon sandwich which, washed down with strong tea, was surprisingly enjoyable.

We talked about relationships and my dating trials and tribulations and it flitted across my mind a couple of times that it came to something when I was seeking relationship advice from my dad who'd been resolutely single since splitting with my mother fourteen years ago.

But then Dad had come out with his line about 'putting your best fruit out to the front of the stall' and once I'd got a silly joke about displaying plums and melons out of the way (I was embracing my temporary regression back into childhood) I found his theory surprisingly interesting.

'What I mean,' said Dad 'is that when you first meet someone and are attracted to them, for the first six months or so you only put your best fruit out. In other words, you make an effort, you shower thoroughly, women perfume and glamorise themselves, while men dress sharply and tidy up their bedrooms. They even change their bed linen which, let me tell you, is not high up on most men's priority list.' For a second he looked genuinely disturbed by the mere thought of having to wrestle a duvet cover on. 'At the start of a relationship,' he continued 'people tell witty stories which portray them in a good light, they downplay the more unpalatable things about themselves and don't act grumpy. I mean, no one in their right mind would dream of breaking wind or going to the loo with the door open in front of someone they'd just met.'

'No, of course not,' I agreed 'but what's your point?'

'Well there isn't one really. Other than that, if you're meeting people on the internet this is going to be even more of a thing. I mean, what's wrong with simply meeting someone in a bar or at work, feeling an attraction, getting to know them a bit and then asking for their number? By which point you have an instinct, having observed them in the flesh, as to what they're all about. Why doesn't that happen anymore? Call me old-fashioned but isn't that easier than trying to decipher what's real and what isn't through a phone or a computer? How much can anyone really glean from a photo and a few 'designed to impress' words?'

I poured myself another tea and knew then it was going to be a day of many teas. In a good way. I was so pleased I'd cancelled my get together. It was such a relief. I decided I might eat loads of cake later too. Being permanently single meant I constantly put myself under pressure to stay in shape. Fat lot of good not being fat did me.

Idly I picked up my phone which was flashing at me.

'What are you doing?' asked Graham.

'Just checking the responses to my last post.'

'Why?'

'Um, so they know I've seen them? You have to engage. But you're right, now's not the time, that was rude.'

Graham looked baffled so I slung my phone into my handbag 'I'm sorry, I'll do it later,' I said, trying not to laugh at how disapproving he looked.

'Yes, I'm sure they'll cope,' he replied. 'God, that thing's never out of your hand.'

'I know, sorry, it's away now. 'Anyway, I know what you're saying about the dating thing,' I added, experiencing a pang of affection for my dad who had recently grown a small, grey, goatee. It suited him. He'd got quite thin lately but looked fine for it. I knew he only ate when he could be bothered. 'But, for what it's worth, you *are* old fashioned. Everyone who's single these days is looking for love online. Don't get me wrong, I'd love to just meet someone but it's not that easy when you get to my age. All the nice blokes have been snapped up. Rotten ones too. The last two men who have propositioned me at work have both been married.'

'Really?'

'Yeah. Plus, have you forgotten about my dalliance with Lucas 'lying cheating scumbag' Harcourt? I met him at work.'

Graham frowned 'I know, but he was always going to be a wrong un. You weren't sure from the start. If he hadn't been so good looking and famous you wouldn't have gone near him with a bargepole.'

'Er, excuse me, that's a bit unfair. I'm not that shallow and actually, I hated that he was famous. That side of it made me cringe. He was good looking though. I'll give him that.' The inevitable snapshots raced through my brain. 'And funny - he did amuse me. He's just landed a big part in a Hollywood movie believe it or not.'

'Yes, I think I read that somewhere,' said Dad, totally underwhelmed by what was in reality a massive deal given how many actors dream of the exact same thing but never achieve it.

'Anyway,' I said, swiftly changing the subject 'In other news, Julie has finally announced that her retirement is imminent. At some point toward the end of next year she said.'

'Oh fantastic,' said Dad who knew I'd been waiting patiently for Julie to vacate her position as Head of Wardrobe and Make Up for Southbank Studios which is where Daytime Live is filmed, along with lots of other shows. I wanted the job so much. It would mean a great salary and a full-time position, something I'd been craving for a long time. I was desperate to be considered. The security of a full-time contract would allow me to start exploring the idea of making products of my own. Only trouble was, nearly all the other freelance make- up artists in the building wanted the position too.

'Do you think you're in with a good chance?' asked Graham.

'Honestly? Yes. I've been very loyal to Daytime Live. I've been there the longest and I've got a pretty good reputation. So, I really, really hope so.'

Graham looked suitably impressed. 'Good,' he said 'Well there you go. You concentrate on getting that then.' He took a small piece of bacon and dangled it under the table. I heard Wallace inhale it in one slobbery gulp.

'Of course I will. I am going to go for it, believe you me, but work shouldn't be everything should it?'

'Well no, but this quest to meet someone shouldn't be either. The whole business is exhausting and, for what it's worth, I think you should call off the search for a while and just enjoy 'being'. Constantly searching is all a bit desperate isn't it?'

Graham said this in a kindly way and with such a lack of judgement that I wasn't offended by his use of a word I dreaded being labelled with.

'One day someone will just notice you for being the gorgeous lovely person you are.'

I tutted, faintly embarrassed.

'You are, you're a very attractive woman. You've got a lovely face, you keep yourself healthy, you don't look anything near your age and you're incredibly bright. In my book that makes you a catch. And you make a bloody good shepherd's pie.'

I could feel a tear threatening to make an appearance. I blinked it away and pulled the scarf I was wearing round my neck up around my mouth. It smelled of the Molton Brown Pink Pepperpod perfume I wear every day.

'And if you meet someone naturally, you won't have to present yourself as the perfect package, or be disappointed when you find out that these chaps aren't anything like the personas they've created.'

'Maybe I should just change my profile totally and see if I get any bites?'

'What do you mean?' asked Dad.

'Well I could just go for the totally honest approach. Put all my bruised, average fruit out to the front instead?' Warming to my theme I continued 'I could write 'I'm a thirty-eight-year-old who calls herself a feminist, yet is desperately looking for a man because I don't feel happy or complete without one. I'm up against the clock fertility wise so need to meet someone pretty sharpish. Oh, and you need to be solvent because I want a baby but am free-lance so won't get any maternity pay. I probably have better general knowledge than you, but I'll try to dumb down in front of your mates as I know a woman with a half decent brain makes some of you feel deeply emasculated. I sometimes snore. Oh, and once a month I get such bad PMT that I fluctuate between wanting to murder someone and wanting to cry. During these days, if you say I'm being mad *because* I've got PMT I won't believe you but will want to hit you and may eat eight wagon wheels on the trot to make myself feel better. I've got a shit tattoo of Donald Duck on my left hip which I regret deeply and, if you meet my mother, she'll probably flirt with you which will be embarrassing for everyone involved. My dad will just be grateful that some mug has finally taken me off his hands.'

'Do it,' said Graham 'What have you got to lose?' Then he winked.

We sat in comfortable silence for a while finishing off our sandwiches until Graham said 'Being single isn't the worse thing in the world you know love. It really isn't. You've got an interesting job with prospects, lovely friends and no responsibilities. Why not enjoy all of that?'

'Because I want a baby. I want a baby *and* the Head of Department job at the studios *and* a nice man to share everything with, which might be terribly unreasonable of me but is also the truth.'

I didn't want to sound petulant but at the same time was fed up with being made to feel bad about wanting what most people my age already seemed to have.

Graham shrugged 'I know. I do know. And it's your right to want it all and it is also fair enough to feel utterly pissed off if some of that doesn't happen. But I want you to understand the greyness of life. You think some man's going to turn up, or you'll have a baby and everything will be perfect, only I'm afraid that's not how life works. Look at your brother.'

My brother, Nathan, had emigrated to Australia with his Melbourne born wife four years previously. Mum had made such a scene at the airport I'd briefly considered buying a flight myself just to get away from her histrionics.

'He's 'got it all'' said Dad ruefully, using his fingers to create the inverted commas 'But we both know his wife's a royal pain in the arse, the twins are hard work and Nathan would far prefer to be here. He's never been the outdoors, barbecuing type.'

'Emily's not that bad,' I fibbed.

Dad grimaced so I didn't bother protesting anymore. We both knew Emily was domineering and difficult. There was a permanent edge of contempt in her voice whenever she addressed Nathan. Being around them was a pretty uncomfortable experience.

'Do you ever get lonely Dad?'

He shrugged in a way which made me feel a bit sad, though I might have been projecting my own feelings onto him. Generally speaking Graham came across as incredibly content and far happier in his own company than I am in mine, and yet I still wanted him to be with someone. If I had to dream up the ideal woman for him, I liked to imagine a big breasted, generous of spirit, ex game show hostess or magician's assistant type, with shiny clothes and a personality to match. I'm not entirely sure why.

'I don't think I do want to meet anyone really. I'm quite happy being able to do what I want when I want,' replied Dad, rather raining on my imaginary stepmother parade. 'And truthfully, I couldn't be bothered to put myself through what you do so often. No, I'm happy as I am. I have a nice easy life, I've got Wallace and plenty of friends, I'm always busy and if I meet someone one day, great, but if I don't, fine.'

I left it. I understood. What I put myself through was pretty soul destroying. Yet if it eventually led to meeting a lovely man it would all be worth it. Wouldn't it?

We spent the rest of the weekend pottering about. We cooked a nice chilli, went for a long walk and even managed to find a pub quiz that was on in nearby Staines. Dad and I won the pot. One hundred and fifty quid and Dad outdid himself by knowing that The Laughing Cavalier was a 1624 Baroque portrait painted by Fran Hals, which clinched our win.

There were far worse ways to spend a weekend and I didn't have work on Monday either so ended up staying Sunday night and not driving back to my flat until Monday afternoon. It was just what I'd needed.

On Tuesday I returned to work calm, rested and focused on getting the promotion when Julie left. I had been listening. I wouldn't call off the search completely but would stop viewing it as my main occupation. It was time to take the pressure off and be more relaxed about it all.

So of course, three months later I met James, eight months after that I was making plans for our future and five months after that I was worse off than I'd ever been before.

9

#INSTADATE

In keeping with my new decision to let Mohammed come to the mountain, I decided The Fox and Grapes, which is a ten-minute walk from my flat, would be the venue for all future first dates. It had taken a while, but I'd finally figured out that if I was going to pursue finding someone to watch telly and breed with (and everything in between), the search might as well take place somewhere I could walk home from.

And here I was, on only my second date post Ryan the racist, with a man called James and things were looking up in such a very hopeful way I hardly dared believe it. Just for once it felt like the dating gods were smiling down on me.

It had all started in the make- up room of Daytime Live, on a deeply average Wednesday when, having made up everyone who needed 'doing,' I'd decided to have a quick flick through Tinder.

Left, left, left, left, left, ooh my word ***LEFT*** I went.

Upon spotting a famous Tinder tiger picture, (for some reason a lot of men seem to think hugging a dangerous, wild animal makes them sexually appealing) I frowned. Given that the 'hugging a tiger thing' is pretty much an in joke amongst online daters it seemed strange that such pictures were still so common. Plus, they always made me wonder how such a large proportion of the masses could afford to go on these 'hands on' safaris. I hated what the photos suggested too. It was like they were saying *'Hey sister, if I can tame this beast, you are going to be putty in my hands.'* Then there was always the nagging doubt that the animals may have been drugged. Awful.

No. Just no. Left. He looked like a proper deviant.

Ooh here's another one. One... no, two...no, three topless pictures and a bio saying he's up for a good time and hook ups only. Unlike this type of internet 'suitor' I personally believe that in order to ascertain whether you want to see someone's genitalia or not, it's best to meet them first and then decide. Left.

Left, left, wow, someone really out of shape in very tight speedos, ***left.***

Ooh.... he looked nice and he's got all his clothes on. Hooray. I had a look at the other pics. Not too bad. Then I read his profile.

> ***If you're after nights filled with smooth jazz, cold Chablis and walks in the moonlight, you know what to do...... swipe right.***

I swiped left.

Next I hovered briefly over a picture of someone called James. Nice face. Friendly. Worth a tap to see his other pics. Hmm, only one more photo. That was disappointing. Showed little effort. I went between the two pics, scanning for clues. Very nice face though. Lovely brown eyes. I flicked up, hoping he'd written something. He had.

> ***My stutter's nearly gone, the Tourette's is under control and my anger management classes are really helping. That's enough about me though... looking for someone creative, attractive and hard-working. If they enjoy a quiz, even better. I'm a secret University Challenge geek and can't stand people who are rude.***

I felt quite taken aback. Ridiculous as it was, it felt like he was looking specifically for me. He obviously had a silly sense of humour too which was good. He was vaguely original. And he liked University Challenge and hated rudeness!

I swiped right.

A ping instantly declared him a match, though I didn't have much time to contemplate this because I was called onto set to do some vital powdering of noses. I left my phone on the side but when I came back I already had a message from 'James 42'

It said: Thanks for the match. I have to admit I was pleased when I saw you'd been inclined to swipe right. And kitchen dancing sounds fun. Though my repertoire might be a bit rusty.

To put this into context my profile said the following-

> ***I'm a makeup artist who is looking for someone sorted, funny, clever and kind, who can see humour in the mundane. Not interested in one night stands. Also, just as a dog needs to be walked, occasionally I need to be danced, but if that's in the kitchen, so be it.***

I smiled at his message and hastily tapped out a response

> *I think the minute someone has a 'repertoire they've strayed quite dangerously into jazz hands territory.*

Send.

I put my phone down and started tidying up my work station, rearranging eyeshadows and so on.

Ping.

> *I'm in a house full of builders and plumbers and this just came through. Made me laugh a lot. And yes, repertoire's probably pushing it a bit anyway.*

Builders and plumbers, I tapped back *Very YMCA.*

> *Ha, yes, though the architects are lessening the camp element which seems a shame. So anyway Charlotte, what are you up to?*

> *At work, not working, messaging someone who I'm now imagining with a big handlebar moustache.*

How did you know?

I giggled. Being able to be instantly silly like this beat the usual standard text messages as far as I was concerned. The standard being *'How are you?'* Or *'How was your weekend*?' Both of which always triggered an immature desire to reply *'None of your bloody business'* as a punishment for being boring and unimaginative. It was instantly obvious James was better than that.

What kind of quizzes do you like? I asked.

> *My favourites are the ones I know all the answers to but I still like to frustrate myself with a bit of Mastermind and the already mentioned University Challenge. Guilty pleasure is Pointless.*

And so it began.

That afternoon, having had a pleasingly high-quality exchange of texts, all of which I was trying and failing not to get too excited about, I asked him if he was on Twitter, Insta or Facebook.

Not on Twitter (too angry) or Insta (too posey)' came back the answer. *'On Facebook but only so I could come on here. I don't use it. Why? Hoping to do some stalking were you?*

Absolutely, only now you've foiled my plans. Which is a shame because I'd put my deerstalker hat on and everything.

I waited for his response but disappointingly it didn't come. I assumed he must be busy and hoped he'd be back.

He was. Eventually. The next day he reappeared and for the next couple of days after that texts flew back and forth, fast and furiously, in a game of intense and compelling text tennis.

Then, just like that, his messages stopped coming again. Suddenly there were no more texts from 'James 42' for three long days. I found myself looking at his profile from time to time and reading our exchanges. They were good exchanges. It was so frustrating.

That night I went out with Lindsay, Claire and some other make- up artists for a drink and after four gin and tonics decided I had precisely nothing to lose and sent him a message. If he wasn't keen he wouldn't reply and that would be that. At least I'd know either way.

Are you there? I wrote.

A few minutes later I got a response. I beamed, mood instantly elevated. I opened the message.

Are you holding a séance?

I giggled out loud and quickly went onto Google images where I downloaded an image of a strange man holding a séance and forwarded it to him.

Yes I am.

He sent back three laughing emojis and then*: How are you my favourite partner in texting crime? You know you come across as faintly ridiculous at times. In a very good way. Has anybody ever told you that?*

Er….noooooooo

So that's a yes then.

Yeeeeeeeessss I sent back, chuckling to myself.

God help me! he tapped back. *Anyway, what do you want my dear?*

I can't remember what I was planning on saying originally. I typed

> *I suppose I was just trying to determine if you'd disappeared for good or not. Seeing as you so rudely stopped messaging me. I've never been one for 'playing it cool.' Too much like hard work.*

There was a short pause.

Then: *well I'm here aren't I?*

Where?

Another laughing emoji appeared.

> *Here. Having this rather odd, very uncool exchange with you. And I MIGHT have been a bit pleased to see your name flash up.*

I'd grinned then and before I had a chance to change my mind, scribbled back *Will you meet me for a drink? On Wednesday?*

There followed a rather more pregnant pause. Then eventually.......

> *Gosh, that was quick. I thought the done thing was that we exchanged messages for at least another month before such extreme pershing took place.*
>
> *Pershing?*

Pursuing! Bloody thumbs.

I paused. Did he want to meet me or not? The fact I was the one who made contact could well mean he wasn't interested and that I was making a spectacular fool of myself.

> Well it's up to you. I wrote eventually Personally I think your texts are great, which means a date with you would probably be soul crushingly shit anyway. That's the law of Tinder you see. But I'd rather get that sense of terrible disappointment out of the way?

Can I think about it?

I felt stupid. He was wasting my time. It was annoying. I considered what to say then, due to having nothing to lose, decided to go with what I really felt.

> *Of course you may. Though know that us fair maidens prefer to be 'pershed' a bit ourselves, so now that I have put myself out there and made the first move, the ball*

> *really is in your court. Apart from anything else I've had a fair few gin and tonics, so am a bit pissed and know I'm going to die of mortification in the morning when I wake up and remember that I 'pershed' you and essentially got rejected. Right, I'm going back to the bar. Fare thee well Mr and sorry for disturbing your peaceful night with my forward ways. You won't be hearing from me again. Yours, a cripplingly embarrassed, rejected idiot. Peace out.*

And with that I escaped back to my friends, face definitely quite hot and wind having rather been taken from my sails.

Half an hour later I felt my phone vibrate in my pocket. It was James. I sort of didn't want to look, expecting him to say *'it's been nice texting with you, stalker but please don't contact me ever again'.*

But he said

> *Read this in the morning. Thanks for the 'pershing'. A drink with a fair maiden would be lovely. You're on for next Wednesday, if you'll still see me. Yours, an idiot.*

If only I'd known then how much trouble I was in.

10

Love Hearts For Eyes Emoji

The following Wednesday, forty-five non awkward minutes into what would turn out to be an historic date, James was talking about ice skating and how much he hated it as an activity. He was telling a story about one Christmas Eve when his mum had made the entire family go and his nephew had ended up breaking his leg. His storytelling was excellent. He was dry, self- deprecating and was managing to conjure up a vivid picture of exactly what his family were all like with just a few well-chosen sentences. They sounded like a family full of characters, whom at times could be irritating and frustrating but who, overall, he clearly loved and had fun with.

At one point I was so drawn in, I imagined meeting them. As he talked I looked at his nose and his mouth and found myself thinking how a casting director could easily cast him as a likeable husband. He wasn't overly trendy but was wearing a great shirt. He'd arrived in a great sweater and jacket too both of which he'd since taken off. (The pub was very warm and cosy with a fire burning in the grate). He wore a flannel shirt in blue and black check. He didn't wear any jewellery at all. No flash watch or anything but he had a good haircut. He obviously went to a hairdresser as opposed to a butchering barber. His hair was dark blonde, his eyes were brown and probably his best feature. They were positively chocolatey. His hairline was receding a bit and he had a few wrinkles but that was because he was forty-two, not twenty-seven and I'd gone on enough dates with twenty- seven-year olds to know that this was for the best.

He was quite tall and carrying a few extra pounds in a way I found attractive. He wasn't *ridiculously* handsome like Lucas but that was a positive. Just easier all round.

James looked like he'd definitely 'give good hug.' He had an ex-wife so was obviously capable of commitment but didn't have any children. It being the first time I'd ever met him I (rightly) decided that *'is that because you're infertile or because you don't want kids'* wasn't an appropriate question to ask him at this stage no matter how tempting.

So far, what I did know was that he was sexy. Tick. And funny. Tick.

Next we got onto the business of 'what we did' and I learned more about his work. He was a builder turned property developer who clearly had an architect's eye for detail and an interior designer's passion for style but with the grounding, rather masculine air and experience of a hands-on builder. I could tell he'd be able to knock up a bookshelf, build a wall or plumb in a bathroom with ease but that furthermore he would then choose tasteful Farrow and Ball to paint it all with. It was a winning combination. My ex- boyfriend, Justin, the poet, had seemed ethereal and interesting at first. For a while I'd enjoyed nothing more than listening to the clever sequences of words he'd written which were always so full of angst, but his creative nature had started to wear thin when I always had to pay for dinner or lend him twenty quid which he never paid back. That one couldn't have changed a lightbulb.

It was reassuring to learn that James was a hard worker and ambitious enough to have started his own business. He clearly had enough money to go on holiday once in a while, to drive a car and to go out for dinner. Tick. And he was useful. Bonus tick.

Such a nice mouth. And teeth. And forearms. Tickety tickety tick.

It was getting better by the minute and only previous experience and cynicism told me not to get too excited. What if he had a cocktail sausage willy? It would be so disappointing but potentially not a dealbreaker, no one's perfect?

Then, with a jolt, I realised that in order to have any chance of marrying this man who would be able to do all the DIY I'm incapable of doing myself, he had to like me back. In which case, I needed to stop sitting there appraising him, wondering about his willy, and start a charm offensive. I pulled myself together, began engaging fully, and it worked.

We gelled. We laughed at the same things. We fancied each other loads. We 'got' what the other one meant just from a look. We shared the same aspirations, the same moral compass, similar political views and I could be as much of an egghead as I liked and he didn't care. Within minutes I knew I'd fallen for him in a swoony, surreal, excited way. Days later the notion I might have found my ideal man seemed like a serious likelihood. In a matter of weeks I was totally hooked, couldn't imagine life without him and was hardly able to think of anything else.

It had happened. Well, it hadn't just 'happened.' Let's face it; it had taken years and years of perseverance, effort, faith, time, knockbacks and determination. But I'd got there in the end, which was why when it all went away, with absolutely no warning, it felt so cruel. Death would have been easier to recover from. Death was certain. Death was an answer. There was no coming back from death.

I would *almost* like to know that James was dead.

11

CURRENT STATUS UPDATE

Apart from blinking I don't move for the longest time. Waves of panic crush my chest while hopelessness simultaneously engulfs me. I hate waking up. Sleep offers sweet escape but isn't permanent. Being awake means another day of trying to fend off a nuclear explosion with a sword. A genuinely hopeless battle.

The room is stiflingly warm. My mouth's dry as a bone. I feel terrible. I only meant to give the heating a blast but it must have been on for hours. The flat's like an oven. I reach for my phone. I've slept all the way through till eleven thirty.

Two missed calls, one from Mum who's at the airport in Venice about to fly back to the UK with Gordon, and one from Keisha. There's a text from Keisha too. No one can say she isn't consistent. I feel guilty about not replying but don't have the energy or words to do so. They're better off without me and my embarrassing disasters.

I get up, switch the heating off, drink water directly from the bathroom tap, then return to bed.

The day stretches before me.

My laptop's on the floor next to the bed. The battery's dead so I plug it in and wait for it to reboot. While it's powering up, I receive another text. This one's from Dad asking if I'm ok and if I'll be able to mind Wallace in a few weeks' time while he's in the Pennines.

I don't know what to say.

I scroll through the handful of emails that have come in overnight. Most of them I can delete without even opening. There's one however from someone called Ben Fitzroy. The name rings a bell.

Reading the email, I remember. Ben's someone I had three fairly enjoyable dates with some years ago but who then wrote to me explaining that he was sorry but that he'd decided to get back together with his ex. Apparently this has transpired to be a mistake. He's wondering if I might be interested in going for a coffee or a drink as he's always remembered me.

My face flames red. I have a very strong notion as to why he might be crawling out of the woodwork after all this time.

I press delete.

No more coffees. No more drinks.

I sniff. My room smells fusty and a bit rank. I do too. I don't care.

I've got work tomorrow. I don't know how I'm going to get through it. I'll put makeup on then. I'll shower in the morning and maybe even book a hair appointment for the following day to get my roots done, though the way I feel today I'm not sure I can face any of it. The only thing getting me through is the knowledge that there is a way out.

Could I really go through with it? Maybe I should write letters to my parents and to Keisha and Lindsay in case it does happen. Then they'd understand. I examine this last thought for a while. Would they understand? Deep inside my psyche I suspect this isn't strictly true but my thoughts are so foggy it's hard to know. They'd be fine. They'd get over it. I'm not doing anyone any favours by being around. Of that I'm sure.

I go to my photos. I'm past pretending I'm going to get better, that I'm going to exercise, ring people, go to the doctors to be given yet more pills and sympathy. I don't want to try to fix the mess anymore. Everything has been infected by what's happened. I see the way people look at me and it makes me feel violated and embarrassed.

I stare at the familiar face I miss so much. There's a picture of the two of us together which I took myself, arm outstretched as I held the phone away. I look so happy and so does he. Was he? I'll never know.

I want him. I want to be the girl in the picture, the one whose whole face is lit up because she believes the man at her side loves her. I had it all then. Perhaps I could have just about coped with losing him if everything else hadn't turned to shit? Or coped with everything else turning to shit if I'd still had him? Don't know. I still love him so much.

'Why did you go?'

I jump out of my skin

The sound of my own voice comes as a shock. I haven't heard another human voice since Friday and my distress cuts through the silence like a knife. The anger takes me by surprise too.

'Where are you?' I cry, entire body wracked in sobs and pain. 'I need you. I need to know you don't hate me.'

But James simply continues to grin at me from the screen and no matter how hard I look for clues they aren't there to be found.

12

The morning after my first date with James all I could think about, from the minute my alarm rudely woke me up at a hideously early hour, was him.

As I heaved my tired body into the shower in preparation for a day of working on a magazine shoot, I had to remind myself via an internal pep talk, why I'd taken the job. It would be great to have some new shots to add to my portfolio. The money when working on editorial content is terrible compared to what you get for TV or commercials but the kudos is greater. Plus, the timing was great. Julie, the woman whose job I was after, wouldn't be leaving until the end of the year but the manager of the studios had already said I was a strong contender for her Head of Department role. It would do no harm to keep my social media looking fresh and current, to remind them that I was still keeping my toe in when it came to different types of shoots.

It was going to be a busy day. I'd been sent the brief a few days before. The 'look' of the fashion spread was 'Victoriana' meets 'Steam Punk,' meaning a lot of time would need to be spent on hair, though thankfully there would be a separate stylist for this. For editorial, skin has to be absolutely immaculate. It's the kind of work I enjoy but which can also be fairly exhausting and pressured, depending on how easy the photographer is to work with. Normally I'd have had a far earlier night in preparation but my date with James had been worth feeling jaded for.

As ever, the amount of kit I had to take was verging on the ridiculous. I brought the car round from the garage and parked outside my flat before manhandling my cases down the stairs and into the boot.

It was too early for rush hour to have begun seeping its way throughout the capital, so the roads were relatively clear. As I drove, I recalled the way James had grinned when I'd recounted a funny story, how good his forearms had looked when he'd rolled his shirtsleeves up and the text I'd received when I'd popped to the loo.

I'd been washing my hands and had been really surprised to see his name pop up on my phone which I'd put down on the side next to the sink. I'd assumed he wanted me to come back via the bar or something but when I'd read it the message had simply said *'You are absolutely beautiful.'*

It had been so unexpected. I'd felt myself becoming a bit flustered and as I'd reapplied my lipstick had noticed I was blushing. I'd realised then I was feeling the definition of one of my favourite words of all time – discombobulated.

Once I'd returned to where we were sitting, the fact I'd read his compliment remained unspoken, yet effectively transformed the atmosphere from friendly and convivial to sweetly flirtatious.

'Do you always take your phone to the loo with you?' he'd asked 'were you in there sending out an 'I'm having an awful date' S-O-S?'

I'd just laughed.

Three vodka and tonics and two hours later, I'd been shocked to find myself on the verge of asking if he wanted to come back to mine. Normally, if I like someone I wouldn't dream of 'doing anything' on the first night, mainly because I don't want to create the wrong impression and end up a one- night stand. After all, if they get their leg 'over' there's nowhere else for it to go the next time.

Common sense had prevailed and once the pub had closed, we made do with standing on the pavement for ages, chatting, until he insisted on walking me right to my door where he chivalrously said goodnight and promised to call. There was no kiss. Very disappointing but I do think he'd wanted there to be.

The next morning, once the shoot was underway, I started to panic. If he never contacted me again I'd be so gutted. I'd had enough Tinder dates in the past to know I wasn't being ridiculous. Not hearing from him ever again could happen. Lesser men I'd had encouraging dates with had seemingly dropped off the face of the planet before. With online dating there's no etiquette you see. In fact, if anything, the rule is that if you meet someone but don't want to see them again you just don't, even if you've been conversing with them for weeks and have shared meals, coffees and life stories. Manners don't come into it, you just disappear into the ether, leaving someone trying to work out what it was they did/said/wore wrong whilst vaguely hoping the other person might have lost their phone or had a fatal accident or something.

Anything to explain away such brutal rejection. *Oh he's been kidnapped by the Russian Mafia THAT explains why I haven't had a reply. Excellent!*

Yet with this one, if our first date turned out to be our last, I suspected brushing myself off and starting again would feel like a gargantuan effort. Also, I'd be forced to start calling my own judgement into question. I'd thought the date had been wonderful, so if he didn't my radar must be faulty, like a dodgy Sky dish or something.

In the end, James tortured me until four thirty that afternoon by which point I was tired and starting to run out of patience with the vaguely vacuous models I was in charge of keeping beautiful. But then it came, a text, which instantly lightened my mood.

I really want to see you again. When's good for you?

I forced myself not to answer immediately, to try and be just a tiny bit cool. I managed an hour. We were on a tea break and I was just typing out what I hoped would be an amusing reply when another message from him came through.

> *Ok, please don't think I'm some kind of stalker. Instead, consider this me 'pershing' you. My friend was supposed to be taking his wife for dinner tonight to an amazing Italian restaurant in Clapham where it's very hard to get a table. She's ill though so, before he cancels, I thought it might be worth checking to see if you might be free? Table's booked for 8. Fancy it? Totally understand if it's too short notice.*

I did some lightening quick calculations before tapping out a response. The whole 'being cool' thing completely forgotten.

> *Dinner would be lovely but I'll have to come straight from work in the car so won't be able to drink.*

I could see that he was typing.

Well that's that then. If you can't drink there's no point.

Over on set I could see the photographer taking his camera back from his assistant. This signalled that our break was coming to an end so I needed to get off my phone and do final checks but I didn't know what to reply. His last text had caught me off balance. I felt a bit insulted. Would it really be that much of an ordeal for him to have dinner with someone who could only have one glass of wine? Christ, talk about bursting my bubble. I was probably too tired to go out tonight anyway. It was a stupid idea. What I really wanted was my bed and an early night. Feeling quite fed up I was just about to sling my phone back in my bag when another text came through.

> *Where've you gone? You obviously know I was joking right? Charlotte, I would love to see you and if you don't drink that's absolutely fine by me. Though it does mean you'll find out how deeply unfunny and boring I am when your judgement isn't*

impaired by booze. But it's a risk I'm willing to take if you are. It would just be nice to see you.

Blimey.

'Can we have final checks please,' called the first assistant sounding a bit tetchy.

I tapped out a hasty response.

Gotta go. Needed on set. Be there at 8. Please text address. Good pershing ;) X

13

DINNER DATE

At ten past eight, I walked into what was a beautiful Italian restaurant full of sparkling wine glasses, starched white tablecloths, exposed brick walls and diners who looked more relaxed than the linen. I felt like a spinning top by comparison.

After packing up my kit the rush hour traffic had been so snarled up, at one point I'd considered driving the car onto the pavement and just leaving it there for someone else to deal with. I was a strange mix of excited, flustered and cross with myself for agreeing to come out without really considering if it was sensible. If I'd thought about it rationally I would have said no, gone home, had a bath, found something on Netflix and had an early night.

By the time I'd found somewhere to park (so badly there was a chance I'd be towed) I was feeling sweaty, crumpled and under dressed. I was wearing grey jeans with scruffy old trainers. My top was nice and obviously I'd been able to do my make up, but as I marched into the restaurant like a woman possessed, I felt unwashed, unhinged and shivery with tiredness.

I quickly spotted James. He was sitting at the table toying with a Peroni beer and a breadstick, blissfully unaware of my stress levels. As our eyes met he grinned broadly.

'Sorry I'm late.'

'Hello you,' he said, standing up to give me a kiss on the cheek 'God don't worry, I know I gave you hardly any notice. Was your journey ok?'

'Erm...yeah...it was...kind of...'

'A nightmare?' prompted James, looking a shade guilty, before sitting down again. He looked really good in jeans that tapered at the ankle and a shirt with a really cool jacket; just my cup of tea sartorially. He smelled lovely too.

I scrunched my nose up 'It wasn't great but never mind. I'm here now so......'

'...so...I'll order a glass of water so I can really relax after my hard day's graft?' he replied, finishing my sentence again, his expression almost comically concerned.

I laughed, deciding to try and relax a bit. He was sweet. He was pleased to see me and appreciated me coming and what it had involved. 'Hmm, you know what, I reckon I can probably be trusted to have one glass of wine.'

'Ok, good,' said James, signalling to the waiter. 'And I am sorry about the short notice. And the fact you had to come straight from work.'

'It's fine,' I said, feeling my shoulders descend.

After half an hour or so during which I told him about my childhood and described my parents I realised he was an incredible listener.

'Sorry,' I said suddenly 'Listen to me going on about myself. I want to know more about you. Tell me about your mum and dad.'

James had smiled 'I like listening to you speak; you've got a lovely voice.'

He looked directly at me when he said this.

I blushed and we both acknowledged a surge of some sort of sexual attraction swishing around between the two of us. 'So, can I ask you something?' I found myself saying, quite on impulse 'Are you seeing lots of people from Tinder?'

James shook his head. 'No, are you?'

'No.'

'Really?' said James, looking genuinely amazed 'I find that hard to believe somehow. A beautiful, smart, funny girl like you, surely you must have hundreds of men 'pershing' you?'

I considered how to respond. I rather liked the sound of the Charlotte he had in his head and didn't want to burst that bubble too quickly. The thing is it wasn't the quantity of suitors that was ever the problem. It was the quality. If I wanted to date the Hunchback of Notre Dame I'd be fine.

'Oh, you know, I get my share of messages and so on, but I suppose I'm just getting increasingly choosy in my old age.'

James raised his eyebrows 'Well, I'm very flattered.'

'You should be,' I agreed cheekily.

'So go on then, tell me about your last relationship?'

I shrugged 'Oh god, not much to tell.'

'There must be some significant other in your past,' insisted James 'Apart from anything else you must meet so many interesting men at work, don't you?'

'Not really.' For a second I debated telling him about Lucas but I couldn't be bothered to dissect my dismal love history. Plus, he'd been in the press a lot lately and I'd hate to sound like I was name- dropping.

'So you're telling me there's not been anyone? That you're like Maria, fresh out of the nunnery?'

I looked him straight in the eye 'Yes, exactly.' Then 'No obviously not, only to be totally honest I can't be arsed to talk about any of my exes. None of them seem particularly worth it and without being rude I'm just too tired to think about them. They're all exes for a reason. Put it that way.'

'Fair enough.'

There was a pause while we both reflected for a second before I added 'Do you mind if I ask you a personal question?'

'Go on.'

'Have you seen anyone else since you split up with your wife?'

James shook his head.

Not ideal. The last thing I wanted was to be his rebound person. It was a shame he hadn't had at least one cathartic 'get over the marriage' experience before meeting me.

'Does that bother you?' asked James, looking a bit bemused as he tried to read me.

I thought of my dad suddenly. Was this what he'd meant about sticking all your best fruit at the front of the stall at the start of a relationship?

For what my brain was screaming directly into my inner ear at that precise moment was *Yes, James, it does. But then everything does. In fact, years and years of unsuccessful, soul destroying dating have rendered me totally insecure and unable to believe I'll ever find happiness, so, frankly you terrify me because oh my word I LIKE YOU and although I've only met you twice and haven't even kissed you yet, I think I might want you to fertilise me because you are the most promising man I've met in years so I'm struggling slightly to believe that A/ you exist B/ you are interested in me and C/ you aren't about to tell me something awful like you're impotent, a murderer or a member of UKIP. Or you're none of the above but kiss like a washing machine.*

I didn't say any of that. Instead I effectively and purposefully rearranged my stall, firmly hiding all the insecure rotten apples at the back where they couldn't be seen, before gazing at him bashfully through thick, heavily mascaraed lashes before saying calmly 'No, not all. Why would it bother me? Anyway, tell me where you live again? I know you said yesterday but I've forgotten.'

'I did tell you yesterday and once by text. It's like having dinner with a beautiful goldfish.'

I giggled. There were worse things to be called.

'I'm currently staying with my best friend Mark and his wife, Jane, at their house in New Malden. It's only temporary till the divorce is finalised at which point Tilly and I will sell the house. It's not ideal to be honest but they've been very kind in letting me stay so... it's fine and paying for two households at the moment just isn't an option sadly so I don't really have much choice.'

'Were they the ones who were supposed to be having dinner here tonight but had to cancel?'

James looked a bit startled and gave me the strangest of looks.

'What?' I said, feeling suddenly unsure. This part of getting to know someone was certainly thrilling but it was hard trying to fathom what the other person was thinking when you hadn't worked out how their brain operated yet.

'Yes, they were,' said James.

'Ok, well good. I'm glad they did.'

'Me too,' said James looking faintly sheepish 'Anyway, that part of the plan wasn't thought out very well. I hope you haven't got another really early start tomorrow or at this rate I'll start becoming bad for your health.'

'I don't. I'm off tomorrow thank goodness so all is well and you should be glad I've got the car here because I can definitely give you a lift home if home is only New Malden. It's not that far from me at all really.'

'You'll do no such bloody thing,' said James, doing the universally recognised gesture to the waiter that he'd like the bill by scribbling in the air with an imaginary pen. Given that no one writes cheques anymore I briefly wondered if it would ever change to someone prodding the air instead, bashing numbers into an imaginary card machine.

'Course I'll drive you home,' I insisted.

'That's a shame. I was hoping you might let me come back to yours for a coffee,' said James, brown eyes not quite meeting mine as he surprised the hell out of me for the third time that day.

'What?' he said, noticing my expression change once he dared to look 'Too much? Too soon?'

I shook my head 'No, it's not that. I've just got a funny feeling……'

'What like a sense of foreboding or dread?'

'No,' I laughed 'I don't know, it'll sound silly.'

He gave me a look and I knew I'd have to tell or it would be too irritating.

'Oh, I don't know, it's weird, I just get this feeling that this all means something.'

'Oh definitely,' agreed James 'But then I think I knew that from your very first text.'

14

You know how they say *'you'll know when you know'*? Well, I knew. I'm not sure what exactly, but then that phrase has always been irritatingly vague, the sort of thing you'd expect Mona Lisa to say if she came to life. Enigmatic, hinting at great wisdom, but ultimately saying nothing and a tad frustrating.

Yet from that first night when James came back for euphemistic coffee I certainly felt like I'd found someone special. A sense of calm descended. I didn't know him yet but could just tell he was cut from the same sort of cloth as me. He would be a good fit. We would be a good fit. There was an air of rightness about it.

In the morning, I woke up before him so took the opportunity to scuttle to the bathroom where I brushed my teeth (and tongue) applied some concealer and a bit of light mascara before getting back into bed to pretend I always wake up minty fresh.

'Morning you,' he'd said sleepily, reaching over to pull me in for a hug. He certainly wasn't in a rush to get away and I didn't have a strong impulse to call him a taxi as I had on previous occasions with others.

And that was it. There was no official 'will you be my girlfriend' moment but given that neither of us are six years' old that was fine. Instead, we just began something. I changed my relationship status on Facebook from 'single' to 'in a relationship' *fist bump, Spanish dancer emoji and massive smug face* We called and texted each other every day. We planned dates then we went on those dates, ergo we were 'seeing one another.'

A few weeks later it was the weekend and James and I had been for a long walk in Bushy Park. This was precisely the sort of thing I'd missed when I was single. Having someone to hang out with and being able to assume that that was what the other person wanted to do too. Afterwards we were treating ourselves to coffees and pastries in my favourite local coffee shop when James started quizzing me about previous boyfriends. It was a subject we hadn't really covered properly yet, probably because whenever he'd asked I'd always tried to change the subject to something less tragic.

I also didn't really want to hear loads about Tilly yet. She was his ex for a reason and that's all that mattered. If I thought too deeply about the fact he'd been so in love he'd married her it made me feel a bit strange.

So I filled him in a bit on Randy Andy and Justin the poet, and then decided to entertain him with one of my favourite ever 'dating disaster' stories. Oh yes, you thought Racist Ryan was it didn't you? Well he was the worst but don't you worry, I've got an entire back catalogue, a full selection pack of funny yet haunting, self-deprecating tales of dating travesties.

'Apart from the fact he was wearing triple denim, a patchwork coat and had smelly hair, he was also ridiculously mean.'

James laughed, face crinkled in amusement. He was always telling me he loved my sense of humour and his obvious enjoyment of the story spurred me on.

'I mean, I can't speak for everyone, but personally I've never found watching someone itemise a fifty-eight-pound bill with their phone calculator that attractive. Especially since I'd already flung thirty pounds down, assuming that meant we were square. Only, not according to Mr Patchwork we weren't. Oh no, he actually had his tongue poking out in concentration as he combed through the bill line by line.'

'He did not.'

'Oh, he did. Only, this backfired when on closer examination he realised that despite me having had two starters as a main and him having had one main, the fact I'd only had a small white wine to his three pints meant he owed me which totally flummoxed him. Suddenly he was in total agreement with me. I was right after all, going halves was just less hassle.'

'What a tight-arse.'

'Yes, I can't say I was massively filled with desire at this point so I told him I was heading for the tube, at which point he insisted on accompanying me whilst doing an impression of a sat nav. It was excruciating. Literally he was marching along, saying in a robotic voice, stuff like 'Charlotte in 500 yards, take the next right.'

James shook his head, chuckling. 'Some of your stories make me embarrassed to be part of the male race.'

I shrugged, hoping I hadn't painted *too* sad a picture. I didn't want James wondering if there was something wrong with me for attracting so many halfwits. 'Yeah, it's been pretty crazy, though I did have one slightly more sensible proper relationship, with someone I met at work. Just so you know I'm not only prone to dating lunatics.'

James' interest was piqued. Until that second, he hadn't known anything about an ex from work. 'Oh, it's all coming out now,' he teased, pushing his empty coffee cup away. 'You've kept very quiet about this mystery man from work. Who was that then?'

'I haven't 'kept quiet' about anything,' I lied, feeling defensive.

'You have,' said James, a grain of something in his voice.

'I have not,' I said, no doubt protesting too much. 'Honestly, it's no big deal, it's just I went out with Lucas Harcourt for a while.'

James raised an eyebrow.

'But it's not something I purposefully haven't mentioned before, there's just not a lot to say about it. We dated, it didn't work out and we haven't stayed friends. In fact, to be honest, I was pretty pissed off with him when we split up so it's never really been worth talking about. Anyway, shall we pay for these?'

James nodded and took a twenty out of his pocket.

'Here,' I said, waggling my purse at him.

He waved my offer away before saying 'Handsome bloke, Lucas Harcourt.'

I didn't know what to say.

It's weird how fame complicates everything. The fact Lucas is a household name is definitely the reason I was so reticent about mentioning him in the first place. Normally people have to snoop on social media or the internet to find out what each other's previous partners look like. With Lucas, people didn't need to do any snooping. They had a fully formed picture and opinion of him already.

I shrugged.

'You must have been like the cat that got the cream.'

Ouch. I didn't like that comment. What was he implying?

Having received his change back from the waiter, James got up from the table. I grabbed my handbag from the back of the chair and followed him out of the shop.

I didn't like how the atmosphere had turned. It's not like I'd done anything wrong. Was it jealousy that was making him act like this? If so it wasn't very attractive.

I decided to nip any silliness in the bud. Start as I meant to carry on.

'Hey Mr, don't walk so fast,' I said, struggling to keep up with his stride 'I don't know what you're getting your knickers in such a twist about and I don't like you intimating I'm some giddy teenager who goes to pieces just because someone's good looking. It's insulting.'

James kept walking at a pace I couldn't keep up with unless I trotted, but I could see his jaw was clenched and that he definitely felt uncomfortable. He probably hadn't expected me to pull him up on his behaviour.

'If you must know,' I continued 'Lucas and I got on quite well but being with a celebrity was difficult and not really for me, so don't judge before you know the whole story.'

James didn't say anything but I knew he'd heard, especially when he asked me where we were going next in an attempt to change the subject.

'Don't know,' I shrugged 'let's just have a walk.'

After ten minutes of slightly strained polite conversation we happened upon a garden square. He led me in and gestured to me to sit next to him on a bench.

'Sorry,' he muttered. 'I guess I was just a bit surprised you hadn't told me but I appreciate you being honest with me. I don't want you to hide anything from me.'

'Ok,' I said, touched both by his apology and by the fact that only after a matter of weeks he seemed to really care about me. 'I won't.'

'And, I just hope you're not disappointed to be with someone so ordinary now, having had a famously handsome ex, I must be a bit of a comedown.'

I'd had no idea James was so insecure. It was a mixture of endearing and slightly worrying. I was clearly going to have to reassure him a lot that Lucas was the last person I was interested in, especially now I'd met him.

Only that wouldn't be the last time I'd have to address the subject. It was something which seemed to raise its head quite frequently. It was a pain.

15

Eye Roll Emoji

I think to some degree James was impressed I didn't view my relationship with Lucas as an opportunity for bragging rights. Overall though I could tell he was jealous and unsettled in a way he wasn't about any of my other exes and this insecurity became a bit of a theme. I understood to an extent, Lucas is extremely good looking and yet, I explained so many times that his beauty really was only skin deep and felt that should have been enough to reassure. Anyway, it was all a bit tricky frankly and from that day onwards every time Lucas cropped up, I could feel James bridling in discomfort at the thought of us together. On a couple of occasions, he even quizzed me about what our sex life had been like which made me desperately uncomfortable.

One night for instance, James and I had just finished having fantastic sex and afterwards, in a post-coital, soporific embrace, I sighed 'That was amazing.'

'God yeah,' James agreed, kissing the top of my head and holding me tight. Only literally seconds later, totally out of the blue, he asked 'Do you find our sex life a bit dull?'

I immediately protested 'No James, of course I don't. What are you on about? Why would you ask that after we've just had such lovely sex?'

'I'm just asking. I mean, is it enough for you? Because you never dress up for me, or suggest anything that unusual.'

I couldn't help it. I giggled 'Oh Christ, is this where you admit to having a fetish for rubber, or for hanging off a trapeze or something? Honestly, I don't understand how your mind operates sometimes. Anyway, why? Is this your way of telling me *you* find our sex life boring? Because that's what this sounds like.'

'No, I'm not complaining. I'm fine,' he said, distinctly huffy. 'Did you do things like dress up with Andy or Justin the Poet?'

'No,' I said, wondering if I could handle going out with someone this insecure. These interrogations weren't that frequent but when they did occur they were so off-putting. Maybe I had to accept that it would take him a while to feel totally loved? Maybe I needed to be more loving?

'Or Lucas?'

I hit my limit. It was a mention too many and clearly what he'd been leading up to all along. I sighed heavily and feeling pissed off about being put in such a position, flung the duvet off and got up to get dressed. I felt really harassed and of course was now faced with a choice of lying or telling him things I knew he'd struggle with. There was nothing I didn't do with Lucas. Maybe I should just say that? Shut him up for good.

'I'll take that as a yes then,' said James.

'This is so unfair,' I protested 'I don't feel at all comfortable with this conversation or the tone of it. It's ridiculous to pretend I was the Virgin Mary when you met me, but you know how much I care about you. I've never felt like this before. About anyone. And if you want me to, of course I'll dress up for you. I'll wear a wetsuit and flippers if it makes you happy. But James, I hate to say it, if you're going to be so jealous over nothing I might start to struggle. I just do not wish to talk about my past. I don't Spanish inquisition you over Tilly, or anyone else. I respect you too much and I wish you would try to do the same. You've been married for god's sakes.'

'Fine,' said James but when I turned around he was getting up and getting dressed.

'What are you doing?'

'I'm going back to Mark's to watch the game,' he said coldly.

I wasn't going to argue. He'd overstepped the mark. 'Fine,' I replied, almost relieved. He was being ridiculous and so out of order. 'Give me a call when you've cooled off and are ready to apologise.'

'Don't hold your breath. Maybe you should be the one to apologise?' he said.

'What the hell for?' I snapped 'For having sex before I met you? Have you had some kind of blow to the head today?'

'You know what for. Your absolute refusal to answer my questions tells me everything I need to know and it's pretty hideous to be honest.'

I shook my head, despairing. 'Just go James. Enjoy the match and I'll speak to you later.'

He didn't say anything, just looked vaguely petulant and sloped off.

I was angry. He was being pathetic. I picked up my phone and checked the schedule at a place where I liked to do yoga in Putney. There was a class in an hour's time. Good.

We'd been in each other's pockets since we'd met. Maybe we both could do with some space. I was absolutely not going to be making the first move to make up on this one.

Fortunately, I didn't need to be.

The next day I was at work feeling pretty fed up. I hadn't really heard from James. Not properly anyway. He'd sent me a text the previous evening but all it had said was 'You OK? Are you working tomorrow?' I'd replied 'I'm ok and yes' and that had been the extent of the exchange.

So when I left the building and saw him standing by my car, holding a ginormous bunch of beautiful, very expensive looking flowers (huge cream and blue hydrangeas with cream roses), I was really pleased. I only allowed myself then to admit quite how upset I'd been and how relieved I was to see him. It was like exhaling.

'Hello you,' he said.

'Hi.'

'The flowers are probably a bit of a giveaway,' he said, all sheepish and handsome. I'd grown to love the familiarity of him. He was a big bear really. 'Charlotte I'm so bloody sorry. Like, properly massively sorry.'

'Ok,' I said, blinking as my eyes watered a little. I wasn't going to fall into his arms just yet though. I was still cross.

'I'm an idiot and you have every right to be furious with me. I can't justify being such a jealous pig and I don't know why I do it. It's not even really like me. I just think I'm so bloody crazy about you that sometimes.... if I let my head go to certain places I find it.... difficult to handle.'

I didn't know what to say. He'd clearly been deeply affected by the whole situation though because the next thing he said was 'Oh god, I've wrecked things, haven't I? Listen, I don't blame you but...'

I raised my hand to interrupt 'It's fine. Let's just go back to mine and thank you for the flowers. They're beautiful. But, what I will say is that I have given you no reason not to trust me and the past is the past. Plus, you were married, so it's totally hypocritical and unfair to give me such a hard time about anything I may or may not have done when in a relationship. So let's just start afresh and draw a line under all of this. Otherwise it's going to start making me not want to tell you anything or feel like I can never recall anything from my past and that is not a healthy place to be.'

James just nodded, seeming to get the message loud and clear.

16

Limerence. It's a word I came across six months into my relationship with James during what can only be described as a summer of love. I was doing a crossword in *The Times* and didn't know what it meant so looked it up. According to the dictionary, limerence is the state of chemical, obsessive, heightened bliss people find themselves in during the first flushes of falling in love. I could relate entirely.

James and I were still very much in the limerence stage. The weather had been unusually good and June and July had passed in a lovely haze with so many memories created along the way. There was a spontaneous weekend away to Bruges where the sun shone the entire time, whistle stop tours of exhibitions and galleries in London that we might not have bothered going to see on our own. There was a 5K in Brockwell Park which involved climbing over giant inflatables, one of the funniest things I've ever done. Then, the day I persuaded James he should try a hot yoga class; another date involving physical exercise which led to laughing so hard we ended up gripping each other in the street afterwards as we recalled how tough it was and how at one point he thought he was going to die. This probably doesn't sound funny, but trust me it was. (I knew he wasn't going to die...)

There were dinners out, picnics and an impromptu meeting with my mum when she turned up at my flat uninvited one day. After the initial shock and relief that we hadn't been naked or shagging on the sofa (she'd brazenly let herself in with a spare key) it had been great. We'd drunk tea, Eleanor had sized James up and he must have got the green light because she started flirting with him and offered to 'do his colours.' Then there was the time we watched University Challenge together and discovered that my general knowledge far surpassed his. He was embarrassed and sweet, but not threatened at all, just impressed, going so far as to concede that his dating bio may have been a little misleading when it came to his 'quizzing' ability.

I'll never forget the day we got last minute tickets for a matinee in the West End and it was so good it moved me to tears. James was definitely a bit weepy too but pretended he had hayfever. Staying in was also bliss, for nights of movies, takeaways and gorgeous, gorgeous sex which kept on getting better. All of these wonderful moments and more became 'us' for what was surely going to be 'it.'

The occasional difficulties we experienced when he felt insecure were only due to the deep intensity of our feelings. All in all, I was so lucky to have found him, or at least I thought I was. Now, with hindsight, I wonder if, when you want something so much, you turn a blind eye to things you don't want to see?

One particular weekend, James and I had agreed to spend the whole of it together. Friday night consisted of box sets and chicken fajitas and after a busy week, just being able to relax and do 'not a lot' was total bliss. Saturday began with a long walk around Richmond Park, a browse round the shops and some lunch out. Then we went home and went to bed for the afternoon, the promise of Saturday night and the whole of Sunday still lying before us. I should have felt totally content yet didn't. The day was being marred by the fact that James was refusing to come out with me that evening to Lindsay's fortieth birthday party. When I'd originally told him about it a month previously, he'd immediately said I should go on my own. Back then I hadn't really minded but now that the day was here, him not coming felt churlish. People at work were starting to think I'd made him up. I really wanted him to come.

I stared at him, naked under the sheets, fast asleep, one arm slung over me, oblivious to what my brain was up to.

The more I thought about it the more I didn't want to go without him. It seemed such a shame to separate on our precious weekend together. More pertinently I wanted to have a fun night out with him, rather than just always hanging out at home, or going out for dinner, or to the movies.

The combination of the lovely sex we'd just had and lunchtime wine meant I felt soporific and fuzzy headed. I should have had a snooze but instead found myself brooding whilst willing him to wake up so we could talk it through. Eventually, feeling hard done by I picked up my phone and looked at Facebook to pass the time.

The first update did nothing to improve my mood. It was from Leo, one of my oldest friend's husband's. I'd met Julia at college many years ago. She and Leo had been out the night before celebrating their tenth wedding anniversary over a romantic dinner. Underneath a glamorous picture of the two of them, which he'd tagged her in he'd written a rather soppy update for all to see. The post read - **Love you to the moon and back baby. It's been a crazy ten years, full of**

unbelievable highs, a few lows and a lot of laughs. Thank you for being my best friend throughout it all. Here's to the next ten. I can't wait x

Ten years. It struck me then how much catching up I had to do with my peers. They were all so settled.

The next post was from someone who had just finished their kitchen extension. I gawped at the photos of the white, glossy, marble- topped shrine to middle class living, wondering if there would ever come a time when I would own a kitchen with a wine fridge and cupboards which weren't falling off their hinges, in a space that wasn't attached to the lounge. I doubted it very much. It never ceased to amaze me that couples I knew could actually afford to build rooms like this when they were neither arms dealers nor born into Arabic royalty. I felt inadequate and un-grown up by comparison.

Disgruntled I scrolled back to the previous post and read it again.

It did occur to me that Leo's public declaration was slightly dubious, given that he could have written the same message in a card, or conveyed the sentiment to Julia face to face. But it was also undeniably romantic. I'd love James to write something meaningful about me but I couldn't even persuade him to come to a party so it didn't seem likely.

By the time James woke up some thirty minutes later I was in a bit of a fug. This baffled him somewhat because the last he'd known we'd had lovely emotional sex and all had been well.

Sleepily he pulled me close until I was wrapped up tightly in his arms, unaware that I was fuming about imaginary messages he should have written to me. I could feel him getting excited again. He was insatiable. But then I'd never had such an appetite for another human being ever in my life before so perhaps it was just 'us'. Or maybe my eggs were just screaming to be fertilised before they gave up the ghost forever. A less romantic but equally plausible idea.

I tried to stop my head swirling and concentrated on being hugged.

I loved every centimetre of his body, from his strong, hairy legs and funny toes, to the mole above his left eyebrow. I loved his sandy coloured hair, brown eyes, soft mouth, uneven teeth, the freckles on his back and how safe I felt when wrapped up in his arms. More than that, I loved how his brain ticked, the way he handled himself, his ways, his likes, his interest in the world around him, his humour, everything about him as a person seemed right for me.

Apart from his reluctance to do much socially. That was fucking annoying.

'Ooh I'm feeling sad,' I protested suddenly, unable to keep my feelings to myself any longer which put paid to any ideas James had been getting.

He stopped caressing my legs and asked somewhat warily 'Why babe?'

I sighed. The last thing I wanted was a scene but why should I pretend I was fine? Wasn't it better to be honest? I'd promised I wouldn't 'nag him about the party' (his words) but as the time to get ready grew closer I felt more and more gutted he wasn't coming. So maybe 'nagging' (AKA an attempt at healthy communication) was in fact warranted, especially if it resulted in him changing his mind and the two of us having a really fun night together? If our relationship was going to progress, surely we needed to start meeting each other's friends and family?

'Ok,' I said, turning to face him. 'I know you said you hate parties but won't you at least come for a tiny bit tonight? For me? Please?'

James tutted and took his hands off my body completely 'No, and please stop going on about it. Why can't you just go and have a good time with your mates? Most women would be delighted not to have to look after their boyfriend all night. I don't want to go to a party where I don't know anyone and if I stay here I can get some work done.'

I wasn't sure I liked how stubborn he was being, or how his face had instantly clouded over. Not coming was mean more than anything. And as for 'most women' if they actually liked their partners, then of course they wanted to spend time with them. Didn't they?

'*Most* women don't have to force their boyfriends to want to spend time with them'

'And what does that mean? We're together now, aren't we?'

I shrugged. The half an hour I'd been left alone with nothing but my own thoughts and evidence of everyone else's perfect relationships had planted seeds that were starting to grow.

'Oh, forget it, I don't know.'

'No, go on, you're obviously alluding to something.'

I reached for my phone and opened Facebook, angling it so he could see.

'Right,' I said 'Ok look, first thing that comes up is Chris and his wife playing happy families. Then there's Sarah Jane, another makeup girl I know, showing off her new engagement ring.' I scrolled through the next lot of updates and only stopped again when I'd found what I was looking for. 'And here's Leo declaring to the world how much he adores Julia. I know it's a bit sad of me to care, but I just wish you were proud to be with me, that you wanted to make more effort. No one else seems to find it so hard. These people all want to show off their relationships. You won't even come to meet my friends.'

James groaned. He looked fed up.

I knew I'd overstepped the mark. He'd hate being compared to people. But then again, if he loved me, it wouldn't take much to reassure me.

'You're obsessed,' he said, not reassuringly at all. 'I'm sorry Charlotte but it's pathetic. We have a perfectly nice day together, great sex and yet it's still not enough for you. Well I'm sorry but I do not believe in posting every bloody thought and feeling I have on the internet. So, if that's what you judge a relationship on, I'm afraid you're going to be sorely disappointed.'

That wasn't what I wanted at all. I'd merely been trying to illustrate a point, admittedly in a bit of a crass and roundabout way. I was hurt that he wasn't making the effort to come out when he knew how much it meant to me. It was selfish and made me feel uncared for.

'Plus,' added James petulantly 'I'm not entirely sure I want to hang out with a bunch of people who all knew you when you were going out with Lucas bloody Harcourt.'

'Oh for goodness sake,' I sighed, frustrated beyond belief, that as ever that name was at the heart of our troubles. It was so boring. 'I honestly wish I'd never told you about him. Are you going to punish me forever, for going out with someone just because he happens to be on telly? It's so unfair and I've had other boyfriends, so why go on and on about him? It's an obsession.'

'I don't have images of the others shoved in my face the whole time.'

I despaired. 'Right, well for the record, no one is praying more than me for his sodding movie to be a massive flop so I don't have to hear you go on about him anymore. I can't reassure you any more than I already have. You know I don't care about him. Don't you?'

James didn't reply. He just lay there, looking vaguely petulant.

I'd had enough. 'Right, I'd better get ready then,' I muttered, hoping my obvious upset would make him want to make things better. He was being ridiculous.

James watched me stomp off without saying a word. His silence spoke volumes and really hurt. Upon reaching the bathroom I found myself shutting the door far harder than was necessary. I actually felt really cross. What was the point of having a boyfriend if you still had to do everything on your own? We'd been together over half a year by now. It was pathetic.

Five minutes later I was in the shower and the soap wasn't the only thing in a lather. I simply couldn't fathom why he was so opposed to going to the party, or why he was being so pathetic about an ancient ex. His refusal to have a sensible conversation about it was so frustrating and I hated that he had accused *me* of being pathetic.

The door opened.

'Shall I get in with you?' asked a sheepish James, looking gorgeous in just his boxers.

I knew this was his way of diffusing the situation but I didn't want to just brush everything under the carpet.

'No. I need a proper wash if you don't mind.'

James looked irritated by my refusal to grab his olive branch (or anything else) with both hands. 'Oh come on. What is it? You're not still being all huffy because I'm not coming, are you?'

'Course I am!' I explained, washing myself vigorously. 'Surely you can understand that after six/ seven months of dating, the man I love refusing to meet any of my friends is upsetting?' I squeezed bodywash into my hand. 'I mean, I'm no expert when it comes to relationships, we all know that, but we've been together ages now and I haven't even met your mum. And yes, I know you said it was a bit awkward because of your ex, but what's the excuse for not meeting any of your mates? Frankly it's starting to feel a bit odd. We're like hermits. And whilst I love spending time with you, just the two of us, your reluctance to do anything else is making me wonder if you're embarrassed to be seen with me or something?'

James' face clouded over 'Don't be ridiculous. Christ, I can't believe we're going over this again. Of course I'm not embarrassed. You know how amazing I think you are. I tell you practically every day.'

I learnt something in that moment. When arguing, if you're in the shower and naked, you definitely feel at a disadvantage. Not that there was much I could do about it so I carried on ranting but with one arm now placed strategically across my boobs. 'You and Tilly must have done stuff together as a couple. Is your reticence because your friends love her so much they don't want anything to do with me? Not that that would explain why you won't meet my friends. Aren't they happy you're happy? If things really were that miserable with Tilly, like you say they were, why wouldn't they want to meet me?'

James had never really said anything negative about his ex-wife, which I appreciated was because he was a decent, dignified human being and yet, if Tilly had been a horrible witch, at least I'd have known James was one hundred percent happy his marriage had ended. As it was, all I knew was that things had 'faded', they'd 'grown apart'. There had been no affair, no drama, just a realisation that they'd come to the end of the road. It all felt a bit wishy washy and ultimately made me think maybe Tilly had really been the one to instigate the split, meaning if he'd had his way, they'd still be together.

James sighed 'Ok, if you're that desperate to meet my bloody mother then fine, let's set it up.'

'Really?' I was stunned. He'd been obstinate about the subject for so long. 'I can really meet her?' I said, picking up an exfoliator.

'Yes, if you're going to go on and on about it then of course you can. Anything to avoid having this conversation again quite frankly, though you'll have to wait till they get back from holiday.'

'Why? Where are they?'

'Lanzarote.'

I felt appeased. I was going to meet his mum and dad. This was a giant leap and I could feel my face spreading into an involuntary beam.

'And what about tonight?' I said, rinsing my hair. Might as well chance my luck while I was on a good run.

James frowned, a clear sign that on that front he wasn't budging, though he did look a bit guilty. So he should. I'd go anywhere with him if he asked me to.

'I've already said. I'd prefer to meet your friends one by one and have no idea why you're insisting I go tonight when all your Daytime Live colleagues will be there en masse?' he spluttered. 'Why would I want to be there?'

Rinsing the last of the conditioner out, I turned the tap off. James passed me a towel.

'It's fine,' I said, climbing out of the shower, happy to drop it now he'd said I could meet his mum. 'I suppose I just didn't get why it would be such a hardship to come to a party that could actually be a real laugh? But it's no biggie so let's forget it.'

'Ugh,' groaned James in such a way I had to look to see if he was being silly or serious. I was dismayed to see he was fuming 'Is this bullshit going to go on all night, because if it is I'm going home? I'm sick of being nagged by you. You can piss off putting so much pressure on me. It's so.... bitchy and unattractive.'

I felt sick.

There was no need to swear at me. I'd thought our discussion had gone well. Why now the fit of horrible temper?

This time it was James' turn to walk out. I watched as he stalked out of the bathroom, clearly very angry.

Dripping wet I decided not to follow, despite this being my natural instinct. He needed to calm down and realise what a pig he'd been and I needed to process what was going on. Towel wrapped firmly round me I went to get changed because no matter what was happening I would not be letting Lindsay down tonight. He could screw himself talking like that to me.

Half an hour later I emerged from my bedroom with my face nicely made up, my new green dress on which I'd teemed with silver heels. My hair was still damp. I'd blow dry it in a bit. Right now I was ready to try and sort things out. I had decided, whilst doing my makeup, that calm honesty was probably the best policy. If he wanted to continue being an arse after that, fine.

James was in the lounge watching telly. I could tell straight away he wasn't really concentrating on the show. He was almost watching too intently. He didn't say anything when I came in so it was left to me to break the ice.

'Right you,' I said sitting down next to him on the sofa 'I'm sorry for moaning at you and I'm sorry for nagging. I've known for ages that you didn't want to come so I don't know why today I've got myself in such a mood about it. Having said that, I'm still upset about your earlier Lucas comments and would really like to draw a line under that for once and for all. He is utterly irrelevant.'

James continued to stare at the screen and in that moment, I learned something new about my boyfriend.

He was a sulker. Great.

'And for my part,' I continued 'Being totally honest, after years of being single it's so nice having a boyfriend, that to some extent I probably want to show you off. Also, I would genuinely rather have your company than not. I know already I'll probably spend most of the night missing you and wishing you were there and that's not to make you feel guilty by the way, I'm just trying to explain.'

I glanced at the TV. Saturday night 'fun' blared back at me. 'Plus, Lindsay is one of my closest friends and has been amazing to me since Keisha moved away, which I'll always be grateful for. I love you and I love her so one day it would mean a lot if the two of you met.'

James' gaze never moved from the screen but I knew he was listening.

'But again, I'm sorry, I should have dropped it. I should have had more empathy and will try to be more patient.'

I was proud of myself for managing to sound so reasonable. But the fact that he was *still* staring at the moronic game show so intently was grating on my nerves. He could at least look at me. Staring at the telly was rude. I took a deep breath.

'Please stay here tonight. I'll be gutted if you don't. I won't be too late in.'

At this point his silence was downright insulting, so before my reasonable tone was replaced by one more representative of what I was really feeling I decided to make a swift exit.

'Ok, so I'm going to go and dry my hair now,' I announced in an unnaturally high voice, experiencing a very real desire to bash him with the remote control.

I got up, gutted that my conciliatory efforts hadn't at least been met with a smile or some kind of acknowledgment. Sod him.

'You look very sexy,' James muttered.

He said it really quietly.

My back was to him but I stopped in my tracks. 'Thank you very much,' I said, grinning despite myself. He was a stubborn sod but I didn't half love him. It would all be fine. I was past caring about the party and just didn't want to leave with any bad feeling between us.

Twenty minutes later and my hair was as good as it was going to get, I was ready to leave and determined to have a great time. I'd been going to parties on my own for years. One more wouldn't make much difference.

'Right, I'll see you later then,' I said to my telly watching boyfriend.

Out of the blue James suddenly looked up and said 'Right, have you got an iron? The shirt I want to wear is totally creased and if I'm going to be paraded round like some kind of show pony I'll need to look like I've made an effort.'

Cool as a cucumber, so as not to put him off or add any more pressure, I went to get the ironing board from out of the cupboard doing an incredible impression of someone who had barely registered what he'd just said. It was only once he was dressed and ready that I allowed myself to do a jubilant jig around the kitchen, which made James laugh his head off. He could be hard work that was for sure, but then every single relationship in the world is and he was worth every second. Or so I thought.

17

As we strode into the crowded, noisy bar the two of us turned heads. I was aware I was getting appreciative looks but for once wasn't altogether surprised. I felt like I was firing pheromones into the ether. I felt powerful, joyful and wanted to dance. I felt like frigging Wonder Woman and was incredibly happy and proud to have James by my side.

And I had no idea why he'd made such a fuss. He was a bit nervous and cagey for the first half an hour or so but as soon as he'd had a drink and got the first few introductions out of the way he visibly relaxed and slowly became the life and soul, charming the pants off everyone. Just as I'd always known he would. And it was so much better having him there than wishing he was. We danced together, we had a laugh and the night was everything I'd hoped it would be. We would share a hangover tomorrow.

At one point when James had gone to the loo, a by now very merry Lindsay seized the opportunity to take me to one side 'Oh my god he's lovely babe. He's really nice and you can tell he's nuts about you,' she yelled over the strains of some disco track.

'Really?'

'Yes, and I've been meaning to tell you all evening, you look bloody amazing. You have an 'in love' cliché glow about you.'

I laughed and before I'd had time to really think about it, found myself admitting what I'd been thinking for weeks. Shouting into my friend's ear I said 'Do you know what? I know it's only been seven months but Lindsay he's the one. I've finally met him.'

My friend smiled 'Well, any idiot can see you've gone loopy for each other so I can't say I'm surprised. And I'm so happy for you, jealous in fact. Paul and I used to be all loved up like you guys. Now his idea of romance is closing the toilet door when he has a poo.' She cackled at her own wit. 'God I'm drunk. But listen, don't go rushing into marrying him yet, I still need to get to know him! And please don't leave early either. I've missed you, so tonight you're mine! Mum's got Ben all day tomorrow and I am getting smashed.'

I laughed, happy to see Lindsay so carefree and able to let her asymmetrical bobbed hair down for once. Lindsay is an amazing person; straight forward with zero agenda and unbelievably caring. We met years ago on a job and hit it off immediately when she took a liking to one of my dresses and in a spontaneous moment we decided to swap outfits. It had been a disaster but a very funny one because we're totally different body shapes. She's the owner of an impressively flat stomach, a big bottom and no chest, whereas I'm curvy, have a tendency to put weight on around my middle and have a definite bosom. We had to accept in that moment that swapping clothes wasn't going to be a feature of an otherwise very promising friendship.

We ended up living together for many years, until she met Paul who is just brilliant. They are my 'pedestal' couple if you like, my blueprint for a healthy, successful relationship. One with only very occasional eye rolling. They never hiss at one another, or get in the car after an event and say 'well, I wish you hadn't done/said X Y or Z'. They like, respect and trust each other implicitly and are totally secure. They support each other doing things separately too. In fact, Paul has always encouraged Lindsay to go away with girlfriends and positively reinforces our friendship to the point where he loves hearing about what we've been up to when we've been out. On this front I'm very lucky and appreciated how often they let me hang out with them, which was why I was so impatient for James to get to know them.

Lindsay is also an incredible mum. She took a year off when Ben was born and was now back at work part time and, due to being one of the most capable people I know, seemed to take motherhood in her stride. She's the absolute best. An all-round legend.

'Promise I'm here for the duration,' I said 'James wouldn't have it any other way.'

'Well then, maybe he is a keeper?' said Lindsay, pulling a ridiculous face and purposefully crossing her eyes. I laughed. I've always had a fairly hearty, quite loud laugh. People tell me it's infectious and along with my love of black eyeliner is probably one of my biggest trademarks. A few short months later I stopped laughing altogether.

'Go and find him,' said Lindsay 'I want a selfie with the two of you.'

I did as I was told and went off in search of my man. It took a while but eventually, after ten minutes I found him at the bar, chatting away to some of my Daytime Live colleagues, Dan, his wife Stacey (who looked like she was in a terrible mood) and Jess the celebrity guest booker.

'There you are,' I said happily 'I've been looking for you for ages.'

James pulled me into him, glad to be found.

'Don't disappear on me again will you,' I said.

'As if, you're stuck with me, I'm afraid.'

18

EGGY

One Sunday, a few weeks after Lindsay's party, James was at my place as usual. We'd decided to get the train into town to see a photography exhibition in Shoreditch and then have something to eat. I was looking forward to it. I like East London. It makes a nice contrast to suburban Middlesex where I'm surrounded by wonderful 'highly rated by Ofsted' schools, green spaces and safe, quiet streets; all great if you're raising small children, only I'm not.

Occasionally I do consider moving to an area more awash with coffee shops, cocktail bars, culture and markets but never do due to hope springing eternal. It's a buggy I've been hankering after, not clothes or furniture and I want a baby keeping me awake at night, not caffeine, so geographically I'm in the right place. Still, that doesn't mean it isn't a tonic to dip into more urban parts of London from time to time. Especially while I can still leave the house unencumbered, unlike my 'mum' friends who at times take so long getting out of the house, that by the time they've got down the road, it's time to go home again.

Anyway, that day it occurred to me that it might be nice to invite some friends to join us.

'Why don't you give Mark a call? Ask if he wants to come with us?' I suggested. I was perched on a barstool at the tiny breakfast bar which divides my kitchen from the lounge, watching as James made us scrambled eggs on toast and coffee. I usually did the cooking, but when James did get stuck in, he tended to move about as though he was catering for a gala dinner, as opposed to heating up some baked beans. He also liked me to praise whatever he'd made, as though what he'd prepared was a culinary phenomenon. I didn't mind humouring him, though suspected it was the sort of thing that would start to become more irritating as time went on. Maybe once we'd been married for twenty-five years, I'd be rolling my eyes behind his back like a cliché, TV sitcom, long suffering type wife?

'Do you like the way I've added a bit of marmite?' he'd asked once.

'Yes,' I'd cooed back, even though I didn't. Spreading marmite on one of my favourite, simple dishes just made it overwhelmingly yeasty. 'It's a really nice touch.'

On another occasion he'd asked 'How's your fish-finger sandwich? They're just right aren't they? Not burnt at the edges but cooked really nicely through.'

'Yeah they're great, perfectly cooked' I'd agreed, secretly thinking there weren't many ways you could get grilling a fish-finger wrong.

Now I watched as he heated milk in a pan and seasoned eggs with such a flourish he may as well have been seasoning a soufflé at The Savoy.

'So, what do you think?' I repeated 'See if they're free?'

'Who?'

'Mark.'

'Why would I do that?' asked James, looking bemused, as if I'd suggested something seriously outlandish.

I giggled 'Why not? Why are you looking like that? Isn't it normal to occasionally meet up with friends? I *still* haven't met any of yours even though you promised after Lindsay's party I would. God, if I don't meet some of them soon I am genuinely going to start thinking you're ashamed of me. Joking!' I exclaimed. Even I knew I was starting to sound like a stuck record.

'I don't know,' replied James, looking irritated and edgy, like he always did whenever the subject of introducing me to anyone came up. It was starting to really do my head in. It was becoming the 'thing' we argued about. 'Jane probably won't be able to find anyone to leave the kids with all day.'

'Of course she won't. So obviously invite them too. I'd love to meet all of them. Or if you think it would be too much of a schlepp across town, we could do something more local?'

I could see James thinking as he spooned scrambled egg onto toast, a look of deep concentration on his face. 'So you want to ruin our nice, romantic day, which I've been looking forward to for ages by inviting other people along? You told me you were dying to see this exhibition but suddenly now you're suggesting we don't bother going and end up in some shit park or something.'

'Thank you,' I said, taking the plate he was handing me. I was determined not to let things escalate and ruin our day. 'Listen,' I said calmly 'You know I love spending time with you on our own. But, that is all we ever do and I have to be honest, I'm a very sociable kind of person and I do find it a bit weird that we never see anyone else. In fact, unless you arrange something with your parents soon, like you said you would, or something with some of your friends I am going to start getting pretty pissed off. As I reached over for my knife and fork, I added laughing 'I'll start thinking you've got a second family or something! Some secret to hide because you act like it sometimes.'

'Don't be so ridiculous,' said James, looking genuinely hurt. 'What a horrible thing to say.'

'I'm joking,' I sighed 'But whilst I don't have a strong desire to go to a park I do want to meet the people who know you best more than I want to see the exhibition, yes.'

I had his attention now.

'Are you blackmailing me?'

Bored of being made to feel unreasonable over things people usually took for granted I looked him straight in the eye and said calmly 'You know what? Call it what you want James. If that's the way you choose to see it, then yes, I'm blackmailing you, because it is odd that you never take me out with anyone. We had a great time at Lindsay's and I know you're not a boring, shy person so there's no excuse, unless, like I mooted earlier, you are ashamed or embarrassed by me. And if that's the case then you need to sort it out, because you shouldn't be. Unless you're still wishing you were married to Tilly and are having doubts.'

James brought my coffee over and fixed me with those deep brown, thoughtful eyes of his. He sighed and for the life of me I had no idea why he looked so pained.

'OK,' he said.

'OK what?'

But he didn't say anything. Instead he left the room, went to the bedroom and came back clutching his work phone. The next thing I knew he was making a call. 'Mark,' he said 'What are you doing today? It's time you met Charlotte......'

I couldn't believe it and as he wandered back into the bedroom to talk to his friend I couldn't resist a little victory fist bump into the air.

Five minutes later he was off the phone and I ran over to him as he shut the bedroom door behind him, flinging my arms round him and wrapping my whole body around him like a cat. 'See, that wasn't that hard, was it?'

'No,' he agreed, rolling his eyes in mock exasperation yet clearly pleased I was so delighted. 'Though, as you probably heard, he can't come today.'

'Why couldn't he, out of interest?'

'They're already going to see friends for lunch. But he's suggested having a drink one night soon, near his work. Only he's based in the city, so if you don't fancy it I'd totally understand.'

I pretended to hit him 'Are you serious? Christ, at this stage I'd pop over to New Zealand for a swift half if it meant actually meeting your best friend.'

'Right. Well I'll text him now and suggest a night then. What are you doing this week?'

'Early starts most days, apart from Friday, so maybe ask if he's free on Thursday? Here's your phone,' I said picking it up and waggling it at him, fearful that if he didn't organise it now he'd end up wriggling out of it.

'Got this one,' he said, retrieving his work phone from his back pocket again and texting.

'Will Jane come too?'

'I don't think so. Not if we're meeting in town. Mark suggested we just go and see him, so let's not muck him about.'

'Right,' I said 'That's sorted then. I'm so happy, thank you, Babe. OK, I'm going to get my handbag and we can go.'

19

Wide Eyed Stunned Emoji

Seven and a half, mainly glorious months after I had first met James, I was finally getting ready to meet his best friend and person he lived with, the one and only Mark. The build up to this event was so great, that in my mind he'd achieved almost legendary status and become a mysterious, mythical figure, as opposed to just......a bloke.

As I gazed into my dressing table mirror, carefully blending my Becca foundation with my most expensive brush in order to create the best finish, I realised what a stress it had been to get to this point. How many mini rows had we had; how much energy had been wasted? Sometimes I did wonder if it should be quite as hard. But perhaps all relationships have their 'thing'?

Make up finished I scrutinised my reflection, pleased with what was staring back. If only men were as reliable as make up.

Still, I'd recently had a long chat with Claire from work. We were having a gossip and she managed to really assuage my anxieties about the fact that James and I were so anti-social.

'What are you worried about?' she'd said, looking totally astounded that I even cared about not having met any of James' friends. 'He sounds bloody amazing and if the only thing wrong with him is that he wants to spend all his time with you, frankly you want to be getting a ring on that finger ASAP. Christ, being a bit anti-social is far preferable to being the other way. I went out with someone once who wanted to spend every waking hour with 'the lads' as he called them. It was pathetic. I felt like I had to make an appointment to see my own boyfriend and if I ever suggested going away, just the two of us, he'd look horrified. So why stress about it?'

I'd laughed, enjoying this new perspective 'I know what you mean, but I just really want to meet his family at least. Isn't that normal? I've been going out with him for ages now.'

But Claire had looked utterly non-plussed 'Again, are you mad? Why do you want to spend time with his boring family who will undoubtedly turn out to be a nightmare by the way? Just law of averages I'm afraid. How do you know he doesn't have the mother from hell, or a really boring dad? Maybe he's not forcing you to hang out with them because he actually loves you. Christ, I had to go to the curtain department of John Lewis with Jason's mum the other day, and when I say 'had to go' I really do mean I had no choice in the matter. All I did was trail obediently after her, carrying all her stuff, while she made it very clear via some barbed, fairly vicious comments that she doesn't think I'm good enough for her precious son. Then later, over tea and dry walnut and coffee cake, she managed to mention that if truth be told, she wished he'd married his last girlfriend Sabina as she'd had such a sweet nature. Honestly, I nearly stuck a curtain pole up her arse.'

The chat did a lot of good. I felt lighter afterwards, like my brain had had a rinse under the cold tap. Why *did* it matter so much as long as we were happy? Jason wanting Claire to spend time with his mother, no matter how difficult she was, still felt more 'normal' to me but I could recognise the 'be careful what you wish for' aspect of her point.

Plus, now of course I was going to meet Mark, so perhaps James had just wanted to take his time and enjoy the honeymoon period.

Of course, having made such an enormous fuss about it happening, I needed the meeting to go well, hence why I spent so much time getting ready. In this instance the expression 'putting on your war paint' felt pretty accurate.

I wanted Mark to like and approve of me. I suspected he'd be comparing and contrasting me to 'the ex' and I wanted James to be proud.

***

We met outside Liverpool Street station.

'Wow, you look great babe,' James said at once.

'Thank you,' I beamed, feeling good in my new green dress, ankle boots and fitted jacket. I'd treated myself to a blow-dry and was really pleased with my new Chanel eyeshadow which gave a lovely smoky eyed, quite sexy look. 'Right, where are we meeting Mark?'

'At a pub called The White Horse. It's on Appold Street. Come on let's go.'

We walked hand in hand through the streets and because of my own nerves it took a while to realise James was a bit tense too.

'Are you not going to give me the lowdown on Mark then, before we meet him?'

'Erm, he's great. Sometimes he can be a bit......'

'Oh god... what?'

'Nothing, he just might be a bit......oh I don't know, he'll be fine. Right, we're here. Let's get this done.'

I was so nervous that as we approached our destination I almost started giggling at his strange choice of words. Let's get this done? He made it sound like this drink was something to be got through or survived. Like an operation, or a tax return.

James pushed open the door of the pub and spotted Mark as soon as we'd walked in. He waved at his friend who was sat at the end of the bar, nursing a pint. He was quite nice looking, dark and quite short but with a charismatic face and wearing a well-cut suit. He leapt up as soon as he saw us. He looked as nervous as I was.

'Hi,' I said, grinning widely, trying to be as friendly as possible without appearing unhinged. There was a fine line.

'Hi,' said Mark. He didn't smile and looked wary. There certainly wasn't going to be a kiss nor handshake.

There was an awkward silence which in the end I broke 'Right, can I get you both a drink then? Mark? Another pint?'

It was as though James had been in a trance because he suddenly said 'Oh god no, don't be silly. Right, I'll get you another one and what do you want sweetheart? Vodka and tonic, white wine?'

'Dry white wine please,' I said, thinking it was going to be a long night unless everyone relaxed a bit.

With James busy at the bar I was left alone with Mark. 'So,' I said, attempting to break the ice 'It's lovely to meet you. James has told me so much about you.'

'Has he?' said Mark, and I got the sense he was really sizing me up.

'Er, yeah. You know, he said you've been friends for years and so on and obviously I know he's living with you at the moment.'

'Indeed,' said Mark, seemingly intrigued by his own hands.

I smiled, waiting for him to pick up the conversation baton, only he didn't.

'So, do you work near here then?'

'Yeah, just around the corner.'

'Lovely.'

Mark nodded awkwardly then looked into the middle distance.

Maybe it wasn't lovely? Maybe he wasn't lovely? I was starting to think he was a bit bloody rude. I tried again.

'So, James mentioned your wife designs children's bed linen. What a great job. It sounds really creative.'

Finally, Mark cracked a half smile 'Yeah, she's pretty good at it.'

'Excellent,' I said. There was another long pause, one which made me so anxious I had to fill it, with anything 'If I had children I'd definitely buy some, but I don't. Though I'm sure James has probably told you that anyway. Or maybe not? Shouldn't assume. Anyway, I'm utterly childless and a bit old to be lying underneath dinosaurs or ballet dancers myself. As in one's which are embroidered onto a duvet cover. Small, sweet ballet dancers as opposed to the big, muscular, male variety. Not that I'd lie under one of those of course, not being single.'

What the actual living fuck was I talking about?

Mark looked genuinely alarmed.

I accepted that what I'd said hadn't been funny but he didn't have to look at me like I was a total maniac. My face was burning.

'You're in telly aren't you?' he said at last, helping me out, possibly due to pity.

'Yes, well kind of. I'm a makeup artist so I do a lot of telly work but I also work on editorial shoots and so on, and if I'm really skint I have been known to do the odd bride.'

James returned with our drinks. I was so pleased to see him I could have cried. By now it was perfectly obvious that Mark didn't want to be there and now I'd said I'd 'done the odd bride' which sounded like another weird innuendo. Had I felt more at ease I would have pointed it out and had a laugh about it but I was too worried about being met by more awkward silence. I hadn't got off to the greatest of starts in terms of making a good impression and yet he wasn't giving me much to work with. I took a large sip of cold wine, trying to ignore the feeling of regret I was experiencing about having insisted on the meet up. Maybe James had had his reservations because the friend he lived with was socially a bit of a fucktard. In my defence, it was Mark being so cold which was making me act so clumsily.

Still, good old alcohol came to our rescue (thank god) and a couple of drinks later the atmosphere relaxed considerably. Mark began to engage and slowly seemed to start accepting that I might be a semi decent human being.

Meanwhile, I decided to 'start again' and did everything in my power to be charming, ingratiating and to avoid any references to the past, because I now knew for sure that up until tonight Mark had been 'team Tilly' and that therefore there must be more to the marriage break up than James had told me. It was just so obvious due to Mark's reticent attitude. His wife probably didn't come because she didn't approve and would probably grill him when he got home. Maybe she was best friends with Tilly? Who knows but the whole evening left me with the impression that contrary to what I'd always imagined, James was the 'villain' in the piece, not Tilly? This in turn meant that she might still want him; competition I could do without. Just thinking about it made me feel insecure and paranoid that he hadn't been totally frank with me about his divorce. The whole experience was draining and left my head feeling fried. I almost missed my single days, when mind reading and psychology weren't necessary life skills.

At ten o clock we all decided to make a move back to the tube which we rode altogether to Waterloo at which point Mark left us to get on a different train home.

As soon as we were alone I pulled a face at James.

'What?' he said.

'Nothing, he's……nice, it's just…'

'What?'

'I don't know…I'm just not sure he really liked me.'

'Course he did,' said James.

We'd just got on the train which was due to sit on the platform for another couple of minutes.

'Really? I'm not so sure you know. Remember how welcoming my mates were at Lindsay's party? And I know for a fact that if Keisha met you she would fling her arms round you and make sure you knew how happy she was for us, whereas Mark seemed to spend the night trying to catch me out or something. To be honest he was quite tricky at the start, when you went to get the first drinks, though things did get easier after that.'

I smiled, an attempt to reassure James that it was all fine, and that I was just bloody exhausted as opposed to anything else. I knew I was speaking plainly but it had been an incredibly stressful night and I fully expected James to sympathise. Any idiot could have seen I'd made considerably more effort than Mark had.

So when it came, James' reaction was not what I'd been expecting at all.

'Well then maybe you won't put so much pressure on me next time to arrange a night that no one can really be arsed with. Because if you didn't enjoy it then there really wasn't any point. And I'm sorry my friends aren't as fucking perfect as yours.'

I remember my jaw practically dropping to the ground. I was absolutely stunned and was about to answer back in the strongest of terms when to my horror James got up and got off the train without so much as a backward glance. It was inexcusable and so harsh that briefly I felt a shot of something which closely resembled hatred.

It wouldn't be the last time.

20
Ex Text

I'd be lying if I said James' behaviour didn't inform how I acted at times which is why, one evening in November I didn't exactly lie but I certainly wasn't as transparent as I would have been if he hadn't been likely to make such a huge deal of things.

We were half way through a particularly gripping episode of a police drama we always saved to watch together. We were on the sofa in our usual positions. He was on the righthand side and I was lying across the rest of it, feet on his lap in the hope that he'd rub them.

My phone was on the coffee table on silent but a text flashed up and the sender's name happened to catch my eye, at which point I sat bolt upright and turned the phone over face down on the table.

'What is it?'

'Don't know. Nothing. I just don't want it distracting me,' I said, as nonchalantly as possible while wondering what the hell Lucas bloody Harcourt was doing texting me. Apart from anything else I thought he was in America. Of course, it didn't matter to me what he wanted but if James saw he'd been in touch, I'd have to undergo something akin to what Tudor prisoners had to go through in the Tower of London and I couldn't be bothered. So I waited 'til he'd gone to the loo to see what it said.

> *Charlotte – I'm in town. Call me as soon as you can. I need to see you. Don't worry! I'm not going to bother you. I just need to ask you something. I really would appreciate it. It's extremely important.*

My heart sunk. It would have been so much easier if he hadn't contacted me. Yet I also resented the fact I felt so conflicted about speaking to him when I had no intention of doing anything wrong. I *should* be able to phone who I liked.

Long story short I phoned Lucas the next morning and, because he sounded utterly reasonable and friendly, agreed to meet him, curious about what it was he wanted. He was being very cloak and dagger and part of me hoped it might be an amazing job opportunity, although if it was, James would hate me working on anything to do with him. Still, he'd just have to understand. My career was important to me and Lucas was moving in A list circles now.

Only it wasn't about that at all.

21
LUCAS

I met Lucas in the Dandelyan bar, in his favourite London hotel, The Mondrian. Lucas owns a beautiful house in Hertfordshire but when he's in town for work he tends to stay in hotels. As all the PR suggested, his career was going from strength to strength. When we were dating, he used to come here for a drink, but stay somewhere cheaper to sleep. Apart from 'special' occasions *blush*.

Not anymore. In fact, he managed to inform me within the first five minutes of seeing him that these days he was quite the regular and that most of the time he didn't even have to foot the bill. Production companies were paying his expenses more and more.

'How are you gorgeous?' he enquired, pouring on the charm once he'd finally exhausted the subject of himself.

He definitely wanted something.

'I'm fine thanks Lucas but would love to know what this is all about.'

'Not interested in a proper catch up then?' he chuckled. I think part of his attraction to me was that, unlike most other females, I was always suspicious of, and vaguely impervious to his charms.

Having said that, I hated myself for feeling a familiar thrill of attraction toward him, even though I would never go there ever, ever again. Not just because James would spontaneously combust but because I'd loathe myself afterwards.

There was a reason I'd refused his advances for so long in the first place. I'm no naïve flower and my instinct with Lucas had always been to avoid. Yet I'd folded because his smile is so intoxicating, he could send a shiver up my spine with a mere glance and he'd known exactly what to say to convince me he was different. When it all went sour it was painfully hard to accept I'd been right all along. Saying 'I told you so' to yourself is no fun.

'What do you want to drink?' he asked as the waiter made an appearance. 'Cocktail? As you know they do make the best ones ever.'

'No,' I laughed. 'Christ Lucas it's 2.30 in the afternoon. I'll have a cappuccino please.'

'And I'll have a beer please. Hey, it was worth a try,' he added, winking as the waiter walked away 'Remember the last time we were here Lottie?'

I met his gaze and indulged him for a second, cheeks hot as I recalled everything in technicolour. It had been a filthy, decadent afternoon. One I'll probably find myself recalling on my deathbed. Even if the person I shared it with did turn out to be a philandering arsehole.

I thought of James suddenly and how upset and hurt he would be if he knew I'd come to meet Lucas today, let alone to end up sitting reminiscing about that passionate afternoon. The thought was sobering and made me feel guilty. I instantly sat up and adopted a more business-like tone, cross with myself for indulging a man who, after all, treated me pretty disrespectfully.

'Right, come on then. I can't stay too long. What was it you wanted to speak about?' I said.

To be fair Lucas took my cue.

'Ok, well it's a bit delicate but as you may or may not have heard I've landed a part in a movie in the States which, all being well, should finally be my really big break. I've got management out there now, as well as an agent who both have a say in what my image should be and how all PR should be handled.'

I gave him a look which said 'get to the point'.

'Ok Lottie, this is the thing. I need to know if you still have any incriminating photos of us.'

I was surprised. This wasn't what I'd been expecting.

'You know the ones I mean.'

I did, of course.

'Why?'

'I just need to know,' said Lucas, looking vaguely sheepish 'I didn't exactly treat you brilliantly and whilst I know you never would use them against me, maybe I...... couldn't blame you if you did?'

'Are you kidding me?' I gasped, truly offended. 'Do you really think I would want anyone to see those?'

'Well no, but then you just never know one hundred percent. And I do trust you but if this movie takes off, those pictures will be worth a lot of money. Probably already are. My agent's worried that journalists are sniffing around for stories because when this film happens there's going to be a lot of heat around it. Anything to do with me will be newsworthy.'

I shook my head, remembering why, despite having some sort of chemical attraction to this man, I also despised him. He was so self-absorbed.

I took my phone out. 'Here,' I said going into my camera roll and scrolling back and back and back for ages until I came across the five or six images I'd kept. 'I'll delete them all and then I'll delete them from the deleted items if you want.'

He took my phone 'Oh my god,' he grinned 'these are so hot. God we were good together.'

I was furious 'Lucas, just delete the bloody things please.'

He nodded and appeared to do as he was told.

'Happy now?' I said, snatching my phone back to check. He had deleted them but I went into the trash bin. They were all still in there where they would be for a certain amount of days so I selected 'delete all' and then they really were gone for good. Good riddance.

Lucas acknowledged what I'd done with a nod, at least having the good grace to look vaguely awkward. 'I'm sorry. I know you wouldn't ever have sold them...... it's just that......'

'It's fine,' I interrupted, just as the waiter arrived with my coffee. 'Here, you have that,' I said, getting up and putting my jacket on 'Listen, it's been good to see you and good luck with your movie and everything but, please don't contact me again. I'm in a new relationship so it's not really appropriate any more. Ok? I'm sorry and I do wish you loads of luck with this film but let's just leave it at that. Anything else is too awkward if I'm honest.'

'Fine,' he said after a pause. 'As a matter of interest, why did you keep them for so long?'

His expression was suddenly knowing, lascivious and infuriating. It turned my stomach. I left without saying anything more as unresolved feelings of betrayal, hurt and embarrassment seeped through me.

As soon as I was back out onto the Southbank I tried to call James, only his phone went straight to voicemail. Seeing Lucas had really disturbed me. It was a brutal reminder that the only person he really cared about was himself. Horrible. On the flipside, seeing him had also thrown how I felt about James sharply into perspective. I was so grateful to be with someone who respected and cared about me; to be in a mature loving relationship which had a future. In that moment I missed him terribly. I was due to see him the following night and couldn't wait to tell him how much I loved and appreciated him.

That evening I went out for a drink with some of the girls from work but still couldn't get hold of James so was pretty distracted throughout, still unsettled by my encounter with Lucas. I remember deciding to tell James about meeting up with him. I had to. If I didn't it would be like admitting I'd done something wrong and I didn't want to lie to him about anything. No doubt there would be a huge row but in time he'd see it for what it was and there would be no secrets between us. Plus, I could tell him quite honestly that I would never be seeing him ever again. It felt like closure.

22

As predicted James wasn't exactly overjoyed when I told him about meeting up with Lucas, but it could have been worse. I couldn't get hold of him until the next morning and it was such a relief when he did finally answer, that I blurted it out almost at once.

'I'm telling you to prove to you how much you can trust me and to show he means precisely nothing to me,' I finished, bracing myself for the inevitable tirade. Yet it didn't really come.

'But why didn't you tell me before you saw him yesterday?' he asked, more shocked than angry. I felt quite on the back foot.

'Well, being honest, I didn't know what he wanted to see me about and I suspected it might be about a job. If it had been I wanted to at least have the opportunity to consider it but I was worried you might tell me not to go at all. I *should* have told you yesterday of course, but I didn't, so I'm telling you now.'

'What did he want?' asked James.

I hated hearing him sound hurt and anxious. I felt so guilty for lying and suddenly quite terrified. If I lost this man over this I'd never forgive myself. I'd known Lucas was his Achilles heel. Had I made a huge mistake?

'He wanted to check that I would never go to the press about our pathetic excuse for a relationship. It was terribly insulting to be honest and typically egotistical. I was offended and pretty pissed off by the whole thing. I've asked him not to contact me again. I told him that I'm in a relationship and that it's not appropriate for us to be in contact. I didn't even stay long enough to drink the coffee I'd ordered.'

Silence.

'I'm sorry baby. I know you're probably really pissed off with me for going but I'm actually glad I did because now he knows exactly where my head is at. Which is with you. I love you so much.'

'I've got to go,' he said.

Shit. My heart sank. I didn't want to end up regretting telling him and hoped he wasn't going to make a big pointless fuss over nothing. Why did doing the right thing feel so difficult?

'Ok, but I'll see you later yes?'

'Yeah, yeah, I'll call you.'

As he rung off I half wondered if he would, but thankfully he did. I remember he was quite emotional and that night turned out to be one of the nicest nights we'd ever had together. He was in a buoyant, romantic mood and surprised me with a gift, a beautiful bracelet. I was so touched. It was a gold links bracelet and he'd bought the letter C as a charm. I loved it. Having anticipated a night of having to reassure him that I didn't fancy Lucas sleazebag Harcourt I was happily surprised and delighted it was otherwise. It felt symbolic and reminded me of all the reasons we fell in in love in the first place.

So it was rather disappointing when a mere day later he went quiet on me. In fact, I hardly saw him for the next week or so. Work had kicked off apparently. There were issues on site and when I did speak to him, he sounded stressed and strained.

Still, I flung myself into my own work, had a rare night out with Lindsay, went out for dinner with Dad and eventually my boyfriend came back, his focus fully on me. I realised then that this was just what being in a mature adult relationship was about. Being there and being patient, through good times and bad. He loved me. I knew that and perhaps we'd come through the teething section of our relationship. Maybe we'd weathered the tricky toddler years during which boundaries are laid down and were now on our way to growing up together. Being honest had been the right thing to do.

It always is.

23

The last time I saw James it was a Tuesday. A Tuesday in December, the eighth of December to be precise and it was cold and grey. These are all facts. But what happened? It was a day I've recalled and recounted so many times since, it's stopped seeming real.

Of course, at the time, it was a normal, unremarkable day like any other so I wasn't concentrating on everything which was said or absorbing every detail. To the point where sometimes I wonder if perhaps my memory has failed me altogether. Have I overlooked or forgotten something vital? There must have been some clue as to what was going to happen because otherwise the whole thing is so weird, precisely because that day felt so normal.

'Will you come back here tonight?' I'd asked, covering my naked body with a towel.

James, who was already half dressed, had bent down and kissed the top of my head. 'You are such a sexy little thing.'

I'd grinned. I loved being called little. I'd never felt little until I met James but the fact he was tall and slightly heavy for his frame made me feel positively petite, even though at this stage I was rounder and softer at the edges than I had been in years. Throughout my many years of being single I often didn't bother with dinner at all and would just make do in the evenings with 'single girl staples' i.e. a yogurt or whatever happened to be in the fridge and half a bottle of white wine. When I got together with James however, my eating habits changed entirely. There was no way a pot of hummus, some crackers and a G and T were going to sate this bear of a man's appetite plus he loved eating out. If we weren't out we were in, getting excited about a night on the sofa with a good series to watch, a Chinese takeaway and lots of wine. The extra pounds were inevitable but I didn't get too worked up about them. I was too content.

'So, will you come here then or do you not fancy it?' I asked him again.

'Erm, yeah that should be ok,' he said 'Though it will mean we've seen each other four nights on the trot. Won't you start getting sick of me?'

'I couldn't get sick of you,' I said, too in love to bother playing it cool. Like any couple we had our little patches and last week when I'd hardly seen him it had been difficult because he'd been stressed with work and so he'd felt a bit distant. But this week he'd been more loving and caring than ever and I was ready to take the relationship up a gear. What was the point in mucking about? I knew. He knew. As far as I was concerned it was a done deal. He'd told me he loved me but so far hadn't made any noises about moving in so, not wanting to be pushy, I'd simply decided to start seeing him more frequently in the hope that this would just segue nicely into moving in together. Packing a bag all the time must be starting to grate. There was no point in him wasting money by continuing to pay Mark rent. And, of course, there was the unsaid but ever-present issue of my ageing eggs.

I'd recently celebrated my thirty ninth birthday and now forty was waving at me, one big, numerical milestone looming in the not distant enough future. I was determined to beat it at its own game though and with James in my life, felt on course to do so.

James pulled a warm sweater on, ready for the day ahead. Working on a building site in December was a chilly business. He and his team were doing up a beautiful town house in Islington. It was a total renovation job. I'd seen the before photos and was dying to see it in the flesh but he was insisting I waited until it was finished which wouldn't be for a fair few months. He'd normally arrive at the site at 8am on the dot with everyone else but yesterday I'd persuaded him to treat himself to a lie in. He was the boss after all. But it was ten thirty now and I could tell he was keen to get on, that his head had gone into work mode.

Briefly he sat down next to me on the edge of the bed and fixed me with the brown eyes I'd grown so fond of. He looked at me so intently sometimes, almost with an air of melancholy. It was very sexy.

'I may have to work a bit later tonight, so can we say that, all being well, I'll be back about eight thirty because I'll have to go to the office after I've been on site? I've got loads of paperwork to catch up on. So, if you'd rather arrange to see a friend or whatever I could always just go home?'

'It's fine,' I said, kissing the tip of his nose whilst experiencing a small pang of guilt. I'd become a bit useless about my wider friendship group since meeting James but overall didn't care. I'd been on the other end enough times to know that the same people had put me second when they'd found love which I had totally understood. So, I was owed and was damn well going to enjoy my lovely relationship whenever

I could. 'And seeing as I'm not working today, I'll do my 'housewifey' bit and cook us a nice dinner for when you get in.'

'Ooh that sounds good,' said James pulling on his desert boots and lacing them up. 'But only if you're sure? You don't have to. You're far too good to me you know.'

'Don't be silly,' I said, laughing at how much he sounded like he meant it. 'You look good today by the way. Very sexy.'

'Shut up,' said James, but he was grinning 'Right you, come on, get dressed. You're making me not want to leave.'

I got up, hugging the towel around me. 'Ok, have a brilliant day and I can't wait to see you later.'

'You too and I'll give you an update when I'm surer of timings.'

'Great,' I said, already half way to the bathroom. I was going to take a shower and then have a constructive day. I'd catch up on my invoices and life admin, maybe make a list of Christmas presents I needed to buy. 'I'll probably make fish cakes later if that's ok,' I called over my shoulder. 'Nice homemade ones. I'm trying to eat less red meat.'

'I could insert a crude joke here,' retorted James from the hallway, checking his bag to make sure he had everything he needed. 'But I won't. Thank you, babe, that sounds great. You are amazing. See you later.'

'See you later,' I called without so much as a backward glance precisely because I was going to see him later.

Only I didn't.

At six thirty that evening I surveyed the flat feeling really pleased. I'd tidied and cleaned, sent off all my invoices, chased ones I was owed, paid bills, gone to the shops and prepped my home-made fish cakes which were sat on a plate waiting to be fried. I'd decided that I was going to spend a fortune on James for Christmas, twice as much as I'd originally been planning and way over the budget we'd mutually agreed. I didn't care a jot. He deserved it all and researching and buying presents for someone I loved was bringing me so much pleasure. I'd bought tickets for a play I knew he was desperate to see and a beautiful shirt. I'd also looked into some country hotels, my plan being to take him away for a romantic weekend in the New Year. The kinds of places I'd been looking at had cosy rooms and gastro pub style restaurants with real fires. It would be something to look forward to in drab January. The whole weekend would be on me. I couldn't wait and of course part of the joy was simply having someone to do that sort of thing with at last.

I'd also phoned and spoken to Keisha about New Year's Eve and was planning on persuading James that night that we should spend it with my oldest friends in Cheshire. Keisha was desperate to meet him and I couldn't wait to introduce him to her either.

I'd still only met Mark, and James had only met a handful of my friends at Lindsay's party. Other than that, we still just stayed in our own little bubble. It did bother me but I'd decided to work on it in the New Year.

At six thirty I sent him a text asking when he was going to be back. When I heard nothing I presumed he must be on a tube and went to have a shower and get ready.

At eight I rang again but his phone went straight to voicemail. I remember feeling the first brief flicker of irritation. Usually he was great at staying in touch but that day I hadn't heard from him at all. I hadn't minded, hadn't thought about it really. I'd been busy and knew he was too, but it was getting a bit annoying. We had an arrangement; he knew I was cooking dinner and apart from anything else I was getting hungry. Still, officially speaking he still wasn't late. He'd said eight thirty so I figured his phone battery must have died.

At nine o clock there was still no word and I was feeling a bit stressed. I made myself some toast to take the edge off my hunger. Where the bloody hell was he?

When my mobile rang I flung myself across the room to answer it.

As soon as I realised it was Mum on the other end I had to exert all my self- control not to just cut her off.

'Hello darling.'

'Hi, listen it's not a great time, can I call you tomorrow?'

'I'm away tomorrow, but this won't take long. I just wanted to talk to you about Christmas and see if you and James had decided where you're going to be yet?'

'Er, no, we haven't, not yet,' I replied truthfully 'but I promise I'll find out and let you know soon.'

'If you would. I need to know what I'm ordering you see, it's only a couple of weeks away now and to get a delivery slot with the supermarket you have to be organised.'

'I know,' I said, putting Mum on speaker so I could check I hadn't missed a text. I hadn't. 'Mum, I will let you know I promise. I'll try and chat to him about it tonight but I've really got to go now. Speak soon.'

I cut my mother off and went to stare at the uncooked fish cakes, wondering what to do. I remember thinking drily that I should have said I was cooking steak. He'd have rushed back then.

It was annoying. All I wanted to know was whether or not I should be forgetting our night or preparing the food? Not letting me know either way was rude and it wasn't like I could ring James at work. His mobile was his work number. Or at least he had a separate mobile for work and one for personal. Absentmindedly I scrolled through my contacts before realising that of course I didn't have his work number. I'd never had any need for it.

Nine fifteen.

He must have gone for a drink and lost track of time, or stayed on to tackle a work issue and got held up.

I resigned myself to the fact that something work related had happened and switched the telly on. There was no point getting cross. He'd ring soon enough and with a bit of luck he'd apologise profusely. I hoped so because if he didn't I'd be very tempted to have a go at him and it would be a shame to row and spoil the night.

At ten o clock I still hadn't heard a thing. By now I'd tried ringing a number of times and every time it had gone straight to voicemail. I was worried and uneasy. It was so unlike him not to phone.

On autopilot I tried him yet again, only this time, instead of getting his answer machine a voice said 'this number is no longer available.'

And that was when I started to panic.

24

When I rang the police, they weren't impressed. Common sense had told me that at this stage, James not turning up for dinner wouldn't count as an emergency, even if it felt like one to me, so I hadn't dialled 999 but instead had googled the number for my nearest police station. It was like they refused to take my concerns seriously though, almost out of obstinacy it felt.

'But I promise you. My boyfriend would not just go out and not bother to ring me. He never does that... ever,' I'd repeated, despite getting the strong impression I was wasting my breath. Apparently, a person wasn't officially missing until a period of twenty-four hours had passed and even then, because James was a grown man and not my husband, they didn't seem concerned by his absence. Maybe he'd gone for a night out and got carried away was what they seemed to be insinuating? Maybe you're being a hysterical, nagging girlfriend who can't cope with the fact that her man is out on the town?

The irony was I thought I'd been quite restrained, having held off from phoning them until midnight by which point I can't lie, I was beside myself with worry. Why on earth was James' phone number not available?

Prior to calling them, at my wits end, I'd phoned Lindsay.

'Oh gosh, that is weird babe. Hey, maybe he just didn't fancy fishcakes for dinner,' she'd added, trying to provide a bit of levity to the situation which at this point she was positive would be rectified by morning. I was too worried to find anything funny, although I'd already noted the potential for future laughs about the fishcakes lack of appeal. It would be funny when James turned up; after I'd yelled at him for not sending me so much as a bloody text.

'I'm only joking, listen, probably the best thing you can do is get some sleep and no doubt by the time you wake up he'll have left you a message and there will be some really innocuous explanation.'

'Do you think?' I'd asked, hoping she was right. 'But why isn't his number available?'

'No idea,' said Lindsay 'But again, it will be something like because he hasn't paid his bill, or he's got a new phone and it hasn't switched over yet. Something like that. Course it will be. You know how much he bloody adores you. He'll be gutted when he finds out how worried you've been.'

My stomach had lurched because this was true. James was so caring which was precisely why him not getting in touch was a worry.

'Was he definitely supposed to be coming round? You did say he was working late and that he'd suggested maybe you should see a friend. Could you have got the wrong end of the stick?'

I forced myself to try and remember, because what Lindsay was saying was helping calm me down and was kind of making sense, apart from the part where she thought I might have got my wires crossed. I was positive our arrangement had been a firm, definite one. But maybe I had got it wrong? It would at least explain his absence.

Eventually there wasn't much more Lindsay could say. I could tell she was tired and wanted to go to bed so we said goodnight. I needed to go to bed too. I was working the next day on Daytime Live so needed to be up at 5.45, but gut instinct made me call the police instead.

At the end of the conversation though I was left with very little choice but to accept defeat and finally go to bed feeling sad and worried. The last thing I did before turning in was to wrap the fishcakes in cellophane and put them in the fridge. I had a horrible feeling in the pit of my stomach so tried some positive visualisation which consisted of imagining James and I sat at the table the next night, enjoying the day old food, laughing about how carried away my imagination had got.

I slept badly. Unable to drop off or to stop fretting I must have checked my phone dozens of times until eventually, at four in the morning, knowing sleep was not going to arrive, I got up to check Facebook. Maybe if he was on some spontaneous night out someone might have tagged him in a picture? But even as I looked I knew deep down it was unlikely. James loathed social media. He was so comfortable in his own skin he didn't suffer from 'fear of missing out' by not being a participant like most people. In fact, he only had a pathetic handful of 'friends' compared to most. I was the only person who ever tagged him in anything. He didn't tweet either but he did use WhatsApp. I'd checked that hundreds of times now. Usually it said what time he'd last been online, but now it no longer said a time when I clicked on our chat thread. Meanwhile, his number, when I rang it, remained unavailable. Having no way of being able to contact him was bizarre. I was aware that I was suffering from the twenty first century disease of panicking because I couldn't instantly communicate with someone, but nevertheless felt I had more than enough reason to be concerned.

Come the morning, despite being grey with exhaustion I was pleased it was time to go to work. With the morning came perspective. It was easier to be rational. Something had happened. He'd explain it all soon enough.

With all my kit packed into the boot of my car I drove to work, almost defiantly listening to the cheery tones of breakfast radio, having deliberately chosen a particularly inane station to listen to.

'So, back to the phone in,' said the DJ 'Sheena from Croydon is on the line, Sheena if you were getting married at the place where you met your partner, where would it be?'

'Costa Coffee in Heathrow airport,' trilled Sheena.

'No way, that's hilarious,' said the DJ.

I felt irritated. It wasn't hilarious.

I switched the radio off.

Anxiety flooded to the surface again. Emotions were oscillating wildly. One moment I was convinced James would ring me later on in the day and all would be well, I'd have a massive go at him for putting me through the mill but then it would all be fine. Seconds later I was livid and wanted to punch him.

At work, Dan, the producer, came to the make- up room to tell me that they'd had to replace one of the guests last minute due to food poisoning.

'It's funny,' he'd said 'but the minute someone says they've got food poisoning I just assume they're lying. The record company would almost be better off saying 'he's got a huge hangover.' It's more rock n roll than having the squits and at least you'd know they were being honest.

I smiled weakly but my heart wasn't in it.

'Hey, you ok? You look a bit pale. Don't tell me, dodgy sausage? Are you going to be stricken down too?'

I smiled weakly but inside was torn. I was reluctant to bring my personal stuff to work. Plus, it was embarrassing to say the least to admit that your boyfriend had gone AWOL. Dan and I had always got on well though, so eventually I decided it probably wouldn't do any harm to confide. At least that way he'd understand if I seemed distracted.

'It's James,' I said, trying to keep my tone light. 'He was supposed to come round last night but was a no show, and I haven't actually heard from him since yesterday morning. It's really weird and.... to tell you the truth, I'm worried.'

Dan frowned, trying to assess quite how worried I was, or should be 'Oh dear,' he said eventually 'us men eh? Bloody useless, aren't we? But don't worry. He'll be right as rain. He'll have had a couple of pints too many, got carried away and forgotten to let you know. We've all done it.'

I wrinkled my nose 'Hmm, I hear you but actually he never forgets to text or call. And it's really odd but for some reason his number isn't working either.'

As Dan regarded me, I experienced a sudden wave of self- consciousness as it occurred to me that I probably looked like death warmed up. I selected my favourite Nars blusher and a brush from my kit, then looked into the mirror and scrutinised my tired face before giving my cheekbones some much needed colour.

In the reflection I could see Dan smiling reassuringly. He was wearing baggy jeans, a navy jumper and trainers and his dark hair was rumpled like he'd literally rolled out of bed and got dressed in five minutes. There's something about Dan that's always made me laugh even when he isn't trying to be funny. He's such a decent bloke, very clever and extremely well respected as a producer yet has a vaguely hapless air permanently surrounding him. Like a male Bridget Jones maybe, only not *quite* as posh.

He gave me a pat on the shoulder which, rather than be helpful, made me register how rigid with stress my entire body was. Bloody James. What was he thinking?

'Honestly Charlotte, don't waste your precious time worrying my sweet. I bet you fifty quid he'll have been in touch by the time the show ends. I remember him from Lindsay's party. Seemed like a really nice guy and was clearly potty about you, as one would totally expect. He'll be in touch begging forgiveness before you know it.'

I nodded, grateful for his kindness and determined to swallow away my true feelings. I was at work so needed to keep a mask on. 'You're right, thank you. Anyway, enough of my boring rubbish,' I'd said, possibly a touch over brightly 'How are you and Stacey? Things a bit better?'

Dan's face instantly clouded over 'Hmm, don't know to be honest……I sometimes think if it wasn't for Billy she'd be off. But there you go. Who can blame her?'

I half wished I hadn't asked. Dan and his wife had been having a 'patch' for as long as I'd known him and at Lindsay's party, Stacey, hadn't come across as the warmest of people. It was my turn to say something nice. 'Well, every marriage has patches. And I'm sure she knows she's got a keeper.'

Dan went red and looked really pleased but slightly embarrassed by the compliment. 'Ah thanks. Right, I'd best head to the gallery and see what's happening with this wretched guest. But we'll catch up later and you can give me that fifty quid you'll owe me.'

I laughed, feeling better. I made a decision. It was time to stop stressing and get on with the day. James had ruined a whole evening and night already. I'd not slept a wink because of him but if he couldn't even be bothered to ring, I wasn't going to allow him to ruin my morning at work too. I switched my phone off and zipped it into my handbag. When James rang he could get a taste of his own medicine and find me unavailable.

Some hours later, once the show was finished and all my stuff had been packed away, I turned my phone on, trying to ignore the butterflies which were flapping around in my stomach in anticipation. I was exhausted by now; my night of no sleep having caught up. My eyes were grainy and sore. I felt cold and shivery, nervous as hell and desperate for a message.

Nothing.

It was crushingly disappointing.

I arrived home just after three o clock. By now I could no longer ignore my instinct which was that something was seriously wrong. I couldn't wait around for the police to spring into action. It was time to call the hospitals.

After an hour or so of fruitless ringing, only to discover that no one called James Ralphs had been checked in anywhere, I considered my options.

As I was doing so Lindsay rang. I was pathetically grateful to see her name.

'Lindsay.'

'Alright darling, I'm assuming you've heard from him?'

I could hear her toddler son Ben singing away to himself in the background 'No. Not a whisper.'

'Oh no,' said Lindsay. Her evident surprise made me feel quite frightened. It was all so bizarre. 'But listen sweetheart, if you think about it, there's still no reason to worry. If he'd forgotten he was supposed to be coming to you last night, then he might well have gone out, woken up really late and then had to go to work the minute he woke up?'

'But he's always up early for work,' I said, trying to sound calm and measured but failing because it just wasn't adding up. 'So even if you're right and he had gone out, he'd have been up at 6.30 because he starts work at 8 every morning. And even if he did wake up really late it's now late afternoon and he would be desperate to speak to me by now. We never go more than a few hours without contact. We're pathetic the pair of us. He knows I'll be worried and, even if his phone is lost or broken and he doesn't know my number off by heart, there's always Facebook or Twitter or email. As long as he was around anyone with a phone or internet he could get in touch somehow.'

'Hmm,' said Lindsay at which point I could tell she was worried too which in turn made my own anxiety multiply and sweep round me like horrible charged electricity.

'Listen, I'm going to have to go. I've got some of my old NCT mums coming round with their toddlers so it's going to be bloody bedlam when they arrive but I reckon he'll definitely have got in contact with you by the end of play tonight. So keep in touch, and let me know when you've heard from him. And, if the very worst comes to the worst and he hasn't appeared by the time I've finished work tomorrow, I'll get Paul to do bath and bed and come straight round to you. Then we can make a plan. Only I'm sure it won't come to that. It'll be alright. Ok?'

'Ok, thank you.' I was starting to feel quite sick. I could have cried. Where the fuck was he? I hated feeling so out of control.

I made myself a cup of coffee. Normally I avoided coffee in the afternon but I was absolutely knackered and needed something to pick me up. As I drank it Mum rang but I ignored the call. She was the last person I wanted to speak to.

After I'd finished my coffee I decided to ring the police again. If James was in trouble I'd never have forgiven myself if no one knew. It had been more than twenty-four hours without contact now so this time I had their attention.

One hour later I was at my local police station, in a room, sat opposite a policeman who was filling out a form. It was surreal and part of me was praying I wasn't making a mountain out of a molehill and wasting their time. He hadn't been gone *that* long yet instinct told me.......

'So, James Ralphs. And Ralphs is spelt...'

'R A L P H S,' I'd said.

'Any middle name?'

'Er... no.'

'Sure?'

'Yes,' I'd replied more definitely, remembering how the two of us had laughed at mine. Mabel was a name that had been consigned to 'out of fashion' a long while ago and it didn't look like it would be coming back in any time soon.

'And his address please?'

I'd scrunched up my nose 'Well.... it's complicated. He's split up with his wife, so he doesn't live at his house anymore.'

'Ok,' said the policeman 'Then where is his house that he doesn't live in anymore?'

'It's in Tooting, but he's been staying with his friend Mark, who lives in New Malden. And then he's with me quite a lot of the time, just till he gets sorted, or until he moves in with me officially.'

'Right,' said the policeman 'Well in order to help we're going to need a bit more information than that. Are you able to provide either of the full addresses please?'

'Er, no,' I admitted, hating myself for going red, though I didn't know why I was. Why the hell would I ever have asked him for the address of the place his ex-wife lived? Why should I care?

'Right, well whereabouts roughly is the friend's house he stays in? Maybe if we look on the map you can show me?' suggested the policeman.

'Oh gosh, I'm really sorry about this, I know I'm not being at all helpful it's just that I haven't been there you see.'

'You've never been to this Mark's house, where your boyfriend lives?'

'No.'

The policeman looked at me blankly, clearly wondering what to ask next.

'The thing is, there's never been any need. We prefer staying at mine because then we've got total privacy.... Mark's married with kids you see and James is actually just staying in the spare room so it's more comfortable and just... easier at mine...you know.'

'Fair enough,' agreed the unruffled policeman. 'Ok, well what *can* you tell me then? Work address maybe? That sort of information would be really handy? Because all we've got to go on at the moment is his name and the photo you provided.'

I swallowed and felt a creeping blush climb my face.

The policeman was only trying to help, yet for some reason was making me feeling guilty and embarrassed, despite the fact I'd done nothing wrong. I desperately tried to recall anything that would not only help but that would also prove how close James and I were as a couple. I could tell the policeman had his doubts and it rankled.

I cleared my throat, sensing it might be best to escape and regroup. 'You know what, I think it might be best if I go home and ring around a few more people.'

'I thought you said you had tried everything,' replied the policeman, a slight edge to his voice. Was it irritation or disdain?

I got to my feet 'I'm really sorry, it's just I think I've got some more numbers at home. I'll go back in case James has turned up. And then I can always come back later if he hasn't.'

'Right, well if you do come back, please be sure to bring more information with you, bank details, driving licence, parent's details, anything would be good. But in the meantime, don't worry too much. Sometimes boyfriends do go wayward...... especially if things are complicated.'

I didn't like what he was implying.

'Things aren't complicated though,' I insisted.

The policeman remained implacable and replied very reasonably 'Ok, well then I'm sure he'll turn up soon. Try not to worry.'

I could tell then he thought I was a phenomenal time waster. I was angry with myself. I'd been worse than useless and felt like I'd let James down. Not being able to answer anything with conviction made me feel like such an idiot. I hadn't even known what bank he was with. Yet that kind of thing was hardly something lovers lay in bed discussing. Unless they were incredibly dull. I tried picturing what his bank card looked like. I was pretty sure it was black but couldn't picture the detail. James often pays for stuff with cash anyway.

If only he'd been testing me on important things, I would have got ten out of ten. Nobody knew James like I did. What he liked to eat, the music he loved to listen to, his views on so many things including who his favourite actors were, which papers were the best to read, how scrambled eggs should be cooked, these were all questions I could have answered in a heartbeat.

The whole experience had been very unedifying and had got me nowhere. I couldn't help it, for a second I found myself imagining how mortified the policeman would be if he were to find out something terrible had happened to James. I was determined, for James' sake, not to leave without some form of result.

'Well, if anyone else rings in,' I said a bit primly, my tone masking my humiliation 'his workmates or his family, or anyone at all who is worried about him, I'd appreciate you letting me know.'

'We will,' said the policeman kindly 'We have your number on file so we'll be in touch if anything comes to light. I've made a note and put it all on the system so if his name comes up anywhere else there will be an alert too. And, of course, if you're still worried in a few days you can always come back. At that point we can decide whether to issue a press release to the media along with his picture and so on. But like I say, perhaps for now he's just having a breather.'

His choice of words said it all.

It was a relief to emerge onto the pavement, only now I had to figure out where the hell James was without any help from the boys in the blue. A breather. Could it be that he would want or need a breather from me?

Lindsay was calling.

'Any word?'

'Not yet.'

'Shit, I don't believe it. Well, there's still this evening. I'm sure he'll show up with some excuse we couldn't possibly have anticipated, tail between his legs.'

My head was mashed. I'd reached the point I didn't know what to think. Maybe I had totally over- reacted? The policeman had certainly implied that James was probably just giving me a wide berth. So why was every cell in my body screaming at me that that couldn't be the case? Could James really have left feeling so irritated by me that he needed a break and had decided to avoid me for a while? The notion seemed alien and unlikely but I was so tired now nothing was making much sense. I didn't even have the energy to tell Lindsay I'd been with the police. I decided to go home and give it till tomorrow. 'I'm sorry if I've been a bit hysterical about it all,' I said, starting to feel like I was going quite mad.

'Not at all,' said Lindsay at once 'I can understand why you're weirded out and listen, like I said, if he doesn't show up by the time I've finished work tomorrow I'll be straight round.'

'Ok, thank you. How was your NCT afternoon?' I asked.

'Hell on earth,' joked Lindsay 'Hanging out with five toddlers who have no social skills and don't know how to share is never pleasant. The house is covered in a sea of plastic toys. I don't know why I bother really, Ben didn't even enjoy it. He spent the whole time apoplectic with rage that a girl called Evie had touched his digger. Not a euphemism.'

I laughed but it was a feeble attempt.

'Don't worry love,' said Lindsay 'He'll turn up and I'm here in the meantime and will be there tomorrow if need be.'

Knowing she was on my side was such a comfort that I certainly wasn't going to argue. Lindsay knew the score because unlike that sceptical policeman she knew James and therefore understood that the situation could potentially be really worrying. In the meantime, I needed to stop panicking and keep reminding myself that he hadn't shown up in any hospital, that he loved me and that therefore he would be in touch as soon as he was able.

25

I would never have envisaged that, in the run up to the Christmas I'd been so looking forward to spending with James, I'd be getting off the phone to the last hospital on a very long list because he'd gone AWOL. Between Lindsay and myself we'd now phoned every single one in the whole of London and Greater London, with no joy.

'Oh god, I know I should be pleased he's not been in some accident but I just want to know what's happened to him. It's doing my head in.' Feeling permanently helpless and frustrated was hideous. Life had become a silent scream.

'I know,' said Lindsay. Whenever I looked at her I felt a twinge of intense guilt. She looked so tired.

It had now been three days (or about fifty-eight hours precisely) since I'd heard from James. The situation had become officially bizarre and inexplicable so I'd called in to work sick. Not ideal with my interview looming which was happening the following Wednesday afternoon. If I got the job in the New Year I would be returning to work as Head of Department. I should have been preparing for it but it was hard to focus on anything other than James' disappearance.

'I'm so sorry about all of this. Honestly, I don't know what I'd do without you,' I said, wide eyed with stress. I hadn't slept properly in days and was tired to the bone. 'I hope you didn't have plans by the way?'

'Christmas drinks with Paul's work.' Spotting what must have been my stricken face, she quickly added 'Don't even give it another thought. I'm glad I'm not going to be honest. You know what December's like. It all gets too much and besides; this is more important. I know you're freaked out and worried so please don't stress. It's not important. Right, what do we do now?'

'Mark, Mark will know where he is. I need to get in touch with him.'

'Ok,' agreed Lindsay 'brilliant, but why haven't you rung him already?'

'I don't have his number. I was thinking today though, I could try and send him a message on Facebook. What do you think? Do you think James will be cross?'

Lindsay looked faintly frustrated. She'd been up the night before with Ben and was clearly feeling quite shredded. I remember thinking then that when James did show up I wouldn't blame her for giving him a piece of her mind. Disappearing like this was so selfish.

'Why would he be cross?' she said slightly impatiently 'Babe, listen, I'm not being funny but either you genuinely think something is up, in which case we have to do something to find him? Or deep down you think he's fine and just being useless which is the only reason you'd be worrying about how you're going to come across to his mates.'

'You're totally right,' I said 'Ignore me, I'm being an idiot. My gut is telling me I need to find him and make sure he's ok so of course I don't care what anyone thinks. Let's just get on Facebook and find out what the hell he's playing at.'

'Good plan,' said Lindsay, relieved to have something else to do which felt like positive action. So far our time together had been frustratingly fruitless. We had so little to go on. Ringing the hospitals had been one of the only things we could do.

'Facebook is a great idea,' encouraged Lindsay 'In fact it amazes me you haven't already done this. 'You'll be able to find all his friends and family and if you have to meet them for the first time on Facebook then so be it. It's his bloody fault for doing a vanishing act,' she added, refilling her wine glass.

I went to my bedroom and returned to the lounge with my laptop. I logged onto Facebook and entered James' name into the search bar. 'I don't know why I haven't done this earlier really,' I admitted. 'But then it's probably because I know he never goes on it. He hates it in fact. He hates all social media and told me he only set his Facebook up so he could create his Tinder profile.'

I felt quite teary when his face came up. I was now missing and worrying about him so acutely it was painful.

Lindsay reached over and squeezed my hand 'Come on you, stop it. He'll be fine. He just deserves a massive bollocking when he finally shows up.'

'I know,' I agreed, blinking hard 'I'm going to kill him. Right, let's go through his friends.'

'Shouldn't take long,' laughed Lindsay. 'He's only got about thirty and you're one of them.'

'I know. He is so anti it all which usually I kind of love him for but right now is just irritating. Right, where's Mark?'

Lindsay shrugged. I'd already reached the end of the list and there was definitely no Mark to be seen.

'Shit,' I said, feeling a bit crazed at this point 'Why the hell isn't he 'friends' with his best friend for god's sake?'

'God knows, right let's see who else is here. Ok, who's Rory Sutton?'

'No idea.'

'Claire McGowan?'

I shook my head.

'Christ, look at Sandra Sulementi,' exclaimed Lindsay 'She looks like a bit of a goer. How the hell does James know her?'

I peered at the profile picture Lindsay had clicked on. Sandra did indeed look like someone you wouldn't want your boyfriend hanging out with. She was pouting provocatively, was essentially wearing a corset and not much else, apart from badly applied lip-liner, (one of my most hated makeup bug bears). Why was James friends with her? She looked like a prostitute. Her makeup was hideous.

'No idea,' I admitted. 'Dread to think. She looks bloody awful. But who knows? Anyway, moving on, who else is there? We need to find someone whose name I recognise. I know, find his sister. She's called Lisa. I could message her.'

We scrolled back to the L's but there was only one and it was a Leonard. I clicked on his picture. He was probably in his late seventies?! It said he lived in Tunbridge Wells.

I was really stressed by now and feeling increasingly vexed. 'Why can't he be like everyone else and just like being on Facebook? Or at least have his nearest and dearest on there. Why would he not have bothered adding his sister? Unless the whole family have an aversion to it, which seems unlikely these days?'

I did a general search for Lisa Ralphs. A few came up but I had no way of knowing if they were his sister.

'Hmm, trouble is she's married and I have no idea what her last name is. It goes without saying she might not be using that name anymore.'

'Could that be his mum?' asked Lindsay doubtfully, staring at one of James' contacts on her phone where she was on the Facebook app.

I regarded the picture she was showing me. The woman in it looked about sixty something years old and was wearing a lurid pink hat and suit, the type a 'woman of a certain age' wore to a wedding. She was called Yvette, there was no second name. She could easily be his mother and yet my instinct was that James' mother would have a better sense of style somehow. At the same time, I knew it wasn't rational making a judgement based on nothing concrete. 'I don't know. I don't think so. It says she's in Oxfordshire.'

'Well where do his mum and dad live?'

'Er, London, I think. I mean I'm sure.'

'What do you mean?'

'Well I don't know one hundred percent when I think about it. But I know James lived in Wales until he was about five, then his Dad got a new job and they came here. I just assume they must be in London somewhere because he tells stories about them being in town. Like when they went skating at Christmas. If they didn't live in London, I doubt they would have gone to the Natural History Museum on Christmas Eve. Every time I ask about them, they always seem to be away somewhere so it hasn't come up specifically... but he's never indicated that they were particularly far away.'

'I remember you telling me about the Christmas Eve story, when you first met him,' said Lindsay who was still concentrating on scrolling through James' Facebook friends. 'Tell me again, why you haven't met his parents yet?'

I shrugged 'I don't know,' I said dolefully 'They're always away on holiday it seems. Then his mum got ill and didn't want to meet me while she was sick, which I totally understand... and James is just....'

'What?'

I shrugged again, perilously close to tears 'He's useless at arranging anything and always says he just loves being with me. I don't know. But yes, I know you think it's a bit shit and I do agree. I think a lot of the problem is guilt though, about his ex who they no doubt loved.'

But Lindsay was still frowning at Facebook 'Babe, he's friends with a very weird mixture of people. Everyone's so scattered and I just would never have some of these people down as friends of his.'

Looking back, that was the moment I knew something was very, very wrong. Only I wasn't anywhere near ready to examine the kernel of suspicion that had suddenly taken root in the pit of my anxious stomach.

26

He left on Tuesday morning but it took until Friday to wrap my head around what had first started to become apparent the night Lindsay and I scrutinised his Facebook.

What I really know about James could be written on a napkin.

I mean, I know what kind of thing makes him laugh. I know he hates hummus and beetroot with a passion but that he has a sweet tooth which hasn't matured since he was about six years old. For James a 'pick n mix' is a wonderful treat. I remember laughing at how excited he was one time at a service station as I watched him salivate over chewy bananas, over size cola bottles and sports mixtures, the type of confectionery my pallet outgrew years ago.

I know he loves having his feet rubbed, that he bites his nails when watching Arsenal and always reads the sports pages of the Sunday papers first, followed by any property section. I know he loves kissing, more than any man I've ever been with, that he closes his eyes and looks totally lost in what he's doing. I know it takes him an hour or so to unwind after work and that when he initially arrives home he's a bit bouncy and wired.

I know he's perfectly capable of going without a drink but that once he does have a beer he finds it hard to only have one or two. I know he hates it when his hair starts to get long and that he likes having it cut every five weeks. I know he used to fancy Sarah Greene from Blue Peter, that he detests social media, can't stand having his photo taken, and despairs at how reliant everyone is on their phones. He's kind to dogs and is physically incapable of passing one in the street without looking at it or patting it. He likes wearing checked shirts. He buys basics from Top Man and River Island but supplements them with bits from Cos and Whistles. He's the best dressed boyfriend I've ever had. I even know his most embarrassing moment. It happened when he was in his twenties. He kissed a girl he'd fancied for ages but failed to mention that he'd eaten a Snickers bar an hour or so before. Which was a shame because what she hadn't told him was that she had a potentially lethal nut allergy which he only discovered when her lips started swelling up and her face went blue. She lived to tell the tale but there wasn't a second date and it's haunted him ever since and put him off nutty chocolate for life. Politically he's a woolly liberal who was far more socialist in his younger years but who's veered more to the centre as he's got older. He accepts and knows he's a cliché in that respect. I know he loves his family and that he had an unusually happy childhood and yet I couldn't tell you the name of his parents or where they live. It's the detail that's missing.

During that night with Lindsay, my growing sense of dread changed. Suddenly I was less worried that something had happened to James, and more concerned something had happened to me. I didn't know what to do. Thank goodness I had Lindsay to talk to because I felt like I was going mad.

The evening we scrutinised James' Facebook my thoughts were already heading in a very dark direction.

Lindsay started to verbally skirt round the edge of things herself 'So,' she said 'Let's look at what we know for sure. You and James didn't have a fight on Tuesday morning. Correct?'

'Correct,' I replied, somewhat feebly.

'When he left everything was great but now it's Thursday night and he's been out of contact since and his number's out of action. So, worst case scenario he's been in an accident, yeah?'

'Yes.'

'But we've called every hospital in central London and greater London and no one by the name of James Ralphs has come in.'

I nodded.

'Ok, so being really bleak, if he had been in an accident and couldn't talk or say his name, maybe they wouldn't have those details yet?'

The thought of James lying in intensive care somewhere, unidentified, made my stomach churn in horror.

'But we've also asked every hospital if there was anyone there who hadn't been identified and there isn't and they all have your contact details in case.'

'True,' I whispered, feeling increasingly like I couldn't handle much more.

'You also asked the police to let you know if he shows up anywhere. So if he hasn't been in an accident or some strange incident of some kind then we have to look at the next likely option which is that for whatever reason he has *chosen* not to turn up or contact you.'

I couldn't dispute her logic but my gut couldn't relate. We'd been so happy on the day we last saw one another.

'Charlotte,' Lindsay continued 'I know this sounds a bit horrible, but is there anything he could have found out about that would have upset him to such a degree that he might want to ignore you for a while? You're not having an affair or anything? He couldn't have seen something on your phone and gone off that morning secretly feeling livid with you?'

'God no! Since I met James I haven't thought about anyone else, let alone looked at anyone. There is nothing he could have found out. Literally nothing. I even told him about meeting up with Lucas that time which he was actually fine about.'

'Ok. I just thought I should check.'

Lindsay almost looked disappointed by my answer. I sympathised, the whole business was infuriating and by ruling out what she'd just suggested, it left the finger pointing at my absent boyfriend. Could he really have deliberately chosen to torture me like this? Was he capable of doing this to me, despite knowing how I felt about him? I was so drained I didn't know what to think. Lindsay looked like she wanted to say something but wasn't sure she should.

'What?'

'Oh, I don't know love. I suppose what's weirding me out is how little you have to go on. You don't know where his work is, where his mates are, where his parents live, or anything? But you've been going out with him for what, ten months?'

She was right. Of course.

Suddenly I needed to be on my own, needed to think. 'I do know where he works,' I cried suddenly 'He's renovating a house in Islington. I'll go there tomorrow, after work, drive around and look everywhere until I find it.'

Lindsay looked doubtful 'Islington is massive love, maybe you should just go to the police again? Let them look? But I'm glad to hear you're going back to work?'

'Yeah,' I said distractedly, wishing I didn't have to.

Lindsay's phone was flashing.

'Ignore it,' said Lindsay 'It's only Paul, he'll be out, again, drunk and no doubt annoying.

'You should speak to him,' I insisted 'and in fact Linds, you look exhausted and you've been so, so amazing, but go home now. I'll be fine. I need to sleep on it I think. My head's mashed and like I told you earlier when I went to the police yesterday, they were really unhelpful, so I'm just not sure. I don't know.'

'Alright,' said Lindsay 'But I'll check in first thing tomorrow ok? I'm sorry I've got work myself tomorrow or I'd come to Islington with you. But I can help on Saturday. Although you'll have heard from him by then,' she quickly added, though I could tell from her expression that something had changed for my friend. She didn't look like she had that much faith in anything James would or wouldn't do anymore.

I saw her out then leapt back onto Facebook, searching feverishly through James' small list of 'friends.' Lindsay was right. There was no rhyme or reason to his social network. It was a completely random assortment of people, none of whom seemed to fit for one reason or another, be it because of their geography or demographic. I'd never heard him mention any of these people and couldn't work out how any of them fitted into his life.

I drained my wine glass, wanting the hit of numbing alcohol.

How was my life unravelling so quickly?

On a whim I sent a friend request from my own Facebook account to Sandra Sulimenti and the man called Leonard. Nothing ventured, nothing gained. James was now more than forty-eight hours late for dinner, something was definitely going on and I needed to find out what it was.

The next morning, after another terrible night's sleep, I woke up to find that James still hadn't been in contact but that both Sandra and Leonard had accepted my requests.

I sat bolt upright and typed out the same message to each of them which would land in their direct messages. It did occur to me that I was lucky they'd accepted my request and a bubble of hope swelled inside me. Perhaps they'd spotted that we had a mutual friend in the form of one James Ralphs. Maybe these people were the key to finding him?

I wrote

> *Hi, I hope you don't mind me contacting you. I'm James Ralphs' girlfriend and I've not seen or heard from him since Tuesday morning. I'm worried about him so am reaching out to friends of his on Facebook to see if they*

can help or have any info. If you know anything please message me here or phone me on the following number....'

After pressing send I left the flat and headed to work in a daze.

27

Having to explain that my boyfriend had disappeared wasn't easy.

I still had no information, no clarity, a pain in my heart and a sense of loss so great I may as well have been told he was dead. Yet because this probably wasn't true, because the stronger likelihood was that he'd done the dirty on me and for some contemptible reason decided to fuck me over completely, I had no choice but to carry on. So I did. Somehow.

The makeup room was strewn with tinsel and other festive decorations and presenter, Logan, was in the chair and in a chatty mood 'What are you up to for Christmas then?' he asked. It was an innocuous enough question and of course he was blissfully unaware what a minefield this had become. I nearly burst into tears as I confronted for the first time that of course I probably wouldn't be having it with James.

'I think I'll be at my mum's,' I muttered, brow furrowed as I made sure Logan's hair was secured in place with a bit of wax.

'And what have you bought the man for Christmas? Anything nice?'

'Oh.... you know......might ...hire a hitman to kill him or something,' I muttered.

Logan looked understandably alarmed.

'Joking!' I said, tone high pitched and strained from the effort of trying to sound light which of course made me sound anything but 'No, it's all fine. It's just we've *sort of* split up. Well.... we haven't split up exactly, more like he's kind of vanished, walked out on me....... I think.'

Talk about a conversation killer. For the millionth time I wondered how he could be putting me through this.

'Shit,' said Logan, clearly wishing he'd never asked.

He wasn't to blame. The Daytime Live team were all aware I'd been unlucky in love for years. They knew (because I'd told them) how much Lucas had hurt me but that now, finally, I was in a relationship and that the wait had been worth it because James was amazing. I was the beacon of hope for singletons everywhere. Wait long enough and it will happen. Even for Charlotte.

As I watched Logan struggling to find something appropriate to say, I felt terrible. His time in the chair is sacrosanct. It's his time to compose himself before presenting a very stressful, long, live show. The last thing he needed was to be counselling me. He's a kind man too so no doubt felt dreadful. Though it won't be anywhere close to how mortified I was feeling. I swallowed hard and patted his shoulder in a bid to communicate that he didn't need to say anything.

'Well... I'm here if you need me. You only have to ask,' he said before escaping to his dressing room.

Claire was also in that day. She was busy making up a boyband member in the next chair. They were engaged in their own conversation but she'd clearly had half an ear out because as soon as Logan had gone, she mouthed 'You ok?'

I nodded yes and mustered a smile as I blinked back tears. I wasn't interested in going into all the details with Claire. I felt like a fool, the office reject. Undesirable Charlotte back on the scrap heap. My 'dream' had gone very sour and no matter how hard I tried to mask it, people would feel spectacularly sorry for me as and when they found out. So much pity and awkwardness lay ahead. It was an awful prospect.

As soon as Mr boyband had gone, having had a minor hissy fit about wanting mascara that didn't look like mascara, Claire shut the door 'What the hell is going on? Are you ok?'

I gave her very edited highlights. Her interest in what was happening felt more motivated by gossip than caring. I didn't like it.

'God that's so out of order, especially when you've got your interview coming up and everything.'

'I know,' I replied, pissed off and wary that that was her first response. I've always been one rung up from Claire, though suspect she'll catch up soon. Her ambition is clear for all to see. That said, I'm the one who's helped her get ahead as quickly as she has. As Madeline Albright, the former US Secretary of State, once said 'There is a special place in hell for women who do not help other women.' I totally adhere to this, which is why I'd have liked her palpable interest in my misery to be toned down a notch.

'Anyway, I'd appreciate it if you didn't tell anyone, you know what it's like round here, everyone knows everything about everybody.'

As if on cue, Dan, the producer of the show, whose own private life is generally regarded as a soap opera, bustled into the room.

'Morning,' he said 'How are you? God I'm glad we're getting the whole week off for Christmas, aren't you? The pre- records are going to be hell, but I'd still rather cope with them if it means getting a proper break. Although I'll be regretting that when Stacey and I are screaming at each other, having had one too many sherries, mother in law giving me daggers. Whereas you Charlotte will be all loved up at mistletoe towers, wearing his and hers matching Christmas jumpers no doubt, like a scene out of a Richard Curtis film. It's so unfair. Same goes for you Claire. What...?' he said, finally noting what must have been mine and Claire's mortified expressions 'Oh god, you haven't split up have you? Shit, I'm such an idiot. I'm so sorry Charlotte; I just totally assumed you guys would have worked it out. Most of us blokes have been on an unnecessarily large bender at one time or another. Could you not forgive him?'

I literally couldn't form words. I managed a shake of the head.

'I'm sure he must feel terrible about it though?'

I needed to tell him, get the humiliation over and done with. I angled my body slightly away from Claire and spoke quietly 'Actually Dan, I don't know if he's been on a bender. I don't know anything, including if I'll be spending Christmas with him. To tell you the truth, I still haven't heard from him.'

'What do you mean? You mean you haven't heard from him at all?' said Dan, looking flummoxed.

'Yes....I mean, no. I don't know where he is.'

'So, have you split up? Or has he just not been in touch?'

I experienced a strong wave of frustration. He was making things harder by failing to grasp what I was saying.

'I don't really know to be honest. I guess I either need to take the hint...... or something dreadful has happened.' I turned away, praying that that would be enough to shut Dan up. I couldn't cope with much more.

'Then you need to call the police,' said Dan and I wasn't sure if it was the concern or the surprise in his voice that was hardest to deal with, or the fact I could see Claire making 'for the love of god please shut up man' actions at him.

And so it went on...... and on, as more and more people enquired in all innocence how James was, how it was all going, or asked what 'we' were doing for Christmas. It was horrendous and with every excruciating explanation it grew harder not to feel utterly desolate and furiously angry. It was a relief when the show ended and I could finally leave and head to Islington.

As I left the building I resolved that no matter what, come Monday morning I needed to be in a better state so that I'd have two good days before my interview. I needed to use the weekend to get my head together and find a way through this so I could pretend I was fine and do my job professionally.

Then I remembered something. The thought hit my scrambled head like a brick. Fuck.

I was supposed to be meeting up with Keisha today and another old school friend, Rebecca, for Christmas lunch. We'd had it booked in for months. I couldn't believe I'd forgotten. I'd been looking forward to it for ages because it was such a rarity for Keisha to get to be, not just in town, but childfree. I was supposed to be in Covent Garden at three o clock for late lunch, shopping and to enjoy London being all twinkly and festive. Keisha would kill me if I didn't make it.

I debated what to do. I didn't feel up to having to explain the situation to my friends. It was too embarrassing, I was exhausted and I still didn't know what was going on anyway. Should I be out of my mind with worry? Should I be furious? I had no idea so looking for James felt like it should take priority, in case he was in trouble.

I simply couldn't sit through a lunch pretending everything was fine. I'd barely slept for days, eating felt like an alien, rather off-putting concept and I was too consumed by what was going on to cope with anything else. I burst into tears. I wasn't just upset, I was also very angry, with James. He was ruining everything.

28

I could easily compose a chart of 'shit moments following James' disappearance'.

For instance:

In at No 3 - *'When the boutique hotel in the Cotswolds phoned to confirm the romantic weekend you'd totally forgotten you'd booked and you cried in Tesco.'*

At No 2 - *'The moment Eleanor rang and you were forced to explain why James probably wouldn't be appearing at Christmas (because you had no idea where the fuck he was) and she actually sounded quite cross and disappointed with you.'*

And at No 1 - *'The reaction you got when you phoned Keisha to cancel lunch with her and Rebecca....'*

Keisha had been quite incandescent with rage.

'But why would you accept a job when this has been in the diary for so long? Do you know what a mission it's been for me to get away? Dave had to turn a job down so I could leave the girls for a night and I've spent a fortune on a hotel so we'd have somewhere to go back to after. And, more than all of that, I've been desperate to see you,' she said, sounding really quite distraught.

'You'll still have Rebecca,' I'd replied, frantically debating whether or not to admit the truth. With hindsight, given how fed up my friend sounded I should have done of course. Only, now I'd lied I didn't want to change my story. I literally didn't have the strength to go through what might or might not have happened.

'Well thanks a lot,' Keisha said, hurt and unimpressed.

I felt terrible but there wasn't much I could do. It was Friday, my boyfriend had walked out of the door on Tuesday morning and I hadn't heard from him since. Going to Islington to look for him took priority. Even if it took all day and night I would find the house he was working on and discover the truth. I'd make things OK with Keisha later. It was the best I could manage. My stress levels were so acute at this point, it felt like insects were crawling through my system. Putting one foot in front of another was challenge enough without Keisha adding to the strain.

***

I hadn't been driving around Islington that long but had already found three houses which were possibilities. I could only vaguely remember the photo I'd been shown so many months ago now, but knew I was looking for a large, grand, town house. Whenever I saw one similar which had skips outside, scaffolding, or any other evidence of builders, I parked up and investigated. But whoever I found just looked at me blankly when I asked if their foreman was called James Ralphs. At one site, the builder I talked to was Polish and after I'd explained why I was there, he looked like he might be going off to get James. My heart positively pounded with anticipation until he returned with a huge black man who definitely wasn't my boyfriend. The man was helpful and sympathetic to a degree but ultimately had no idea what to tell me. He'd never heard of a James Ralphs.

I returned to the car, determined to carry on.

I checked my phone. A text from Keisha. I could hardly bear to read it but did.

> In Covent Garden wishing you hadn't blown me out. I know work is important but so is our friendship and it would have been nice if you'd given me more notice. I would have cancelled and come down on a different day when you were free. Anyway, I've said my piece, have a good day.

My heart sunk with genuine regret for upsetting my friend. I'd handled things badly but Keisha's anger only piled more pressure on and I was already dangerously close to being utterly overwhelmed. My phone pinged again. A Facebook notification.

Adrenaline whooshed around my system as it did every time my phone beeped. Could it be from James? *Surely* this would be him now?

My hands were shaking. It wasn't James but I did have a message from one Sandra Sulimenti, which at least meant information. I clicked to open the message.

> *I don't know your boyfriend. I've never met him. I just accepted his friend request because he looked cute. Same reason I accepted yours ;)*

For lots of reasons which I have spent the last few months deciphering, those words freaked me out so much, the next thing I knew, I was flinging open my car door and puking violently onto the kerb.

***

I gave up on my mission and drove home, sobbing the entire way. By the time I got in the door I had a pounding headache but undeterred went straight to my computer and logged onto Facebook. I had a sick feeling in my stomach. Alarm bells weren't just ringing anymore they were clanging but I needed more proof before I gave in. I went to James' page and sent a friend request to every other single one of his 'friends.' Alarmingly, a mere two hours later nearly all of them had accepted, at which point twenty-three individuals then received messages back from me, all saying the same thing.

> *My name is Charlotte. You are friends on here with my boyfriend James Ralphs. How do you know him? Please do answer. He's gone missing.*

I sat staring at the screen. I wasn't going to move until at least three of them had replied. I didn't have to wait long. After a few minutes I had eight replies sitting in my inbox.

I sensed I was at a crossroads; there would be no going back after reading them. Slowly I opened them one by one at which point something became crystal clear. My boyfriend, the man who less than a week ago had been my entire future and world, didn't know any of these people at all. They were strangers, all of whom he had randomly sent friend requests to, which indicated that all the others would be saying the same thing. I knew then for sure, that there was a huge possibility that apart from me and Lindsay, not one person on there was connected to him in any real way. Meaning he had artfully constructed a fake life. Why?

I also knew then, that in reality, I knew nothing about James. Nothing at all. Not where he lived, not where his family lived, where he worked or who his friends were. The trail was therefore cold as I had no way of knowing where to look for him and, what seemed glaringly obvious for the first time, was that that was the way he'd always wanted it.

I ran to the bathroom and for the second time that day was violently sick. The rest of the day was a blur.

29

Saturday was a write off. I spent the whole day in the flat weeping, raging and feeling entirely sorry for myself. In the end I did try to ring Keisha to tell her what was going on but she didn't pick up and instead sent a terse text saying:

Can't speak. Rebecca and I about to go to hotel spa.
She was well within her rights to be angry, but I ended up feeling furious with her, furious with the world. It was a day spent getting a lot out of my system.

By Sunday though I'd calmed down. I'd had my day of wallowing. Enough was enough. I decided to pack my day with distracting but wholesome activities. There was nothing more I could do in terms of trying to find out where my bastard boyfriend was. I was facing my future alone once again, heartbroken, devastated and having to process the fact that James had lied to me from start to finish.

I only knew one thing for sure. I was giving up. There would be no more dating, no more searching. I'd found love and it had chewed me up and spat me out. Had it been worth it? No. The pain was indescribable and I was under no illusions about how much this latest disaster had damaged me or how long it would take to get over.

So, what to do? Hit the bottle? Escape? These were the most tempting options. Yet, underpinning the pain and heartbreak I was experiencing, visceral anger was pumping through my veins, providing me with quite an alarming amount of strength. I hadn't slept much, yet felt like I could do eight rounds in a boxing ring and come out bouncing. I was choosing to survive this. I wasn't going to let him win. He had lied and he had conned me. He didn't deserve my grief. I wouldn't let him pull me under.

So, as hard as it was, that Sunday I climbed out of bed at ten and started packing a bag for a hot yoga session. That would take me up until lunchtime, at which point I planned to go to Lindsay's. She'd kindly invited me over to join them for Sunday lunch. I planned to not drink and then, later that evening, I was going to attempt a long run around Marble Hill Park. I wanted to wear myself out so entirely that with a bit of luck sleep would come. Then I could turn all my attentions to my interview which was now just days away. It was hard, the pain was borderline physical but I wasn't going to let James ruin anything else for me.

I switched my phone on and threw it on the bed in order to finish packing my bag. It rang almost instantly.

When I think back to this point, this moment in time, my memory takes on a sort of hazy, dreamlike quality. Maybe because I was about to experience the precise second when my already fragile world would implode irrevocably.

I went to answer, oblivious for a few more glorious seconds. It was strange, my phone was positively reverberating with notifications. At a glance it looked like I had loads of Twitter notifications plus numerous Instagram notifications, emails and voicemails. What the hell was going on?

'Hello,' I said, still protected by ignorance, though by now I was prickling with a sickening sixth sense. Something bad was about to happen.

'Charlotte.'

It was Dad, his voice full of warning and upset 'Have you seen the papers? What were you thinking?'

30

Will you do something for me?

It involves summoning up all the empathy you have.

Now, try to imagine everyone you know, I'm talking *everyone*, including your parents and all other relations (including elderly ones), your friends, your parents' friends, all your work colleagues, the man at the dry cleaners, your hairdresser, the creepy man with the bulgy eyes from No.42 and millions of strangers seeing you *having sex*.

As I ran down to the newsagents at the end of my road I hoped Dad had gone insane. I'd almost forgotten how to breathe. My whole system was pumping adrenaline. I prayed he'd made a mistake. He hadn't.

I saw it immediately, in the plastic containers at the front of the shop. The biggest selling Sunday tabloid emblazoned with the headline

WILL LUCAS HARCOURT KISS AND 'MAKE UP' AFTER DAYTIME LIVE ROMPS WITH MAKEUP GIRL CHARLOTTE?

I felt like my legs were going to collapse. This revoltingly sleazy sentence was accompanied by a clear image of Lucas having sex with me while I was bent over. The whole scene was reflected back in the big mirror at the end of the bed and according to the same front page the 'full story' could be read from page five in a four-page spread.

I wanted to die.

My first thought was to grab every paper they had and to destroy them but, even in the state of shock I was in, I knew it was pointless. This was the biggest selling Sunday rag. The one you bought alongside your broadsheet for the salacious gossip. The one couples argued over because they both wanted it first. There would be millions of copies all over the UK. Getting rid of these ones would make zero difference. My life was over. How could Lucas live with himself? How could he do this to me? *Why* would he do this? Not just to me but to himself? It was so grim. The bastard.

I rushed back up the road, hot tears sliding down my face. I was utterly distraught, panicking, mortified with shame. I didn't want to be seen, by anyone.

Back in the flat, ignoring the fact that the world and its mother (and my mother) were trying to contact me, I dialled Lucas' number.

No answer.

I left a message.

'How could you?' I screamed like a banshee, my fury white in colour. I needed to convey the pain I was experiencing; transfer some of it to him. 'How could you do this to me? Why bother lying about deleting them? And why bother meeting me to tell your pathetic lies when your intention was to sell them all along? Or did you send them to yourself that day in the hotel somehow? Is that what that was all about? Either way I will *never* forgive you and I will sue you for this. Even if I have to sell my fucking flat.'

I flung the phone down and paced, aware I was making a very strange sound, as my body and brain tried to work out if it was going to scream or cry. I was so freaked out and felt out of control physically, like I might be on the brink of a heart or panic attack.

Dad had sounded so disappointed, and furious. At the thought of him being subjected to seeing what I'd only been able to handle glimpsing, I burst into loud frightened sobs. Shit, shit, shit. This was so fucking serious. How would I ever face anyone again?

I glanced towards my phone. Terrifyingly it was still vibrating continuously.

Eventually, almost gasping for breath and convulsing with sobs, I picked it up. Thirty-five missed calls. In a moment of exquisite horror, I noticed that eleven of them were from the Executive Producer of Daytime Live. Until now this particular consequence hadn't even occurred to me. I'd been too busy picturing my parents and friends and what they would think. But work would be furious beyond belief. It wasn't exactly great publicity for a daytime show. Everyone would know.

And, wherever he was, James would know.

This thought repulsed me. I threw the phone onto my sofa as if it had just burned my hand then fled to my room where I climbed under the duvet, trying to make sense of everything. I couldn't though so I just stayed there, silently sobbing, grief stricken, ashamed, fully aware that when I did emerge, life would never be the same again.

31

During that bleak, dark Sunday my head went to places I never want to revisit.

Needless to say, I never made it to yoga, or Lindsay's, and I certainly didn't run around the park. I'd learn later that Lindsay found out what I look like during copulation, whilst eating her fried eggs on toast and therefore had a clue as to why I didn't answer any of her subsequent calls.

Monday arrived. I was still struggling to process what had happened and was terrified of what the fallout might be. I'd spoken to no one. I had no desire to speak to Mum, or Dad, or Keisha only to hear the disappointment and disgust in their voices. The only person I'd tried to make contact with was the one person who wasn't desperate to speak to me and didn't pick up. Lucas, who I wanted to kill.

The only 'crime' I'd committed was consensual sex with my boyfriend, but the minute it was splashed all over the papers it became something different. Something seedy, shameful and embarrassing.

How would I handle bumping into anyone who might have seen it? Should I act normally, or confront the situation head on by trying to explain my side of the story? I didn't have the answers to any of these questions but ultimately, my instinct was that no matter how hard it was going to be I should probably face the music. Staying at home would look like an admission of guilt and I didn't want anyone at work thinking I'd sold the story, like a prostitute. I had my interview coming up. I needed my job. My job was the one good thing in my life and maybe, just maybe, not everyone would have heard about it and I could persuade the powers to be that it wasn't my doing.

Not long after arriving at the studio, I realised my sleep deprived brain had been clutching at straws.

I hadn't needed to set my alarm. At 5:25, rather than lying in bed awake a moment longer I'd accepted defeat and got up twenty minutes earlier than I needed to. I don't know how I drove. I was wired and sick with nerves. I arrived at 7.00 am which gave me enough time to set up the room before seeing Logan at 8.00. I always make him up first so he has plenty of time to rehearse and prep before the show goes live at 11.20. The guests are done as and when they arrive and after that I obviously make sure all hair and faces stay immaculate and un-shiny under the lights.

I could hear people starting to arrive but kept the makeup room door firmly shut. I concentrated on laying out all my various brushes and organising my foundations, powders and everything else I needed, so that no matter what the skin tone of the guest I could lay my hand on the right product quickly and efficiently. Then I went to make myself a coffee. I couldn't avoid everyone forever.

In the green room (where the guests hang out) there's always a large platter of pastries and croissants which the runners go out to buy first thing (runners being the youngsters who do all the menial tasks, plus anything else the team need doing). I felt like shit. I was shattered and hadn't eaten properly for days. Stress was gnawing away at me. My bust had already shrunk and my jeans were feeling loose around the waistband.

I grabbed a pastry and banana. I needed stodge to get me through. As I approached I could hear the unmistakeable tones of a clearly delighted Ricky (one of the young researchers) whooping, about what I had no idea. As soon as I walked in the door though he instantly fell quiet and sprung apart from the three other younger members of the team he was with, Sam (researcher), Colin (lighting assistant) and the new runner, a girl who can't have been more than about nineteen. She went bright red the minute she saw me then smirked.

It was a hideous moment. I was exhausted and felt so vulnerable I didn't know what to do or say. It was blatantly obvious they'd been talking about me.

It was too late to turn back so, avoiding eye contact, I ignored them and went over to the coffee percolator. Janice, the production manager who's worked on the show for years, was standing there drinking from the mug she insists nobody else uses. It's got a picture of Justin Bieber on it. She's a perfectly nice woman but that's just one of the small reasons we'll never be soulmates. I also know for a fact she still has cuddly toys on her bed. I know this because she said she and her husband had a row about them one day during which he threatened to throw them out. She said if he did, she'd throw *him* out. I remember thinking that was a bit odd.

'Morning Charlotte,' Janice said hastily, shooting Ricky and Co a filthy look. 'How are you darling? Are you alright?'

I just stared back, terrified I was about to cry.

'Why?' I mumbled.

Janice's face coloured but her expression remained full of sympathy 'Oh come on honey, I think we both know why. Listen, I've been telling this lot to calm down about it. I said there's every chance you might have been stitched up. No one should make assumptions.'

Her direct approach was excruciating, though ironically, I also realised how kind she was being and decided her husband was a lucky man after all.

'It had nothing to do with me,' I replied quietly, keenly aware that Ed, the accountant, was earwigging, as were the handful of other people in the room.

I made my coffee, desperate to get out before anyone said anything else. I wasn't quick enough though. Ricky couldn't help himself. His initial shock at seeing me had turned into glee and perhaps to show off, or just because he's an immature little shit, he swaggered over.

'Here she is, the dark horse of Daytime Live. I hope they wedged you up good and proper for those pics. And, please don't think we judge. What you do in your spare time is your own business. Though I'm not sure Shelley's particularly happy about it.'

Shelley was the office manager. Fuck! *Literally. Every. One. Knew.*

I stared back blankly. In retrospect I think my frontal lobe was so overwhelmed I'd lost cognitive ability.

I found myself looking about the room, my thoughts abstract. I knew what so many of them had been up to over the weekend. I'd seen it all on Facebook. Janice had taken her slightly odd looking four-year-old twin boys (they have very big heads) to a trampolining park on Sunday morning where she'd taken a selfie of herself and her husband, with the boys bouncing up and down in the background. She'd made some reference to hangovers being a thing of the past with 'these two to wear out'. She posted a lot of pictures of her 'boys'.

Ricky had posted a succession of pictures of him and the 'lads' over the course of their night out which had ended up at some club, all making the same face down the lens. This one had got a lot of likes and a lot of comments, mainly from girls. Ricky goes to the gym a lot and is what his mates would describe as 'pumped.' He's got dark hair. I think his Dad is Greek Cypriot. Either way he's got lovely olive skin and a nice face. The problem is he knows it. I suspect it'll be many, many years before Ricky loves a woman as much as he loves himself. As a result, even if I wasn't closer in age to his mum, I'd never find him remotely attractive.

Only Ed, the quiet, lanky, head of accounts with his excellent afro and penchant for tweed jackets, (who isn't normally in this early so must have come in to do some overtime) hadn't posted anything on social media about his weekend. When he does appear on Facebook, he usually only posts links to songs by obscure Ska or reggae bands anyway. I know nothing about his personal life other than that his partner's called Martin. He's more of an acquaintance than a friend but I like Ed very much. He doesn't intrude.

He had the decency to look embarrassed on my behalf. Ricky however, further demonstrating that his emotional intelligence was on a par with a frog's, continued to pursue the subject, despite my distress.

'So, Charlotte, come on, tell us,' he said, as if the newspaper story had suddenly given him the right to talk to me with an utter lack of respect. His eyes gave me the once over, something else he wouldn't have contemplated doing the day before. It felt lecherous and made me want to join the Amish. Flat shoes, a shapeless tunic and bonnet, even no makeup would be a small price to pay for not having to deal with this kind of blatant disrespect.

'You and Lucas, what was that like? Did he know you were going to sell your story?'

'I don't want to talk about it,' I managed, quivering with anger 'but just so you know, not that it's anyone's business, but because you're clearly all talking about it, I did not sell my story. I wouldn't do that in a million years. I knew nothing about the so called 'story' until it was out and I'm totally gutted that anyone here has assumed I would have.'

Janice gasped 'Oh my god, that's awful Charlotte. See,' she said to the others 'I said she wasn't the type and, for the record, I think that's obvious. Ricky, you should be ashamed of yourself. You shouldn't be speaking to any woman like that. This is a warning and if you continue to pass that thing on your phone around anymore I will report you to Dan and to HR.'

What was she talking about? What thing?

There was an awful, prolonged silence.

'What did you get up to over the weekend?' asked Ed, doing his best to diffuse things.

I looked at him blankly, mind spinning. 'What thing on your phone,' I said to Ricky who suddenly looked sheepish.

'Nothing,' he said defensively 'it was just a laugh.'

'What is on your phone?' I repeated icily, hands shaking. In fact, my whole body had started to tremble.

Finally, Ricky caught up and realised, firstly what kind of state I was in and secondly that I hadn't waltzed in triumphantly, looking proud of the story which painted me as a cheap slut.

'It's nothing. Don't worry about it. I'll send a WhatsApp asking people to delete it.'

'Tell me,' I said to Janice. At this point you could have heard a pin drop. 'What has he sent?'

Janice tutted and shot Ricky a furious look 'It's an immature stupid.... what is it you call those things? Not a vine, a GIF I think. I don't know. Some stupid thing Ricky made, doctoring the pictures from the paper. You really don't need to see it and I will personally make sure the whole group is deleted. You are in trouble Ricky, mark my words.'

'It was a meme and I deleted it straight away,' piped up Ed. 'I thought it was out of order and smacked of bullying.'

This really shocked Ricky who was looking increasingly nervous.

Janice and Ed's kindness, was harder to cope with than Ricky's vulgarity. It made me want to cry, only that wouldn't do. If I started, I wouldn't stop.

'Eh? I wasn't bullying,' said Ricky, who by now had visibly lost his swagger and was squirming at his public dressing down. His mates looked mutinous and embarrassed on his behalf. 'If I've upset you Charlotte, I'm sorry. I didn't mean to. I dunno. I just assumed you didn't care. It was just a bit of a laugh. I didn't realise you didn't know anything about it.... or...... I wouldn't have done it......'

'Right,' I muttered, wondering quite how much other unsavoury, salacious material featuring me was flying about the internet. I felt completely violated.

After a while, Sam, who had been staring at the floor for most of the exchange, said 'Are you coming to quiz next week Charlotte?'

'No,' I replied. I think it was her way of apologising but I remember wondering how she could possibly think I might. With pricks like Ricky about I'd never be able to show my face anywhere. I would be the talk of the whole production team and though they wouldn't all show it in the same brazen way, the vast majority would be thinking what he had been vile enough to express to my face.

Then Dan walked in, pale and embarrassed, followed closely by Shelley the office manager and David Robinson, the Executive Producer.

As my heart rate accelerated, every single person in the room stared at me, expressions ranging from worried, to bemused, to enthralled.

'Could we have a word?' asked Dan.

'Sure, can we go somewhere else though?'

'I tell you what,' interjected Shelley 'if you wouldn't mind making up Logan who's waiting now in makeup, then we can all have a chat in my office after. Your assistant can do checks.'

I agreed of course.

It was a struggle. My hands were shaking and although he studiously avoided saying anything, I could tell Logan knew what was going on. He must think I attract drama constantly. He'd be bound to want to get someone new.

As soon as he'd gone through to the studio I went to Shelley's office where it became apparent that she and David had already discussed my fate over the weekend. Dan just stood there looking awkward and desperately sorry for me. They'd agreed there was no way they could consider me for promotion now, what with so much negative press attention having been brought upon the show. They said they would discuss everything else once I'd had some sleep and felt better. I burst into tears at which point they all looked hugely uncomfortable.

It was beyond humiliating and I knew I needed to get it together but I couldn't. I felt like a twelve-year-old being wrongly accused of something, my only mistake having been to get mixed up in the wrong crowd. And yet I *had* done something wrong.

I was disgusting.

And it was there, for all to see.

Dan led me out of the office, through the building, into the lifts and through reception, cooing platitudes as you would to a distressed child. 'I'm so sorry,' I kept saying, over and over again, almost in a trance of shock. Though I did notice that he'd somehow managed to retrieve my handbag from somewhere. He had it slung over his shoulder. Ordinarily I would have found the sight faintly amusing but I was so distressed I really didn't know what was going on.

Dan was kind and gentle. Outside he put me in a pre-paid cab which had been conjured up, all part of project 'get the embarrassing whore out of the building'. His expression as we pulled away said it all. I've never seen anyone look so sorry or worried for anyone and there was nothing I could say or do to reassure him.

32

Before James disappeared, back when I was deluded and happy, I used to day dream about waking up next to him on Christmas Day. On more than one occasion I imagined how happy and excited I'd be feeling. Happy in the knowledge I'd be starting as Head of Department in the New Year, my own cosmetics brand an ever-closer possibility. After some festive sex I'd serve a special Christmas morning breakfast, something involving smoked salmon and Bucks Fizz before giving my amazingly well-chosen presents, which he'd love, hardly able to believe my thoughtfulness and generosity. I'd even pictured getting dressed to go to my mum's where we would endure her and Gordon and whomever else she'd invited. Only, because we were together it would actually be fun for once and of course, when we left, sometime later, we'd laugh and joke about my dysfunctional yet hilarious upbringing. Then, we'd snuggle up on the sofa and watch precisely the kind of Christmas movie I'd come to despise, whilst eating chocolates and feeling as happy, cosy and peaceful as the characters on the screen.

Well fuck that, fuck Christmas and fuck my fucking fuckety life.

In reality, the lead up to Jesus' birthday felt like a viciously cruel joke. My disappointment was acute. Not only was James gone, but my entire life had unravelled beyond repair. I was officially 'off' until the New Year. Work said they were 'only thinking of me' and that they thoroughly sympathised given that I hadn't sold 'the' pictures. Nevertheless, I'm not so sure the (unpaid) 'time off' was totally altruistic. They just didn't want me around until the story had settled, and who could blame them? We agreed to talk in January.

Before James left, London seemed beautiful and festive. Everywhere I'd looked there had been signs of love and life and vibrant happiness. Now, when I walked down the street, it no longer felt like that. All I saw were the homeless people suffering in the cold, lying in doorways in filthy sleeping bags. I noticed how dirty the streets were, the litter, the garish commercialism and tinny music. Whereas before the department stores seemed warm and inviting, now, the very same shops felt like unholy places, hoodwinking everyone out of their cash and exploiting gullible customers. I started feeling claustrophobic and panicky anywhere other than my flat.

Not that it was easy being there either. Every time I turned on the TV there was some sentimental Christmas film on, so saccharine and romantic it was as if it had been scheduled purely to mock sad, lonely people like myself. The radio, the TV, the shops, Facebook, *everywhere* I looked, all that was being talked about was how it was the time of year for being with people you loved and the importance of family and fun. The only reason I didn't book a one-way ticket to somewhere remote was in case James suddenly picked up the phone and I missed his call. Illogical and crazy I know, but despite everything, hearing from him was all I wanted.

Mum was angry with me (*'It's the humiliation that's so hard to take Charlotte'*) Dad was palpably disappointed and my phone was filled with notifications from perverts, newspapers, journalists and nosey acquaintances. I pushed everyone away, even Keisha and Lindsay, both of whom kept checking in to see if I was OK.

I didn't know what to say.

Lindsay had proved herself to be a great friend but ultimately had her own family and there was only so much she could say or do. She'd done so much listening the friendship was in serious debt. I needed to give her a break from it all.

Keisha had been really sympathetic and kind too, especially about the 'story' which she kept saying would blow over and be forgotten, but she also berated me for not having told her sooner about James disappearing. In the grand scheme of things, I couldn't see how it mattered and our once easy friendship felt strained and unnatural. Maybe I wanted it to be? Part of me wanted to put distance between me and everyone I knew and to destroy what little I had left before they did it to me.

My sense of self-loathing grew stronger by the day and no matter how hard I tried I didn't feel able to draw on the resilience I'd initially felt when James had left. Perhaps because then, the rest of my life had still been intact.

Every day, after yet another patchy night's sleep, I'd check my phone to see if James had rung. At this point I would have welcomed even some disgust from him about the story. At least I'd know he was alive.

Before the scandal, getting over him felt possible and was what I wanted to do. My perspective was different now though. I started to doubt he was wrong for leaving. Maybe he'd gone because I'm such a disaster? This thinking may not sound rational but depression isn't and by this point I think I knew I was struggling but couldn't do anything about it. I was out of puff. My soul, unable to take anymore, appeared to have given up, which is why I also gave up trying to reach Lucas. What was the point? I didn't have the money or the energy to take him on anyway.

Meanwhile, everybody else's worlds kept turning. Facebook continued to be awash with pictures of baby's in Christmas pudding outfits, happy couples at parties, friends looking gorgeous in specially purchased sparkly dresses to be worn at seasonal parties, and sentimental updates gushing about the joy of family at this time of year.

I suspended my Twitter and Instagram accounts; the followings I'd spent years building up and cultivating were gone in a second. I had no choice. I'd been plagued by trolls and seedy men sending me revolting images and followed by perverts galore. It was very upsetting. Another part of my identity destroyed. I was tempted to delete my email account which was full of requests from other papers, magazines, even TV shows but instead I just stopped checking it. I just wanted it to all go away.

There was no escaping Christmas day of course. It was going to happen, despite what was happening to me. And suddenly here it was. The 25th December.

33

I woke up low, lonely, ashamed and unbearably disgusted at myself.

I'd lost everything.

Why couldn't I just be normal?

A day at Mum's lay ahead. She'd been insistent that I come to her for Christmas so she could 'look after me a bit'.

It wasn't like I had many other options. Dad was going to his sisters so I'd said yes to Mum, knowing she wouldn't allow me to spend the day on my own. My brother, Nathan, Facetimed me from Australia. I quickly regretted answering when it became clear that he and wife Emily had already formed opinions on what had happened to me, without waiting to hear my side. I didn't really care. Thankfully my Wi-Fi connection was weak because I couldn't muster up the energy to give my account anyway. We'd never been close and I wasn't convinced he really cared. In fact, it felt like he and his bossy wife had been very quick to judge something which had happened on the other side of the planet and had taken the papers version as gospel. I got rid of them as soon as was polite.

Despite being tempted to get back into bed and rot until the whole bloody thing was over, I started getting ready. A few hours later I sincerely wished I'd gone with my instincts.

***

As soon as Mum opened the door, I could tell she was on her way to being quite drunk. My mother's always been a pretty pathetic drinker. Couple of glasses and she becomes very 'forthright' and a bit screechy. She was wearing a kaftan which she must have picked up on her travels at some point, probably from her trip to India with Jeff, her boyfriend before Gordon. Eleanor is an attractive woman for her age and emanates an earthiness which a certain kind of man finds beguilingly attractive. She wears a lot of silver jewellery, her hair is long and tends to be either down or up in a bun, held in place by things which remind me of chopsticks. She's given to sometimes going without a bra which, with bosoms as large as hers I find a bit embarrassing. I was pleased to note my mother had put one on today. I could do without seeing them swinging about.

'Darling, I'm so glad you're here. Happy Christmas. Come in, come in. Gosh you're thin, we'll have to fatten you up on nuts and booze today. Now, you know everybody I think. Gordon, get my lovely girl a drink and make sure it's a large one.'

I followed Mum through the hall into the sitting room of her modest Victorian semi. My godmother Linda was there, Gordon of course, Gordon's very elderly and extremely frail mother and the next-door neighbour Bertrand, who Eleanor had an affair with when she was married to Dad. It was all rather bohemian.

For a surreal second I looked forward to laughing about it all with James. It had still only been a few weeks since he'd gone and occasionally, I'd forget. A pang of hurt almost toppled me. So much shit had happened in such a short space of time, my brain couldn't keep up.

'Hello gorgeous girl,' said Linda, getting up and looking genuinely pleased to see me, even if the elephant in the room was positively enormous. I couldn't look her in the eye I was so mortified with shame. 'Hi,' I muttered, summoning up a smile.

Linda is a handsome woman in her early sixties and reasonably famous. She's a newsreader and on screen frequently enough for people to often do double takes when they see her in the street. I'm fond of her and whenever I see her always vow to try to spend more time with her than I do. Despite being Mum's oldest friend, Linda has always felt like an ally to me and handles being around us with incredible diplomacy, thus helping rather than hindering our tricky relationship. What must she be thinking now? It was painfully embarrassing to contemplate.

She was looking glamorous with a new shorter haircut, tight suede trousers and a soft grey cashmere sweater. Sensing my discomfort, she marched over and embraced me and when we drew apart, she gave me a wink, designed to reassure. It did and yet it also left me wondering how much she knew. Had mum told her about James or did my mere appearance reveal the extent of the trauma I was experiencing on every front? Everyone had probably been expecting James to be here today so the absence of my much-heralded new partner probably gave the game away anyway. Hopefully Mum had briefed everyone before I arrived so I wouldn't have to talk about it.

'Prosecco?' asked Gordon, approaching with a bottle and a flute.

'Er, yes please,' I said dully, wondering if I really wanted it. I'd been drinking too much for days and wasn't sure it was a good idea but couldn't think how to refuse one on Christmas day. It would only draw attention or, god forbid, have them asking if I was pregnant.

'How are you Bertrand?' I asked politely, going to perch on the end of the floral sofa where Linda had also gone to sit.

'Oh, you know, not too bad,' he said, looking quite flushed in the face. Bertrand was wearing a too tight, three-piece suit and a bow tie. He had combed what hair he had left over the top of his bald pate. The effect was truly awful. Poor Bertrand.

I nodded at Gordon's mother too 'Hello Jane,' I said. Jane didn't reply so I tried again. 'Hi Jane, happy Christmas.'

'Deaf as a post,' said Gordon cheerily.

'Charlotte, come and help in the kitchen,' yelled mum down the hall. It was a relief. I was struggling on the small talk front and it was too warm in the small room with the gas fire blasting.

'I'll come too' said Linda, giving me another little wink, understandably desperate for an escape route.

In the kitchen Eleanor looked slightly out of control on the cooking front. She'd wound her hair up on top of her head into a topknot but it was coming loose, her face was puce and there wasn't one bit of surface free.

'Bloody hell,' I muttered.

'Don't you start,' huffed Eleanor, bending down to peer into the stove 'I don't know who deemed it sensible to have to prepare ten thousand different side dishes on the day when it's also traditional to start drinking at eleven in the morning. Right, that's alright I think,' she said poking the turkey quite viciously with a fork 'So Charlotte, have you told Linda what's been going on with you?'

I stared at my mother, dazzled by her insensitivity.

'I'm so sorry about Lucas,' interjected Linda quickly 'and for what it's worth, everyone who knows you, knows you've been utterly exploited and betrayed.'

I blinked away hot tears of mortification.

'What you do in your personal life is for no one else to judge and of course, what you've done isn't a big deal anyway. He's just made it into one by making it public.'

'Yes,' agreed Eleanor testily 'though I'm not sure we'd condone letting someone take degrading pictures of us. Imagine how any partner you have in the future will feel about it? Not a great advert is it? Your brother agrees by the way. We spoke this morning and he's pretty embarrassed in case people from his work find out.'

I couldn't bear it. My whole body was drenched in 'flight' hormones, yet my legs appeared to have turned to lead.

Linda changed the subject 'Yes, well, I'm sure Nathan will survive. Right, on a happier note, how's James then? It is James isn't it? I'd hoped he'd be here actually but when you turned up on your own looking so sad, I did wonder if perhaps you might have had a row over all this business. If you have, I'm sure a bit of time will work wonders.'

I was at an utter loss. Why hadn't my mother done what any normal person would have done in this situation which would be to warn everyone before I arrived about what had happened. Alternatively, she could have kept her mouth shut and purposefully steered clear of the whole mess. That's what I'd needed. Either/or would have been fine. But of course, my mother wasn't a normal person.

'It's complicated,' I managed.

Eleanor snorted. 'Not from where I'm standing.'

I glared at her but she refused to take any notice.

'If you're just going to stand there looking gormless Charlotte then I'll have to fill you in Linda,' she continued, peeling carrots in a fairly demented fashion.

Linda looked deeply uncomfortable, but Eleanor bulldozed on 'So, Charlotte's delightful boyfriend has only gone and done a bunk. It turns out he was absolutely full of crap, was lying to her and taking her for an absolute idiot. And this is *before* this scandal, so it's not exactly been the best time in terms of people asking how my daughter is.'

I swallowed.

Linda who had been trying to tidy up a bit turned to look at me, her face incredulous 'Really? Oh darling. I'm so sorry. You must be so upset.'

'Course she is,' said Eleanor 'I mean, what a toe rag. I'm upset too! I'm really cross and frustrated.'

'Well don't be,' I said flatly, desperate to escape. Claustrophobia was making its presence felt. 'You being like that doesn't help anyone.'

Eleanor turned around, peeler in one hand, other hand on hip just as Gordon shuffled in to join us 'Hello you lot,' he said 'I've just come to get some drinks, ginger ale for mother and a gin and tonic for Bertrand.'

'We were just telling Linda here about the awful business with that James and how poor old Charlotte fell for his rubbish hook, line and sinker.'

'Hang on a minute,' I said 'If you're going to stand here discussing me and my business would you mind dialling it down a notch please. I mean, is that really what you think?'

Eleanor was about to reply but thought better of it and turned her attention back to the veg.

'Your mum was really upset about it,' said Gordon, thinking he was helping.

Linda tried to come to the rescue 'Listen, I don't know the detail of what's gone on Charlotte, and I'm sure you'd probably rather we didn't all stand around discussing your private business. But one thing I do know is that we have all had relationships before where things haven't worked out and it can be very painful. You've obviously had a really tough time lately and I'm so sorry it hasn't worked out with James. It's his loss.'

'It hasn't 'not worked out',' said Eleanor 'it's been a bloody disaster and I hate to say it...'

'Then don't...' For a second I felt quite murderous. If Mum carried on like this I would leave. She was a disgrace.

'.... but the problem is, Charlotte here was single for so long she left herself very vulnerable to something like this happening. He could probably tell she was easy prey.'

'Prey?' I spluttered, putting my glass of Prosecco down. I didn't want it. It was sour and acidic and I was so hungover from my Christmas Eve, block out reality, vodka binge for one, it was making me feel sick. 'Why would you use language like that? You know nothing about our relationship. We were happy and he loved me. And the fact is we still don't know anything for certain.'

Eleanor rolled her eyes which made me feel quite violent towards her and very distressed.

'Oh, I'm sorry,' she said in a mean tone, hands on hips again, face flushed from alcohol. I wondered at what point she was going to 'look after me' like she'd said she wanted to all week.

'I think we do know lots for certain actually because I'm afraid darling, in a normal relationship people don't create fake Facebook accounts. They also don't not introduce you to anyone and then disappear into thin air. We know that for certain.'

Having prepared the drinks and put them on a tray with a bowl of crisps Gordon was ready to take them through but stopped at the door to say 'Perhaps leave this for now Eleanor, it's Christmas day and I'm sure Charlotte doesn't want the whole nasty business raked up.'

Eleanor couldn't have shot him a filthier look if she'd tried.

Linda chipped in 'I agree with Gordon. Leave poor Charlotte alone. Honestly Eleanor I think you're being incredibly insensitive and should stick to drinking water for a bit. Now, please, let's change the subject. Tell me Charlotte, how's work? Are you still getting lots of shifts on Daytime Live? It must be wonderful to have something fairly regular.

'Yeah, it's fine thanks,' I said, trying desperately not to cry. I could feel my whole body shaking. 'I mean I could have been sacked so, they've been quite understanding I guess.' My voice betrayed me. It was really wobbly and on the verge.

'Good,' said Linda 'Well that's amazing and a testament to how good your work is. I'd love you to get some shifts with me but as you know Deborah has been there since the dawn of time.'

'Mm, I'm not sure if anyone new will want to employ me right now,' I said, smiling weakly.

'Right,' said Eleanor sulkily, slamming something into the oven 'that's all done now. I'll come back in ten minutes or so, do the last few bits, and then we'll be there. Shall we go back through?' She shot Linda a shitty look.

Linda rolled her eyes at me before following her. I trailed after, trying to decide what to do.

'I think it's time for some presents,' said Eleanor, who was squatting by the tree now. Bertrand's eyes were on stalks looking at her bottom. 'Charlotte, this one's for you.'

'Thanks,' I said taking her envelope with very little interest. I was still smarting from the scene in the kitchen.

'I got it a while ago but I think you'll still like it,' said Eleanor looking slightly shifty. 'Well, hopefully you will anyway.'

I felt like I was stuck in the middle of a bad dream but as I opened the envelope I tried to look suitably excited and grateful instead of like I wanted to leave and run home. 'Theatre vouchers. Oh, that's great,' I said, as enthusiastically as I was able.

'Good,' said Eleanor 'Of course I had thought you could go to see something with James but you can take a girlfriend I suppose.'

Everyone stared at her. Well, everyone except poor old Gordon's mother whose head was so bent that she couldn't really see what was going on. As they all stared I was filled with wave after wave of terrible fear that before I knew it I would also be a very old woman, bent double with no one to look after me, having lived alone for years, unloved and unwanted. To my horror I could feel tears threatening.

'Well, are you pleased?'

'Yes, thank you. I said thank you.'

'Only they were very expensive you know so if you're not keen on using them Gordon and I can always go and give you a bit of cash instead.'

'Yeah maybe.'

'Oh right, so you don't really want them then?'

Something inside me snapped 'Look mum, I'm very grateful but as you know full well my boyfriend left me recently, so being totally honest, planning a trip out that would have been with him doesn't make me feel that wonderful right now. Plus, I don't really want to go out much until everything's blown over. I can't bear anyone to recognise me.'

It was what Eleanor had been waiting for. Some form of comeback she could react to, so that she could get what she really wanted to say off her chest.

'Oh well that's bloody charming. Now, look Charlotte, I'm sorry to say this on Christmas Day but I'm afraid a bit of tough love seems to be in order because you need to snap out of this mood you're in. You need to accept that in this instance you've been a bit of a fool and your judgment hasn't been great. It's not your fault, not your fault at all. It's just, like I was trying to say earlier, you've been single for far too long, so when the first half decent bloke's come along and acted all interested you've been grateful and pleased. I get that. But at the end of the day he was a bad egg. Just like Lucas, who has embarrassed us all. Your judgement is appalling and I'm worried about you. You're thin, you're down and I just know that, if it were me, I wouldn't let these idiots get the better of me. So don't let them win. Plenty of fish and all that. Move on. And don't take things out on me.'

'Your mother's never been one to mince her words has she?' laughed Bertrand.

Everyone else looked vaguely horrified and sorry for me.

'No, she hasn't,' I said, at the end of my tether. How dare she speak to me like that?

'Right, have a nice day everyone. I'm not going to say what I make of that little speech but I hope you all have a really great lunch. There's a bag of gifts from me to each of you under the tree. Not you though Bertrand, but only because I didn't know you were going to be here......sorry.'

'Oh, don't go,' said Linda, looking really fed up. I didn't blame her and felt bad for abandoning her but couldn't stay.

'Oh for god's sakes,' spluttered Eleanor 'Don't be so over sensitive. This is precisely what I'm talking about. Grow some balls girl and don't ruin the day for everyone.'

I shot her a look which said it all 'Bye everyone, have a nice day.'

And with that I fled, cheeks burning hot, feeling like my bruised heart which was already on the floor had just taken yet another kicking.

34

Current Status Update: 3 weeks later

I've been walking for hours. The dark has descended as if by stealth. I hate how short the days are. As I storm along the towpath my phone rings and only because I'm so engrossed in my thoughts, I answer.

'Charlotte, it's Lindsay, I've been trying to get hold of you for days. Why haven't you called me? What are you doing? I just got a phone call from Claire saying you were supposed to pop into work today for a chat about your return date. What's going on? I thought you'd be keen to get back?'

I wish I hadn't picked up.

'Claire,' I manage. 'They gave Claire my job.'

'I know darling,' says Lindsay, who can appreciate more than anyone what a kick in the teeth this is.

'Anyway, nothing's going on, I just didn't feel well. They probably won't want me back for ages anyway, so there's not a lot to talk about.'

'Where are you now?'

'Nowhere... out for a walk.'

'In the dark?'

I look about. It is pretty gloomy now, and cold. 'It's not that dark.'

Lindsay tuts 'It will be pitch black in five minutes.'

There's a long pause during which my heart literally aches with sadness. I feel so distressed I don't trust myself to speak.

'Right...' says Lindsay. 'Enough is enough. Get over here now.'

I want to say no, want to pretend I'm fine and that I can't because I'm busy, but I can't speak. The pain and sadness are overwhelming and the inevitable tears are sliding down my face at an alarmingly fast rate.

'Charlotte,' says Lindsay softly 'Please babe. It's going to be alright. I know you've been through such a lot, but it's going to be fine. It's like anything, people will move on, they'll all forget soon enough.'

'Maybe, but anyone I ever meet in the future only has to google my name to see stuff that will always be there. There's no escaping that.'

'Listen,' said Lindsay, at least not denying what I'd just said which would have annoyed me 'I know you're in a bad place. I don't care where you are or what you're doing, you're to find a cab, get in it and get to me. I would come to you but I'd have to bring Ben and he's going to be ready for tea soon. Now I'm not asking, I'm telling.'

'But I'm fine,' I lie.

'You're not. You're wandering around in the dark. In the freezing cold. On your own.'

I can't go to hers. I just can't. I won't be able to act OK. I'm in too much of a state. I improvise 'It's sweet of you Linds, but I'm literally going home in a minute. Honestly, Mum's coming round soon.... for dinner.'

This seems to appease her, but only just. 'Ok, well that's good, I'm glad you're seeing her and that you're on good terms again. Listen, I know I've not been around much lately, but I want you to know that I'm always here. It's just hard when you never reply or pick up.........'

'Sorry,' I mumble.

'It's OK. I know you're still sad about the bastard.'

No one dares even say his name around me anymore.

35

I can't dismiss how I feel as the January blues anymore. I go the doctors to ask for some sleeping pills. I'm desperate, not having had a proper night's sleep in weeks.

'Why do you think you aren't sleeping?' asks the kindly doctor, an Asian woman in her fifties with silver glasses and a clip in her jet-black hair, keeping it off her face.

Her tone's so caring.

I start to cry.

'That's ok,' soothes the doctor, passing over a box of tissues. 'Take your time.'

I don't have any choice. It's a good few minutes before I can speak properly. The kindness of strangers. It's an absolute killer.

'My boyfriend left me,' I say eventually 'and.... I'm just.... struggling a bit with being on my own and.......'

'Go on,' the doctor gently encourages.

'There was something else that happened but it's so awful and......I'm so ashamed....'

'Ok,' says the doctor softly 'You don't have to talk about it if you'd rather not, though if it helps, know that everything you tell me is confidential.'

I can't speak.

She waits until I can.

'I don't know,' I manage eventually 'It's everything. My whole life's a mess. I'm on my own. Work's a disaster. Everything I do is wrong and my family are so ashamed of me. I'm going to be totally skint soon and I'm just......useless.'

She hands me another tissue. 'I very much doubt that's true Charlotte. But it sounds like you're having a very hard time right now and when so many areas of our lives are going badly it's extremely hard to know what to deal with first. Now, I'm going to ask you to fill out a form please. Just answer everything honestly and let's see if perhaps you might need something to help you through this difficult period in your life.'

I did as I was told. I went through the form answering honestly, until I reached question 9 at which point I lied.

HAVE YOU THOUGHT THAT YOU'D BE BETTER OFF DEAD OR HURTING YOURSELF IN SOME WAY?

Instead of answering option D - NEARLY EVERY DAY

I ticked option A – NO, NOT AT ALL.

Despite my omission the doctor still sees fit to prescribe me anti-depressants. She also says I'll receive a letter in the post with an appointment to speak to someone. I leave the surgery grateful. I want something to work.

36
FEBRUARY

At first, I take the meds religiously. A week or so later however, I reason that perhaps pills aren't the answer. I know I'm depressed but the pills make me feel nauseous and rough, and besides, maybe I wasn't clinically depressed? Maybe life was just depres*sing*, in which case I probably needed to feel my way through things as opposed to numbing it all out?

So I stop taking them, despite the doctor having told me this was the very worst thing I could do. She said the consequences of not coming off them gradually could be very serious, even resulting in suicidal thoughts but I simply couldn't see how such tiny little pills could make that much difference. I felt desperate before and only feel suicidal now because I am a piece of shit and my life is in ruins.

I pray something will change but I'm not counting on it. For now, it's a case of waiting and finding out how much more I can take. One foot in front of the other. That's all I can do.

Anyway, even if there was a grain of truth in what she'd said, by now the tablets will I be in some rubbish tip somewhere, rotting away, the warning out of sight out of mind.

> **Withdrawal symptoms:**
>
> *When you stop taking your medicine you may experience withdrawal symptoms. This is most likely if you stop taking your medicine suddenly. Some patients have experienced the following:*
>
> *Dizziness . sleep disturbances. tremor. confusion . emotional instability . One of these symptoms could be a worsening of your depression or anxiety disorder: Thoughts of suicide may occur.If this happens see your doctor* ***immediately.***

37

'So what's going on?' my mother, Eleanor, demands to know in a voice I recognise well, having heard it during all the most crucial stages of my life, the stages when things aren't going according to plan and she wants to 'get to the bottom of things.'

It's Wednesday and I'm at home. It's February and I still haven't been to work to discuss a return date. I keep blowing them out, telling them I've got flu. I don't think they believe me. I'll probably be fired but the alternative (having to be there), feels worse.

I'm in a state. I've just been holed up in the flat. I do Tesco delivery shops so I don't even have to go out for food. I buy cheap wine, vodka and ready meals.

I decided to write some letters. Partly as an exercise to work out how I feel. I want to have a realisation that I do have things to live for because at the moment I don't feel like I do. I get up and plod to the fridge to fill up my wine glass. It's 11.30 am.

So far, I've written one letter to Dad.

It reads -

Dear Dad,

I know you must be so ashamed of me. I'm ashamed of myself. I've been a naïve stupid fool.

I've ruined what has been a great life in many ways and I really want to thank you for the good bits. Apart from you and Eleanor breaking up I had a pretty happy childhood and, let's face it, how many people can say that? I loved school and college and enjoyed my twenties. I've had a lot of fun and I do appreciate that. But, I guess the last ten years haven't been the easiest. Maybe not meeting someone, falling in love, being loved in return and having a baby sounds like a first world problem? Maybe I am extremely selfish to have expected any of those things? Who knows? But along with a good career it's all I ever wanted. For a time I thought I'd done it. I had it all. But I've managed to mess it all up. I thought I'd got where I wanted to be and then it was all taken away and I'm afraid since then I haven't been coping brilliantly. Forgive me. I love you very much. You've been a brilliant Dad. I'm so sorry I've been not such a great daughter and I'm sorry for the embarrassment and shame I've caused.

I'd like you to have my flat. I know you won't want to take on another mortgage, so just sell it and use whatever you get to have a nice time. Sorry I couldn't help look after Wallace.

It really is for the best. I'm so tired of everything that I just want to sleep. Think of it like that. I love you.

Charlotte xx

Is that what I really want to do? Would it be for the best? I was about to start writing one to Mum which would be tricky to say the least, only now she's rung and is giving me a hard time. I wish I hadn't picked up.

'What do you mean?' I ask flatly, wiping silent tears from my face.

'What do you mean what do I mean? Unless you've put on weight since I last saw you then you're too thin. You're so pale, the flat's a mess, which isn't like you and you never ring. You never even asked about my trip to Venice with Gordon. Your dad and I understand that you're sad but you've got to start looking after yourself better. We're worried about you. You don't seem yourself.'

'You've spoken to Dad about me?'

'Yes Charlotte, I have spoken to your father about you, because when our daughter is having some sort of breakdown we are capable of having an adult conversation.'

'Well you needn't. I'm fine.' Was it any surprise I avoided calls these days?

'You can say you're fine till you're blue in the face. We both know it isn't true and you've been avoiding our calls. Your Dad's distraught. You have to put all this nonsense behind you.'

My mum has an incredible knack of playing things down with old fashioned euphemisms.

There's a long pause during which Eleanor considers her next tack.

'Right, Charlotte, I probably should have said this sooner, but you know what I'm like, I'm a stubborn old goat, but the point is, if I've contributed towards you being so low, then I'm sorry.'

I don't reply. This is probably....no... it's definitely, the first time my mother has ever admitted her behaviour has been dubious. Now she has, I recognise quite how much damage she's done over the past few months. The hurt seeps through me.

As she continues, her tone is measured and quiet. She's clearly desperate not to say the wrong thing again. It's unnerving, and unlike her to be so delicate.

'Gordon thinks that maybe when someone tells you they feel something, that you shouldn't discount it. I underestimated how badly James hurt you and also how strongly you felt for one another.'

I swallow. 'You did.'

Another pause while Eleanor fights to control her every natural instinct which is usually to be both on the defence and the attack.

'I also know that the other awful business wasn't your fault so I'm ...sorry, if I was a bit...fraught about it at the time. I was just embarrassed. Finding out from bloody Helen wasn't ideal. But I get that you had nothing to do with it.'

I can't hide the fact I'm crying anymore.

'Oh Charlotte,' Mum says, sounding sad and despairing 'Come on now, you've got to pull yourself together. I may have made some mistakes but, in my way, I was just trying to help. I was trying to make you understand that you aren't the first, and won't be the last, woman to be taken for a ride by a man. It happens. It happens all the time and I suppose I got a bit.... brusque because I hated seeing you so damaged by everything and in so much shock when James left.'

'Brusque?' I whisper, tears pouring down my face 'I hardly think that covers it.'

'What are you talking about?'

'I was at such a low ebb when James went. I was grieving for what could have been and you told me I'd been a fool. In front of people. You said I'd never had any idea about men. You accused me of being vulnerable and naïve. And, when everything happened, you said I was disgusting and that you were embarrassed by me. You said all of that and more, during what was one of the most heart-breaking, confusing and difficult times of my life.'

I remember verbatim everything that's been said because it's etched across my heart and brain and hurts almost more than James' betrayal.

Almost.

'I've said I'm sorry,' repeats Mum, who at least now has the good grace to sound ashamed 'I do regret not being more sensitive at the time. But Charlotte you are letting this bastard defeat you and he simply isn't worth it. That I know for sure.'

'But *how* do you know? You met him for all of about twenty minutes after which you told me he was charming and wonderful. And besides.......'

'What? Besides what?'

'Nothing.'

'Just say it Charlotte.'

I don't want to though. I know I'll only be met with derision. Everybody thinks I'm an idiot. My mother is no exception.

'Please?'

Fuck it. I have nothing to lose and am past caring what anyone thinks.

'The thing is, we don't know for sure. We don't know anything. Maybe he didn't take me for a ride? What if he's in trouble? Or dead? Because I know you don't believe me Mum, no one does, but I was the one in that relationship and I know he loved me. He did.'

I wait for the inevitable onslaught but it doesn't come. Instead, what I've just said is met with heavy sadness and frustration. It's palpable, even down the phone.

'Right,' says Mum eventually 'we can talk more about this face to face because there's no point while you're in this kind of mood. I can tell you're very down my love and I don't want to dredge everything up when you're on your own. So, come round this weekend. I'll tell Gordon to stay away so we can spend some time together and we'll work out a plan. Ok? And don't tell me you're busy because I know you're not.'

'I am.'

Eleanor sighs. 'You are coming to mine. That's final.'

'Mum, you can't dictate my weekend.'

'I can. You're not well darling and I'm worried you'll do something silly. I mean why aren't you at work? You should be fighting to be back there, not letting them think you're not coping. If they fire you, then where will you be? You have to go in and hold your head up high and eventually everyone will forget.'

'It's fine. I'm fine. I'll ring you next week.'

'No Charlotte, you won't you'll.....'

I hang up. She's right, I won't. But I also won't do anything drastic. I look down at the letter I wrote to Dad and put it to one side, not quite ready to tear it up. She's right though. No matter how lost I feel I can't let James Ralphs or Lucas Harcourt or any other bastard man get the better of me.

I have to go back to work. I have to try.

38

There's a meme I used to see time and again on social media and never gave much thought to, but now it keeps popping into my head.

> EVERYONE YOU MEET IS FIGHTING A BATTLE YOU KNOW NOTHING ABOUT. BE KIND. **ALWAYS.**

I wish I'd paid more attention to the people who had posted it. Maybe they'd been going through something I could never have imagined or comprehended.

I've gone back to work. For weeks now I've been getting up, getting dressed, getting in and getting on with it. But I'm not there really.

Today I've woken up before the alarm. I think I've had about two hours sleep. Pretty standard these days. I switch my phone on. The constant barrage of abuse and attention I received after Lucas gate has subsided. The relative silence is easier, but also very lonely.

My family have tried. My friends have tried and more poignantly, I've tried. Nothing works. I've run out of hope.

Maybe I needed to get to this point. Maybe I've reached acceptance? Having been on a scenic tour of misery, anger and despair I'm now nearly pulling in to my final destination. So that's that. I'll go on, until I don't.

***

At work everyone's looking forward to a night out to the pub quiz the next evening.

'Please come,' Dan tries 'I'd really like you to be there. You're not just brilliant at quizzes, I wouldn't only be exploiting your ridiculously impressive knowledge, it would just be nice to hang out again. We haven't seen you socially in so long.'

For a second I find myself debating going. It's not like I have anything else planned, but the prospect is too frightening. I still find it excruciatingly hard to be around people who know about Lucas. Plus, Claire would be there and though I hate myself for it I feel bitter resentment every time I see her. Despite the fact I helped get her last three jobs she's fundamentally my boss now. She isn't as talented as me, or as experienced, but she also hasn't disgraced herself with one of the guests. She isn't viewed as unprofessional or sleazy.

It's easier to deflect, to tell people I'm under the weather, that I have plans; anything to put them off. Dan seems particularly disappointed that I won't come but I stick to my guns and before I know it the day is done and it's time to head home.

Later that night I log onto Facebook. It's a mind-numbing activity in a sense. It stops me thinking about myself and my own life and allows me to observe how life should be led, which in turn helps reinforce my decisions to keep away from everyone. The contrast between my pathetic existence and everyone else's is so marked.

There's a picture of Janice and her twins sitting in a patch of early March daffodils. I stare at them, numb. Janice is so fulfilled and clearly loves them to death. She's found someone to love her. I haven't.

Next is a post from Dan. He must have had an afternoon nap after the show because there's a photo of him standing locked out of his flat wearing only his pyjamas. He and Saskia have finally split up and Dan's renting a pokey studio flat while she stays in the marital home. I know he's trying to fight for joint custody of their son Billy. When he locked himself out (according to his first post), he was stuck outside with nothing on him but his phone. He has since posted however that a neighbour spotted him and took him in until someone else could arrive with a spare key. Poor Dan I think with sad affection. He's an idiot. A lovely idiot.

I learn that Lindsay's going out for the night with her friend, Ruby. They're going to the cinema. I experience a brief flash of hurt that I haven't been asked but know I'm being irrational. Lindsay will have grown sick of me always saying no.

Another status. My godmother, Linda, has been asked to be a contestant on quiz show Pointless. This is by far the most interesting post of the night.

Other than that, there's nothing, just boring, mindless, dull, never-ending posts from people having fun, showing off, being smug or looking happy and gorgeous in glamorous selfies. Human beings, who, unlike me, have places to go, people to love and stuff to do.

At two a.m. I fall into a restless sleep, exhausted and drained, dead but alive.

39

Saturday's a write off. Bored of my own head's dark thoughts I got completely annihilated on booze and ended up staring at Facebook, sobbing. People from work had started posting pictures from the quiz the night before. The last thing I remember is feeling very angry about something Claire had posted.

On Sunday I get up. This is harder than it sounds. I'm so hungover my whole body's aching. I reach for the vodka and drain the last of it. Inflicting a different kind of pain brings fleeting relief. I stagger over to my closet which is where I keep my 'James' bag. In it are three cards he wrote to me, a few notes he left on my bed as surprises and the clothes he left here. There are clean boxers, socks, t shirts and one grey, fleecy, sweatshirt which even now carries the very faint but unmistakable scent of him. I bury my face in it, infused with indescribable pain.

The vodka's all gone so I stumble to the fridge and grab a bottle of wine. I pour an enormous glass and swallow back a couple of sleeping tablets. It does the trick. Sleep will do for now.

40

I open one eye and then the other, groggy, rancid. I've been asleep for much of the day.

I can't do this anymore.

In this moment I know. It's over. I'm done. I didn't know if I'd get here, but I'm certain. It's the only option left.

I get up as quickly as my pounding head will allow and pull on knickers, bra, jeans and one of James' t-shirts. Part of me hates myself for wanting to wear it, a bigger part is way past caring. I prepare a bag to take to the garages. Blankets, car keys, photos, a scribbled note for my windscreen, my iPod and headphones.

The note says:

> *My name is Charlotte Woodward. I live at 42B Acacia Close. Please contact my father Graham on the number below to tell him I'm dead. There's a letter in my flat which explains everything. He knows where the spare key is kept. Thanks, and sorry.*

I find the letter I wrote to my dad, stick it in an envelope and leave it out to be found, propped up on the kitchen surface.

I make my bed, have a quick tidy up and debate whether or not to have a cup of tea. Seeing to basic human needs feels odd and pointless given that I've decided to stop caring for myself on a permanent basis. I'll have one though. I'm dehydrated and my headache is incredibly painful. While the kettle boils I recognise how jittery I feel. I can't keep still and am doing laps of the flat. A million tiny spiders are running through my veins. I examine what state my bedroom is in, imagine people looking at it. It's bad. Think 'Tracey Emin's bed.' But I don't have the wherewithal to do anything about it.

Right.

I'm about to shut my bedroom door when I spot my laptop's still on. I wander over to close it down and log off when I notice I have a notification on Facebook. A direct message.

From James Ralphs……

I sink onto the bed, legs shaking, instantly nauseous.

It can't be.

My brain must be playing cruel tricks.

I look again and this time can't prevent my stomach from heaving. I run to the bathroom and retch bitter tasting bile.

My body heaves so violently my brain constricts and my ribs ache.

Eventually, feeling faint I manage to stagger back to my computer.

I hadn't imagined it. It definitely says I have a message from James.

I feel like I'm going to have a heart attack and for a second actually look around my room, half expecting to see a camera, or someone laughing at me but I'm very much alone.

Now I feel scared.

For so long I've been desperate to hear anything from him, so why today, of all days? It was so twisted; the universe was insane. Should I read the message? If someone had hacked his account, I wasn't sure I could cope with how disturbing that would be. But what if it was actually him, somewhere, waiting for me to reply….

I wasn't sure I could handle that either yet, deep down, knew I didn't have a choice. Unanswered questions had driven me mad for so long. Perhaps I was at last destined to glean some idea as to why he disappeared. It's not like things can get any worse. I'm lower than rock bottom already.

Whole body trembling, I steady myself by taking a deep breath. My hand shakes. I click.

The message reads

Hello you. I'm so sorry.

My eyes flick over the words multiple times, hungry for detail, expecting more. That's it though.

Hello you. I'm so sorry.

My brain can't quite compute that that's all he's written.

That's the best he can come up with after months of living hell.

I stare at the screen.

Hello you. I'm so sorry.

I want to scream with rage and frustration but I've frozen completely.

How many times over the months must I have checked and checked my phone, praying for some word, a message, an explanation, any kind of indication that he was either alive or dead? The constant yearning I've had for answers has placed me in purgatory. I've been tortured by the never-ending silence and again, the timing seems too coincidental to be true.

I'm so angry. Why am I always out of control? I feel like a puppet, having my strings pulled by someone heartless and cruel. What the hell am I supposed to reply to this pathetic, meaningless message?

And yet my fingers seem to know what they want to do before my brain does and are positively itching to type. So, I do.

Are you fucking kidding me?

Send.

I wait and when the little green light comes on, indicating that James Ralphs is actually online it's beyond weird. It's so outrageous that he's dared to get in touch after all this time. I can still hardly believe it's happening. I want to kill him. Why now?

I really am sorry. I had no choice.

Bullshit I reply, fast as lightening. Send

I deserve that.

NO I type, punching the keys far harder than was really necessary *You deserve far far worse. I hate you. I don't even know who you are.*

Don't say that

It's the truth. Though we both know that's something you don't value very much

For a while he doesn't type anything.

I'm nervous. On the one hand, now I have his attention I want to berate him, punish him, wail at him, make him understand just a fraction of the pain he's caused, on the other, I don't want him disappearing again, before I've had the chance to vent. Plus, another part of my brain feels like I deserve to be treated badly because I'm so worthless. It's almost a fitting torture and somehow justifies my decision to end things. This is what I have been reduced to. It's pitiful.

Eventually he types.

Will you let me explain?

Go for it

No. Not on here. Face to face.

Not going to happen.

Why?

I don't have time

Ok, well tomorrow – meet me somewhere

> *Fuck you James (or whatever your name really is) fuck you. I won't be meeting you tomorrow. I'll be dead.*

Once again it transpires that my fingers are ahead of the game. I stare blankly at what I've just written. I've written instinctively, from my gut, without agonising over whether it was the right thing to say or not, because I don't care anymore. His feelings are simply not ones I want to take into account.

It occurs to me in that moment that whatever his excuses are they wouldn't make anything alright anyway. He's alive. That's all I needed to know. Why would I meet him? It would just be incredibly painful and *what was the point*? To absolve *his* conscience? Hearing why he decided to string me along won't change the fact he did. Nothing can solve the fact that I'm alone, having wasted precious months of my life on someone who didn't care about me one iota. My career's in tatters, I'll never escape what's on the internet for all to see for eternity and I can't bear the thought of meeting anyone new and having to explain my past. I can't handle anybody looking at me and judging me anymore. Everyday feels unbearable. The mere thought of dating again makes me want to kill myself, so I may as well just do it.

On some level, I'm pleased he's been in touch. It's given me an element of peace. He's alive. He's confirmed what I knew already. He screwed me over. Like Lucas did. Like everyone does.

I close my laptop down, despite the fact I can see he's typing a reply, stand up and grab my bag. Time to go. Anger has given me the energy required to end this shit.

Was there a tiny part of me that liked the thought of him panicking? Yes, there was.

I'm a despicable human being.

The garages are at the end of my road. Each flat in my block owns one unit each, something which makes my flat infinitely more valuable. It pleases me, in an abstract way, to think of Dad acquiring my flat. It'll ensure he's OK in his dotage.

Feeling almost like I'm having an out of body experience, having raced down the road, I unlock the garage and heave up the heavy metal door. It makes so much noise I look about to see if anyone's seen me. The street's empty. Good.

I find myself taking one last glance up into the sky. I'm so used to crying I hardly register the tears rolling down my cheeks as I take a few quiet moments to watch the clouds scudding along their ethereal background. Part of me hopes I'll end up out there somewhere, but if there's nothing, that's OK too. I inhale deeply, noting and appreciating the warmth of the pale March sun on my face for what will be the last time. Then, I pull the metal garage door down behind me. It makes a racket as it slams into place, leaving me standing in the cold, dark garage. I retrieve the blankets from my bag then, without hesitation, arrange them along the bottom of the door, making sure there are no gaps.

The only really bizarre thing is how calm I am. I feel leaden, drained, and heavy with a hopelessness I can no longer live with. The tidal wave of depression knows it has me where it wants me. I'm on the very edge of the ledge now, toes hanging over. It waits patiently because the outcome is certain. A few minutes will change nothing.

I climb into the front seat of my car and fetch my iPod from my bag. My phone stays in there. I don't have any desire to look at what James might have written. My last, admittedly feeble act of revenge is to not read it. He can know what it feels like to be ignored and cast away. Fuck him. I'm sick of it all.

I switch the engine on and open the car windows fully. I'm not sure how long it will be before I fall unconscious but, according to the internet searches I've done on my darkest days, it shouldn't be too long. My car's quite old so won't have a very good catalytic convertor and the space is relatively small. All things considered I probably have about half an hour left.

I'm suddenly overwhelmed by pain, grief and terror. With shaking hands, I put my earphones in and find the playlist I've compiled on my iPod. It's two hours long so there are more than enough tunes to see me through. I put it on shuffle. The first song that comes on is one which reminds me of my mum. It's Private Dancer by Tina Turner. When I was a kid she used to dance around the kitchen singing it with real gusto, dancing in her own inimitable way, with enthusiasm, basic rhythm and lots of middle aged, white woman cringe factor. I used to like seeing her so happy though and always thought it was such a lovely tune. I was only a kid so had literally no idea it was about a lap dancer until many years later at which point the memory took on a slightly less 'warm, fuzzy, nostalgic' hue. How odd to be thinking about this now. Yet perhaps it was a metaphor for my entire life. Thinking things or people were wonderful and sweet, blind to reality.

I recline back in the seat and try and fail to think of nothing. At some point, I reach over for my bag again and retrieve from it a framed photo of me and James that's been hidden in a drawer for months. I want to die remembering the happiest I ever was.

The smell from the exhaust is now very unpleasant. It's making me cough and I already feel quite woozy. As the next track comes on, I feel myself slipping slowly away.

Thank goodness for that.

41

Air slaps my skin in a cold burst which feels both heavenly and shocking. This is it. I must be dead. I didn't think death would be this violent. It's like a hand is reaching inside my throat and down my oesophagus before grabbing me by the intestines and yanking hard, pulling my insides out. Colours and outlines swim before my eyes but it's difficult to know what it is I'm seeing. There's noise too.

And a voice.

Nausea, sudden and violent, comes as a wave, crashing through me. The vomit exits in a torrent, the smell of it acrid and sour. Too real for it to have occurred in death.

The blurry outlines swimming before my eyes quickly became solid, joined up shapes. To my horror I find myself looking at James.

I'm lucid again. He appears to be cradling me on the ground, in the street. My back hurts. My head does too. My legs are grazed, scraped and painful. My mouth tastes rank.

He stares at me. He looks distraught, wild with fear. I have a pounding head suddenly. Everything's foggy.

'Why?' he asks. He sounds angry with me.

I pass out.

***

I can't remember much about getting here, but A & E is a nightmare. All I want is to go home and sleep. I'm more depressed than ever because it *didn't work*. I can't even get dying right.

Apparently I'm very lucky.

Apparently, if I had breathed in another couple of minutes of CO2 filled air, it would have been a different story. According to the medics, at that point I could have been brain damaged on a permanent basis. James 'saved' my life they said, as if he's some kind of hero, when what he's actually done is ruin it. For the second time in a row.

I **hate** him.

After dragging me out of my car and out of the fume filled garage, it transpires that James bundled me into his car and drove at breakneck speed to the hospital, threatening me with an ambulance if I didn't cooperate. Not that I was in any fit state to argue at that point. When we arrived at A & E I felt horrific and once James had explained at reception what had happened, I was rushed off for a blood test. My bloods were fine though so, because I didn't need to be rushed off for treatment in a hyperbaric chamber, I was no longer considered an emergency case, meaning we were in for an interminable wait.

We were taken to a curtained cubicle containing a bed and a plastic chair and left. We're still here now. For hours and hours nothing much has happened and I've had nothing to look at but James, who just sits there, looking miserable and saying little. It's hell. Every now and then a nurse pops in to examine me which I grow increasingly resentful of. I know that's so unreasonable. I know they're only doing their job but I'm wrecked with exhaustion and want to go home. I'm hungry, I've got a headache and feel shivery and hungover, and that's about it. But due to the fact my notes say I've attempted suicide, no one's letting me go anywhere. At one point I declared I was leaving but a nurse got quite heavy handed and informed me that if I tried to go anywhere before having been seen by the psychiatric team, they would have no choice but to section me under the mental health act. That was when I realised I was going to have to change my attitude or risk being here even longer.

As we waited to be seen by the doctor who wanted to do a second set of blood tests James kept saying that not being high up on their list of priorities was a great sign, that it meant I must be fine, that they could obviously tell that my 'attempt' was just a 'cry for help'. Every time he says this, it's obvious he's longing for confirmation from me. Was it a 'cry for help'? Don't know. After all, I'd had no idea he was going to pitch up. But, if it helps him to believe that my attempt wasn't serious, then fine. I just have to give the appearance that I'm not going to do it again in order to get out.

James tries a few times to engage with me, but everything he says is white noise. I've deliberately retreated into some kind of numb state in order to cope. I need to. The enormity of the fact he's here is too overwhelming to confront at the moment. There's a massive chance I'm in shock.

When we do finally get seen, the doctor is more concerned about *why* I'm here than any after effects of my attempt. Again, there's a lot of talk of how lucky I am. There's also a lot of talk of counselling and so on. I feel numb throughout but concentrate on saying whatever I think they want to hear. I must not be sectioned. I'm taken into a room to fill out a form I'm already very familiar with, having filled it out at the GP's multiple times now. It's the one used to determine how depressed someone is and to ascertain whether they are at risk to themselves. I try to make all my answers less extreme than they are in reality, without making it obvious I'm lying.

Meanwhile, I'm vaguely aware that James is acting as my mouthpiece in a way that's so ironic it almost has me amused. He's acting like a concerned boyfriend, having slipped back into the role of someone who gives a shit when of course I haven't seen him for months.

I watch him talking to the doctors on my behalf. Feelings start to seep in, melting the edges of cold shock at which point my heart aches with distress. I look at him properly for the first time and he's deliciously familiar. I've spent so much time concentrating on the negatives in a bid to get over him, so the fact that everything about him looks lovely to me is devastating. He's wearing a blue and red check shirt I've never seen before, with jeans and a pair of trainers that I do know. His hair is the same, he's the same. He looks the same and yet, so different. When I last saw him, that morning when he left for work, I would never have imagined in a thousand years he'd be capable of hurting me. It's all too much.

Eventually, mercifully, the psychiatric team seem satisfied that I knew that James would save me, that I hadn't really wanted to die and that I'm feeling far better and regretful about my actions. On some level there may be some truth in that. I'm already starting to feel like I want to just cry and cry with relief that I'm not dead. I realise then how much I need help. The doctors decree that as long as I'm with someone constantly for the next forty-eight hours, I can be discharged, once I've been given some more oxygen.

The ordeal isn't quite over.

Back in A&E and it's just James and I again at which point I'm unable to control the (probably) inevitable tsunami of grief. I begin to weep and the tears don't stop even when they put a tight-fitting oxygen mask on my face which forces me to breathe pure air for an hour or so, revitalising my blood, making up for what I've put it through, albeit briefly.

Trapped with his wailing, unhinged ex, James looks helpless and sheepish. He obviously doesn't know what to do or say but he also doesn't leave. Instead he sits in a chair with his head in his hands, saying nothing but obviously thinking hard about what to do next.

Once we've ascertained from a *third* set of blood tests that the levels of CO2 in my blood stream are at a safe level the doctor says I can be discharged, on the proviso that James stays with me. He reassures them (I'm guessing for appearances sake) that I won't be left alone for at least forty-eight hours by which point I should have been seen by a doctor again and been assigned a new counsellor (because I never showed up to the one the GP organised) and put on strong medication. This doesn't sound negotiable.

The minute we step through the revolving doors and out onto the pavement, without saying a word I walk as quickly as I can away from James, almost breaking into a half run. I'll either have to walk home or get the bus. I've got a fiver on me which will get me an oyster card and fortunately my flat keys are still in the pocket of my very grubby jeans.

'What are you doing?' calls James.

I frown but can't be bothered to reply. I carry on. Only James runs after me and grabs my arm.

'Get off me,' I shout, loudly enough that passers-by stare.

James drops my arm, wary. 'Listen,' he says, both hands up to show he's not going to hurt me 'no matter how angry you are with me, you cannot go off on your own. You heard what the hospital said. You're not to be on your own for forty-eight hours.'

I spin round, eyes blazing with fury 'Are you for real?' I hiss 'Do you honestly think I would go anywhere with you after what you've done? You've done your bit. Now piss off.'

James looks horrified 'Charlotte, you're being totally ridiculous. You have just tried to kill yourself, which I know was a cry for help. But I've listened. I know you're upset and I'm so sorry for everything. I want to explain.'

I stop again and this time the fury is so intense it fills every cell in the way I'd hoped the carbon monoxide would.

In that moment I despise him so intensely. I speak calmly, my voice full of loathing 'You have no right to claim to know anything about the way I feel. Now, I'm not standing here demanding to know anything or having a go at you. I just want you to leave me alone. Just as you have for the last however many weeks. Now leave me alone, fuck off, and don't contact me again. Please.'

I'm beyond desperate to go to bed, where I'll stay until I have enough strength to figure out what the hell to do next. I set off but can hear him behind me, following.

'Right,' I say, turning around. He jumps, clearly terrified of what I might say or do next. 'Here's the deal. Maybe it was a cry for help. Who knows? Who cares? It makes no difference because you came. So that's fine. But now I know you're alive, which is all I needed to know. So, I'll be fine. Ok? Goodbye.'

Hopefully that'll do it. And for the thirty seconds during which I don't hear any footsteps I allow myself to believe he's gone. But, like a dog with a bone, the next thing I know he's at my elbow again, looking irritatingly determined. It's so annoying!

'Charlotte, like it or lump it, I'm not going anywhere. You can shout and scream if you want, or phone the police, only if you do, I'll tell them you've just tried to commit suicide and I'll also make sure they ring both your parents and tell them what's happened.'

I might explode with frustration. This man I think. This man is making me so mad. He will definitely destroy me.

42

As soon as I'm in the door I march straight through the lounge and into my bedroom, slamming the door hard behind me. I flop onto my bed. The physical relief is intense. I'm utterly spent.

I stare at the ceiling despairing at how absurd the whole situation is. I've spent months wishing James was here, and now he is, I want him to fuck off. I'm clearly not going to shake him off though, so for now I accept that if I play things right, hopefully I'll be rid of him soon enough. Then I can do what I want. Work out what that is. The most important thing is that he doesn't tell my family I tried to kill myself.

'Can I make you something?' he calls through from the lounge, like he's my bloody husband or something. In a minute he'd be asking if I wanted anything putting in the wash. I can hardly believe he's in my flat again. It's weird and is making me feel deeply suspicious and on edge. I wondered briefly if he'd dare berate me about Lucas? He may have done wrong by me, deeply wrong of course, but I still wouldn't put it past him to get angry. Maybe his intention was even to kill me? I experience a wave of fear which might be sleep deprived paranoia. Hard to tell.

'I don't want anything,' I say, getting up and then actually into bed, under the duvet, still in my filthy clothes, too beaten and exhausted to bother getting undressed. I smell of fumes, my hair is lank and dirty but I'm too wiped out to care. I'm furious with myself and furious with him too. I've failed and am back at square one, alive, depressed and useless.

As I continue to stare at the ceiling, I hear him putting the kettle on and moving around the kitchen.

Ten minutes later there's a feeble tap at the door and he walks in carrying a tray. His lack of awareness is so staggering it's almost comical. Almost.

'I've made you a tea and there's a sandwich and a cake bar thing, though that might have possibly gone off. There wasn't much else in the fridge.'

I glare at him and pull the duvet further up around myself. 'I'm not hungry.'

'Charlotte, we need to talk,' says James, looking truly pained. To my horror, I watch as his whole face sort of crumples strangely. For a split second I wonder if he's having a stroke but then realise, he's crying.

He tries to put the tray down on my dressing table but it's so littered with make-up and other detritus it's an impossible task, so he staggers around with it, tea slopping everywhere.

'Just put it on the floor,' I snap.

He does as he's told, squatting down carefully within about the only patch of clear floor space there is. Gingerly he places the tray down before standing up again, at which point, he wipes his face with his hands, clearly mortified with himself for crying. I'm finding the whole episode mightily uncomfortable. I'll also admit that, surprisingly, I'm gleaning no pleasure from seeing him so all over the shop. Thinking about it I didn't think I'd ever seen him cry before. Like really cry.

'I'm sorry,' he manages eventually, trying to gulp away his emotion.

I sigh heavily. My heart is literally aching. It seems so unfair that after everything I still care. No matter how hard I try, I simply don't relish seeing him so upset.

'I need to sleep. But sit down if you want,' I say wearily, motioning to the foot of the bed.

James does as I instruct, still sniffing, trying to pull himself together.

'I'm sorry. I know this isn't about me. It's just the truth is, finding you in that garage...'

I wait for him to recover from yet another wave of emotion.

'It was so frightening. I thought I was too late. I thought you were dead and you see.......... I just......well.... I just hadn't realised till that moment how much I'd fucked you up.'

I blink hard, looking everywhere but at him. 'Don't flatter yourself. It's not all about you.'

James looks at me. 'Oh. Right.'

I can't speak. It's too hard.

'Anyway, aren't you going to ask me why I went? Don't you want to know why I've come back?'

I shake my head. 'I can't do this now.'

'Ok,' he says, seeming to understand. He clears his throat and in that second reverts back to carer mode again 'right, I'm going to leave you to get some rest but I'll be next door if you need me. I know you don't want me here but I'm afraid you're stuck with me, unless you're happy with someone else knowing what's going on.'

I turn over and wrap the duvet around me even more tightly, indicating by doing so that for now the situation would have to do.

James stops at the door having had a thought 'There aren't any pills or anything in here are there?'

'No,' I manage, determined not to let him see the tears which are rolling down my exhausted, grey face.

'No rope or anything?'

Was he for real?

'OK, well you get some sleep,' he replies quickly and, for the first time in a long time, I do.

43

I wake with a start and my first thought is that when I went to sleep, James was in my flat. My second thought is that I must have slept all day. According to my phone it's five o clock in the afternoon.

James isn't dead.

I'm not dead.

James is here.

Still groggy, I stare at the wall contemplating. It takes a while to 'come round' but I can feel how grateful my brain is for some unbroken hours of solid sleep.

Eventually though my mind starts whirring again and anxiety rises in my chest. Maybe it's time James answered some questions now? But do I even want to know why he left anymore? I'm not sure. As for my botched attempt to end my life, I don't want to examine that. It's too terrifying. It's imperative James doesn't tell anyone. I need to work out what's going on and process what's happened. I feel vulnerable, scared and devastated and ashamed.

I slowly clamber out of bed, still fully clothed and reeking of petrol which is gross. My body feels sweaty, grim and in desperate need for a shower.

I'm absolutely starving too. What a mess I am. In so many ways.

I poke my head round my bedroom door and peer into the living area.

'James?'

There's no reply though and due to the size of my compact flat it's easy to tell he's gone.

Again.

A wave of disappointment rises up inside me but I refuse to submit to it. What had I expected? That he'd be sitting there, waiting for me to wake up? I'm a fool. It's for the best he's gone. He's done nothing but cause me pain.

Just then my heart lurches inside my rib cage as I hear the sound of a key in the front door.

Who the hell's that? Only Eleanor has a spare key. Or has Dad found the spare? I can't let either of them see me like this. Seconds later however, I'm stunned to see James blithely letting himself in, staggering through the door with two bags of shopping, both of which look ridiculously heavy.

'Hi,' he says sheepishly. 'Sorry if I scared you. I just popped out to get some supplies. Thought you might be hungry and your cupboards are pretty bare. I've spent all day thinking you were going to wake up any moment. Typically, you have while I was out. Sorry.'

As my frayed nerves settle, I consider my options. For now, hunger beats pride.

'Right,' I say eventually, not giving away how surprised I am to see him back 'Fine. Whatever. I'm going to have a shower.'

He looks relieved not to have been screamed at.

I stalk my way to the bathroom where I lock the door behind me, heart pounding and head swimming. Where has he been? Why turn up now? Why hasn't he said anything about the photos? Maybe he didn't see the newspaper or hear about my 'sex scandal'? I experience a healthy dollop of irritation at myself for being pleased he hasn't disappeared again. It's all like being in a weird dream.

The hot water feels extraordinary and I end up showering for far longer than I need to. Twenty minutes later I'm squeaky clean and any toxic reminder of the garage and what happened in it has been washed down the plughole. The shower felt very good.

A good shower. It's something.

When I turn the water off, I can hear James moving about in the kitchen.

The sound transports me back to the days when hearing him busying himself around my home was the happiest sound in the world, one which ironically used to make me feel safe and loved. Tears threaten. What had been so terrible about our set up that he had felt moved to abandon me in the cruel way that he did? I *didn't* imagine our happiness. We were perfect and he threw it all away.

Logic shows up not a moment too soon, jostling sentiment to the back of the queue. We weren't happy. *I* was happy. We weren't even real. He was lying the whole time. I had no real idea what was going on.

God, I'm sick of feeling like my brain's being fried in a pan.

As I dry myself I realise I've only got my filthy dirty clothes to change back into, which frankly I don't even want to touch. They need burning. I'll have to change my bedsheets too, they're rank. In the meantime, I certainly don't want James seeing me in just a towel. It would feel too weird, even if there was a time when I would have pranced out completely naked without a care. Months of distance, multiplied by no contact, plus lies, is an equation which equals awkwardness and damage. There may have been a time when it was more than acceptable for us to see each other's bits but that time has long gone.

In the end, I make a run for it. One, two, three, go. Towel held tightly round me, I open the door and scamper as quickly as I can towards my bedroom without so much as glancing in his direction.

In the privacy of my room I get dressed. It feels good to be clean. I'm about to put a white and blue smock type top on when I remember James once telling me he liked me in it. I swiftly take it off again and plump for a boring, plain grey t shirt and ripped black jeans which feel far looser than normal. I go to the mirror, moisturise my face and quickly brush my hair and put a bit of eyeliner and mascara on. I look like shit. Whenever I used to fantasise about bumping into James or seeing him again, in any capacity, my imagination was always generous enough to have me in full makeup looking my best. In reality, the first time he saw me again I was nearly dead and I puked on him. Life's such a bitch. I look pretty ravaged now and my skin is the worst it's ever been, but I guess you get the face you deserve and I've been subsisting on vodka, wine and junk for weeks.

I hesitate before adding some peach blusher to my cheeks and filling in my brows a bit.

When I finally open the door, feeling strangely nervous, James looks up. His face drops.

'What?' I say, on the defence.

'Nothing, it's just you're so... thin. I noticed a bit yesterday too.'

I bite my lip, not sure what to say. I hate the way he's looking at me, all appalled and worried, like I'm a freak-show. I shrug and glare at him, hating myself for caring what he thinks.

'Ok, right,' he says, in that weird over the top carer voice again 'I wasn't sure what to make and I know it's closer to dinner time but I've made sort of brunchy stuff. Is that OK? There's a tonne of bacon, mushrooms, toast, juice, and I can do eggs as well if you like?'

It's only then that I notice the loaded plates arranged on the breakfast bar. What was he up to? Why go so over the top? I was too weak and hungry to question anything out loud, though, and the smell of bacon was making my mouth water.

Avoiding eye contact, I perch on one of the two stools and reach tentatively for a plate.

'Shall I make you a bacon sarnie, with a bit of ketchup? Oh, and here's a tea,' he says handing me a mug. He's made it just the colour I like it and I know there'll be half a sugar in it. It's like being in a time warp.

'Or if you'd rather have something else, just say. Or perhaps you want to drink your juice first?'

'Look,' I say eventually 'would you mind not fussing quite so much. This is fine but we both know we're not having some kind of date so...... please stop acting like we are.'

James' shoulders visibly drop.

I grab some bacon and stuff it in my mouth. The saltiness and taste are ridiculously good. I eat three pieces in a row then start tearing into the toast. I can feel my entire system thanking me as my blood sugar levels adjust. James watches me eating. I don't stop until I feel sated. Then I sit, sipping my tea, aware that the atmosphere has turned very awkward.

'I'm so sorry,' he says suddenly.

I leave a long pregnant pause before replying quietly 'For what? Which bit?'

James walks around to my side of the breakfast bar and sits on the other stool. 'Tell me you meant me to find you yesterday,' he says, brown eyes pleading with me to say yes.

I blink, feeling like he's invading my personal space. It's all about him when it comes down to it. All he wants is for his guilt to be absolved.

A thought occurs to me 'Out of interest, how did you find me so quickly?'

James holds my gaze, clearly still hoping to know what the answer to his question is but reluctantly acknowledging that I've heard but don't want to say. 'I was pretty nearby when I messaged you on Facebook. I've been thinking about you constantly lately. I've driven by the flat a few times to be honest, trying to pluck up the courage to knock, wondering how you are, wanting to see you. Anyway, I was sitting in the car just a few roads away when I messaged. I didn't want you to spot me in case it looked I was stalking you but I was hoping you might reply and agree to see me. When you sent that last message saying you were going to be dead, I panicked and sped over. I banged on the door and when there was no answer I……. well, I used my keys to get in.'

My face must register the shock and unease I feel upon hearing this because James lifts a hand up 'I know but, I thought you might have done something stupid. Then I saw you'd left a letter to your Dad on the table and knew you had, or were trying to. So I'm bloody glad I did use the keys.' His turn to sound defensive.

I'd forgotten about the letter. I look over. It's still sat propped up on the coffee table, unopened. I feel embarrassed suddenly. James has been exposed to my grief in a way no one else has.

'When I saw it, I had to assume you were actually trying to kill yourself, so once I'd checked you definitely weren't here, I ran to the garage to see if you'd taken your car or not. Thank god I did. Another five minutes and………'

His eyes well up again, like they did yesterday. It's irritating. If he cared so much why did he walk out on me without so much as a note?

'The thing is,' he begins 'before yesterday if anyone had asked me if I thought you would ever even consider killing yourself, I would have placed everything I own on no. Happy Charlotte, kill herself? Charlotte who can find humour in anything and who is so glass half full about life? It just doesn't add up.'

I'm absolutely incredulous. 'Are you kidding me?' I shove my plate away. 'Happy Charlotte? Are you insane? Have you forgotten the part where we were in a relationship and one day you said 'see you later' only I never did? Or am I imagining that ever happened?'

James shakes his head and tries to protest but I'm done listening to him. He's making my blood boil. I slide from the stool and start pacing. 'I'm sorry James but hearing you label me as 'Happy Charlotte' is too much to take. You need to get real about what you did. You just walked out, with no warning, breaking my heart in the process. How the hell did you think I'd deal with it? You didn't even have the common courtesy to ring, or even text. Nothing. After nine months together, I had no explanation. Not so much as a poxy WhatsApp. Instead I was left to figure things out for myself when I couldn't be totally sure you hadn't had an accident, or died of a heart attack. How the hell did you think I was going to cope with such extreme cruelty and humiliation? Did you think I would have just sat there that night, looking at the food I'd made saying blithely 'Ah well, I thought we were in love and had a future, which by the way is all I've ever wanted, but I guess I got it wrong, so onwards. In fact, give me five minutes and I'll reinstall Tinder and find another person who can lie to me continuously.'

Finally James looks appropriately mortified. He sits there blinking hard, processing what I'm saying, while I try to comprehend why on earth I'm having to spell things out?

'Ok but....'

'But what?'

'Nothing.'

'No, I get it. You want me to tell you that trying to kill myself had nothing to do with you at all. You want me to make you feel better?'

'It's not like that,' says James shaking his head.

At this point I have truly had enough.

'Do you know what? I really want you to leave now please. This isn't healthy, being here with you like this. To be honest it's creepy. I don't even know what your real name is. Please get out.' My whole body is trembling with rage. 'And leave my keys on the table. It's weird that you've kept them all this time.'

Our eyes lock, both of us daring the other one to speak first.

'No,' says James.

I despair and briefly consider killing him instead of myself.

44

There's only so much one person's brain can absorb and mine feels like it's in danger of combusting but then it's had a lot to cope with over the last twenty-four hours. No one knows this more than James yet, despite that, I can tell he's gearing up to tell me things I'm not sure my frazzled grey matter's up to hearing. His selfishness is astounding.

I can tell he's preparing to 'confess'. The atmosphere is tinged with it, only the more whatever 'it' is casts its shadow, the less sure I am I want to know. I'm sick of never being in control. James left when he felt like it, he reappeared when he felt like it and by 'saving' me seems to think he can do what he likes. But why should I have to listen to him now, just because *he's* decided it's the right time to spill his guts?

'I can't leave you alone and actually I won't leave you alone,' he argues 'How do I know you won't do something stupid?'

I head for my bedroom, but stop at the door and say wearily 'You don't, but I won't ok? So please just go. Leave me alone. Piss off. Go away. Thanks.'

'My real name is James.'

'Great,' I say 'Good for you.'

'But Ralphs isn't my surname. Ralph is my middle name. My real last name is Samuels. I'm James Samuels.'

He must have no respect for me whatsoever. In my already fragile state he's forcing me to go through this? I despair.

'And I didn't lie about everything. I did....I do....love you.'

'Don't,' I warn, face grim. I'm trying not to get wound up but can feel my heart rate accelerating. How dare he? If he loved me so much he wouldn't have left and maybe, just maybe, if he'd been around to support me when the whole Lucas thing blew up I might have coped better? Maybe I wouldn't have reached such a desperate point? As it is, I'm weak, gaunt, ill, a shadow of the person I'd been before meeting James Ralphs. Or whatever his stupid name is.

'But why don't you want to know?'

I shrug, eyes brimming with tears. 'Why should I care anymore? Whatever it is you want to tell me it's not going to be good news. I do admit it's strange. For ages I would have paid anything to know why you did what you did. But the minute you got in contact and I knew you were alive, it didn't seem to matter anymore. What I don't know can't hurt me more than I've already been hurt type of thing. And besides, I can guess the basics. No doubt you're married and our relationship was some kind of sadistic joke, or some form of con, or bet or...... who knows. In fact, thinking about it now, I honestly am just past caring. Now *please* get out of my flat and my life.'

If I could I'd remove him physically but obviously I can't and for whatever reason he seems hell-bent on ignoring me. He just stands there, a stubborn hateful lump. I could scream.

'Listen,' I try again, sounding far more patient than I feel 'if it makes you feel better, my suicide attempt wasn't all about you. I was devastated when you left but other shit has happened too. I've been humiliated. My family and friends think I'm disgusting and I didn't get promoted. In fact, it's probably only a matter of time before I'm fired altogether from Daytime Live. I've lost all respect I ever had from my colleagues and people within the industry. So, there you go. Does that make you feel better, knowing it's not all about you? Is that what you want to hear?'

I watch him, waiting for him to react, still curious despite myself to know if he already knows about the Lucas 'story' or not.

'It was just a story,' he says evenly 'not a nice one admittedly but people forget about these things eventually.'

So he does know.

I'm surprised and feel quite taken aback. Though I don't know why. He was in no position to criticise anything given that he disappeared on me. Was it the reason he took so long to get in touch though?

I'm starting to feel panicky and anxious. His evident calm about the photos is unnerving. The James I knew would have been at least a little jealous and upset. My desire to get rid of him becomes urgent once again. I want him gone.

'No one will remember in the fullness of time,' he says.

He doesn't get it. 'No, James. Sadly, the trolls and the perverts take a lot longer to forget than a few hours. All that shit will be online forever. And, if you must know, I received a load of disgusting online abuse, like I was a prostitute, some of it very aggressive and frightening. My parents are embarrassed and repelled. Work were, and still are, pretty livid. My reputation is in tatters and I've been incredibly ill. I'm permanently anxious and stressed and I have depression. I barely eat, I drink every day and I hate my life and myself. People think I'm a starry eyed, gold digging slut and no doubt you think I'm disgusting too? And you know what, maybe I am? The photos prove it.'

James' face is ashen. The next thing I know he collapses onto the sofa, covering his face in his hands and shaking his head.

I realise he's crying.

'I don't think you're disgusting and I can't believe you'd say that about yourself. That's not the Charlotte I know,' he sobs.

I wonder about that. Feeling worthless and full of self-loathing has become normal. I can't recall not hating myself.

'Charlotte, listen, I need to tell you something.'

'Please don't,' I beg, starting to cry myself.

'I have to because I did something bad.'

Tears pour down my exhausted face as I plead with him 'I'm sorry, I can't handle this right now. Can you not see how much this is distressing me? How many times do I have to tell you that I don't want to hear about some other woman or have my nose rubbed in the fact that I was totally and utterly naïve and stupid to have let you into my heart like I did. So, for the very last time, have a tiny bit of respect for my feelings and go.'

I race into my bedroom and slam the door. If he hasn't left in the next five minutes I'll call the police.

'But you don't understand,' wails James.

Christ alive. He's certifiable. We both are.

'Please just hear me out and then I swear I'll go.'

I stand rigid, back against the door, trying to decide what to do. I owe him nothing but if I want to get rid of him, I don't think I have any other choice but to do as he's asking and listen. He's utterly impossible.

I turn and wrench open the door again 'You've got five minutes,' I yell, eyes wild, brimming with tears and rage. 'After that I am phoning the police.'

James nods and wipes his face with his shirt sleeve, visibly struggling to compose himself 'Right, ok,' he begins, taking a deep inhalation of breath, seeming to have at least grasped that he only has a very small window before I lose it completely.

'So,' he begins 'the thing is, I'm not really a builder.'

This is why I do not want to be doing this now. I feel faint and collapse onto the sofa, right in the corner, hugging my knees to my chest, making a shield with my body between him and me.

'I'm a journalist.'

It takes a few seconds to register what he's just said.

'I don't understand.'

'Charlotte, I'm so truly sorry and I swear I never meant to hurt you like I have. But you see I wasn't supposed to fall in love with you. But I did. You know I did and I still love you now. I love you so much and I......'

'Shut up,' I say in a tone that does indeed silence him. Even I'm shocked by how cold I sound. 'Stop snivelling and tell me what you've done because if it's what I think it might be, I won't be responsible for my actions.'

'Charlotte please, you have to understand, it's not what it seems like, it was a nightmare and I tried to make it stop and I did stop it, for ages but..........'

'Was it you? Did you give the photos to the newspaper?'

James just stands there, sobbing, looking pathetic.

My blood runs cold.

'Answer me.'

After an agonising minute or so, his face covered in snot and tears he simply whispers 'Yes.'

45

I feel like I've been punched in the guts.

'But why tell me you were a builder on our first date? We met on Tinder. You were a builder then. There's no way you can have known you were going to ruin my life at that point?'

My head races as it tries to work out the extent of his despicable betrayal.

James just stands there looking pained.

'Tell me everything. Now!' My rage is so visceral at this point I no longer feel remotely wary of him. 'Tell me every sordid detail before I go insane. More insane than I am already.'

James nods, bottom lip wobbling.

'From the beginning. I'm deadly serious. Do not waste a second more of my time.'

James swallows 'Right, so I'm a journalist. I've been at The Sunday Globe for a couple of years now. It's a bit of a rag but whilst numbers are on the decrease for just about every other paper, ours have always been OK, mainly because of our weekend stories. We have a reputation for exposing celebs before anyone else has got even a sniff of a story.'

'I know what The Sunday Globe is James. Sometimes we looked at it together,' I snap, fearful my heart might actually break, the pain of betrayal is so intense.

'Lucas Harcourt has been dodging paying as much tax as he should have been for years. We found that out ages ago but the story had no value when he was just a third-rate soap actor. There was always something juicier to print to be honest. But the political climate has changed since then. People hate tax dodgers more than ever before, plus, his career suddenly started going stellar, at which point his business became of interest to a far wider audience. His reputation's way more important now too, particularly given that his next film role has him playing this moral crusader type. Anyway, we first told his agent we were going to run the tax story about a year ago and of course she begged us not to. Eventually my editor agreed to withhold the story but only if they gave us something else.'

I shake my head, not quite able to compute 'Are you telling me I've been used as some sort of bargaining tool for your revolting, immoral paper? Are you kidding me? Is that not totally illegal? To take someone who's not even famous and just ruin their life?'

James looks ashamed but mumbles 'it's not actually illegal. The pictures were taken by Lucas so if he gives his permission for them to be used.......'

'But I deleted them and anyway, I don't understand. What did you have to do with it exactly? Where does the bit where you dated me for months on end come into it, convincing me along the way you actually gave a shit? What the hell were you doing?'

James swallows again and in that moment, I see him for what he is. Maybe you need to peel away enough layers of the onion skin in order to truly know someone? I could see now. At the heart of James was a cowardly, pathetic, lily livered, spineless git.

'When I first met you, Lucas didn't have the pictures anymore. He'd deleted them so his new girlfriend wouldn't find them in his camera roll. But he was desperate for us to run that story instead of the tax evasion one.'

'Why the hell would he want that?'

James shrugs 'The public will usually forgive a man for being promiscuous. It can even enhance their image. Sad but true I'm afraid. A good-looking makeup girl having consenting, wild sex within a relationship. It's win win for him. Nothing's really happened but the association with such a safe, daytime show which is supposed to be so wholesome makes it scandalous and newsworthy.'

He says that last bit in such a monotone he may as well be reading instructions off the back of a ready meal.

I'm filled with a renewed sense of revulsion. His world-view is so jaded, so amoral.

'Lucas was desperate to squash the tax dodging story which could have been career suicide, so he told us how we could get to you. He said you'd still have the pictures so we had to plan a way to get to them. He suggested finding you on Tinder, I think a mate of Lucas' had seen you on there or something, so he advised us what to write on the Tinder profile, told us how much you loved quizzes and stuff.'

It's official. The world is a dark and awful place.

I've been so used.

'You entrapped me?'

James can't look at me.

'All that time I thought you were wooing me, that you were right for me, that we got on, you were in fact just conning me?'

'No Charlotte. Well, ok, yes at first, I guess I was. But very, very quickly I realised how amazing you were and how right for one another we were. You can't fake a connection like that.'

For all these months my imagination had been spinning, trying to resolve the mystery of his disappearance to the point where I'd come up with far bigger, even more dramatic scenarios than this. Courtesy of my imagination, at one time or another James had been an illegal immigrant, a criminal on the run, a polygamist, dying of a terminal illness. Turns out I never could have imagined how frighteningly cruel the truth was. This was actually worse.

'But how could you possibly guarantee I'd come across you on Tinder, or that I'd swipe you?'

James looks deeply uncomfortable.

'Well?' I demand, my anger gathering in strength. 'Tell me!' I yell.

James flinches before mumbling 'If you make sure your location settings are set at the very lowest and you're nearby it's inevitable you'll come up and.......the paper often use me if they need to.....you know.....get the attention of a woman.'

Once I've registered what he's said and what it means, I find myself laughing vaguely hysterically. 'Wow, I see, so A/ you've done this before B/ you think you're god's gift and C/ I'm a sad, pathetic, gullible cliché because I fucking well fell for it.'

'No... that's not.......'

'Don't,' I say icily, blinking back tears 'I don't want to hear it. Just tell me what happened next?'

James gulped 'I was supposed to get the photos out of your phone that first night. That was the plan. Lucas had given me your pin number and we were all hoping you wouldn't have changed it since the break-up. Most people don't so we had high hopes. But that night it was like you were surgically attached to your phone so I quickly arranged the date for the following day. I already thought you were a nice person and not the kind of girl I'd imagined at all. To be honest I just wanted to get the job done.'

I omit a sort of low moan as it all starts to sink in.

'I know,' says James 'I know this is a lot to take in but you have to believe me when I say that, looking back, I genuinely think I was falling for you hook, line and sinker as quickly as on that second date. Even then I was having major doubts about whether I could go through with the job. It just didn't sit right.'

'Oh well, well done you,' I say tearfully, feeling possibly more broken hearted now than I did when he first disappeared. Everything had been a sham.

'How could you be so cruel? You say you fell in love with me but you still did it. Why?'

James sighs and goes to sit on an armchair opposite me, looking defeated by the whole situation.

'Tell me,' I shout 'This is like torture and I can't take much more. So just finish off this horrible disgusting story so I can get some peace. Please,' I beg him.

James rubs his face with his hands and continues, accepting he has no choice but to keep ploughing on 'By the time I managed to get the photos out of your phone I had really strong feelings for you. So, I kept delaying and making excuses to my editor. Then eventually I told him there was no point running them. I said they weren't any good but he saw right through that. He accused me of being unprofessional and we had a huge bust up. He said it was his job to decide whether they were usable or not but I refused to show them to him. Charlotte, I was in love with you by then so I hated those pictures. Imagine how hideous it was for me to see them. I didn't want anyone to see them. Ever. I nearly lost my job over it and Tilly was suspicious by this point and wanting to know what was going on too so life was a mess. But I kept insisting that the tax story was better. Only by then, John, my editor, had made so many deals with Lucas' agent he was hell-bent on getting you. It was just better for business all round. You see if we pissed off Lucas over this, he would never co- operate with us ever again and neither would his very powerful agent. His very powerful agent who represents all kinds of newsworthy stars we need relationships with. It rumbled on for ages.'

He looks up and realises I'm struggling to formulate a sentence.

'Rewind a second. Tilly was starting to get suspicious?'

I didn't think it possible that James could look anymore guilty, but apparently, he can. He's actually squirming.

'Still with her now?' I ask flatly.

'No,' he says, shaking his head vehemently.

I go to the sink and pour myself a glass of water. I feel incredibly faint and exhausted.

'Are you ok? You look pale.'

I don't answer, instead I just return to the sofa and slump down.

He comes over and kneels on the floor beside me. 'Charlotte, you have to understand. I've never met anyone like you before when doing this kind of thing. Tilly always knew about my undercover work and never cared because she understands that it's part of being that type of journalist. As long as I was paying the bills and didn't get 'involved' she was fine. I've never had sex with anyone else outside of the marriage before.'

'Bullshit,' I muttered.

James looks taken aback and almost offended but carries on. 'I know you're very angry, understandably so, but you must know that my feelings were genuine. I left Tilly for you for Christ's sakes, I left her really soon after we got together and you know how jealous I was of Lucas, who by the way, started getting quite heavy with me personally. He's not stupid. He soon guessed I was the only thing blocking the story. He knew we were seeing each other. I'm not sure how but it probably didn't take a genius. I suspect he might have done some sniffing around people at Daytime Live.'

'Which is why you were so anti going to Lindsay's party.'

James just nods. 'Yes. Anyway, he turned up at the office one day and was quite threatening, truth be told. He said I was a fool for protecting you and that if he wanted he could have you back in an instant.'

'He what?'

'I know,' placates James 'And I didn't believe him at all. I knew he was just desperate. But he kept on and on until eventually he said he'd prove it. He said that he would be able to get you to meet him at The Mondrian at four o clock the following Thursday. I said fine because I didn't think you would ever do that to me.'

'Do what to you?' I splutter 'I went for a fucking coffee.'

'I know,' says James, looking tortured 'I know that now. But I didn't at the time and when you arrived, I was so upset. I was there you see, watching to see if you'd come. Jealousy is such a horrible emotion and honestly, I was devastated. I couldn't get the images of you and him together out of my head at the best of times and I just assumed you were meeting him because you were still into him. I thought you were going to end up in bed together and I couldn't handle it. It made me mad and I got into a real state. I felt betrayed and gutted and I wanted to lash out. I wanted to hurt you like you were hurting me, so I wrote an email to my editor, attached the images and pressed send. Out on the Southbank, I remember, I stood there and debated doing it for about five minutes. I can even recall now, my thumb hovering over send and eventually I thought about him touching you and kissing you, I allowed the images of those photos to flood my brain and that was that. I experienced a sense of regret the very second I'd done it though. I remember wishing you could recall emails. I regretted it almost immediately but I was just so hurt you see.'

'But I told you about my meeting with Lucas,' I wept, struggling to come to terms with the fact that this man who I had loved so much and who I thought had loved me was the one who had caused my demise and inflicted all this pain on me. Lucas had been despicable too but I hadn't been in love with Lucas. The pain of his disgusting behaviour paled by comparison.

'I know, you did,' blubs James inhaling deeply, tears pricking his eyes 'But not until after, by which point it was too late.'

'You bastard,' I sob.

'I know, I know Charlotte and I will never forgive myself and I tried to fix it, believe you me I tried. When you called and told me about meeting up with him, I cannot tell you how awful I felt. I was disgusted with myself, desperate. I begged my boss not to run the story. Begged. I practically got on my bloody hands and knees if you must know and you know what, I thought he wouldn't run it. I honestly thought I'd had a reprieve and I made a promise to myself at that moment to sort my life out. I decided to tell you the truth about who I was and that if you forgave me I'd propose. I didn't want to run the risk of losing you ever again.'

'What made you think I'd forgive you?' I asked.

James sighed, shaking his head 'I didn't. I mean, I didn't know if you would or not and I knew I'd just have to accept it if you couldn't and spend the rest of my life full of regret. I was going to tell you that Tuesday night, the night you'd said you'd cook dinner for me, but when I went into work that day they were formatting the story. My boss sold me out totally, putting the story before our friendship, or what I had always believed was a friendship.'

'And how did that feel?' I wail 'being betrayed by someone you trusted who you thought cared about you? Eh? Did that hurt?'

'Please Charlotte, don't. Trust me when I say I couldn't feel worse than I already do. I just got myself into such a pickle.' As he utters this understatement of the year his voice cracks and he begins to sob.

'So why not at least warn me?' I say, my heart almost breaking with pain 'Why didn't you come and see me and tell me what you'd done?'

James shrugs as he tries to stem tears with his hands 'I don't know. I just couldn't. At that point I knew the story would be running the following Sunday and there was nothing I could do. So, I decided it would be best for you if I just disappeared from your life.'

'But how could you possibly think that was best for me? It was so cowardly. Do you have any idea what you put me through? I've been through utter hell. The pain of not knowing anything was far worse than anything else.'

'Maybe,' James says 'I don't know. Or maybe it was the sensible thing to do? There was nothing I could do or say to take back what was about to happen and you were hardly going to want me around once you knew I was responsible and that I'd lied.'

'All those months,' I say 'all those times I asked why you wouldn't introduce me to anyone, why you were so anxious about going anywhere with me. My instincts were right the whole time, yet you made me feel bad about it, made me feel like a nag when really you were lying about everything, taking me for a complete and utter fool.'

'I never thought you were a fool. Ever.'

'And all those times you were so cross about Lucas, when you were in fact living with another woman. The hypocrisy is unbelievable.'

James looks shame faced 'I know and I know it seems so unfair but the jealousy was corrosive. There wasn't a day during our relationship when I didn't wish I hadn't seen those fucking photos.'

I thought I'd hit rock bottom. Turns out, I was only scratching the surface.

46

For a while we both just sit and cry, oblivious to one another, wrapped up in our own pain. I'm struggling to absorb everything. It's all so surreal. At a certain point James looks up. His face is wet and swollen, his nose unattractively snotty. I can't bear to look at it and suspect mine must be as bad so I get up to find some tissues. I can't find any so I rip off pieces of kitchen towel instead.

I shove some towards him, ignoring a strong urge to smash his face with it, oscillating wildly between anger and grief 'So, what else were you lying about?'

'What do you mean?' sniffs James, before blowing his nose hard.

'Were you ever really living at Mark's? Or was that bullshit too? And what was that weird drink with him all about? Or perhaps that wasn't even Mark? Perhaps it was someone else entirely?'

James shakes his head, desolate and ashamed. 'That was Mark, of course it was, and I really did want you to meet him. But it was always going to be awkward. I was living with him by then because Tilly had found about 'us' but he didn't really approve I suppose. Charlotte, so much of what I told you was true, it's just I suppose there was a lot I also... didn't, or couldn't tell you......'

There are so many things I could say.

'Please try to understand. I know my job is devious and a bit shady but when I first met you I didn't know anything about you other than that you'd had a fling with Lucas 'sleazebag' Harcourt and that you were on Tinder.'

'So bloody what?' I exclaim. 'And it wasn't a fling, it was a relationship. And being on Tinder hardly makes me a terrible person. Everyone's on it these days.'

'I've never been on it,' says James, sounding pompous and disdainful 'I'm probably a bit old fashioned about things like that. I've always viewed it as something people only go on if they're looking for sex. It's an app designed for people wanting one- night stands. At work, whenever I hear guys mentioning it, either they're moaning about how they hardly get any matches, or they're bragging about their conquests.' He glances at me briefly 'Me not caring about social media is true by the way. I find everyone's obsession with it dull beyond belief.'

I march over to the breakfast bar, impressed with myself for managing to remain so calm when inside I feel so murderous. 'I've never heard anything so judgemental in all my life. How dare you sit on your high horse? You, the man who's quite happy to prostitute himself on Tinder as long as he's getting paid. The man who will happily steal then sell private, personal photos and lie to someone he claims to 'love'. *You* are morally bankrupt so do not get to preach to me. Everyone who's single uses dating apps. You probably haven't been on them because you're married! Being on them is nothing to be ashamed of and besides, what has any of this mess got to do with bloody Tinder?'

It's interesting to note suddenly that my intense fury has penetrated the thick cloak of depression I've been wearing for so long. It can't shrug it off entirely but outrage is giving me back some vague sense of self-worth.

'Because you were on it and I suppose I judged you for that, which again I'm just trying to be honest about.'

The irony of his effort to be totally transparent doesn't escape me. I'm starting to wonder if there's something very deeply wrong with him.

'Anyway, Lucas knew you very well. He came up with the status I put on Tinder. He said you'd like it and he was right.'

Even *now* I can hear jealousy in James' voice.

'And suddenly there you were, and I remember thinking, what a beautiful face this girl has. It was your eyes I loved. Your eyes and the fact that your profile was just honest and simple but also hinted at fun. Kitchen dancing. It made me smile and I remember thinking god, what was a girl like this doing letting Lucas Harcourt take pictures of her? And I messaged you of course and you messaged back and I was glad because that was what needed to happen.'

My expression must be changing because he rushes on 'And I know that sounds harsh and it is, it's awful but I am only going to tell you the truth from now on and at that stage I still hadn't met you. But of course, your message was dry, funny and made me smile and from that second onwards, although I didn't realise it at the time, I was screwed really. You were sunshine, instant sunshine.'

I can't believe his choice of words 'I beg your pardon? *You* were screwed?'

'Yes,' nodded James 'and I will never ever forgive myself for not being stronger and for not telling you straight away what was going on.'

I think I've hit some kind of wall. It's quite possible my brain has caved in.

'Right, great.'

'What do you mean?'

I shrug, borderline hysterical. 'I don't know. I just think at this stage whatever you say is pointless because I'm no longer really listening. In fact, all I am wondering is at what point you realised that instead of being someone for you to exploit, that I was an actual human being, with feelings?'

James looks deeply shifty and uncomfortable. 'Please don't.'

'Don't what?'

'Do this. I know I've made a mess of everything.'

'I'm not entirely sure you do though.'

I slide off the bar stool and approach James. I need him to get this. And then he will go.

'Firstly,' I say, face inches away from his 'your assumptions about people on Tinder aren't just pathetic and mean, they also represent what I hate about the world the most.'

'What do you mean?'

'I mean I hate how we all, and I include myself in this, judge everyone else. You see, you have your pompous, lofty attitude about a 'girl like me,' someone who, god forbid, has had a good time in bed with a man she was in a consensual relationship with and been on a dating site. But what exactly is my crime? What have I done that's actually wrong? Apart from being a well-meaning, naïve, idiot who went on Tinder because I was single and looking for happiness.'

James looks on the back foot.

I move out of his personal space and start pacing 'Only what I didn't realise, but understand perfectly now, is that there are loads of people, like you, who are on there for entirely self-serving or duplicitous reasons, hiding behind the fact it's online. Like that makes it ok to be a lying scumbag. It actually explains a lot.'

'What does it explain?' asks James, looking at me like I've gone mad. And there's a massive chance I have.

'Oh, so many things,' I say, arms flailing 'Like why sometimes I'd be enjoying texting with someone for a few days and then suddenly they'd just disappear into the ether. I used to assume they'd met someone better but perhaps they'd only just split up with someone and realised they weren't ready to meet anyone else? Or maybe some of them were still in relationships, married, or there under false pretences? Like you were, playing with other people's lives because apparently, they don't matter because of course online they're not real. Only they are.'

James tries to interrupt. I don't let him.

'I'm a real person James and look what you've done to me and the assumptions you've made. Slutty? Happy? I don't think so. I was fine before I met you, but yes, I was also lonely at times, and a bit sad because for years I longed to meet someone special. I wanted a family, a sense of belonging, a shared history and then you walked into my life and for a few naïve months I thought I might have actually found someone to have all that with. I thought I might be a mum one day. Only it was all a load of shit. In fact, worse than that, I was being used and conned. My phone was being hacked into, my personal photos were being stolen and I was being fed an endless stream of bullshit which frankly nearly drove me mad. I have been treated like a piece of inconsequential shit by you. You used me to sell papers and then ran, the minute things got tough. You left me on my own, in utter hell, beyond scared about what might or might not have happened to you. I went to the police James. Did you know that? I spent hours phoning hospitals and god knows what else.'

Now I've started I can't stop. It's cathartic.

'I haven't slept properly in months because when that story came out my whole world collapsed. It was excruciating. Imagine what it was like having to go in to work? All those people saw private, intimate pictures of me. Because of you. And I didn't get my promotion. Did you know that? You know I worked for years towards that and now, my 'pie in the sky' dreams of having my own brand are just that. I'll be lucky to be employed anywhere and have to live with the fact that those photos and the accompanying story will be on the internet forever. So, what I want to know is this. What gives you the right to be dishonest, exploitative, cowardly and selfish? Who the hell do you think you are treating anyone like that? And why didn't you at any stage just tell me the fucking truth?'

James stares at me wide eyed, unsure whether I've finished or not. After a long pause he realises I have and that I am waiting for an answer.

'Because I didn't want to lose you and if I'd told you the truth you might never have seen me again,' he says eventually, his tone flat, defeated.

'How do you know?' I scream, frustrated beyond belief. 'At least it would have been my choice to make. I could have decided how *I* felt about everything. And maybe I would have been furious and unable to forgive you. Or, maybe, after some time, I might have weighed up the fact that despite behaving like a monumental prick, you did at least care enough to 'fess' up. As it is, you have destroyed my life and turned me into a joke. So now, for the last time, get out of my flat and don't claim to imagine you know even the last thing about me, because you don't.'

'But I do,' pleads James 'you know I do and that's why I came back, because deep down I know that despite everything you must still love me. I still love you and I know I'll have to spend the rest of my life making things up to you but it's you I want. I love you. I know it doesn't feel like it and I know I should never have done a disappearing act but I needed to be certain. I got freaked out one day. I didn't know how to tell you or how to find the words. I just panicked. Please let me explain properly...'

'No, I don't want to hear it. The day you pressed send is the day you ended everything, our relationship, my job, my life as I knew it.'

'Alright,' pleads James 'But I'm not going to give up. Please don't push me away. I know I can make you better. I can fix us. I can fix you.'

I shake my head vigorously 'No James. This isn't a fucking Coldplay song. In fact, the whole business is the most unpoetic, unromantic, vile, insidious mess. So, take your empty words and go. I hate you.

James looks horrified 'I need to show you that I am worth a second chance. I want to woo you. I want to be the man you deserve. I want to introduce you to my family, to everyone ......'

I put a hand up 'Stop. This is insane talk. Now, if you care for me even one iota, you will leave and if you don't, the police will be getting a phone call. You have precisely thirty seconds to make up your mind.'

For a second he looks like he's going to argue but then...... 'Ok,' he sniffs 'I tried and I'm sorry you hate me so much. For what it's worth I know what a huge mistake I've made. And I will leave you alone now but I'll also be back, because you have to realise how much we love each other and how that should not be thrown away.'

He stands up to go but then stops as if something has just occurred to him.

'And I know I may have got it wrong about Tinder and made some very big assumptions, but I'm not the only one in this room who's guilty of that to be fair.'

I glare at him. He cannot be for real.

'It's true. You were obsessed with what everyone else was up to on Facebook and Twitter and would project all sorts of things onto it.'

My jaw drops. I'm flabbergasted. What is he on about? 'Are you seriously going to do this James? Do you honestly believe you have any right to criticise *my* behaviour?'

'You used to nag me about not being on Facebook, Twitter and Instagram, whatever. You made me download WhatsApp, all things I couldn't give a toss about, and what did we row about most?'

'Er, never meeting your friends and family, which obviously I couldn't because you'd created a fake life?'

'No, well yes, we did row about that the most, I stand corrected,' he acknowledges 'but after that, what we rowed about most was WhatsApp. If I was online but didn't reply to you, all of that nonsense. And the amount of times I'd see you and you'd be nettled about something you'd seen on Facebook. According to you the whole world was having a better time than you. Everyone was in love, had the perfect family, the best careers and the answers to bloody life. Why? Because their status update said so.'

I feel like I'm under attack. 'I'm sorry, but what the hell is this? This is not about me James. Today is about me realising what a self- centred, lying, duplicitous, cheating selfish *married* scumbag twat you are.'

'Alright Charlotte, please, I'm not trying to hurt you more than I have already, but I need to know that *you* are not going to be a selfish cow tonight. If you die, your parents, your friends, everyone who knows you will be devastated. That includes me, although I know you don't care about my feelings. In fact, knowing it would hurt me might give you a reason to do it, so pretend I didn't say that.'

I blink hard.

'All I'm asking is that tonight you reflect. Please. Whatever you may think, you *have* spent too much time thinking the grass is greener.'

'Why are you being so cruel to me, even now?'

'I'm not,' he says, his tone gentler 'I'm just worried and you need to realise other people's lives aren't as perfect as you think. One of the reasons I fell for you in the first place was because compared to so many people I've met in the past, it felt like you had such a strong sense of identity. You were your own person and it was refreshing to meet someone who loves what they do. You had life plans, ambitions, goals and knew exactly what you liked and disliked. But I soon realised you were just as fallible as everyone else to the bullshit we're all capable of subjecting ourselves to. Because you're right. What people present on dating apps doesn't tell the whole story. But neither does social media which you're obsessed with. In fact, there's a huge gap between actual reality and people's constructed realities and for what it's worth I think the gap is constantly widening for you. You're always on your phone and you're always comparing yourself to others. Only as far as I'm concerned being plugged in to hundreds of people doesn't mean you're not alone. Having loads of followers on Twitter isn't a substitute for a handful of close relationships with friends you see in the flesh and interact with face to face.'

'I'm not on fucking Twitter or Instagram any more thanks to you,' I snap. 'I'm a social media pariah. I've been trolled so much I doubt I'll ever go on it again and frankly this is irrelevant. How dare you stand there and lecture me about anything when you should be jailed for what you've done to me.' I'm so angry I feel like I might combust.

He raises his hands 'Look, I know my timing's up the spout but like I said, I'm worried about you so I'm saying it because I care. Your inability to be at peace in the day without checking your phone all the time started to really bother me. Everyone's need for constant validation online these days mystifies me and I definitely think it was getting out of hand for you. Maybe because you're the only person who doesn't truly get how special you are. Whereas I do, and I also know now, without a shadow of a doubt, that you are it for me Charlotte. You are the person I want to be with forever. I just need the chance to make things up to you.'

Just then the door buzzer goes.

'Who the hell is that?' I say tearfully, head spinning.

James ignores me and goes to answer it. He presses the button which opens the main door downstairs. 'It's Lindsay, I'll check in tomorrow. You know you have a doctor's appointment, right?'

'Shit,' I say, panicking 'You bastard.'

'Couldn't have put it better myself,' says Lindsay who, having run up the stairs, shoots James the dirtiest look she can muster as she charges into the flat.

Suddenly it becomes apparent that someone else is running up the stairs behind her. The next thing I know, my breathless Dad appears in the doorway.

I watch in horror as he barges past Lindsay, looking quite crazed. It's obvious who he's looking for. James suddenly seems to be rooted to the spot.

'You bloody animal,' Dad shouts, and then, before anyone can stop him, he swings his fist back and throws a punch. Only, due to the height difference, plus poor execution of said punch, Graham's fist lands squarely, not on James' chin as had probably been the plan, but on his chest.

There follows a loud cry of pain and anguish. Not from James.

'Fuck,' gasps Dad, who never usually uses the 'f' word. He sinks to his knees, clutching his hand. 'I think I've broken my wrist.'

James, who doesn't seem to have been affected physically at all by Graham's attempt to thump him, goes to help him off the floor.

'Don't touch me you evil bastard. Don't you come anywhere near me or I will kill you,' Graham protests, eyes bulging and we all believe him.

I've never seen Dad like this before. It's awful. I feel so guilty for causing all of this drama and pain for everyone around me.

I begin to cry.

'Oh Charlotte,' says Lindsay coming over and scooping me up into a big hug, her expression having changed completely from the one she was wearing when she first arrived. 'My poor love,' she soothes, looking utterly distressed and worried. 'What the hell has been going on? He said you tried to kill yourself. How could you even think of it?'

'I'm sorry,' I sob, despising James with every fibre of my being. For the life of me I cannot understand why he's still standing there, looking mortified. Why doesn't he just go? And why phone everyone? The fact I tried to kill myself feels more shocking when confronted with it as part of other people's reality.

'You idiot,' Lindsay says softly.

'I'm sorry,' I repeat.

'It's alright. It's alright. I'm here now. And you're going, aren't you?' she says. This last comment is directed at James.

'Yes, but please let me know how it goes at the doctor's tomorrow,' he nods, looking distraught

'Urgh,' roars Graham, words obviously failing him completely for a second. He gets onto his feet and yells 'I'd suggest you leave right this second you scumbag, or I will not be responsible for my actions. You have caused my daughter nothing but pain and I don't wish to hear your name ever again, let alone see you. You stay away from her. Do you hear me?'

It occurs to me that when I was going out with James, I'd never imagined his first meeting with Dad would go quite like this.

James nods 'Ok, I'm so, so sorry everybody.'

And with that, finally, he leaves.

And then there are three. Three devastated people, left to work out how the jigsaw has got quite so broken and how we can even begin trying to piece it back together.

'Only good thing that pig has ever done was ring me,' says Lindsay, leading me to the sofa where she sits me down. She strokes my hair as I weep quietly. 'I genuinely nearly fainted when he rang. He said you were in the shower and that he needed someone else to know in case you slung him out. I phoned your dad because I thought he had the right to know what had happened. We came as quick as we could and we're not leaving till we've got you sorted. This has to end Charlotte, it has to end.'

'It does,' says Graham, face ashen and wrist still sore, judging by the way he's holding it. 'My little girl. Don't you ever do anything like this again,' he says before bursting into tears. My heart breaks all over again and before I know it we're all crying. I hold my arms out and Graham sits down on the other side of me and gives me a cuddle.

'It'll be ok,' says Graham 'It'll be ok.'

I have no idea if it will be or not but the words are undeniably good to hear.

47

Two Weeks Later

I wake up after a deep, twelve-hour slumber. My sleep situation's gone from the sublime to the ridiculous. At night I can barely keep my eyes open past nine pm and I'm sleeping in for Britain. I'm not sure if this is a sign that my meds are making their way into my system, or if months of sleepless nights have caught up. Either way, the doctor said the pills would take a few weeks to take effect though I've started to notice my anxiety levels improving during the last few days. The fluttery breathing in my chest has calmed. Nothing is quite as intense.

Rationally I know I need the pills, in the same way a person suffering from a migraine needs tablets. Something my therapist said really resonated. She said that there are natural responses to unnatural events. So, in the event of James going for instance, it was normal and natural to feel devastated and grief stricken. It was also normal and natural to feel horrified and broken after the newspaper story came out. Add to that, feeling ashamed and like I'd failed, and being bullied online and it's perhaps not surprising that things escalated. However, a suicide attempt was a disproportionate reaction. One borne from desperation and being too ill to rationalise anything. There's always a better way. And that, in a nutshell, is depression and why I need to take tablets and talk to a stranger about difficult things.

I reach over for my phone and stare at the colourful boxes on it. I know my way round them so instinctively. For years my morning routine has been; wake up, reach for phone, press the Mail envelope to see if any work has come in, press the little bird icon to see what people are twittering about, then the green WhatsApp symbol for streams of conversation from various groups. Then to dark blue with a white F to see what my social circle were up to and the Instagram symbol to check overnight 'likes.' Of course, there also used to be the red flame icon, or the yellow one with white stripes for swiping and messages. These ones were wonderful to say goodbye to. I got rid of them as soon as I met James. I remember deleting the icons, pressing on them until the little crosses danced about on the screen before sending both apps into the ether, thinking my life was sorted.

For the last couple of weeks, I've been trying to change my ways. Now, I wake up, have breakfast, then spend ten minutes meditating before going anywhere near my phone. It's been surprisingly hard. Like many of us, I'm pretty much addicted to my phone. It governs me in a sense, not the other way around. If I leave home without it or it runs out of battery, I feel positively itchy. What James said that day unsettled me.

Is it possible that all the information, images and gossip contributed to my crash too? Did they amplify the negative thoughts I was having? Virtual living provides us with instant gratification but just as the 'post can of coke' sugar rush is quick to run out so is that type of high. Has being 'connected' yet feeling so disconnected contributed to my depression?

Apologies if this sounds a lot like naval gazing. This is what therapy does to you. It forces you to examine all sorts of things you normally wouldn't.

I still haven't reinstalled Twitter or Instagram but, breaking my own rules, I open Facebook now, analysing my reactions whilst trying to be as dispassionate as possible. I scroll through. Erica, a friend I originally met years ago when travelling, is tagged in a picture from what was obviously a night out with a load of school mums. I experience a faint stab of envy. Erica's done it. She has a happy family and a husband who earns a fortune in the city. Though admittedly he's quite boorish, has terrible dandruff and once bought her a pressure washer for Christmas. She admitted this when very drunk one night. She doesn't usually swear but was so angry about it she called him a c**t. So, swings and roundabouts I suppose

I admit I haven't made much effort to see her for years, but that isn't strictly my fault. Erica never invites me to any of the lavish dinner parties she throws which she posts so many photos of on Facebook. Although, thinking about it, she did ask me to their son's christening and the drinks afterwards but I declined the invitation. I recall now pretending to have a shoot then spending the day on my own at home, watching soppy films.

Why didn't I go? I force myself to really think about the answer.

Firstly, I probably knew that going to something like that, on my own, would mean making an effort with people I didn't know and I didn't necessarily feel like doing that on a precious day off. Secondly, it would have been expensive. I'd have to have bought an appropriately generous gift for a child I barely knew. Lastly, going to a christening would have been yet another reminder that everyone except me was married and having babies and that would have made me feel jealous and inadequate.

Gosh. That's not a nice thing to admit. Am I really so selfish that I couldn't just be happy for an old friend? Should I have gone to spend time with Erica, been more grateful for the invite and focused on feeling special to have been asked? Could I have framed it differently?

I frown.

Next on my timeline is Chris, the vicar I used to go to university with. We used to be such great mates, drinking buddies, confidantes; we were inseparable and completely and gloriously platonic. Back in the day we'd told each other everything, always grateful to get the 'other sides' point of view on affairs of the heart. We even spent many a night in the same bed, crashed out in my student digs, top to toe, drunk on snakebite and black, happy and grateful for such a rare friendship with a member of the opposite sex. He always wanted to be a vicar and was doing a degree in theology. When he finally got his collar, he was the coolest example of a vicar you could ever imagine. Until he met Camilla that is. She seemed to change him the minute they became an item. Under her influence our friendship became tricky to maintain, and we slowly grew apart.

He has a tendency to come across as rather smug on Facebook, to the point where *anyone* would feel slightly resentful reading his posts. Sure enough, here he, is boasting about some table he and his wife have constructed out of copper piping. Copper piping? Why would anyone even have access to copper piping, let alone want to fashion a table out of it? The table's a monstrosity really but they look exceedingly pleased with their efforts. He's written underneath. **Amazing what you can do when you put your mind to it and when you have the help of your brilliant and very creative wife.**

I examine how I feel again. Irritated, slightly resentful, sad? What else? No, the overriding feeling is probably sadness that he's changed so much, along with a smattering of irritation. Why has he changed so much? The old Chris would hate the new Chris. I miss Chris.

Oh god. It's confirmed. I'm a hideous person. No wonder I'm on my own. Maybe I just miss my friend yet in order to get there it seems my brain insists on taking all manner of mean detours.

There follow a few totally inoffensive, fairly uninteresting updates.

The next one to properly grab my attention is from my godmother. She's posted a picture of herself at an awards dinner, looking extremely glamourous in a blue satin, full length evening gown.

I observe how I feel and am relieved to note it's mainly pride and admiration for how wonderful she looks. I dig deeper. Possibly there's a very small anxiety that I'll never be as strong or dynamic as her or as at peace about being single.

There's a knock on my bedroom door. For a brief second I try to recall which of my bouncers/nannies I'm expecting today.

The last fortnight has been interesting to say the least. By ringing Lindsay, James ensured I'd be watched like a hawk every day. Lindsay didn't fancy being in sole charge of making sure I didn't do anything stupid so passed the responsibility buck around.

I don't think anybody had comprehended quite how severely depressed I was but, once they'd got over the immediate shock, they decided I needed policing and organised shifts. I think a spreadsheet may even have been drawn up and now Lindsay, Mum, Dad, even Gordon, take it in turns to keep an eye on me. I'm basically under house arrest and what's really telling is, I don't mind. Despite feeling guilty about having upset everyone so much, my nearest and dearest knowing out what's really been going on has really helped. I'd become so solitary, I'd shut them all out, whereas now, although I'm still not great, I feel safer. Everyone else is in charge and it's a relief. Plus, finally knowing the truth about James, no matter how horrific it is, has changed things. It's the not knowing that kills you.

So maybe, my 'attempt' *was* a huge shout for help because, now that everything's out in the open, it feels like the emergency stop button has been pressed on the petrifying treadmill I was on. In turn this has enabled me to finally get off and admit that I wasn't getting anywhere fast.

48

James knows better than to show up when my parents are around but that hasn't stopped him from texting me every five minutes, desperate for titbits of information. How am I? Will I meet him? Do I feel better? He even phoned Lindsay begging to let him help. He received very short shrift. Sometimes I reply with something suitably cutting. Sometimes I'm friendlier. Sometimes I don't reply at all.

If I had any dignity, I'd block him, but at times, a WhatsApp exchange during which I can be as acerbic as I like with no shred of guilt, feels vaguely satisfying. Not that I'd dare tell anyone how much communication I'm having with him. They'd thoroughly disapprove and yet, I can't see how it does any harm. The harm was done ages ago.

There's also no work to worry about. There wasn't much in the diary anyway but one of the 'help fairies' (Lindsay) decided I should be absolved of all grown up responsibility for a time. She placed a call to *Daytime Live* and to my booking agent to say I'm on a sabbatical for the foreseeable due to health issues.

Meals appear three times a day, whether I want them or not. I'm driven to the doctors for my appointments and watched over to make sure I swallow my anti-depressants every day.

Eleanor came with me to the councillor's and sat outside while I had my first consultation, then drove me home wordlessly once I'd emerged, tear stained and quiet. I have to admit, Mum's been pretty amazing. Or at least she has been ever since she dialled down her initial histrionics. I think to some degree my 'attempt' has acted like a hard slap for us both, rendering us more cautious and respectful of one another.

Dad's struggling though. He's taken it all extremely badly and makes me feel excruciatingly guilty every time I see him. He simply can't fathom how I could have reached the point of thinking I'd be better off dead and seems to be taking it as a personal failure as opposed to a sign that I was just desperate. Fortunately, he didn't break his hand when punching James but it was bruised and sore for a while and he still can't get over the audacity of his reappearance. Of course, it's very bittersweet and confusing for everybody because, if he hadn't reappeared, I'd be dead, and yet they blame him for everything in the first place.

Meanwhile, my head whirls away, trying to work out what the future holds. Things got as bad as they ever could, so maybe, just maybe, the only way is up? Even that thought is an indicator that things are improving. For the opposite of depression isn't happiness, it's hope, and when things were at their worst that's what was missing completely.

49

A week or so later I phone James. It's the first time I've called him since his return. He picks up after half a ring

'Are you OK?' He sounds frantic, probably imagining I'm calling him from the top of a high rise building or something.

'Get me Lucas' number?'

'Sorry?'

'You said you'd do anything to help me, anything to make me forgive you. Well, this won't do that but I won't hate you quite as much. I need Lucas' new number. I need to tell him what I think of him. It's eating me up inside.'

'I'm not in touch with him though. I don't have it.'

'You're an undercover reporter. Find a way. Please.'

50

Some Weeks Later: April

I'm bored. I've got more energy than I've had in ages and Mum's irritating me. We've actually been getting on really well but today she's in a bad mood because Gordon hasn't done exactly as she wants this week. I've seen her like this plenty of times before. If her boyfriend isn't towing the line completely she starts getting twitchy and begins unlatching herself from the relationship. No doubt she's already got her next victim lined up. The last person to know will be Gordon.

Poor Gordon.

I've grown fond of him. He's kind and gentle and due to the unprecedented amount of time we've spent together lately we've begun to form a relationship of our own. I don't mind his company at all and he's besotted with Mum yet, unlike some of her previous boyfriends, he also recognises her shortcomings and refuses to let her *completely* rule the roost. Personally, I think this is extremely healthy and good for her.

I find myself blinking. I don't like thinking about Gordon being left. I know what heartbreak feels like.

'He didn't need to go to Tunbridge Wells to see his boring friend,' Mum says now as she scrubs the inside of my kitchen cupboards. The flat's never been so clean. 'I told him I'd rather he didn't and he was quite rude in his response really.'

'How was he rude?' I sigh.

'Well, he just ignored me, said he was going to go anyway and that me wanting to hold a bridge night could happen anytime.'

'Well it could, couldn't it?' I challenge, knowing full well she knows that. This is about her having control, nothing else.

Eleanor shoots me a look but doesn't say anything like she usually would. We're still on eggshells.

My phone flashes. A WhatsApp, from James.

I've got number for Lucas

Finally. Yes.

Great I reply *Ping it over then*

No, I need to see you. Give me ten minutes of your time and I'll give it to you. Please Charlotte. I'm so desperate here. I know you're angry but you're being so cruel. I have to see you. Please. I love you.

How dare he call *me* cruel? I roll my eyes. It was pathetic. Nothing for months and months then an endless stream of correspondence. It's been non-stop.

I debate what to do. I'm feeling claustrophobic in the flat. It would be good to get out.

'Mum,' I say, making sure my voice doesn't betray anything.

'Yes dear,' says Eleanor, now busy rearranging my herbs and spices back into the scrubbed cupboard.

'I'm going to pop out for a bit of fresh air, to the park.'

'Are you?' I have her attention now. She puts her cloth down and turns to face me 'Oh good. That's great that you want to get out. Layla said you should start going for more walks.'

Layla is my therapist, an incredible Jewish lady, who's wise but slightly scary. You can tell she has the measure of you before you've even said anything. I think of her as 'Yiddish Yoda.'

'Just give me ten minutes. Once I've done this and hung the washing out I'll come with you.'

'It's alright,' I say, tapping out a response to James 'I'll be fine. I promise. Layla said getting out on my own for a bit was important. I can't be babysat for the rest of my life.'

Mum looks like she's weighing up what damage I could do to myself at the park. Garrotte myself on a see- saw maybe.

'Sure?'

'Sure,' I say, getting up to get dressed, in a way that doesn't invite further debate.

Forty minutes later and I'm with James, walking round the almost empty park. The crocuses and daffodils are out and the fresh Spring air is a natural mood enhancer. It's chilly though. I wrap my jacket tighter around me.

'You cold?'

'I'm fine.'

It's so surreal. If you'd told me a few weeks ago that James and I would be strolling along together I'd never have believed you. To some extent, it feels more normal than anything has in weeks, which makes me sad. Despite all the bullshit and lies, I was so happy to be in a relationship with him. When he vanished, I was terrified I'd imagined that. I know now I hadn't. He was the one with the issues, not me, for treating something so special so shabbily.

Meanwhile, James seems entirely relaxed in my company. I begrudgingly respect him for it. I appreciate why, but my parents, and Lindsay, watch me with a permanent hint of unease, worried what I might do next I suppose. At times it's tiring to be around.

'So, did you love your flowers?' he asks now.

'They went in the bin.'

He looks hurt.

'What did you expect? Dad was there when they arrived. He was livid you'd sent them.'

James looks crestfallen 'Oh shit. Sorry. And I understand. You're angry still.'

'Angry doesn't cover it,' I say, despairing. 'I'm afraid, lovely as they were, in this instance sending a bunch of flowers is a bit like punching someone in the head then offering them an aspirin.'

'Oh, I see. Sorry.'

I can't help it. I smile and shake my head.

'What?'

'James,' I say, stopping for a second 'I don't know what you think is happening, but I haven't come out to meet you because I've forgiven you, or because I want to get back together. I just needed some air. Let's be honest about that. And, let's not forget the facts. You entrapped me, you conned me, you lied to me *and* your wife, and you left me, but only after you'd made money out of ruining my life.'

James holds his hands up 'I'm not deluded. I deserve that and I'm expecting you to be angry and upset with me for a long time, but I won't accept we don't have a chance. I know it all came to a head the other day but I'm here now, far too late of course, but I am here and I won't leave you again. We're worth fighting for.'

It's ridiculous. He's acting like before I know it, we'll be back together, as if nothing ever happened.

'So, just so I know where your head's at,' he says now 'are you still having *those* kinds of thoughts?'

No one's asked me this directly. Well, no one except Layla, who's professionally obliged to ask me every time I see her for a session. Everyone's just hoped, or assumed, that by loving me so much, they're loving me better. But things aren't that straight forward. I never actively wanted to be dead. I just reached a point where it felt like there was no other option. I don't feel anything about much still, just a bit blank. It's hard to explain.

'Ok, well the fact you haven't answered straight away is bloody disturbing,' says James. 'And you know as well as I do, this rota everyone's got going can't carry on forever. You can't be nannied for the rest of your life.'

'I agree,' I say, lifting my face to the sky. 'Look, there's no point me saying things just to make you feel better so, the truth is, I can't see a time where I would ever try to kill myself again. But.... I don't know.... I feel numb to some extent. When I think about today, I'm OK. But if I look to the future, it's pretty overwhelming.'

I look at James. He looks stressed beyond belief, frustrated by me. He keeps running his hands through his hair.

'Can we sit?' I ask, motioning toward a bench.

We sit, a foot or so of space between us. I stare steadfastly ahead, trying to employ a bit of mindfulness as I gaze right out across the park and watch the trees swaying in the distance, the sound of them audible from so far away. I'm aware of my mind leaping around from one thought to another. How bizarre to be sitting next to James when for so long I wondered if he was dead. It's strange that events have conspired to have me arrive at this point. What if I'd simply swiped left and never met him? Would I be happy now? Would life have carried on as it was? Or would I have met someone special? Do I invite this kind of drama? Is it my fault somehow? Have I attracted it by putting the wrong sorts of signs out into the universe? I desperately try to still my thoughts.

'So, here's what I suggest,' says James suddenly, who seems to have taken it upon himself to 'fix' me. 'You need to get out of that flat, you need to work out what it is you want and come up with some strategies to make that happen. I know it's a cliché but no one else can make you happy, it has to come from you.'

This is rich, James thinking he knows what's good for me.

'You think everyone has better or more sorted lives than you, right?'

I shrug. He's so black and white about everything, so reductive.

'Find out if it's true,' he says, his tone challenging. 'See people. Stop staring at Facebook and go and actually spend time with these 'friends' instead of just gazing at them online, making everything up in your head.'

'Excuse me? I splutter 'I was the one trying to get you to be more sociable the entire time we were together.'

James doesn't look convinced 'Yes, you wanted me to meet Keisha and your work friends and so on, but only because you wanted to show them you were in a relationship. But you also admitted that before we met, you'd stopped making much of an effort to see anyone, apart from Lindsay and a handful of others. You used to avoid certain people because being around their families made you feel sad. No?'

'No,' I reply instantly, wondering why I'd bothered to come. I could really do without a lecture, from him of all people.

'I'm not saying it to be mean. I'm saying it because I care. You're my beautiful Charlotte,' he whispers, reaching over and taking my cold hand in his. I pull it away and am about to retaliate and tell him to get lost when I make the mistake of turning and looking at him, like really looking at him, at which point all I can see is the familiar face of the man I'd loved so much. He'd been my happiness, my present, my future and now, in this precise second, what he did to me was inexplicably cruel.

'Come here,' he says, arms open.

I shake my head, tears threatening.

'Come on, I won't bite,' he insists 'You need a hug.'

I feel vulnerable and conflicted. I want a hug but also don't want to give the wrong impression. Sensing my confusion, he pulls me gently to him. It's so painful but I give in and stay where I am until sadness has run its course. He gently strokes my hair, telling me it's going to be OK.

'You're going to be alright Charlotte. I promise. I'm so sorry and I know it's hard to trust me again.'

I stay where I am for ages, head buried into him, quietly weeping. Being like this feels familiar and safe to a degree, but I also know I'll never be able to recapture the joy I'd felt with him before. He thinks we could pick up and carry on. He honestly believes that if he helps me now, we can reconnect and start again, but we can't. He's broken it. We are broken. I'm crying for something that's gone.

'Come on,' he says 'I love you Charlotte and we're going to get you better. I know this is all my fault and I know you wish you hadn't met me, but you did, so you have to let me help now.'

'I don't have to do anything and I don't think anyone can make it better anyway,' I mutter, talking very specifically about my life, not our relationship. Nothing could make that better.

'You can sweetheart,' he soothes 'You can make it better. We can make it better.'

I unbury my face from his jumper and stare into the brown eyes I wasted so much time dreaming about. I must look blotchy and puffy and ugly. I don't care.

'Start with Keisha.'

'What are you talking about?'

'Keisha, you were always saying how much you loved her and how much you wanted me to meet her, but in the same breath would make comments about her posts on Facebook.'

'I did not. Why the hell are you going on about this again? Don't you understand? My friends are the least of my worries right now. My main worry's my career. You know how much I wanted to start a makeup brand one day but, thanks to you, my reputation is totally destroyed and it'll never happen.'

James gives me a look.

'What?' I snap.

'Well it won't if you think like that, and yes, I do know I've messed things up but it's all salvageable. Only you have to be in the right mindset before you can embark on anything and maybe working on how you perceive things, starting with your friendships, will help.'

'But I love Keisha and I'm happy for her. There's nothing to 'work on',' I insist 'So stop lecturing me. After everything you've put me through, you have absolutely no right.'

'When was the last time you saw her?'

'Not for a while,' I admit, feeling more ambushed by the second.

James looks at me, as if what I've just said spoke volumes. He stands up 'Come on, let's walk a bit more. I'm freezing.'

I shrug but stand up and follow him down the path. If he carries on like this I'm going home.

'Actually, where do you get off suggesting anything to me?' I fume suddenly, outrage having fully caught up. How dare he? 'Before you carry on criticising and advising me, shall we dissect your recent behaviour? Honestly, it's insulting.'

'It's not meant to be,' James insists 'It's meant to be constructive.'

I'm stomping along the path at quite a pace now 'It's like you've come back thinking you're some kind of lifestyle guru, which frankly is patronising and absurd. And this whole notion is so simplistic it's absurd. Ring a few pals and all will be well. Seriously James you need to get a grip and…….'

My phone vibrates in my pocket. It'll be Eleanor, no doubt worried I might have thrown myself in the river.

I look. It is.

'Forget it, I'm going home,' I say, having had more than enough of James' cod psychology for one day. I text Mum to say I'm on my way back. I don't want her stressing. 'Give me Lucas' number please.'

He reaches for his own phone and sends it to me.

'Please be careful. Maybe ask your mum and dad what they think before contacting him. You don't need further stress.' Then, far more tentatively he adds 'Listen, I'm really not trying to upset you. I just worry about how isolated you're becoming and know that you feeling suicidal was my fault. I have to live with that. Do you know how hard that is?'

'Do I know how hard *me* being suicidal was for *you*?' I ask, sounding as incredulous as I feel.

That shuts him up momentarily. 'Ok, that came out badly,' he admits 'You're right, this isn't about how I feel, but it is about me helping you. It's all I want. Well, you're all I want but if I can't have you, I'll settle for seeing you smile again, or hearing you laugh.'

'And you honestly think that me making more effort to see people is going to make that happen?' I say, as sarcastically as possible.

James seriously considers the question 'I think it's worth a go, yes,' he says solemnly 'If nothing else I think being busy and having some distraction would be healthier than sitting around in the flat. What have you got to lose? You've become very introverted and that's not you. I'm not saying visiting Keisha for instance would be like waving a magic wand and would stop you feeling depressed ever again but wouldn't it be good to think about something that……'

'What?'

'Nothing,' says James, appearing to have changed his mind. He was obviously going to say something he knows will annoy me.

'Just say it,' I sigh audibly. I find it so annoying when people start saying something but don't finish.

'Ok, I was going to say, wouldn't it be good to think about something that wasn't me and all the shit that's happened, but then I stopped because it sounds arrogant. I mean obviously I'm not the only thing you've thought about while I've been gone. Course I'm not.'

I say nothing.

51

The next day, Graham is 'on duty.' When he arrives it's clear he's made a conscious decision to be terribly upbeat.

'Good morning,' he says, announcing himself as he lets himself in. The 'carers gang' all have their own key to my flat. I've essentially been institutionalised and seem to have surrendered all basic rights.

'Hi,' I call, from the sofa where I'm writing my journal. This is a 'Layla' initiative, one I was reluctant to start at first, but now that I have, I am surprised by how useful it is. Purging thoughts onto a page makes me feel, not only like I've off loaded, but also that my brain has transferred some of its worries and feelings to another place, one where I can view them more objectively.

Dad can't hide it. He's visibly surprised but also really pleased to see me up and about, dressed in something which can't be classified as 'leisurewear'.

'Gosh, you're up. Well good, because it's time we got you out and about more. I was going to suggest we take a drive out to the country.'

He waits for me to refuse, to say why it's a bad idea and is clearly ready to argue so looks quite wrong footed when I simply put my journal down and say 'Ok.'

***

As we climb Box Hill in Surrey, the view grows more and more magnificent the higher we get. Having thought about it for much of the night, I decide to have a chat with Dad about the things James said, only I'm bright enough to realise that mentioning his name would be a terribly bad idea.

'How are you?' I ask out of the blue, in a way which makes it obvious I'm not asking in passing. I actually want to know.

He stops, panting slightly 'I'm alright thanks.'

'Sure?'

'Yes, why?'

'I know you've been really worried about me, so I'm just checking I suppose and I wanted to say sorry. For everything.'

Still out of breath he touches his hand to his mouth and throws me a kiss, which manages to convey that he's heard, accepted and appreciated my apology.

We carry on in comfortable silence for a while, drinking in the view and concentrating our energies on getting up the hill.

Once we reach a flat bit again we both take a while to get our breath back at which point I say 'So, I've been thinking about things a lot recently, and one of the things I think I need to work on is not letting everyone else's lives affect me so much.'

'What do you mean?' says Graham 'Whose lives?'

'Well,' I pause, drinking in the vista that's spread before us. It's a clear day and the morning sun has produced a hazy glow which seems to envelope the scenery in what resembles a layer of natural Clingfilm. It's beautiful, quite ethereal. 'Keisha for instance. We've grown apart and yet she used to be my closest friend, a sister really.'

Graham considers this. Like everyone else, he's desperate not to say the wrong thing 'Well, to be fair,' he replies eventually 'lots of friendships suffer when one person moves away.'

I appreciate what he's saying but deep down I'm not sure I can blame distance entirely and one thing I've learned lately is that there's no point being anything but honest. 'I'm not sure her moving away is what's changed our friendship.'

'No?'

'No, you see *some* of my old friends, once they got married and had kids, gradually sort of dropped me from their social circle. Not in a particularly conscious way but I suppose people feel more comfortable hanging out with their own. Sad as it may sound I know loads of couples who are only capable of hanging out with other couples. As though us 'singletons' pose some sort of threat to their set up, like we're incapable of normal, age appropriate social behaviour. By the same token, I haven't exactly made any effort to have dinner parties where I've invited lots of couples round. Instead I tend to go out with single friends, or see my married friends on their own. But Keisha's never been like that. She's always made effort to maintain our friendship. She never changed who she was when she got married, or stopped inviting me to stuff. Instead it's me who's been useless with her which deep down I feel bad about. She's always tried to make me feel like a part of her family and to still be my friend individually but I've found myself shying away from her.'

'Why do you think that is?'

I've been pondering this very question a lot so already have an answer formed. It's one I'm not very keen on.

'I think I just want, or wanted, what she had so much that at some stage I started finding it hard to be around her. Our lives were always so in sync before, the contrast in our lifestyles felt more acute with her than with other people. Not when she met Dave necessarily, but when she had the girls.'

I feel my eyes becoming a bit glassy. Being envious is a horrible thing to admit. Jealousy in any form is a vile, unattractive emotion, one which will never evoke any admiration from others. But it's also pretty unbearable for the person experiencing it.

Graham places a comforting hand on my shoulder 'Oh love, you're only human. Please don't get yourself too worked up about this. We can't help our feelings, none of us can but as long as we all retain a modicum of self-awareness about why we feel the things we do, it's OK.'

I exhale. His kind words act like balm.

'Maybe,' I clear my throat 'Anyway, I think I'm going to try to go and see her, to see if I can rectify things a bit. Then, there's something else.'

'Go on,' says Graham, motioning with his head that we should carry on walking.

'Ok, so Layla thinks, and other people have also suggested, that maybe I pay too much attention to social media. I end up focussing on what everyone else has got, or on what they're doing, then end up comparing their lives to mine and feeling miserable.'

'With all due respect it doesn't take Einstein to work that one out,' chuckles Graham 'How many times have I said something similar? Not that I'm saying there aren't tremendous upsides of social media too. Being able to stay in touch with your brother in Australia for instance, is far easier than it would have been years ago. And online dating works really successfully in some instances. And yet we don't need to look far to see a terrible example of what can happen when someone uses it disrespectfully. And I strongly believe that none of it should replace proper, human interaction because if people aren't in a good place it will only ever amplify that.'

I suspect he's right. When I was happy and healthy, I only ever benefitted from online activity. It amused and informed. When I was low and depressed however, feeding on what other people were projecting made me feel worse.

With regard to dating online I'd been an innocent really, trying to swipe my way toward true love and a man to share my life with.

It makes me feel tired just thinking about it.

'I'm going to make more effort with people,' I conclude dolefully. 'And then I need to concentrate on what I'm going to do about work.'

'Can't do any harm,' says Graham 'on both fronts. As long as the people you make the effort with are ones you can be honest with. There's no point pretending everything's wonderful at the moment. And the most important thing is that you don't neglect your therapy or stop taking your meds. Who apart from Keisha is on the list?'

'I'm not sure yet. I think it's more about me shifting my attitude a bit, about being more inclined to say yes than no I suppose, and about not creating excuses not to see people. Oh, and one last thing. I've got Lucas' new number. I want to phone and give him hell but I suppose you're going to tell me not to.'

'I certainly am not,' says Dad emphatically. I'll have it after you and I'll be telling him to expect a writ. We both know I can't afford it but it makes my blood boil that he's got away with such disgusting behaviour scot-free.'

'Me too,' I agree 'and I'm glad you said that. It's good to know that feeling so much anger towards him is natural and not me being mad.'

'God no,' reassures Dad 'I'd say your rage is a good sign on that front.'

***

The next day, when I check in with Layla and say I'm going to reconnect with Keisha, she sounds really pleased, victorious almost. 'Charlotte this is such progress. I think it would do no harm at all to reach out to people you've been keeping at bay. If they love you and are real friends they'll only be pleased to hear from you and the fact that you have thought to explore this idea is encouraging to say the least. Sometimes none of us know why we feel the way we do, so to take some time trying to work it out is healthy and to be admired. Furthermore, it shows something.'

I wasn't sure what she meant.

'That you want to try, and that basic urge, wanting to try, means you're on the path to recovery, and I think you know that deep down. As for contacting Lucas though, be careful. You won't get the reaction you'd like I suspect and you are still vulnerable.'

As a result, I decide not to ring him.... yet.

That evening, taking a deep breath, I pick up my phone, press contacts and then 'Keisha.'

52

When Keisha answers the phone, she isn't as instantly warm as she once might have been. I can hardly blame her. For too long now Keisha has made all the running with our friendship. She's texted and emailed and phoned religiously, persevering long after my return efforts dwindled to a fairly embarrassing amount. Since my suicide attempt, I hadn't responded to even one of her texts. I just felt like too much of a failure. It was always going to be an awkward call to make now, on many levels.

'Hi,' says Keisha.

'How are you?' I ask, undeniably nervous.

'I'm alright,' she says, tone polite but a little reserved. I've known her long enough to know she's furious with me. I swallow. Someone else I've hurt. It doesn't feel good.

'Ok, Keisha, listen, I need to tell you some stuff.'

'Has something happened? Are your parents alright?' she asks, immediately sounding on edge as her mind races, wondering suddenly what on earth this phone call is in aid of.

'They're fine,' I reassure her 'everyone's fine, it's nothing like that. Oh gosh,' I exhale 'Look, there's no easy way to tell you this so I'm just going to plough on if you don't mind.'

Keisha keeps quiet, listening hard.

'Ok, so I know I haven't been in touch for ages and I know I've been a shit friend, not that that's an excuse....' I'm rambling. 'But I do need to talk about that in more depth at some point, only not on the phone. But anyway, and this is all vaguely connected...... James leaving, it just hit me really, really hard. Not knowing what had happened or why he left sort of...... tipped me over the edge a bit.'

'I know,' says Keisha softly 'it must have been really awful.'

'Yeah,' I agree, swallowing. 'And then the thing in the papers was so damaging and embarrassing and I didn't get my promotion......'

The next bit is going to be so hard to say but I have to be straight or there's no point in anything.

Right, over the cliff I go....

'Ok, so I...... er, well what with all of that, I got really ill to be honest, very depressed, like properly clinically depressed and um, well to tell you the truth I ended up in hospital, having been found in my car, in a bit of a state shall we say.'

I pause, blinking hard, waiting for Keisha to say something, but she's silent. No sound comes down the phone whatsoever.

'Are you there?' I ask, feeling dreadfully unsure. Is she angry? Maybe she doesn't believe me?'

'I'm here,' says Keisha eventually, sounding remarkably calm, given what she's just been told 'So, what happened?'

'Um, well I just reached a point where things felt very bleak and I just felt desperate. With hindsight I wasn't in my right mind of course but I just couldn't face anything anymore. I'd had enough. But anyway, James came back, that day of all days. He found me as it goes. So.......so that's that and obviously since then I've realised what a desperate act it was and.... you know....... everyone's sort of rallied round and I'm on medication and I've just been working really hard on getting better.'

More silence. I end up looking round the flat not sure what to do or say next. Keisha not saying anything is difficult because I can't tell how she's reacted.

But then she speaks and it's clear the only reason she hasn't said anything is because she hasn't been able to.

'I need to see you,' she says and it's obvious then that she's crying.

I feel tears threatening myself; the relief is so immense 'Really? Ok cool. I'm glad you said that. Excellent.'

'I'll come tomorrow. I'll just tell Dave he has to have the kids. End of.'

'No,' I say 'Don't do that. Why don't I come there? Please? Then you don't have to worry about the kids.'

I can hear her thinking.

'Apart from anything else I need to get out of this flat and, like I said, I've got a lot I need to talk to you about.'

'OK, done.'

Twenty minutes later I'm off the phone having made a plan and booked a train ticket. The most surprising thing isn't how easy it's all been but how much better I feel already for having done it.

53

Keisha collects me from Runcorn station. I spot her immediately. She's got Jasmine and Freya in tow. Freya's in the buggy asleep, wrapped in various warm layers, oblivious to anything other than the cocoon she's ensconced in. Four-year-old Jasmine's hopping from one foot to another, drowning in a grey duffle coat that her mum must be hoping she'll 'grow into'. I can't believe how much both children have grown.

'Hey Jas, look at you all grown up,' I say, hurrying up the platform, dragging my wheelie case behind me. I want to give my goddaughter a hug, only I'm not totally sure Jasmine will want one given how long I haven't seen her for. I needn't have worried though. Jasmine bounds up quite happily, arms outstretched 'Have you brought sweets Aunty Charlotte?'

'Jasmine,' remonstrates Keisha 'You don't ask that, that's really rude. You never ask if people have bought you presents. Sorry love,' she says to me now, slinging an arm around my neck and kissing me hard on the cheek.

I embrace her back then reach into my handbag which is over my shoulder and pull out two huge bags of Haribo, or 'kids crack' as I like to call them. To be fair I always bring sweets so it was a sensible enough question. 'Here you are angel; though don't eat them till your mum says it's ok.'

'Yay,' squeals Jasmine in delight, taking her stash and sizing it up. 'Can I have one now please Mummy?'

'Go on then,' says Keisha, opening one of the bags for her 'but only one or two now. You can have more later if you eat your tea. How are you then?' she asks me 'Journey ok?'

'Yeah fine,' I reply, happy to see Keisha but also acknowledging that it really has been too long. I definitely feel a bit nervous about seeing her and I can tell the apprehension's mutual. It's good having the kids here for now. They're a comforting buffer.

'Right, well let's get back to the house and get sorted. I made a Bolognese sauce yesterday as I thought we could all have that, but I'll feed these two first. Then, once they're in bed we can have a proper catch up.'

'Is Dave about?'

'Yeah,' says Keisha 'and he's really looking forward to seeing you, though I'm not totally sure when he'll be back from work. He's been getting home so late recently. To be honest it'll be a lovely change to have someone to hang out with and talk to while I sort these two out. Speaking of which, I'd better wake Freya up if you can bear it. Otherwise she won't fall asleep at seven and that will cut into our gossiping time.'

***

It's nearly eight by the time both girls are finally in bed and settled. Freya's longer than usual afternoon nap did indeed mean the toddler wasn't looking particularly tired at seven. In fact, she was bouncing off the walls and incredibly excited about having 'Aunty Charlotte' there. This was sweet and amusing for me but less so for Keisha who was clearly eager to get them down so we could talk. Still, I pitch in with everything, spooning pasta into mouths, wiping sauce off hands and highchair, bathing, delivering bottles of milk, reading stories, the lot.

By the time the girls are tucked up in their bed and cot I feel quite whacked. I don't know how Keisha does it, day in, day out and there's an undeniable sense of relief once the house is quiet and the promise of wine and adult conversation is finally tangible. They're so adorable though, such pretty, sweet children and very affectionate. When I bent down into Freya's cot and kissed her chubby, soft cheeks I melted a bit but noticed that the painful angst I usually feel around other people's offspring had faded, or softened.

Before James had disappeared, being here would probably have made me feel feverish with anxiety about wanting to experience motherhood for myself. Every time I heard one of the girls calling Keisha 'Mummy' or witnessed another sign of their dependence on her, I would have felt an almost physical ache and a sharp sense of injustice that for some it just happens and yet for me it was out of reach. I wonder what's changed. Has depression dampened my lust for life? Or is not feeling so desperate actually a positive?

My suicide attempt failed but maybe, instead of an end, it might mark a new beginning of sorts? One where I come to terms with the fact that being a mother isn't my destiny. Maybe that's the shift?

Keisha flops onto one of the eight kitchen chairs which surround her oak dining table, bottle of Pinot Grigio in hand. 'I can't tell you how much I look forward to this moment every day,' she admits. 'Wine o clock, I'm such a bloody cliché.'

'I don't blame you. It's hard work when they're so little but you're doing an amazing job. They're such good girls and so sweet. The house looks incredible too Keish, I can't believe how much you've done since I was last here.'

The house has indeed been transformed from a slightly rundown farmhouse with a very dated interior to a beautifully restored building with a modern extension on one end, which is where we're sitting now, in the kitchen which has glass doors all along one side. The sun is starting its descent but you can still see into their enormous garden which segues into a serene vista of never-ending fields. On a clear day it's quite idyllic.

'It is nice, we're very lucky' says Keisha 'I always find it hard to get my head round the fact that in London you couldn't get a tiny two bed house in Wandsworth for what we paid for this. Silly isn't it really?'

I take in the Aga, the walls which are painted in tasteful, dove grey paint, the Shaker style units in off white and the beautiful flagstone floor. It's all achingly gorgeous and yet there's also just the right amount of kids clutter strewn around to make it feel homely as opposed to a sterile spread from an interiors magazine. I think of my own modest flat with its ancient kitchen units and no outside space and wait for a pang of something to arrive. No pang appears though. I don't really mind my flat. In fact, that isn't accurate. I love my flat. It suits me.

'But anyway, you didn't come here to talk about the house. It's time, finally, to talk about you. I still can't believe you're actually here. I've really missed you. I'd got to the point I thought you didn't want to know me now I was boring and living in the country.'

'As if,' I say, genuinely shocked at the suggestion 'god hardly, if anything I'm the boring one never having anything good to tell you. I know I've been rubbish and I'm so sorry.'

'So, fill me in,' says Keisha, not wasting any more time and getting straight to the nitty gritty 'This James, I just don't get what on earth's gone on and I am so devastated that things got so unbearable for you.......'

She doesn't need to finish the sentence; we both know what she means.

'All I know is that one minute you were madly in love, the next he'd disappeared on you, and now you say he's back. So, what the hell's going on? What was his excuse for disappearing and does this mean you're back together?'

'Oh gosh, where to begin?' I say 'I think you need to pour that first.'

'Oh god yes,' laughs Keisha 'here I am hugging it like some kind of weirdo. Let's drink the bloody thing and sorry for the interrogation it's just I'm so desperate to know what's been going on.'

Just then though, as if on some kind of irony cue, the lights on the monitor flare up and Freya starts to cry.

Keisha looks disproportionately fed up and, in that moment, I truly see the extent of how exhausted she is.

'I'll go,' I say, immediately, springing up, not giving Keisha time to object.

I'm back within twenty minutes, having surprised Freya back to sleep more than anything. Someone who wasn't her mum appearing and being really calm and soothing seems to have done the trick.

'God sorry,' says Keisha, who's at the stove boiling us some pasta when I return 'The last thing you need is to be running around after those two, I'm supposed to be looking after you.'

'It's fine, don't be silly,' I insist 'You forget it's a novelty for me. I like it, so stop looking worried. It's so good to be here I can't tell you. Just being away from the flat is a tonic and frankly something I should have done a long time ago.'

OK,' says Keisha looking vaguely appeased. As she drains the spaghetti, clouds of steam billow from the sink 'Right, let's try again, you were telling me about James.'

'OK,' I say sitting down again 'so in a nutshell, he lied to me from day one. He's a journalist and met me by design with a whole fake story worked out so that he could hack into my phone and steal the photos which, as you know, ended up in the papers.'

Keisha looks utterly stunned to the point where it's obvious she's struggling for words.

'Oh Charlotte,' she manages eventually 'that's awful. What a bastard.'

Her face is so shocked I suddenly experience a vague desire to laugh. It is so horrendously outrageous it almost feels unreal when I say it.

'I know. It's the worst thing anyone could do to you really. A total betrayal of trust on every level.

'God, I want to kill him,' says Keisha, furious on my behalf 'and anyway isn't it illegal to steal pictures.'

'You'd think so,' I say 'but the law is all rather blurred unfortunately. Trouble is, it could be argued in court that the copyright is Lucas' because he's the one who took the pictures and he gave permission to print them. My face was blurred out, but by saying that I was the make-up lady from Daytime Live it didn't take a genius for people to work out who it was, given that I'm the only make-up artist from Daytime Live to have dated him. It took about nought point five seconds for the press to figure out my identity. Having said that, there's a chance a jury could side with me due to the duplicitous way the photos were obtained. But it would cost thousands.'

Keisha, who's spooning sauce onto our pasta, looks incredulous 'What has that bastard Lucas said about it. I always thought he was a bit up himself but that deep down he was a nice guy. How the hell can he think this is OK? And if James was just trying to entrap you, how come you went out with each other for so long? Did he really love you? I'm guessing he must have done or why else would he have come back?'

'God knows,' I say, not sure which bit to explain first 'I'm still finding it hard to get any real objectivity. All I know is that at a certain stage he cared enough to have decided not to run the photos but then he ended up doing so because he thought I'd lied about meeting up with Lucas and he was very jealous. So, the short answer is yes, to some extent he did love me, the longer one is that whilst he definitely had feelings for me, what he did was so awful he clearly doesn't understand the true meaning of the word love. Anyway, life just became unbearable in every way. Everything was fucked. My career was over, my reputation was in tatters, I was so ashamed and embarrassed and of course my boyfriend had disappeared and I had no idea why. It was all too much and I got ill and ended up in total self- destruct mode. But the most bizarre thing of all was that he eventually came back the precise day I'd decided to end things, hence why he was the one to find me, so now he's on a one-man mission to sort me out. He *says* he loves me but I don't believe a word that comes out of his mouth and I don't even really care. I think I've gone through too much to be honest.'

‘I still can’t get my head round how bad things got for you if I’m honest,’ says Keisha looking stricken ‘Your life always looks so amazing. I never could have imagined how bad things actually were.’

‘What do you mean?’

Keisha looks worried in case she’s said something that might have upset me ‘I’m just saying that you always look so glamorous on Instagram and from the outside looking in it looks like you’ve got everything sorted.’

‘Does it really look that great? A single make up girl, living on her own, approaching forty?’

Keisha frowns ‘Er, I think you’ll find most women of our age would love to look as good as you do and to have such a glamorous existence. You work in the media, you often have celebs in your pics and to be honest yes, it does all look pretty great and exciting.’

I ponder this while she dishes up the food. What she’s said comes as such a shock that at that precise second I have the beginning of an idea. Nothing fully formed but the kernel of something I definitely want to think about properly.

‘I hate the fact I’ve made other women think my life is all glamorous parties and celebs and great make up. For a start it’s bullshit and secondly it was never my intention you know.’

‘I know,’ says Keisha ‘But it’s probably my fault, not yours, for not questioning what’s really happening behind the picture, if you know what I mean?’

‘But that’s not what any of us do,’ I say thoughtfully, feeling a flicker of real excitement as my idea continues to take hold. Still, it’s not for now. It would have to wait till I got back to London.

‘Anyway, how are you doing now?’ Keisha asks, pulling her chair in and motioning that I should start my spaghetti. Her face looks fearful of what the answer might be.

‘Better,’ I reply truthfully ‘Much better. I’m still sad obviously and I still feel a bit lost but I’m far more at peace with things than I’ve been in a long time. Knowing what was going on has helped enormously. That ‘not knowing’ aspect of things was horrific. I don’t know. In a way I can see now that I’ve been searching for something for years and I suppose I thought James was it and that he made my life complete which is why it hit me so hard. But I literally feel like I can’t be bothered with men anymore, which makes things far easier. And the pills are helping. God bless drugs and all that.'

'What have you been searching for do you think?'

I take a moment to find the right words 'Um, this I suppose,' I say lightly. 'What you've got. A lovely family. Someone to share stuff with.'

Keisha's face creases in sympathy. She places one hand on mine 'Oh babe, I'm so sorry. I hate knowing you've been so unhappy and since you're being so honest with me, I know you've found it a bit difficult being around me and Dave and the girls sometimes. I'm not stupid, I know how much you've wanted to meet someone, but then in a way that's meant I haven't been totally honest with you.'

'What do you mean? This pasta is delicious by the way, thank you.'

'I mean that when things have been tough for me, I haven't really felt I can tell you because I always knew that from your point of view whatever I said might come across as ungrateful, or spoilt. I know I'm lucky to have Dave and obviously I'm incredibly blessed to have the girls but honestly Charlotte I cannot tell you how hard it is at times and maybe I should have been more honest about that.'

I consider what she's saying. As I do I feel prickles of guilt. 'I hate thinking you couldn't confide in me. That's awful and probably my fault. I haven't made things easy. I do know having kids is knackering though because you don't get enough sleep or any time to yourself. But then again it must be so rewarding.'

Keisha sighs and looks like she's debating whether or not to say what she really wants to say.

'Isn't it?' I prompt, my question genuine. I really want to know.

'Yes, of course it is. In some ways. I adore the girls. But Charlotte, I can't tell you how shit it's been since we moved here. I hate it at times and believe it or not, most days I wish I was back in our cramped flat, swearing because I've just trodden on another plastic toy.'

'But why?' I exclaim, mouth full of spaghetti, gesturing around, to the house, to the luxurious kitchen, to the dream.

'Well, firstly I'm sodding lonely. Dave has had to up his hours in this new job so I never see him and when I do he's grumpy and miserable and boring. The whole point of moving here was to get help from his mum, only I can't stand her half the time. She says she wants to help but doesn't really. If she's got a better offer that always comes first and when she does help she always has something critical to say to me. I'm in the middle of pigging nowhere so if it's a nice day, fine, we can tramp around the fields but if it's raining, we're trapped and bored and at least half an hour away from civilisation. I'm permanently exhausted, the girls wear me out and if I was in London, I'd pay for someone to help out a bit. I'd go onto Gumtree and find someone who lived locally and have a break. I'd get a babysitter sometimes and drag Dave out for a curry or a drink at the pub. I'd try to get a job and I would spend time with you. As it is, there is no one local. I spend my life in the car, shepherding them to a nursery which is so far away that by the time I've dropped them off, the thought of driving home and having to come back out a couple of hours later feels pointless. I feel so lonely at times. Also, sometimes when I go into the village I feel really uncomfortable.'

'Why?'

Keisha shrugs, and I can see her shoulders tensing up.

'One or two people are quite racist round here and once I heard the girls described as half casts.'

I must look as shocked and appalled as I feel.

'Yup,' confirms Keisha 'how hideous is that? It's not everyone of course. But one is all it takes and I feel constantly aware that people are looking at the 'black' woman when I go out to be honest. So I spend the vast majority of time here, in this admittedly stunning house that I am so lucky to have, only that doesn't make me happy, at which point I feel spoilt and hideous. I spend a lot of time daydreaming about what other women my age are up to and regretting that I gave up my career. Sometimes, and this is going to make me sound like an absolutely awful person Charlotte, especially in light of how wrong I've got things, but sometimes….'

'Go on,' I encourage, wondering what on earth she's about to say.

'….ok, but please don't think badly of me because it's embarrassing.'

'I won't.'

'Well, I think I've hinted at it already but sometimes I've seen pictures on Facebook or Instagram of you and Lindsay out together and felt so left out and jealous. I've felt like a boring, frumpy, dull person who has nothing interesting to say which is why even my best friend doesn't want to know me anymore. I always think how much I would love to be out with you, having fun like we used to. And of course, I know now I've been an idiot because you've been having such a difficult time so I've even managed to get that totally wrong.'

I squeeze her hand. I had no idea she was so unhappy and feel awful that my 'online persona' has caused my friend genuine misery.

'And in the meantime,' Keisha continues 'I'm bored to tell you the truth. I miss London. I miss being invisible. I miss traffic. I miss my husband, which is tragic given that I live with him. I miss fun. I miss company. I miss being able to walk up the road to get an overpriced coffee as a treat. I miss our crummy flat and most of all, I really miss you.'

I don't know what to say so I don't say anything. Instead I put down my fork and get up and go to give her the most enormous, heartfelt hug.

'I'm so sorry,' I say, 'I had no idea, I honestly thought you had it all sorted.'

'No babe,' says Keisha, half crying, half laughing 'God, does anyone?'

'Well neither of us do, that's for sure,' I exclaim, also laughing now. What a pair we were. 'Maybe that's why we get on so well, two idiots together, fumbling their way through life.'

Keisha wipes away her tears and laughs again. As I go to sit down again I shake my head, marvelling at our idiocy.

'So what are you going to do?' I ask eventually.

'I don't know. There never seems to be a good time to talk to Dave, who for the record is doing my bloody head in. God it's good to say that out loud.'

'Say it again then. Don't mind me.'

'Ok. Dave is doing my bloody head in,' she says, this time with real feeling. 'Ugh, I want to bash him for making me come here and then doing nothing to make me feel settled.'

I can tell Keisha's trying not to cry. She's obviously been repressing everything, stuck in the house on her own with no one but Dave's family to talk to. What a nightmare. I feel awful for not having been more aware. Things have to change starting from now.

'Since we came here he's started completely taking me for granted, like he's regressed back to being the spoilt mummy's boy he once was. I've tried to talk to him but when I told him how uncomfortable I feel with his mum's friends or with some of the nursery friends he seems to not care in the slightest. We haven't had sex for about four months Charlotte.'

'Four months?'

'I know,' sniffs Keisha 'I know, that's just not like us but I'm so pissed off with him I just don't want to. Then the more I don't want to the more frustrated and moody he gets. Then I start panicking that he's going to have an affair. It's all such a mess.'

'Come home,' I say. 'Tell him you've tried and it hasn't worked.'

'Don't think I haven't thought about it,' replies Keisha 'but we can't. We've put so much into this place and I just know Dave won't want to. But anyway, Christ, that's enough of my rubbish. Gosh I'm so sorry for going on and on, though just being able to say all of that out loud is amazing. I actually feel a lot better already. But it's nothing compared to what you've been through and I just want to make sure you get better. If you had died......' Her whole face crumples at the thought 'Sorry,' she says 'Sorry I'm such an emotional wreck, but seriously I don't know what I would have done.'

'I know,' I say, stroking her hand 'but I was just really ill and I'm here now and I'm so sorry for not being there for you. I want to be here for you now.'

'Thank you for coming, for making everything good with us again,' says Keisha now.

'Don't you dare thank me,' I say, shaking my head 'I've been an idiot and I'm just so glad I'm here now. This may sound weird but I feel more like me again.'

'Me too,' says Keisha. Then in an attempt to lighten the atmosphere adds 'Right, pudding?'

I nod and just as she gets up, a WhatsApp notification from James appears on the screen of my phone. The bit I can read just says 'How's it going?'

I can't help but smile as it crosses my mind that it wasn't me Keisha should be thanking. Ironically it was down to James that I was here, James, the lying toe-rag who had, on this occasion, done me a favour of sorts.

54

JUNE

As the weeks go by, the 'carer crew' wind down their rota. Everyone has their own lives to lead and I guess they're confident I'm not in any imminent danger of wanting to harm myself. My therapist is pleased with my progress and there's talk of returning to work. This is becoming a financial imperative. I've been glibly working my way through my savings and having no money is becoming a source of high anxiety, and high anxiety is exactly what my therapist and I are working towards preventing. It's agreed that returning to work in August seems like a sensible idea. I can manage another couple of months. Just.

Lindsay has suggested that to start with I should only go back to Daytime Live where they know me well enough that I can explain a little of what's happened. It would be the best place to dip my toe back into the working waters, plus Lindsay's happy to have a preliminary conversation with Dan, meaning that when I phone him, I won't have to go into too much detail about what's gone on.

'Charlotte, you're the best make up person we've ever had,' he says warmly when I do finally pick up the phone 'I know it was awkward when the story first broke but it's old news now and no one really cares. Not in a horrible way but because everyone's got their own stuff going on.'

'I know,' I say 'It's still so embarrassing though.'

'Look,' says Dan 'I can't lie, at the time it was spectacular gossip, of course it was and there was certainly an element of 'gosh, she's a one,' going on. But anyone who actually knows you also felt terrible for you, especially when you came in and it was evident how much it had hurt you. I can only imagine how upset you were. So don't even think about it. Logan wants you to come back too, especially because the girl who's been doing him while you've been off irritates him beyond belief, the guests love you and we all miss you. So, please come back, you'd be doing us a favour. In fact, if you tell me what dates you want to work I'll make sure Sadie schedules them in now.'

'That's brilliant,' I say, heart aching with gratitude 'Thank you.'

'And listen, I know you probably don't want to talk about it but, are you ok?' he adds 'Lindsay explained that things got really quite difficult and I don't need to know the finer details but when you stopped accepting bookings I was really sad because I do care about you and have always considered you to be a mate. You had so much going on it was enough to affect anyone, but I feel terrible I didn't do more to check you were alright.'

'Oh god, you did your best,' I say quickly 'and I'm sorry I didn't reply to your messages. If it makes you feel any better, I was avoiding everyone, so please don't take it personally. I just got myself into a right old state,' I say, infused with guilt as I recall the amount of Facebook messages I artfully ignored.

'It's fine,' he says instantly. 'But, when you come back, if you have any inkling that you're having a bad day you have to promise you'll talk to me.'

I swallow. He was always so kind to me. God knows why, but whatever the reason, it was very much appreciated.

'Thank you, that means a lot. It really does.'

'Good,' he says 'I mean it, you've never realised it, or you have and have just been so horrified you've chosen to ignore it, but I've always had a soft spot for you Charlotte and not just because you're bloody gorgeous. You're a good person and for what it's worth I truly believe good things will happen for you.'

I'm quite taken aback and don't really know what to say so go for the easy option and deflect 'Thank you Dan, I really appreciate it. So, how are things with you? Are you Ok?'

'I'm fine,' he replies 'Well, work's fine anyway. This place keeps me sane really. Stacey is just awful though. And yes, you did hear that right. The scales have rather fallen from my eyes with regards to my dear wife but we're still figuring all that out. It's quite stressful and obviously I worry about Billy a lot.'

'I'm sorry to hear that,' I say. I pause before adding 'I know I've been totally useless for ages but genuinely if ever you want to talk things through I'm also only ever at the end of the phone.'

'Oh god, don't offer that,' says Dan 'you'll have me ringing at two a.m. bemoaning my life after I've drunk half a bottle of whiskey. But seriously, thank you. Anyway, my misery aside, there is a condition to your coming back,' he says suddenly.

'Er, what's that?' I ask, slightly anxious about what he's going to say. I hope he isn't going to ask me out on a date. After the lovely conversation we've just had I thought we'd understood one another.

'That before you come back to work you come to a quiz night. It would break the ice and, in the meantime, I can just tell everyone you've been having time off for personal reasons. No one needs to know anything else and no one will care any way, they'll just be pleased to see you. What do you say? Not that I'm exploiting your quiz talents or anything.'

Ok, no date. That's a relief, but a quiz night? With everyone from work, all in one place, asking questions about where I've been? My instinct is to say no, to run, to avoid, to fabricate an excuse. It would be easy to say that I don't feel ready. He'd understand. But then I think about the promises I've made to myself to try harder, to say yes. Even if yes is more difficult than saying no.

'When?' I ask.

'In a few weeks. I'll text you the date?'

'Ok,' I agree, feeling faintly terrified.

55

A week or so later I'm staring at my computer. The weather's grey but clammy and I haven't been for a run or a walk yet, which I've noticed does affect my mood. On Layla's advice I'm trying to incorporate fitness into my life as much as possible. I've already started to notice the difference in mood if I miss out on exercise. I've grown addicted to the endorphins probably. I'll try and go later.

A notification pops up. A message, via Facebook messenger, from my old friend Chris the vicar.

He'll be able to see I'm online so I can't really pretend I haven't seen it. It says.

> *Charlie!! How are you? It's been far too long. This is a huge longshot but I'm coming to town for a few days and it's so rare that I escape the countryside I want to make the most of it. Don't suppose you'd be around for a drink on the 12th would you?*

My heart sinks a bit. Meeting Chris is the last thing I feel like really. I haven't seen him for years and I'm not sure what we'd talk about.

I don't reply immediately, the answer requires proper thought.

I already feel like if I say no (my natural instinct) I'll feel really guilty but in turn that makes me feel resentful of the mere invitation. It would have been easier if he hadn't asked. Still, maybe I should just do what I want and make an excuse; I've been so good. I've not missed one therapy session, I'm taking my pills religiously, I'm working on my relationship with Keisha (very successfully) and I've put a date in for pub quiz with work. Surely I can allow myself to duck out of this?

I come to a decision. If Chris' wife Camilla's going to be there I won't go, if it's just Chris I will.

I type a response

> It would be great to see you, just need to check that date though.
> Would it be you plus family or just you?

Just me

After a polite enough amount of time during which I could have been going off to find my diary, feeling slightly anxious about the whole thing I reply

Ok, you're on, I can do it.

56

'Chris,' I say, pleasantly surprised by how nice it is to see him in the flesh after so many years. He's sitting at the bar, where we agreed to meet on the Kings Road, distinctly middle aged yet the same.

I wonder what Chris makes of the nearly forty-year-old me. This is where Facebook is actually very helpful. A steady stream of photos of a person whom you last saw when they were young, fresh faced and thin, lessens the shock. Chris is actually in quite good shape. In some ways his face is more handsome now. His edges are harder and a little creased but this means he looks more rugged than when he was enveloped in the sheen of plump youth.

It's six thirty and the place is full of people having an after- work drink.

'You look amazing,' he says, leaping to his feet and giving me a huge bear hug.

This demonstration of affection takes me a bit by surprise but breaks the ice and is an instant reminder of how close we used to be.

'What do you want to drink?' he asks, looking all excited, blue eyes darting about as if they can hardly believe they're seeing me again. It really has been too long and his obvious excitement is contagious. 'I've nearly finished this pint so, happy to get a bottle of wine? Let's get some bar snacks too.'

Twenty minutes later and we're sharing a bottle of Sancerre and some nibbles. The conversation's flowing easily and the atmosphere is so comfortable it truly feels like we saw each other only last week. I have to admit, it's nice and I'm so glad I made the effort. It's great to be in town too, to see the smart tourists milling about, the Chelsea set heading in and out of Peter Jones across the road.

'Buzzy isn't it?' says Chris, following my gaze 'I miss this sort of thing sometimes, living in the country.'

'You've got an idyllic set- up there haven't you?

'Yes, to be fair it's great.'

I remember something and giggle out loud, the wine having gone to my head a bit 'I can't believe you made a table out of copper piping. I saw it on Facebook a while back and it just seemed so.... out of character somehow.'

'Why?' says a flummoxed Chris, looking for all the world like he can't believe everyone isn't making tables out of copper piping on a day to day basis.

His face makes me laugh even harder 'You have to remember; I saw your DIY attempts when we were students. They were all unmitigated disasters.'

'Oh gosh that's true,' agrees Chris 'I seem to remember you sitting on a chair in the kitchen once that I'd put together from Ikea and your arse going straight through it. Do you remember, it had a sort of woven seat and I hadn't attached it properly?'

I throw my head back in delight at the memory. It had been hilarious at the time.

'But actually, I still can't take any DIY credit. It's Camilla who's the creative one. She really is a bit of a genius at stuff like that.'

I regard my old friend affectionately. His voice is so full of love and respect for his wife, even after all these years. It's lovely. Rare. And suddenly making tables out of copper piping doesn't seem quite so tragic; it seems great. If anything, I feel petty for sneering. Whatever makes, and keeps them so happy, good for them.

I wait. Nothing negative arrives. No wistful pang or stab of envy, or sadness. It's a relief, just to be happy for someone else and not reflecting everything back to myself all the time.

'You adore her, don't you?' I say now.

'I do. To be honest I feel sad you don't know her better really. The thing is though, she's not like you. She's not a 'fall in love with instantly' kind of person. She's amazing once you get to know her but she's a bit shy and I think she was always rather intimidated by you.'

'By me?' I exclaim, horrified 'Are you kidding?'

'Not in a bad way,' reassures Chris 'it's just you have to understand that you've always been quite worldly compared to people like me and Camilla, probably as a result of having been born and raised in London. Plus, if you think about it, it's not surprising she felt slightly wary given how close we were. You've always been a pretty lethal combination of blonde hair, a filthy laugh and clever brains and for a long time she was definitely a bit jealous of our relationship. Nowadays she still sees you as extremely glamorous, what with all your TV work and the circles you mix in. I've even caught her snooping on your Instagram before. Of course, I've always told her that whilst you do indeed lead a rather glitzy lifestyle, you're as down to earth as they come. Only, when we were young, I was a bit weak about it. Rather than insist she accepted our relationship because she had nothing to be jealous of, I took the road of least hassle and didn't protest or defend our friendship enough.' He lets out a big sigh and looks quite cut up. 'Inevitably I allowed us to drift apart and I regret that greatly.'

'Gosh,' I say, surprised both by their perception of me and what he's saying.

'I know. An apology is probably long overdue but I really am sorry.'

I consider everything he's just told me while munching on some very tasty fat green olives. I hadn't been expecting any of what he had just said and feel really touched and incredibly surprised. I'd read the situation differently for so long. The truth is so much kinder than my imagined version of it and far more flattering. I don't like the fact that some of my closest friends have misread my 'glitzy' lifestyle because I occasionally posted photos of C-list celebs getting their make- up done.

'Right,' I say eventually 'how about this for an idea. How about the two of you either come down to London and we all do something together? Or, I come to you for a night and we show Camilla that A/ she has nothing to be jealous about and B/ that I'm actually not glitzy in the slightest. In fact, give her ten minutes in my company and she'll soon see I'm a total idiot who's utterly incapable of finding a boyfriend, who has suffered from terrible depression and gone through all sorts of stuff, none of which is glamorous I can assure you.'

'I'd love that,' says Chris, looking delighted '*We'd* really love it. Done. She'll be so happy to make the effort too. She knows we're meeting tonight and she was really pleased. I think she feels a bit guilty about her insecurities causing so much space between us. I guess we're all a lot older and wiser now and she'll be nothing but welcoming and friendly. I actually think the two of you might get on really well.'

'Good,' I say feeling disproportionately pleased and a bit choked. How extraordinary that one honest chat can shed so much light, reframing how you've viewed something for years. I've always wondered why Chris went so distant on me and as a result of not knowing, ended up feeling quite resentful towards his wife. Now, I'm determined to make sure Camilla and I meet and that it goes well. It would make all three of us really happy I suspect. It hadn't been 'me' after all, it had been insecurity, on Camilla's part, and I know how horrible it feels to be insecure so will do everything in my power to vanquish her fears completely. I will drown her in warmth and sisterly friendship.

'When did you have depression?' asks Chris 'I'm so sad to hear that by the way. I had no idea.'

'Yeah, well I didn't exactly share any of what I was going through on Facebook. It's been a weird couple of years that's for sure,' I admit 'You must know about what was in the papers?'

Chris looks blank.

'The scandal? With Lucas?'

'Who?' says Chris 'Who's Lucas?'

'Lucas Harcourt, the actor,' I say, half wondering if he's winding me up. 'He's going to be in that film soon 'Redemption Battle.'

Chris continues to look mystified 'Sorry, I'm hopeless with that sort of thing. I only really watch the news, sport and whatever drama Camilla's roped me into watching. We're on *Succession* at the moment. It's quite good actually.'

I could honestly hug him.

'Ok, well don't worry about it then. It's just someone who badly let me down but I'm having therapy and it's really helping. I'm starting to get to the root of why I got so depressed.'

'And what was it, if you don't mind talking about it? If you do, I totally understand.'

I have nothing to hide. I fill him in. On everything.

'You poor thing,' says Chris gently, once I've finished. 'Gosh, isn't it amazing the things that go on in people's heads that, as you say, we have no idea about. Well, not until we actually interact properly, that is to say see one another.'

'Exactly,' I nod, the irony not lost on me 'but anyway, we can talk more about all of that another time. What I really want to talk about right this second is, why now? Why after all this time did you decide to look me up?'

Chris looks terribly grave all of a sudden, to the point where I start feeling a bit panicked. It looks like there might be a big serious reason behind this meeting after all.

'Oh Charlotte, I don't know who to turn to,' says Chris, face stricken. 'As much as I love and adore Cam, this isn't something I can talk to her about yet. Not until I've got it straight in my own head.'

'What? What is it?'

Suddenly Chris can't even look at me. It's awful. Was he ill?

'This is probably going to sound a bit strange but I had the most vivid dream about us recently. I woke up in the middle of the night experiencing such a fierce pang for our friendship. It was like I was craving a chat with you, like I'd had a vision almost. I knew then that what I needed most of all was a Charlotte perspective. You were always my favourite person to talk to.'

He looks directly at me and his expression is so sad and full of regret it makes me feel quite tearful.

'Hey, me too,' I say, squeezing his hand, unaware of the hovering waiter who finally, realising a 'moment' is occurring, retreats altogether, probably having sensed it wasn't a good time to ask if we wanted more olives.

Chris inhales, visibly trying to compose himself.

'Oh god, are you ok? Chris you're really worrying me now.'

Chris shakes his head, face tortured.

'I haven't told anybody this,' he says, voice little more than a whisper which in the noisy bar makes it quite difficult to hear. 'Oh Charlotte, I don't think I believe in God anymore.'

Of all the things he could have said I could never have anticipated that.

'What do you mean?'

'I mean.... just that,' he says, looking utterly ashamed 'And I don't know what to do about it.'

I take a moment before replying 'OK, but your faith has been rock solid, ever since I've known you. So, I don't know, maybe this is just a phase or a time of reflection that you're *supposed* to experience? Maybe questioning your faith from time to time is a good thing? Maybe it's natural? Perhaps you'll even come out the other side with renewed conviction.'

'Do you believe in God?' asks Chris, staring at me intently.

'No,' I answer quietly 'I don't. But then I never have really, apart from when I was a little girl and liked the idea of heaven and hell. Now I guess I'm pretty much an atheist though I do believe in living by some form of moral code and in making sure our time here is spent not deliberately hurting or harming our fellow humans. More and more I think I believe in fate too. But Chris, this isn't about me. What's shaken your belief?'

Chris looks distraught as he tries to explain 'A few things I think, but one specifically.'

'Go on.'

'My eldest, my daughter, Laurel, has been diagnosed with anorexia.'

'Shit.' I know immediately how serious this is. 'Oh Chris, I'm so sorry to hear that. That's awful. Is she going to be ok?'

He shrugs. The weight of his grief is plain to see. 'I don't know. She was in hospital for months at one stage. Had to be force fed with a tube. It's been horrific in all truthfulness and I just worry so much that it's the kind of disease that can stay within someone for life. It's been a very stressful time and, of course, Cam and I blame ourselves for not spotting the signs earlier. We're constantly asking ourselves if we've done or said something to trigger it and so on?'

I reach over and squeeze his hand again. 'I'm sure you didn't. Your other children are fine aren't they and I'd imagine they've all had the same kind of parenting and influence from you? It's just an awful mental illness, so who knows what the trigger was. I can't imagine how hard it's been but isn't this precisely the time when your belief system should be helping you?'

He sighs heavily 'Probably, yes, and that's the thing you see. Over the years, as a vicar, I've had so many different people come to me with all sorts of horrific things having happened to them. I've met abused women, people with cancer, the sick and the needy. So many people have turned to me, seeking reassurance, guidance and comfort and I've been the one telling them that God has a plan, that they just need to stay faithful and to pray. Yet the minute I'm tested, like really tested, because let's face it, up to now I've had a miraculously wonderful life, I feel differently. How weak and hypocritical is that? I've tried to stay strong Charlotte. I've wrestled with it, night after night after night. But the truth is I just can't see Laurel having this disgusting, traumatising mental illness as anything other than the shittiest, cruellest blow. You see, maybe we did 'do' something wrong to make it happen and yet deep down I don't really believe that. So that means it's just bad luck. Awful, crappy, unfair luck. So why would God do this to me, and to a girl like her who's good and sweet? It's rocked everything for me. I watch the news at night and consider all the atrocities that are happening and whereas before I was able to reconcile how unfair life can be in my head, now I can't. I've lost my way completely Charlotte and I'm angry because without my faith I'm nothing.'

I find myself struggling to know what to say. 'Listen, I do want to talk to you about this but how am I supposed to come up with the right thing to say in terms of the theology? I mean, I'm tempted to say isn't that the point? As a Christian aren't you supposed to believe that he sacrificed his own son for the greater good? So therefore, like you've told your parishioners, God has a plan.'

'But I just don't believe it Charlotte and you're so kind but let's face it, you don't either. I simply don't feel it anymore. I'm a fake and a liar and feel like the worst kind of hypocrite. Plus, the practical repercussions of me losing my faith are enormous. Being a vicar is my job. Working for the church is all I've ever known. How can I tell Cam I'm having some sort of mid- life spiritual crisis which involves me probably needing to make myself redundant?'

I sigh and take his hand in mine again 'Right you. This is what I think. You've sat here tonight and told me how much you love Camilla and it's blindingly obvious that she loves you too. That was clear from the minute you both got together and became totally inseparable. And all these years on you are still together, making bloody copper piping tables or whatever else it is you get up to in the country.'

Chris smiles, eyes watering like mad.

'So, I suspect that if you tell her what you've just told me and stop trying to deal with this on your own, she will understand. I can sit here and help you as much as I can, but Chris, you need your wife. What you're going through is huge and I know from experience that things can only be faced and worked out if you're being honest about them. Trust me, if she finds out, which eventually she will when you have some kind of related breakdown, what she's going to be cross about isn't the fact you're struggling with your faith but the fact you've not told her. You can't carry all of this alone. Like I say, it'll be the fact you haven't been honest which will upset her most and she'll be within her rights to be angry because you aren't giving her any credit for understanding. Give her a chance. Let her show you that, when the chips are down, she loves her husband. I suspect she'll surprise you. Sure, she might be a bit worried or shocked at first, and that's fine too, it's a lot for her to get her head around, but let her process it and get used to the idea and then work things out as a couple.'

Chris nods, looking choked.

'You haven't done anything wrong,' I say, making him look me in the eye so he can see how serious I am about this. 'You haven't hurt anyone or been mean. You're just using your brain to make sense of something really hard that's happened to you and your family. If you end up realising that you don't believe in God anymore well then that's fine too, you're still one of the kindest people I've ever known. It wouldn't make any difference to me.'

A stray tear rolls down Chris' face which he immediately wipes away. He swallows and clears his throat, just about managing to say 'Thank you. I feel about a stone lighter already. You're right. I'm bloody terrified of telling her, but you're talking total sense. I'll do it. Oh gosh, I feel so emotional, can we get some more wine?'

I laugh 'How many years have you known me? What do you think the answer to that one is?'

***

Hours later, world having been put firmly to rights, I arrive home having got an indulgent Uber I can't afford all the way to my front door. I have had the most amazing night and feel full to the brim with something I can't quite put my finger on. What is it?

As I lie in bed recalling the evening, the penny suddenly drops. I feel needed. Chris needed me tonight and I know beyond a shadow of a doubt I helped him. Yet I nearly hadn't gone to see him because I'd put barriers up, just as I had with Keisha.

Now, two friendships have been reignited and that's made me so happy. Maybe I'm not so awful after all? Not as hopeless as I'd started to believe? I can be a good friend and I am loved.

That night I find myself crying as I have done so many times during recent years, only this time the tears are of a different type. Tonight, I'm crying with a kind of sweet relief. I could have died. I could have died thinking I was useless and not needed by anyone. Now I have hope again. I have reasons to stay alive.

James nearly killed me, but in another respect, he also might have saved me.

57

JULY

I take a final look in the mirror. I look absolutely dreadful.

Perfect.

I'm not wearing one scrap of make- up and my hair is tied back off my face. I'm letting the summer sunshine flood into the room and the camera, which is sitting on the tripod, is on an extreme close up. My complexion isn't too bad. At least I've got some colour. But the fine lines I have are very evident in the stark sunlight and without mascara and eyeliner I'm unrecognisable from the everyday version of me that I normally present to the world. My eyelashes look sparse and short and my brows are so fine they provide no frame whatsoever. My nose is shiny.

Good.

'Ready?' says Lindsay from behind the camera. It's a small, broadcast quality Canon C300 which we borrowed from work.

I nod and stand on the cross I've marked on the floor with masking tape. 'Remember to pull back into a wide when I start referencing the products,' I instruct.

'Got you,' she replies, pressing record 'Ok, in three, two, one.'

'Hi,' I begin 'my name's Charlotte, I'm a professional makeup artist and this is Bare Faced, a new channel where you're only allowed to join the conversation if you've got something honest to say. Because no one ever posts that they're feeling sad, or inadequate, or can't get a job, or are worried about their relationship. No one ever shows how fat their thighs are or posts a picture of themselves sitting on the sofa tucking into a family size bar of chocolate because they've got their period. But maybe, occasionally we should? Just to even things out and to remind everyone else that we all have great days where we look and feel gorgeous but also have days when we'd rather not bump into any exes because we've got a spot on our nose or have popped to the shops in our pyjamas and a coat. I'm going to start proceedings by admitting a couple of things myself.'

I take a pause because this is the point in the vlog where we'll edit in various selfies from my old Instagram feed. I've already worked out which ones.

From behind the camera Lindsay gives me an encouraging thumbs up and a grin.

'The day I posted this, three years ago now, I'd just come back from one of the worst dates of my life with a man who was wearing a patchwork coat and triple denim, had terrible personal hygiene and who pretended to be a human sat nav for the entire time it took him to walk me to the tube. I posted it afterwards because I felt so down and needed affirmation that I was still attractive and therefore wasn't going to die alone.

And then there's this one – where even I think I look pretty good. I posted it because I was hoping that someone I'd met on Tinder might be checking me out. It was about the eighty fifth 'spontaneous' shot I'd taken, I filtered it massively and although I never heard from my Tinder crush ever again it did lead to one anonymous person sending me a picture of his revolting penis. I blocked him but only after ten minutes or so because at first, I genuinely could not figure out what I was looking at.

This is a picture I posted on Instagram just before I went on an horrific date with someone I now refer to as 'Ryan the Racist'. I probably don't need to say much more than that in terms of how truly freaked out I felt after that experience.

So why am I sharing this with you?

Well, recently I was in the news, for all the wrong reasons. A man I was dating gave pictures of me that were taken within what I had thought was a good, healthy relationship to a newspaper. They were fairly explicit pictures so, needless to say, it was devastating. I had never imagined for a second that anyone else would ever see them. I felt completely violated. The man in the pictures is very well known and his career has suffered not a jot because of them. I however ended up missing out on a promotion and was trolled all over the internet. I'm not ashamed to admit that my mental health suffered a lot and I became incredibly depressed.

A lot of people thought I'd made money out of the pictures, that I had no self-respect and that perhaps I was a different type of person to the one I appeared to be. None of these things are true but I guess I don't blame them. I'm guilty of doing the same thing all the time. I often see something on social media and assume that what I'm seeing tells the whole story.

And this is why I'm going Bare Faced. I want to create a community where there's no pretence, no trickery, no airbrushing, no lies and therefore, hopefully, no 'making you feel inadequate or bad' in the process. Before everything happened to me I think I subconsciously used social media to make *myself* feel better. From now on I want to use it to make other people feel great.

Of course, one way of feeling better is to look good and no one is more of a fan of makeup than me. Makeup is wonderful. Wearing it gives us confidence and enhances what we already have. In truth, showing you what I look like with none on is terrifying. As you can see, I'm not awful looking but I'm also definitely not a model. I'm approaching forty and with no eye makeup on personally think I resemble a guinea pig, so this is taking courage on my part I assure you. But there you go. I'm sure many of you can relate. Or I hope you can anyway. So, what I'm going to do now is make myself over using this selection of products and hopefully at that point you'll see how good these products I've chosen really are.'

Lindsay pans the camera down to the table where I've set everything up.

'Within this selection we have one of the best mascaras currently on the market, a really affordable primer which will make fine lines virtually disappear and an eyeshadow so great that no matter what your budget it's a great investment.........'

I spend the next half an hour making myself up and chatting about why each product is such a find, a process which we'll edit down so that ultimately my 'makeover' will take only minutes to demonstrate.

Fully made up and looking so much better than I did at the beginning, I close the piece by saying. *'If you enjoyed this please share and you can also find me on Twitter and Instagram* ***@Barefacedworld.*** *There I'll be sharing, not only more honest makeup tips and before and afters but also other aspects of my life with no filters or showing off.*

So that's me, and if you want to share anything brave, honest and/or funny Bare Faced is for you. See you soon.'

A couple of hours later we have edited and added the graphics on my Mac and the first ever Bare Faced vlog has been uploaded to YouTube. There are hundreds and thousands of vlogs out there but fortunately I know exactly how to make this one stand out from the crowd. Call it cheating, call it savvy or call it spotting an opportunity and going for it. Whatever you call it I've got nothing to lose and it's not like the internet can make me feel any worse than it has before.

It's time to be in charge.

58

AUGUST

At my most ill there was no rhythm to my days. Now, a natural, normal ebb and flow has returned. It's lovely and I'm so grateful to everyone who's helped nurture me back to normality. I'd list them all but this is starting to sound like a third-rate Oscar acceptance speech already so I won't, but the gratitude is there.

What's become very apparent though is that in terms of my recovery, routine has been my friend. I have structure back in my life and my days are packed and productive. You see, against all the odds, Bare Faced appears to have gone viral. *high kick*

Well, I say against all the odds, referring to 'Lucasgate' did no harm at all. (manicured nails emoji) Plus, I went out of my way to ensure I didn't get lost in the sea of blogs, vlogs and Instagram feeds which are out there by making a conscious decision to exploit what happened to me. Firstly, because regaining some control of the situation made me feel less like a victim. Being honest about what happened goes some way to addressing the balance when people google me. Secondly, because I knew full well that the truth being made public would piss Lucas off more than an unhappy phone call from me ever would.

And so it was that I went into my long ignored inbox and emailed back all the journalists who had been in contact when I'd been in the papers. If the media and Lucas could exploit me, I decided I was within my rights to do the same back. Graham, Eleanor, Keisha and Lindsay all agreed when I did a straw poll.

I sent every journalist the link to my first vlog post with a note explaining who I was and that was that. Pretty much all of them wrote something about it and suddenly it became front page news. Only this time it was Lucas and The Sunday Globe that came across as revolting and sleazy, not me.

The publicity didn't do Bare Faced any harm either. Today's vlog has had 500,000 hits and counting. The first one reached two million hits after a week.

Is any of this sinking to his level? I'm sure a Buddhist monk would argue, yes. But I'm not a Buddhist monk and no one has, or ever will, describe me as zen, so I prefer to see it as intelligent revenge. What Lucas did was far more unscrupulous and, by explaining my side of the story, I'm a more successful, more fulfilled and ultimately happier person who's had the satisfaction of knowing that for a couple of weeks it was Lucas and his team of PR's who felt what it was like to receive unwanted press attention.

Women and men of all ages have responded to Bare Faced, and now I feature not just *my* bare face but many other people's too, plus hundreds of online dating disaster stories. Make up brands are clamouring to have their products featured and I guess Bare Faced feels like a refreshing place to be, the antithesis of everything we've been fed for so long. It certainly brings me a lot of happiness and a sense of real pride as more and more people get involved and start to almost relish outdoing one another in the honesty stakes. Only this morning, a woman tweeted a picture she'd posted on Facebook of her and some friends having 'an amazing time' in a nightclub. Only in reality she'd left at eleven having only gone in the first place in the hope of making her ex- boyfriend jealous. Only the ex-boyfriend was there… with someone else. Someone very gorgeous. So one hour after the photo was taken, she was crying at home and in her state of distress managed to post his name on her Facebook page, as a status, as opposed to writing it in the search bar as intended. Cringe.

No one who goes onto Bare Faced is after pity. It's a self-deprecating, warm community which enables people to laugh at themselves knowing that these things happen to us all. It feels like I'm only at the start of developing what could end up being a huge brand with a great message. I've already had enquiries from various companies who want to give me sponsorship.

My career is rocketing. I can hardly believe it.

I still have a session with Layla once a week and continue to take my meds but I'm living honestly, with no pretence. My brilliant family and friends are here for me despite everything and the future looks exciting. At one point I didn't think I even had a future so this feels nothing short of miraculous and at times I feel quite overwhelmed with emotion about it all.

I also experienced a beautiful sense of irony when in the end it was Lucas who picked up the phone to call me. I can't be bothered to recount what he said in his ten-minute voicemail, but let's just say he wasn't happy….

As for James, he's still sniffing about, determined not to get the message, but I keep him at a distance. I don't give either of them a lot of headspace these days.

I spend time with people I can trust, time passes and that in itself changes everything.

59
Late August

'So, the final question of the night is coming up and after that I would ask you all to exchange your sheets for marking,' instructs the quizmaster over his microphone.

'Come on Charlotte,' encourages Dan. He's three sheets to the wind by now and looking a bit sweaty. Everyone is. The weather's been tropical today and the pub is boiling hot, despite the fact everyone's in shorts and t-shirts.

So far, the quiz has been a particularly riotous affair. More alcohol than usual is being consumed because Daytime Live is on a rare transmission break due to horse racing being shown next week instead. Drinks are on the company and the night's tinged with an end of term sense of celebration. I'm enjoying myself. People seem to have forgotten about the pictures. In fact, they all seem far more interested in Bare Faced and what's happening with that.

I nearly didn't make it through the door. As I arrived at the pub I suddenly felt intensely nervous about seeing everyone for the first time in ages and almost turned around and went home again. However, Ricky spotted me across the road and from that moment on, going home wasn't an option.

'Charlotte!' I heard him yelling, as he darted across the road to join me, only narrowly avoiding getting hit by a car.

'What do you want?' I'd said, instantly wary. Out of everyone Ricky was the one who had really made me feel cheap.

'To say sorry,' he said, looking genuinely contrite 'I should have said it months ago but I know you were angry, so I thought it best to let things calm down a bit. I was out of order. You're a lovely girl, everyone knows that and I shouldn't have behaved like I did. I really am sorry.'

'Ok,' I said 'thank you.'

He nodded 'Ok, so we're good then. And massive congrats on Bare Faced and all that. I've followed you on it all. Feel free to follow me back won't you? You're turning into a bit of a celeb now, so a follow from you would be good actually.'

I rolled my eyes and shook my head but had to smile. Cheeky bugger.

'Now, don't go thinking you're going to just swan in and beat us. I've been taking 'quiz' very seriously lately and have been swotting up like mad. We are going to smash you lot.'

'Oh, are you now?' I said drily, allowing him to manhandle me in the direction of the pub door.

'Yeah babe, last time we got 'who is the only player to have scored in a Champions League final, FA Cup final, UEFA Cup final and League Cup final?'

'I have no idea,' I admitted 'I'm shit on sport, as you well know.'

'Yes,' said Ricky 'you are. Whereas I am a total legend so knew it was Steven Gerrard.'

As we burst into the pub a fug of heat hit me and I instantly spotted the Daytime Live team standing around in one enormous group, drinks in hand.

'Hey, look everyone,' Ricky yelled, making a discreet entrance a total impossibility 'Charlotte's here.'

Ricky's voice was so loud his announcement managed to carry and as a result more than a dozen faces or so turned to look, the rest of them following suit once they'd realised something interesting was happening. As soon as people registered my arrival, everyone, without exception, looked really pleased and a rather touching cheer went up. The next thing I knew I was surrounded in a scrum of hugs and goodwill.

All week I'd been planning on sneaking in and saying a quiet hello to people, but actually, Ricky's way was better. My jangled nerves dissipated and the demonstrations of love and warmth shown toward me filled me with emotion. One big hello also meant the elephant in the room was acknowledged to some extent too. They all knew I'd had a terrible time so showing their pleasure at my return, as opposed to all politely pretending it hadn't happened, was more truthful, more real.

Twenty minutes later it was like I'd never been away and everyone was treating me as they always had before the Lucas debacle. I was struck yet again by how kind people could be. The only person who was super awkward was Claire but I singled her out before the quiz began.

'Hey. How's it all going?'

'Er fine,' she said 'It's good to see you and I'm so sorry about.... you know, what happened.'

'Don't worry,' I say. 'I can't lie, I was upset at not getting the promotion at first but I promise it's all water under the bridge and I genuinely hope it's going well for you.'

'Thanks,' she said, blushing to her roots but flashing me an appreciative smile.

Three hours later and the quiz is almost complete. We're on the seventh round out of seven and, having marked three of the previous rounds already, I know my team, which is made up of Dan, Sadie the production manager and Ed the accountant, stand a great chance of winning.

The other teams are no competition. Only Ricky's could potentially beat us now, though that could only happen if they get the next three right and we get one wrong.

'So, the next question is history.'

'Shit,' says Ricky.

I grin, full of anticipation. My love for a quiz hasn't gone away and as I've discovered tonight, neither has my competitive streak.

'Who was the first ever British prime minister?'

Dan makes a noise of frustration 'Dammit, not sure. Anyone?'

'William Pitt?' suggests Ed, not sounding sure at all.

'Not a bloody clue,' says Sadie.

I take the pen and the sheet and write something.

'Oh my god, do you know or is that just an educated guess?' asks Dan.

'Educated guess,' I say because I'm not one hundred percent sure I'm right. 'Though I do know William Pitt isn't right. Sorry Ed, are you happy to go with my answer?'

'Go for it,' says Ed. 'Ricky looks like he's sucking a lemon so it's safe to say they don't have a clue.'

'Next question,' says the quizmaster 'And it's sport.'

'Yes, you beauty!' yells Ricky, making offensive hand gestures in our direction.

My heart drops. How annoying, plus I hate Ricky's assumption I won't know an answer just because it's sport. I pray it won't be a football question. When it comes down to it, that's the only sport he's really hot on.

'Which Italian city is home to the San Siro Stadium?'

I shoot a look at Ricky to see if he knows. I can see him grimacing, trying to recall.

'I know this,' he's yelling 'I fucking know this.'

I don't care if he does or doesn't. I know it and so does Dan who whispers the correct answer into my ear.

'And finally,' says the quizmaster 'the last question is this. Which American President said the following 'In the end, it's not the years in your life that count. It's the life in your years.'

I can't help it. I look straight at Ricky and grin. What are the chances?

At my most depressed, desperate to find both inspiration and comfort I devoured all kinds of literature but was particularly drawn to reading about great historical figures who suffered from 'melancholy.' The man who said this was one of them. I can't even be bothered to consult my team. I know I'm right.

Sir Robert Walpole, Milan and Abraham Lincoln win our team the quiz making us overall victors by a clear five points. Dan declares me a hero.

Twenty minutes later, having been plied with congratulations and copious drinks I'm at the bar half considering leaving. It's been a brilliant night but I'm exhausted. Maybe it's time to call it a day.

I retrieve my phone from my bag, half thinking about ordering an Uber and am surprised to see I have a stream of WhatsApp messages. All from James. There are seven of them. It doesn't take long to deduce that he's probably had a few drinks. He seems to have worked out via my colleagues' social media where I am and what I'm doing. The first message is pretty reasonable and coherent. The last one isn't and could well have been typed with his nose. What I can glean is that he's outside the pub and 'needs' to talk to me. He'd written this two minutes ago.

My heart sinks. All I want is to go home. I certainly don't want a scene. What was he thinking?

I sneak out of the pub. The air outside is cooler and fresher.

With a start I realise James is indeed there, waiting for me, leaning against the wall in the car park, hands in pockets.

'What are you doing here?'

'Did you win?'

'Yeah, we did.'

'Good, you deserve it,' says James, staggering a bit as he lurches towards me.

I stare studiously at the ground 'James, what do you want?'

'I need you to give me another chance,' he says. My heart sinks further. I thought he'd got the message by now.

'I've been waiting patiently for months, trying to do the right thing, trying to help and I can see you're better now. So why won't you just go back out with me?'

I tut 'Oh for god's sakes James. Why do you think?'

'I don't know,' he wails, looking genuinely baffled 'I know I was an idiot but can't you see how sorry I am? Haven't I proved to you how much I care and that I would never do anything like that ever again? I want you Charlotte. I love you so much.'

To my horror he starts sobbing. I feel deeply uncomfortable and also fed up that I'm having to deal with this after such a great night.

'I've been punished enough now. I want you so, so much.'

I shake my head 'If that's what you really think then you don't know me at all James. I'm not trying to punish you. The truth is, I just don't want to be with you. I don't love you anymore and I don't think I've given you any other impression since you came back.'

'You do love me,' he wails unattractively 'you're just not letting yourself.'

'James,' I say firmly, knowing I have to make things crystal clear, once and for all. This sort of behaviour isn't fair, on either of us. 'I'm grateful you turned up when you did. You saved my life. But that's it. I could never have a relationship with you, ever again. Our relationship is dead. You hurt me so much. You lied to such an extent that I don't even know what we really were. I was in love with something that didn't exist, with a lie. That's the only way I can explain it. So, I'm afraid there's no going back and what's more I don't want there to be. I feel like a different person after everything that's happened. I am a different person. I don't think I could have gone through what I have without changing to some degree and what I've learned is that I'm OK on my own and I don't want to be with someone like you. I'm sorry.'

'No, you're not,' says James 'you're a bitch for treating me like this.'

It's as shocking as a slap.

'You're a selfish bitch and just trying to get revenge. We both know deep down that you were desperate to be with me because no one else wanted you until I came along. And now, just because you've had a bit of success you're being selfish.'

I feel sick. I need a brilliant riposte but the truth is whilst my self -esteem is in a much fitter state than it was, it's still not perfect and what he's saying is hurtful and vile.

I don't want to be anywhere near him.

I order an Uber. Three minutes. Thank god for that.

James groans 'Oh god, I'm sorry, I'm really sorry, I don't mean that. I'm being an idiot because you are making me so frustrated.'

I don't answer or look at him. I just keep staring down the road, looking for a Toyota Prius. I haven't actually checked what the car is but it's bound to be a Prius, they usually are.

'Ok, you *are* being a bitch. How can you act like this? Like you don't care at all? Don't you dare just get in a taxi and walk out on me.'

At this point I *have* to react.

Slowly I turn to face him 'Are you kidding me?'

'Don't walk out on me,' he repeats, bottom lip trembling unattractively. Right now, he's about as sexually attractive as Abu Hamza. I hate him.

'Don't walk out on me....*Think* about what you're saying James,' I say calmly, incredulous at his lack of irony 'just think about it, and then go home.'

'So that's it. You're saying there's no way we can be together again, despite everything I've done to try and show you what we've got.'

'That's correct,' I confirm 'we will never be together.'

'Give me three good reasons.'

I snap. I have one hundred percent had enough.

'Oh I can do better than that,' I say icily 'I can do loads. So, reasons I don't want to be with you are as follows - A/ you lied B/ you lied C/ you lied and then D/ you disappeared, causing me to basically have a nervous breakdown E/ you betrayed me by selling private, explicit photographs to a national newspaper, despite having proclaimed that you loved me. This despicable act ensured my nervous breakdown was as bad as it gets F/ you lied and G/ you're an undercover reporter which is sort of revolting really, oh and H/ you lied and I/ you've just been horrifically aggressive, abusive and rude to me and whilst it might be true that I was largely unwanted before we met, I know now that I would rather be single for the rest of my life then settle for someone I cannot trust, who I have zero respect for and who clearly does not understand what love really means And...shit what letter am I on? Can't remember but just add on that I don't like you and don't fancy you anymore. And your thing where you put marmite underneath beans on toast. Gross. You never actually asked me if I wanted it but I ate it to be kind. Because kind is good. And I don't think you're a very kind person and so I think I could do better. And, even if I can't, I *deserve* better.'

And on that pretty emphatic note I leave James swaying, looking utterly crushed and hop into a now awaiting Toyota Prius.

60

NOVEMBER

Suddenly it's November. I'm forty years old.

Forty.

Four. O.

O for old.

O Four fuck's sake.

Lindsay tries everything in her power to make me mark the day in some way suggesting a drink out, a meal, having a party, a trip to the cinema but I flatly refuse. I'm not unhappy, I just don't feel like celebrating.

In the end I agree to meet Lindsay for a birthday brunch to which she inevitably invites a handful of other people. I'm completely surprised but in a really joyful way and I end up making a speech during which I tell everyone how she's the most legendary friend in the world and how much I love her at which point she cries. That sets me off and when we've stopped crying, we start laughing and it turns out to be a really lovely way to spend the day. After, I choose to spend the rest of it in the flat with Mum. A game of Scrabble is as exciting as it gets.

Later, Gordon joins us to watch a film and eat Thai takeaway. It could all be so much worse. I even post a picture on the Bare Faced Insta feed saying 'Feeling grateful for good friends and family. Forty years old today and totally un rock n roll celebrations have taken place but surprisingly content about that.' It gets thousands of likes.

I'm deluged with messages on Facebook which makes me feel vaguely pleased and vaguely cynical. I'm pretty sure only about three of the fifty-eight people who have written something would know it was my birthday if Facebook hadn't told them it was.

Dad gives me a beautiful locket which he drops round, giving me yet another chance to feel weepy and touched. Then yet another highlight of the day is when Keisha Facetimes me, and the children sing Happy Birthday. I'm in bed by eleven.

61

DECEMBER

'If it's alright with both of you I think I'm going to go to Keisha's for Christmas,' I tell both Mum and Dad who have managed to 'pop in' for a cup of tea at the same time one Saturday afternoon. 'Is that OK Dad? I know I spent it with Mum last year, so would you mind? If you do I won't go.'

'No,' says Graham 'I'm happy as long as you are. As long as you being there doesn't make you feel upset in any way.'

'It won't,' I promise 'To be honest, I think Keisha could really do with the company and I can help make sure she has a bit of a break by helping with the kids and stuff. It'll be good. We're really close at the moment and I love spending time with her girls.' I get up to go and switch the kettle on at this point so I don't have to look at my parents as I say the next bit 'To be honest, if I'm not going to have kids of my own I want to be more a part of Jasmine and Freya's lives, not less.'

It's the truth and even I know I've come far. As I sit down again Eleanor squeezes my hand 'Atta girl. I'm proud of you. Sounds like a great plan and actually that means I might say I will go to India then.'

'India? Who with? Gordon?' I ask. This is the first time I've heard anything about India.

Mum's cheeks flame red.

'Oh god, poor Gordon. Who've you met?'

'Don't you dare 'poor Gordon',' she splutters 'It's his own bloody fault. He's grown really quite complacent lately. Anyway, I probably will go to India with him but.........'

'What?' I sigh 'Go on, you might as well tell us.'

Eleanor's expression is that of a fifteen-year-old school girl who's just been caught smoking. 'Well, I happened to meet a lovely chap, a widower called Derek, when I did that massage course with my friend Liz and we just clicked.'

I look at Dad to see what he makes of his ex- wife's flightiness and inability to commit for longer than two years, or to be on her own, ever, but he doesn't look upset, more mildly amused.

'Eleanor, I have to hand it to you,' he says now, a rueful but affectionate smile on his lips 'there's life in the old dog etc. Plus, I'm starting to feel quite flattered, I mean, with me you managed what, a whole fifteen years or so? Must be a record.'

I can literally see Eleanor puffing up, getting ready to retaliate with a comment that will no doubt be unnecessarily harsh but she seems to think better of it. She visibly deflates, like she's lost all her bluster.

'Hmm,' she mutters 'Well I don't know for sure. Nothing's.... happened yet. I'm still thinking about it.'

'Mum,' I say 'Far be it for me to tell you what to do, especially about relationships, given that I clearly know nothing about how to conduct them, but what I will say is that Gordon has been extremely kind to me lately and to us as a family. So please, just have a think before you kick him into touch. You were so excited when you first got to know him and who's to say what can of worms Derek would come with? Perhaps you'd be exchanging one set of problems for another, without having really explored whether or not you can make things work with Gordon first?'

Eleanor looks a bit pouty 'I might think about it. I do feel a bit sorry for Gordon if truth be known. He got rather wobbly when I hinted that I may have had enough the other day. I don't know. And yes Graham, as men go you're the only one I've managed a decade with. Don't know what's wrong with me.'

She sounds quite vulnerable and I can tell she's feeling unsure. Something she finds practically impossible to admit. I get up to make the tea. It's interesting, only a year ago I'd have been focussed on the fact that my mother has managed to meet yet another romantic contender in stark contrast to my own inability to meet anyone. Now, I appreciate far better that everyone's built a bit differently, that everyone operates in their own way and that being my mother doesn't come without its own unique set of difficulties.

'There's nothing wrong with you Mum,' I say now. 'You're just you and that's fine. I mean, I do despair a *bit* and your pulling power should be one of the wonders of the world, but who's to say you're doing anything 'wrong'. It's only society which dictates that we all try to find the human equivalent of a Holy Grail and stick with them forever. But who's to say that's right for everyone or even right for anyone? The only thing I do think is that if you decide to take up with Derek, please make sure you look after Gordon a bit in the aftermath. He really is the kindest one you've had, apart from Dad obviously, and I've come to the conclusion that kindness is the most important quality in a partner.'

Mum fails to suppress a mischievous grin.

I roll my eyes, wondering who is the parent and who is the child 'And that includes having a big willy Mum,' I say firmly.

She cackles, confirming that I had translated her look correctly.

'Oh Christ, I'm going to go for a walk in a minute if this carries on,' says Dad, though you can tell he's amused really.

'Don't you start,' remonstrates Eleanor 'I know you think I'm a 'serial monogamist' or whatever the label is but at least I'm not so terrified of rejection and so stubborn that I refuse to be with anyone.'

'Who says I'm not with anyone?' replies Graham.

'Dad,' I laugh, mouth open with shock 'You never said.'

'You never asked,' he says primly but he's grinning like a Cheshire cat.

'Well,' says Eleanor who looks quite thrown by this turn up 'Who is she then? What's her name?'

'*She's* called Sarah and that's all you two need to know for now. It's very early days.'

I get up to give him a big hug. 'Good on you.'

Eleanor doesn't look quite so sure and I suspect a part of her is a bit jealous.

'And as for you Mum, for what it's worth, I think you could do far worse than by staying with Gordon. I think he's good for you. Just because he doesn't do every tiny thing you tell him to do doesn't mean he doesn't care. In fact, the opposite is true.'

'Here, here to all of that,' agrees Graham.

For the first time in years Eleanor is rendered speechless. She sits blinking for the longest time before saying primly 'I'll think about it.' Then 'By the way you haven't got any of that magic blusher stuff you were talking about on Bare Faced a couple of days ago. You know I don't normally bother with all of that but it did look good. You were so pasty before you put it on, almost grey. It was quite transformative.'

Coming from her this is a huge compliment. I get up 'You can have one. I got sent a box of them as a thank you.'

62

Six Months Later

Summer Again

I heave the last of my kit up the stairs and into my flat. It's only five thirty in the afternoon but I've been up since five a.m. on a shoot for the publicity photos for Bare Faced which will be soon adorning every branch of the most well-known chemists on the high street. Soon I'll be able to put my flat on the market and buy a house if I want to, but I'm in no rush.

It's been the most incredible day, emotional and fun and exhilarating but now I'm exhausted and my plan is simply to collapse on the sofa. However, once I've put things away, on the spur of the moment, I change my mind. It's too much of a nice evening to be indoors.

It's June and today the sun has cast its joyful energy over London, transforming everything, including people's moods. You can feel it in the air. I suspect tonight the pubs will be full to the brim as everyone decides to go for a spontaneous pint, glass of wine or maybe even an Aperol spritz. I might text Lindsay and see if she's about.

The sky is still and cornflower blue and the promise of more sun and warmth lies ahead. It's a beautiful evening. I wander down my street till I reach the main road which I cross before heading for the park.

I'm alright.

More than alright. Everything is good in my world.

I walk until I reach my favourite bench, the one which has a view of the whole park. I recall sitting here with James that cold day when the landscape looked so different and I had felt so desolate and lost. In some ways it feels like decades ago.

As the park shimmers in the early evening sunshine I feel peaceful, healthy, realistic and calm as I reflect on how much things have changed.

It's strange, for so many years I was actively trying to find love. Now I've got used to being on my own and have learned that not only am I fine as I am, but that it's actually pretty good. I like not having to compromise and being able to do what I want when I want. I like not having any of the stresses that being in a relationship can bring. I do miss sex though, sex and intimacy. But I'd rather be on my own than in the wrong relationship.

Still, on days like today I suppose it would be nice to have someone to ring and tell about my day. I'd still like to have that one person to check in with, no matter what was happening. I miss cuddling up in bed with someone on the weekend and having someone to make a special effort for. I miss feeling like the centre of someone's world and having someone to love. I miss sex. A lot.

Ultimately, I still believe it's part of the human condition to want to search for a match, to want to pair up, to need to be part of something. My world is good now but could it be even better?

So, what's the answer? Inevitably if one day I 'try again' it means allowing myself to be vulnerable. Looking for love comes with no guarantees and could I cope with another setback? Is it even worth it? Perhaps if I do ever look again, I'd be better off joining a dating agency, one people joined for the right reasons. Tinder was so instant and accessible it attracted all sorts for all reasons.

Would it have changed much since the days when I was on it? I doubted it.

When I get home, out of curiosity more than anything I decide to have a look before saying goodbye to it forever. I go into the App store on my phone and install Tinder for <u>the last ever time</u>.

Once the icon's downloaded, I press it and am stunned to see that my profile's still there, preserved exactly as it had been when I met James. I feel totally stunned and a bit nauseous. What the hell was it still doing there when I deleted it so long ago?

Instinctively I call Ricky, guessing he might fully understand the ins and outs of Tinder. He picks up straight away.

'What can I do you for my favourite viral sensation?'

'Quick question. I was on Tinder many moons ago but I deleted the app. Only I've just reinstalled it and my profile's still there. What's that all about?'

'You numpty,' he says immediately 'You can't just delete the icon on your phone. You have to actually go into the settings in the app and delete the account. If you didn't, you'll have been there all this time. I'd have swiped you myself, only I've set mine to only see girls aged between twenty and thirty, so obviously I'll never have come across you.' He laughs delightedly at his own wit.

'Ha bloody ha,' I say, feeling irritated that how to leave hasn't been made clearer to luddites like me. It's creepy discovering I've been there this whole time.

'Anything else I can do you for?'

'No, that was it thanks love.'

'See you soon then Tinderella,' he says before going.

I look at the app again and scroll through for one last look.

As I swipe I find myself wondering how many hours I must have wasted in the past doing exactly this. ***Left left left.***

Quite quickly a fairly nice-looking guy crops up. He's incredibly good looking, though clearly knows it and doesn't have much to say on his profile. Lindsay recently suggested during one of our makeup room chats that perhaps I should set about finding someone I could have no strings sex with. Only I'm not convinced that kind of set up would work for me. I've got full respect for women who can manage it but in my personal experience, whenever I've slept with someone and there hasn't been an emotional connection, it's left me feeling empty and a bit sad afterwards.

I carry on swiping.

The next person I click on (Bradley, 46) has written the following

Favourite roast dinner – chicken. Why? Because I LOVE a good leg and
breast.
Christ.

I stop on the next picture.

Conor, 42 – nice face. Not overtly good looking but pleasant. Beard. Friendly looking. Nice smile. I look at his other pictures. Not bad. Nothing weird stands out. The last picture is of him and a boy who looks about nine. Must be his son?

What's he written, if anything?

Irish, London living, divorced father of one. That wasn't the plan but these things happen, so here I am, warmly embracing risk taking and hoping to poke failure in the eye. I'm optimistic and believe in fate and happenstance. Form an orderly queue, please. (Can't wait to delete this app.)
Hmm. Not sure.

The 'form an orderly queue' bit is off putting. Would he be big headed? He wasn't *so* great looking he could assume women would be stampeding to get at him, like people trying to grab tellies on Black Friday. It's nice that he's so honest and upfront about being a dad though. I also like that he's only featured the boy in one photo as opposed to all of them. I always used to find it a bit odd when people displayed their children on a dating site to that extent. It felt far too 'buy one get one free' whereas just the one picture tells the whole story. He's a parent. Another person's feelings are at stake. He comes with another person attached. He's made his statement but is still selling himself primarily as an individual.

I wonder what it would be like to date someone who's got kids. I've never considered it before but now my eggs are getting so ancient maybe it's exactly what I should be thinking about? If I met someone who had already done their breeding and it turned out I couldn't produce, there wouldn't be any pressure. Plus, if I'm not going to have any of my own it would be lovely to contribute in some way, shape or form to a child's life, even if only as a step-parent.

Of course, these thoughts are formed and processed in seconds not minutes, as all Tinder based decisions tend to be. I laugh at myself. I've been on the app for no time at all and my brain's already starting to spin.

Still……what am I worrying about? I'm going to delete it anyway.

I swipe right. It's a match. Instantly. Oh….. How weird.

I smile wryly. What a ridiculous circus.

I close it. I can't be bothered to look anymore, let alone message anyone. I'm suddenly flooded with memories of having to deal with umpteen dull messages saying 'How are you?' or 'Having a nice weekend?' and it's already making me feel slightly anxious. I really don't have the desire or energy to invite any of that back into my life. In a few months' time, if I'm feeling ready, I might research into some other dating options, but not yet.

Right now, I'll do what I've been doing successfully for ages. I'll see who's around and form plans to spend time with someone who I like and care for, who feels the same way about me.

Ten minutes later I have a plan for the evening. Lindsay can't get away but my godmother, Linda, is free and delighted to have been asked out for a glass of wine. We decide to meet in Putney, by the river.

Good. I have a nice life. I'm far more social these days and don't suffer from any relationship angst or stress, or have to worry about why someone hasn't texted me or returned my call.

I don't need a man.

The next morning, I wake up to a notification from Tinder and a message from Conor 42.

Hi Charlotte – well, you're totally out of my league. I have a feeling I 'swiped' you light years ago. I remember being a bit sad I didn't get a match. But, hey, isn't that what this app is designed for? Toe curling rejection and disappointment? Perhaps my hideous face required a lot of extra thought. Either way here I am, knowing that I'll probably never hear back (in reality you probably tripped over and swiped entirely by accident) wanting to say that you have a lovely smile, are very attractive and that I wish I was the sort of bloke who could twirl you about dancing, in the kitchen or anywhere else for that matter.
Only, when I dance I look like I'm having some kind of an attack so I'm not going to pretend I'm really good on the tiny off chance we ever do meet. I'd hate to spot you watching my best efforts, looking really disturbed whilst frantically calling an ambulance. Having said all that, I'm not a totally useless idiot. I work, am solvent, know my way around the bars of, not just Soho, but also North London where I fit in beautifully now that I've grown this (hopefully anti-ageing) beard, so if you fancy being bought a cocktail of your choice I'd love to hear from you. And yes, I am bribing you with free drinks. I've never come up with anything better or that seems to be more effective to be honest.

I smile, get up, take my pills and get ready for a day of Bare Faced meetings.

***

Two days later, I'm at home having a cup of tea and a biscuit while I take a short break from writing a product review. I have another quick look at the app. There aren't any more messages from Conor but suddenly I feel horrible and rude for not replying given that he took the time to write something so long and so decent. I tap out a message.

Hello Conor, sorry for the late reply. Your message is very sweet but in truth I meandered back onto this app prematurely. I am not in the right headspace for online dating after all. Have had my fingers burnt rather badly in the past. Sorry for wasting your time, Charlotte

By the time I've drunk my tea I've had a reply -

Sorry to hear that. To be honest, my fingers have been burnt pretty badly too. In fact, they're pretty much charred stumps. My wife left me which was the first rather big blow to the ego and then I had a date with someone from here who told me I reminded her of a cross between Peter Sutcliffe and Andrea Bocelli. A murdering blind opera singer wasn't the image I'd been intending so this came as a shock. There was no date two.

Anyway, if you do fancy changing your mind I'd be quite happy to provide a bucket of water to plunge our burnt fingers into if things didn't work out?

I giggle. He's funny.

I type

Peter Sutcliffe and Andrea Bocelli? Now you've said that I'm tempted!

Ha. Yes, I really am truly crap at this aren't I. Ok Charlotte, I'll level with you. I'm giving up. I came on here in good faith but so far all being on Tinder has achieved is to make me doubt the female race. So, I bid you farewell and really hope you have better luck than me and that you find happiness. You do look lovely. You were my last bastion of hope ;)

I consider my position feeling really torn. The last thing I want is to complicate my life now that things are so much more back on track but there's something about this man that's making me curious.

Ok, here's the deal I type swiftly before I can chicken out. *It sounds like we've both had similarly traumatic Tinder experiences, although mine will trump yours in terms of scale and awfulness I promise, so maybe we should just throw caution to the wind and meet for a drink? Perhaps we could think of it as a Tinder support group meeting as opposed to a date and take it from there?*

There's a bit of a pause before his reply and I realise I'm eager to see his response.

Well, it's not the kind of offer I've dreamed of if I'm totally honest, but if it means meeting you then fine. Support group for the dating damaged it is. But if this is going to happen then please can we go to WhatsApp so we aren't constantly reminded of our Tinder woes. I truly am sick of this app.

We exchange numbers and over the next couple of days much texting ensues.

I can't help it. I'm instantly engaged by him and like everything he has to say. The experience is bittersweet though because it does remind me a bit of when I first met James. We had also had great text 'banter' only look how that had ended. Still, I keep reminding myself that Conor isn't the same person and that I'm mainly interested in meeting him as a friend. I'm cautious, wiser, more cynical, not so desperate to meet someone. The experience will be different. Still, I certainly revert to type when it comes to organising the date.

I suggest we meet at The Fox and Grapes I type one afternoon. *It's near me and it's a nice pub.*

Er no comes the reply.

I frown. It hadn't been a question.

Why?

Because I'm old fashioned and want to take you somewhere a bit more exciting than your local boozer, where I imagine you've conducted all your dates, one at least of which has left you with a nasty taste in your mouth. Let's ring the changes.

I blink. Hmm. What to do? Losing control of the situation makes me a bit nervous but at the same time I like that he knows his own mind. It's attractive. Plus of course, he's right.

Ok I text, wondering what I'm letting myself in for.

The Saturday after is the day we've arranged to meet. I wake up in a cold sweat, terrified I'm doing the wrong thing.

I go to text Conor straight away as has almost become habit over the last few days. Last night we'd been messaging for about two hours.

Are you still sure about this? I write.

Morning dear, er yes, though you're clearly not. I'll try not to be offended by yet another deeply unromantic overture and hope that if I tell you (again) that we can meet as friends you might be reassured/calm down.

I laugh, instantly appeased. *I think I got the fear because I sent you that Bare Faced picture last night. The one of me with no make-up on. Thought you might have run for the hills.*

I did. I'm here now, just approaching the first hill.

I send a laughing emoji

Not really, I know you're doing your hardest to put me off but I'm afraid it's going to take more than that. I thought comparing yourself to a guinea pig was a bit strong too. Maybe a hamster's more apt? I jest of course. To be honest I was very impressed with the whole concept, though discovering you're some kind of a celebrity makes me feel rather inadequate. (Cheers google) Plus you look perfectly acceptable with no slap on. Naturally pretty. My only concern is, do I now have to send you something equally revealing? I hope not. A picture of me taking Gaviscon to alleviate my middle-aged heartburn might put you off.

He makes me laugh so much. Out loud at times. He makes me feel at ease and seems able to deal with whatever I throw at him. I swallow. Shit. Of course, by telling him about Bare Faced he'll now 'know' about Lucas. My stomach lurches.

Still there? He types.

Yeah. So what else did you learn on google. Anything that's put you off completely?

He's still online but takes ages to type. I'm so nervous that by the time he starts to reply I'm convinced he's building up to something I don't want to hear.

Sorry. Door went. Parcel for next door. Anyway, where were we? Oh yes, you were doubting my integrity as a human being. Charlotte – don't be a doughnut. The only thing I discovered is that you're a woman to be reckoned with, who at one point in your life had the misfortune to get involved with a horrible arsehole. Hardly anything ground breaking 😉

I exhale, and type

Good reassurance thank you. And thanks too for calling me a doughnut. A very under used insult I think. But seriously oh bearded one, given that some of your texts have amused me greatly I do want to meet you, of course. So where are we meeting? Or do I need to attend a séance to find out? Just head out and guess using psychic powers? It's the day of THE DATE and I still don't know where we're going…..

You're a clever girl, bring your divining rod and work it out comes the response.

If I said that to you it would sound like a Carry On Film – And don't call me Rod. I shoot back.

The next thing to appear on my screen is a hilarious picture of a very strange man carrying a divining rod.

Then - *Here you are this evening at 7.30, around Charlotte Street stopping off for a white wine spritzer at the Charlotte Street Hotel where they'll say 'No rods on the bar please Charlotte.'*

I laugh out loud as I so often do at our exchanges. I'm also delighted by his choice of venue. *Will they put my rods in the cloakroom?*

Rods plural? You have more than one divining rod – is there no end to your spirit world talents?

I've got bloody loads – some are more tube friendly than others. And, by the way, in the spirit of honesty here's a picture of what I really look like. And my name's really Margaret, not Charlotte.

I quickly ping over a picture I've found via google. It's of a very stout woman with a divining rod. She's got long grey hair, some of which is entwined in a scrunchie. She's wearing a tunic and a huge pair of crocs.

Margaret, you are just my type! Although does this require a change of venue? Is there a bar on Margaret Street that has a cloakroom big enough to accommodate rods? Actually, we'll stick to the plan and deal with it. Hmm and by the way I've just noticed, earlier on you said 'some' of my texts amuse you greatly. More annoyed some have not!! Can we talk about those instead please?

I giggle. I'm looking forward to our date, a lot, which in turn is a bit terrifying. Deciding I have nothing to lose I type....

We can – but before I waste a lot of good lipstick on getting dolled up for this date, please promise me you're not A/ married B/ a liar C/ in a relationship of any kind. Please put your rotten fruit out to the front of the stall now. If there is some. I don't want to waste my time you see.

He replies

Oh Margaret, you really have had your fingers burnt, haven't you? Right, truth time. I'll do my 'Bare Faced' bit. All the rotten fruit coming your way....now. I'm about ten pounds overweight. The reason my wife left me is because she fell in love with someone younger, arguably better looking and because we'd gone rather stale. I have a son who I love. A lot. I'm a nice man. Too nice. I also don't want to get hurt. I'm bloody nervous about tonight too if you must know. I worry that I won't do my mildly amusing texts justice. But you sound fun. And you look pretty in your pictures. Less so in the most recent one (scrunchie/grey hair one not bare faced one) and I'm slightly alarmed by the crocs, yet you're interesting enough for me to be prepared to overlook them.

I read the message a few times pondering what to reply. I like him so much and I haven't even met him yet. It's so weird.

I've got a funny feeling we might get on you know? I type.

Undoubtedly, Margaret, undoubtedly. I've got a funny feeling in my waters too it has to be said (sort of a euphemism). Listen, I can tell you're wary, but I promise I've got no agenda, other than wanting to meet someone who shares my slightly warped sense of humour who one day I can hopefully be romantic with, and domestic and optimistic. All the 'ics'. So, I'm going to slather my own burnt fingers in lotion, wrap them in bandages, turn up with a copy of the trades descriptions act and give this drink business a chance if you are. You never know, it might be as good as these texts and besides, what have we got to lose eh Margaret/ Charlotte?

I grin from ear to ear.

I type back. *Nothing. Absolutely nothing at all. See you at 7.30 x*

PRAISE FOR JEMMA FORTE'S BOOKS

'An unmissable read.'
– Abby Clements

'A witty account of rollercoaster events that will get you thinking about the 'what ifs' in life.'
- Heat

'A must read for all'
—Digital Spy

'A story which bristles with warmth and humour.'
—Hello

'The most imaginative romcom we've read in a while.'
—Now

'An engrossing and magical read with romance at its core.'
—OK!

'The perfect mix of funny and emotional.'
—One More Page

'Addictive, heart-warming yet funny.'
—Chick Lit Uncovered.

JEMMA FORTE grew up wanting to write for glossy magazines, be a famous actress or work in Clarks shoe shop (she loved the foot measuring device). Her parents didn't want her to go to stage school because, according to them, she was 'precocious enough already.' However, they actively encouraged her obsession with reading and writing and she wrote her first book, 'Mizzy the Germ,' when she was eight. She even sent it to a publisher (unwittingly backing up the precocious theory).

In 1998 she became a Disney Channel presenter and after five years leaping about there, went on to present shows for ITV, BBC1 and BBC2 and Channel 4.

These days she can be found on C5's Jeremy Vine Show where she is a regular panellist, on QVC where she guests for *Molton Brown*, as a contributor on shows such as GMB, and on the radio. She lives in London with her children, Lily and Freddie.

Be Careful What You Swipe For is Jemma's fifth novel.

Printed in Poland
by Amazon Fulfillment
Poland Sp. z o.o., Wrocław

61254574R00171